SEASONS OF TOMORROW

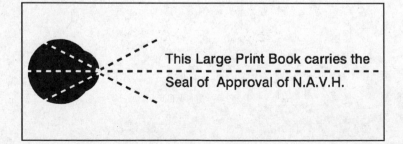

This Large Print Book carries the
Seal of Approval of N.A.V.H.

Seasons of Tomorrow

Cindy Woodsmall

THORNDIKE PRESS

A part of Gale, Cengage Learning

GALE
CENGAGE Learning·

Farmington Hills, Mich • San Francisco • New York • Waterville, Maine
Meriden, Conn • Mason, Ohio • Chicago

LIBRARY OF CONGRESS CATALOGING-IN-PUBLICATION DATA

Woodsmall, Cindy.
    Seasons of tomorrow / by Cindy Woodsmall. — Large print edition.
        pages ; cm. — (Amish vines and orchards ; 4) (Thorndike Press large print Christian fiction)
        ISBN 978-1-4104-6573-3 (hardcover) — ISBN 1-4104-6573-X (hardcover)
        1. Amish—Fiction. 2. Large type books. I. Title.
    PS3623.O678S434 2014b
    813'.6—dc23
                                                    2014010062

Published in 2014 by arrangement with WaterBrook Press, an imprint of the Crown Publishing Group, a division of Random House LLC, a Penguin Random House Company

Printed in the United States of America
1 2 3 4 5 6 7 18 17 16 15 14

To my brother Mark
one of the most exceptional,
steadfast, honorable men
I've ever been privileged to know

AMISH VINES AND ORCHARDS SERIES

The story so far . . .

In *A Season for Tending,* Rhoda Byler, a twenty-two-year-old Amish girl, struggles to suppress the God-given insights she receives. Her people don't approve of such intuitions. Because of their superstitions and fears, Rhoda spends most of her time alone in her bountiful fruit and herb garden or with her assistant, Landon, canning her produce for her business — Rhode Side Stands. Although she lives with her parents, two married brothers, and their families, Rhoda is isolated and haunted by guilt over the death of her sister two years ago.

Thirty miles away, in the Amish district of Harvest Mills, three brothers — Samuel, Jacob, and Eli King — are caretakers of their family's apple orchard. Samuel has been responsible for the success of Kings' Orchard since he was a young teen, but due to Eli's negligence, one-third of their orchard has produced apples that are only good for canning. If Samuel doesn't find a way to turn more profit on those apples, he'll have to sell part of the orchard, resulting in even smaller harvests in the future.

When Samuel and Rhoda meet, they see eye to eye on very little until she shows him her fruit garden. He soon realizes that her horticultural skills are just what he needs to restore the orchard, and her canning business could provide an established outlet for their apples — if he can convince her to partner with them. Without telling his girlfriend, Catherine, he asks Rhoda to work with Kings' Orchard.

Rhoda declines . . . until someone maliciously destroys her garden and her livelihood. She gives her land to her brothers and commits to partnering with Kings' Orchard. Before long she and Jacob begin courting, and Samuel severs his relationship with Catherine.

Just as they begin to harvest the apples, a tornado destroys most of the orchard and almost costs Samuel his life. In an effort to make a new start, Jacob, Samuel, Rhoda, Landon, and others decide to buy an abandoned apple orchard in Maine that they can restore. As the families commit to establishing an Amish community in Maine, Samuel realizes he's in love with Rhoda.

As *The Winnowing Season* opens, a small group is preparing to move to Maine — Rhoda Byler, her brother Steven, his family, her assistant Landon Olson, brothers Samuel and Jacob King, and their sister Leah. Their goal is to establish a new Amish community and to cultivate an abandoned apple orchard to replace the income from the orchard the tornado destroyed.

But the day before they leave, Rhoda's church leaders insist she attend a meeting, because Samuel has reported Rueben Glick for vandalizing her garden. She's upset with Samuel and dreads going, but to make matters worse, Jacob, her boyfriend, is called away at the last minute. Samuel goes with her and is outraged at the hostility and suspicion they express toward Rhoda. Although the meeting does not go well, Rhoda is given permission to move to Maine in good standing with the church.

The following day the Bylers and Kings leave, except for Jacob, who never returned. Rhoda feels alone in her new surroundings as she continues to see her late sister and begins to hear music and a new voice calling her to meet an isolated couple, Camilla and Bob Cranford. She tries to confide in

Samuel, but he pushes her away for fear she'll discover he's in love with her.

When Jacob arrives, Rhoda begins to learn about his past and his connection to a non-Amish woman named Sandra. Jacob and Rhonda's love and loyalty to each other are unshaken, and everyone at the farm soon settles in to revitalizing the orchard. Whenever Jacob's past calls him away, the others work extra to make up for his absence.

Although most of their neighbors welcome the Amish, Rhoda finds herself in legal trouble as three teenagers from powerful families accuse her of giving them drugs. That forces Jacob into hiding to protect Rhoda from negative scrutiny because of his past. As pressures mount, Samuel helps her find strength.

Months pass with Jacob gone, and Samuel continues to withhold his feelings from Rhoda. After she is finally cleared of charges, Samuel is alone with her in the barn, and the conversation turns personal. His emotions get the best of him, and he kisses her. Rhoda is swept up in the moment before pushing him away. Almost immediately Jacob arrives home and discovers what has happened. He breaks up with her and is furious with his brother. Without explanation, Samuel withdraws from her.

Rhoda realizes she has lost both men, so she moves in with Bob and Camilla, hoping Jacob will eventually forgive her.

As *For Every Season* opens, Rhoda is still living with Camilla and Bob while she sorts out the difficult situation with Jacob, Samuel, and her. Her intuition tells her that Camilla has a son, and Rhoda tries to find out what happened to the family. At the farm Leah sees the work piling up and takes the initiative to hire a new worker, a young Amish woman named Iva.

The need for the Maine orchard to survive forces Rhoda, Jacob, and Samuel to confront their complicated relationships, and Rhoda tells Jacob that she wants to give their courtship another chance and that even though she and Samuel share a deep bond, she doesn't have any romantic interest in him. Leah and Landon decide they are officially dating, but he doesn't want to influence her decision on whether to leave the Amish faith.

Jacob confronts Sandra about lying to him and convinces her to go with him to see his lawyer. They learn they are not legally responsible for the incident that led to the deaths of two women, but because Sandra witnessed an unrelated violent crime, she must remain in hiding. In order to clear his name, Jacob agrees to go to Virginia to give a deposition and to testify at the upcoming trials involving Jones' Construction. Once Jacob and Sandra are back at the farmhouse, the group decides that the best way to keep Sandra and Casey safe is to move them to a new, secure place to live.

As Rhoda and Samuel's friendship slowly heals, she shares with him her visions concerning Camilla's son and possible grandchild. Samuel encourages her to see that the intuitions must come from God. When Camilla is in a car accident, Rhoda and Samuel work together to keep her calm until help arrives. Steven tells Rhoda that Samuel is the better match for her. Phoebe, Steven's wife, shares that she lost the baby she was carrying.

Iva helps Sandra move while Jacob goes to Virginia to testify, and Samuel and Rhoda grow closer as they work to keep the budding orchard from frost damage. After Jacob testifies, he realizes three things: his desire to work construction has been revived, his brother is in love with Rhoda, and Rhoda may have hidden feelings for Samuel. Jacob resolves to get Rhoda off the farm as quickly as possible.

When Jacob returns to Maine, he tries to

persuade her that they need to leave the farm. Even though the farm is home and she's needed here, she recognizes that her feelings for Samuel have developed into romantic love. So she agrees to go with Jacob. When he realizes she loves Samuel, he frees her from their engagement and leaves. Rhoda is broken over the pain she's caused Jacob, but she knows that Samuel is the one who holds her heart, and she feels a measure of peace for their future.

For a list of main characters in the Amish Vines and Orchards series, see page 577.

ONE

Rhoda stood over the forty-gallon copper kettle filled with apple butter, slowly pushing and pulling the paddle. Bubbles gently broke the silky, dark-brown surface into soft craters as steam carried the heady scents of cloves, cinnamon, and nutmeg. Cool mid-October air rushed in through the open doors and windows, dispersing the heat of canning.

At one of the long worktables, Leah rapidly prepared apples for another kettle. Apple peelers, which also cored and sliced the apples, were bolted to the table. In another part of the kitchen, Iva used a long-handled scoop to pour cooked apple butter into canning jars, while a newly hired helper, Mary Yoder, cleaned any drips from the jars, put the metal sealing lids on, and screwed on the band.

Although Orchard Bend Farms had been established only a year ago, everyone rolled through the day with the kind of expertise one would expect after several seasons of hard work tending to the orchard and canning — Samuel; his sister Leah; Rhoda; her brother Steven; his wife, Phoebe; Rhoda's longtime *Englisch* assistant, Landon; and hired, live-in helper Iva. All of them were really good at doing whatever task faced them.

The newer helpers from the Amish families who had moved to Maine only a couple of months ago, like Crist and Mary, weren't as useful yet, but they were eager to learn and were very pleasant to be around.

Migrant workers filled the orchard, picking the trees clean, and they had another month of work to do.

But a huge part of what made the canning season such a success was this kitchen. The longer Rhoda worked in it, the more she realized that Jacob had thought of every possible canning need — like the gas-powered eyes that were sunk into the floors and surrounded with bricks. The sunken eyes worked much like in-ground firepits, and her kettles fit right over the heat sources. He'd also built massive worktables, oversize sinks, and numerous storage shelves, pantries, and spice racks.

A dull ache mixed with guilt throbbed

inside her chest.

Jacob. How was he faring?

In the three months since he'd left, she and Samuel had talked about him and prayed for him often. If only he would contact them. He had a cell phone. His uncle Mervin, the man Jacob had gone to work for after the breakup, had given Jacob's number to Samuel. But Jacob hadn't responded to a single call they'd made or so much as sent a postcard.

Although she longed to hear from him, she didn't blame him for ignoring her. She'd said some really harsh things as they'd hurtled toward the breakup. If she could go back, she'd be kinder. Oh, so very much gentler. They still would have broken up, and he'd have left hurt and angry. But she wouldn't be carrying the guilt of having dumped on him her anger and mounting disappointments. And she wouldn't be continually rehashing the unkind words she'd spoken.

Only a few people knew where Jacob was working these days, and no one at Orchard Bend Farms was privy to his whereabouts. What had she and Samuel done to the man?

"Rhoda." Crist stepped into the harvest kitchen, holding up a clipboard.

She shooed the heartache and remorse

back into their hiding place. *"Ya?"*

"I ran the inventory like Samuel said, and we're missing fifty cases of jars. He said that's not possible. But I've checked everything three times."

Samuel strode into the kitchen, and her heart turned a flip at the sight of him. Despite their grief and guilt over Jacob, they navigated it together, and the rare and genuine honesty they shared was helping their hearts to mend. The distraction of this busy harvest season helped too. Samuel's brown eyes moved to hers, making her heart race even more.

"He's right." She held Samuel's gaze. "It's not possible."

In the evenings after she and all the others retired to their rooms, her thoughts of Samuel and her hopes for their future lingered long into the night. When she did finally go to sleep, she saw him in her dreams. When would he ask her out? Would she have to wait until Jacob had forgiven them?

But the truth was, Samuel didn't have to use words to say all she needed to hear. Staring into his eyes like this, she could forget the world and every problem that faced them.

Crist tapped the clipboard against the

palm of his hand. "Then do you have any idea where the missing jars are?"

She couldn't manage to break eye contact. Was that what caused a slight blush to cross Samuel's cheeks before he lowered his head, smiling?

Some semblance of thinking returned to her, and she focused on Crist. "Did you check my loft like I said to?"

"Ya. The barn has no crates of jars left."

"Crist," — Iva pointed to the ceiling — "she meant her sleeping loft."

"Oh. Sorry. I didn't check that one." He shrugged. "You actually want me to go into your bedroom?"

"It's not really a bedroom." It was a small space where Rhoda slept some nights. Samuel's uncle Mervin had come for a visit a few weeks after the harvest began. When he realized Rhoda was climbing a ladder and sleeping on the floor of the attic some nights, he built her a set of stairs and turned the attic into sleeping quarters with what might be the smallest half bathroom ever. Although a man couldn't stand up straight there, she managed just fine. But she would sleep there only during the busiest canning times, like now, when she started her day before sunrise and worked late into the night. In the slower seasons she returned to her bedroom in the farmhouse she shared with her brother, his family, Samuel, Leah, and Iva.

"*Kumm,* Crist." Iva rinsed her hands. "I'll count boxes. You take notes."

Crist glanced at Leah before nodding. "Sure."

Did Leah realize Crist liked her? Rhoda doubted it. Crist was a broad-shouldered, good-looking man who was even tempered and had a lot of energy, but Leah seemed as taken with Landon as Rhoda was with Samuel. Unfortunately, if Leah chose an Englisch man over an Amish one, Rhoda would be blamed because she'd kept an outsider as a worker even after partnering with the King family business — as if Samuel's *Daed* needed another reason to dislike her.

As Crist and Iva went up the narrow stairs that led to the small attic, Samuel dug oranges out of his coat pocket and set them on the counter near her. Rhoda used grated orange peel for flavoring in one of the apple butter recipes. As he continued to pull the fruit from his pockets, she grabbed a clean, long-handled wooden spoon from the counter, dipped it into the kettle, and waited for the apple butter to cool.

She wished Landon and Leah hadn't

fallen in love, but people couldn't dictate to their hearts who they wanted to spend a lifetime with. She and Samuel knew that all too well. But it did hamper their business decisions. They wanted and needed to make Landon a partner, and at times Amish businesses partnered with the Englisch. An Englisch partner could bring certain modernization to the business that Rhoda and Samuel were forbidden to implement — like having electricity in the harvest kitchen or using motorized vehicles to haul apples and tend the orchard. Landon knew they wanted him to become a partner, but they couldn't pursue it right now, and he was willing to wait.

The problem was that the approval of such a venture would have to go through Samuel's church leaders in Pennsylvania, because that's where the original business started, and the founding owner, Samuel's grandfather, had been a church member in Pennsylvania. The scrutiny and visits from those church leaders would soon reveal that Landon was going out with Leah, and under those circumstances the ministers wouldn't approve Landon as a partner. And once Samuel was turned down, he couldn't appeal. So Rhoda had no idea how many years they'd need to wait or what would have to transpire before they could make Landon a partner.

Samuel set two more oranges on the counter. "That's all Phoebe had. She said if you need more, Landon will have to run to the store."

"That's plenty for today." She and Samuel weren't yet skilled in knowing how much of certain items they would need for the kitchen or the orchard. Those calculations had been Jacob's forte. "But Landon has no time to make a run to the store today or tomorrow. If I need more, maybe Camilla still has some from the bag she bought." Despite how busy everyone stayed, Rhoda found a way to snatch a bit of time here and there with her Englisch neighbor, and Camilla drove Rhoda whenever she needed to shop for canning supplies.

Samuel kept an orange from rolling off the countertop. "Speaking of Camilla, she left a voice mail asking if you had time to meet with the private investigator this Sunday evening."

Fresh guilt pushed in on Rhoda.

"Don't." Samuel pointed at her, reading her face. "Trust me. They will find Sophia and her mother. I know they will."

She forced herself to nod, but she had good reasons to feel culpable in this. God had given Rhoda several insights concerning Sophia even before Camilla knew she had a granddaughter. But out of fear that the leadings might not be from God, Rhoda had held on to them for so long she'd botched what God had wanted to accomplish through her. The investigator the Cranfords had hired had yet to find Sophia and her mom, and Rhoda felt more uneasy with each passing month, concerned that something may have happened to them.

Unlike working in the orchard or the harvest kitchen, she could do nothing physical to fix the problem. Like the situation with Jacob, she could only pray about it.

Rhoda drew a deep breath, aiming to find her cheerful self. She couldn't let grief and guilt over her yesterdays snatch all the good God gave her today. She held out the end of the spoon to Samuel.

He inched forward and took a taste of the apple butter. "Perfect."

She sampled it too, verifying his novice opinion. "It is, and it'll be ready for the jars in an hour." She went to the sink and dropped the spoon into the sudsy water.

In an odd way what happened to her and Jacob reminded her of the Bible saying that a person cannot serve two masters without loving one and hating the other. In her

23

experience a woman couldn't keep a healthy relationship with one man while harboring tenderness for his brother. But Jacob shouldn't have been the one to call the situation what it was. She should have. If she had, she would've freed him sooner with more of his heart and self-respect intact.

Samuel stirred the concoction for her. "Phoebe is setting up lunch on one of the tables outside. Let Mary do the stirring while we eat."

"I wish I could." Would she always long for every possible minute with Samuel? "We have to get the batch Mary is working on into the jars before it cools. Leah's prepping another batch, and this batch has to be stirred nonstop for another hour until it'll be ready to put into jars. I'll eat later."

"I'll help you get to a stopping point."

"There isn't one, not today. Just have her put sandwiches on the porch like usual, and we'll grab bites while working."

"Rhoda," — Samuel's tone said he was ready to argue if need be — "it's the halfway point of the harvest, and Phoebe wants the core group, plus anyone else who can, to eat a picnic lunch together."

"This is the first I've heard of it."

"That's because you missed dinner the

last two nights, and I forgot to tell you about it."

"Ah, makes sense, but like I said, we can't stop for lunch."

He turned his back to the others. "Find the time. Do we need to dump out the batches that are cooking?"

Even as their love grew, they still managed to argue easily. Would that go away with time, or was it part of who they were together? "You wouldn't dare!"

He raised his eyebrows, and the firm look in his eyes said he would. "Then be reasonable, please."

"You can't breeze in here, Samuel King, and start telling me how to run my kitchen."

"I don't see why not. You don't mind telling me how *we* need to run the orchard." He studied her, waiting for her rebuttal.

She wanted to put her hands on her hips and set him straight, except . . . he was right. She drew a breath. "I guess I should be grateful that you insist I take breaks."

"You should, but that would be asking too much." He grinned. "I would settle for begrudgingly agreeable . . . and for lunch, with everyone together."

Regardless of how much work there was to do, how could she argue with his reasoning? "We need to get the batch Mary is working with into jars. While we do that, she can eat, and then she can take over stirring this batch."

He nodded. "That's a plan I can live with. What do you want me to do to help?"

"You stir." She passed him the apple butter paddle and turned to Leah. "It appears we're having a picnic, so let's stop preparing apples for another vat. We'll delay starting the next batch."

"Works for me." Leah set down the knife and began to clean her work station.

Rhoda went to the foot of the stairs. "Iva? Crist?"

Iva peered down. "Ya?"

"You two are needed down here, and you can return to that later, okay?"

"Sure." Iva hurried down the steps, and Crist followed her.

Rhoda gave instructions. Bringing most of the kitchen to a halt during the day wasn't easy. It's why they ate in shifts.

"Mr. King." The foreman of the migrant workers stood at the door of the kitchen. Samuel had told the man not to call him mister, but it was no use. Perhaps the man's English wasn't that good, or perhaps using titles was part of his culture.

"Coming." Samuel went outside to see what he needed.

26

She and Samuel had rented a home not too far from here for the migrant workers to sleep in, and they'd hired two cooks to feed them. The overhead of running an orchard seemed crushing to her, but Samuel was used to it.

They could use extra workers to help in the spring too, but the migrant workers would be long gone by then. Samuel had hired some workers from the new Amish families in the area to help this fall, but since farming their own land was their main goal, they wouldn't be available during the spring or summer. Orchard Bend Farms might not have much help during spring and summer for a few more years yet.

Within thirty minutes Leah, Iva, and Crist were washing their hands. They passed around a hand towel to one another and then left the harvest kitchen.

Leah paused. "You coming?"

"Ya." Rhoda passed the paddle to Mary. "I'll be back in a bit to check on you."

"I won't let it burn. I promise."

"Denki."

When Rhoda stepped onto the porch, she paused, soaking in the lovely fall day. A canopy of clouds hung overhead. Trees were filled with the splendor of the fall colors.

Landon brought a wagon to a halt, jumped

down, and looped the lead over the hitching post. "Hey, Rhodes, I brought a bushel basket of McIntosh from cold storage."

"Thanks." She used the sweetness of a McIntosh to mix with the tarter apples, which cut down on the need to add sugar to the apple butter. "You're joining us for lunch, right?"

"Definitely." He left the apples in the wagon and headed for the table.

Could the day be any more gorgeous? Her five-year-old nephew, Isaac, and his three-year-old sister, Arie, were sneaking food to the dogs under the picnic table, and Rhoda laughed. As she watched her loved ones under a harvest sky, she saw Samuel take a box from Phoebe, and then he paused, staring at Rhoda. He walked toward her, his boots echoing against the wooden porch. "Hi." His deep voice rumbled softly. "You joining us for lunch?" He winked, and warmth ran through her all the way to her toes.

She raised an eyebrow, aiming to look defiant as she teased. "Maybe. If you're lucky."

He chuckled. Since Jacob had left, she and Samuel hadn't held hands or kissed, yet they were — dare she think it? — intimate.

How long would she have to wait to begin a life with him?

Two

The late-November sky spit snow as Jacob carried one end of the panel of Sheetrock toward the half-built home. At least a dozen Amish workers from his uncle's construction business buzzed in every direction.

"Jacob!" His uncle's voice rose above the hammering and sawing.

Jacob glanced around and spotted Uncle Mervin on the dirt driveway, standing beside a young Amish woman who had a little one on her hip and a toddler hanging on to her dress. Jacob gave a nod. What could an Amish woman possibly want on a construction site? "I'll be right with you." He and a coworker carried the Sheetrock into the house and set it down.

The house had plumbing, a good foundation, skeleton walls, and a finished roof. Jacob's current goal was to get the exterior insulation on before a wintery blast hit Virginia. But the supply truck with the wall cladding had yet to arrive.

This house was one of two he was working on. Each sat on a bluff overlooking a valley with the Appalachian Mountains on the horizon. The view was spectacular, and even as he worked, the desire to do construction burned within him, which was good, because not much else interested him.

He volunteered to work out of town on every available construction job and was the only member of his uncle's construction crew who didn't rotate with other men in order to get weeks or months at home. He worked out of state all the time by choice. Sort of . . . Could he consider anything that had caused him to land in such a lonely place to actually be a choice?

Between doing construction work and helping build mission homes, he worked long, hard days and fell into a sound sleep the moment he crawled into bed. Funny, or maybe just sad, but he'd never noticed how long twenty-four hours were until Rhoda handed his heart back to him.

It'd been more than four months, and he was starting to feel a little more like himself again. Whatever that meant. For now he was content to work here. He paid an Amish family for room and board, and he'd be here until these two houses were lock-and-key ready.

He went into the garage, heading for the driveway.

"Hey, Jacob." A young Amish worker, maybe eighteen years old, stopped him while filling his tool belt with nails. "Want to go to the singing with me this Sunday? There are some really pretty Amish girls around these parts."

Jacob shook his head. "Not me. Thanks."

"Kumm on." The young man's forehead wrinkled. "It'd shake up this sleepy little Amish community if a group of us visitors went."

Jacob wasn't interested in shaking up anything, but he could at least give the boy some hope. "I'll think about it." When Jacob got to the driveway, his uncle and the woman were gone. He looked past the multitude of work trucks and Amish carriages.

The toddler ran from behind a red Chevy truck parked at the curb and headed toward the house.

"Amos." The woman lunged, grabbing the little boy's wrist while holding on firmly to the child in her arms. *Duh net geh neh die Haus.*

The boy complained at her refusal to let

him go near the house, but Jacob appreciated it. Any construction area was really dangerous for children.

The woman and his uncle were looking at what appeared to be a transport trailer for riding lawn mowers that was loaded with old wood flooring and doors. A black man was leaning against the cab of the truck, watching the workers. Jacob would bet money that the man was the Amish woman's driver. But what did she want?

"Jacob." His uncle gestured toward the woman. "Esther salvages items from old homes and repurposes them. I was telling her that you would be helping the owner make decisions about floor finishing and such."

Was his uncle trying to pawn the woman off on Jacob? Mervin knew the answer to this woman's query as well as Jacob did — no, but thank you. Besides, this was his uncle's job, so why wasn't he giving the answer?

Despite himself, Jacob picked up a piece of flooring. It was gorgeous, and once it was sanded, stained, and shellacked, it would regain its luster.

"It's two-hundred-year-old pine." The woman's voice quavered as the toddler tried to tug free of her.

"It's nice, but —"

The black man moved in closer and crouched, facing them. Esther released the little boy, and he flew into the man's hands. He picked up Amos and walked off with him.

Esther breathed a sigh of relief. "You won't find this quality in anything new." She shifted the baby to the other hip. "I can give you a good deal on it."

Jacob glanced at his uncle. Mervin would've said no to a man in a heartbeat, but apparently this pretty, blond-haired, doe-eyed woman with two young children was too much for him to refuse.

Jacob shook his head. "Sorry, but we use all new materials when we build a home."

"But I have pieces — flooring, windows, bricks, doorknobs, and cabinets — that can add character to a new home. It's the perfect combination, new construction with old-world character."

"The owners are Englisch. They expect new-world character."

"How do you know that's what they want?"

Jacob stifled a sigh. Maybe his newly acquired jaded attitude was influencing him, but he didn't want to deal with a young Amish businesswoman. Was her kind a growing trend? "It takes a lot of reclaimed wood to complete a room."

"You're right, but how large is the kitchen?"

"It's twenty by twenty."

"A four-hundred-square-foot kitchen." Her eyes grew wide. "Wow. Okay, but I have enough of this" — she tapped a strip of pine — "to cover a two-hundred-square-foot floor. That could probably do two small bathrooms, one for sure. Or" — she picked up an old brick — "you could use the pine in the kitchen and then put rows of hundred-year-old brick around the edges to make up the difference. Or slate. I have some wonderful old slate in my work shed."

"Our schedule is very tight, and it would take a lot longer to install repurposed items. Whatever you've salvaged will come in odd sizes, and probably a third of the best you have will still be too damaged to use once we try to place it."

"But I make allowances for those things. That's my responsibility, not yours."

Her responsibility? He seriously doubted she knew that much about flooring a room, which meant he'd get stuck trying to make the limited supplies fit the space.

When Jacob's phone buzzed, he was glad for the interruption. He didn't wish to be rude, but she would have to take no for an answer. It's how the business world worked, and if she wanted to dabble in it, she needed to figure that out. He pulled the phone from his pocket and looked at the number. The barn office in Maine, probably his brother.

Again.

Jacob rejected the call and slid the phone back into his pocket.

"You have to answer him at some point, you know." His uncle's matter-of-fact tone didn't fool Jacob. Mervin would walk the Appalachian Trail in winter if he thought it'd help Jacob and Samuel work things out.

"You want to talk to my brother?" Jacob held out the phone to him. "Or maybe you want the phone back that you gave me?"

"No." His uncle shook his head.

Esther shifted, looking like a stranger caught in a rift between relatives, which she was. But she should've left before now. If she and her husband needed a handout, he'd dig deep into his pockets, but business was business, and he didn't need anything the woman was offering.

The phone in his pocket buzzed again. He didn't get back-to-back calls from the farm in Maine. Someone, probably his brother, called once a week and left a message — none of which Jacob had listened to. He glanced at caller ID.

Sandra.

Any thought of possibly reaching out to Esther fled. He had all the responsibilities of helping others that he could manage right now.

When he'd stepped into the Englisch world as an older teen, Sandra and her husband had taken Jacob under their wing. But that'd been a long time ago, before her husband disappeared. Since then Jacob had spent too much time helping *her* cope in the very world she belonged to — the Englisch one. The one good thing in the situation was Sandra's daughter, Casey. Jacob loved her like she was his own, and she was doing well despite her mother's issues. He declined the call. He'd already talked to Sandra twice today. Surely he could ignore her call this time.

Jacob returned the phone to his pocket. "Your goods are nice, but we don't use reclaimed products. I'm sorry."

Disappointment flitted through her eyes, but her smile said she understood. "I appreciate your time."

He nodded and walked back to the house. Is this all that life had to offer him in the way of relationships — needy ones that heaped guilt and responsibility onto him?

Maybe he should go to the singing this Sunday after all. At least it'd offer a few hours of fun with no one needing anything from him.

THREE

The wind howled, and the shutters on the old farmhouse quaked, but the chill of winter could not reach into the home. Or into Samuel's heart. He glanced from the cards in his hands to the fire dancing in the hearth. The blue heelers, Ziggy and Zara, were stretched out on the floor near the fire, sleeping soundly. The logs shifted, sending sparks flying toward those sitting on the floor playing cards.

Life . . . It made his heart pound of late. Is this what being in love did — take the ordinary and make it feel amazing? They had a lot less pressure this winter than last. No doubt about that. After months of working from before dawn until after dark, all of them had been able to relax and enjoy the past few months. But his feelings had more to do with everyone in this room than anything on the farm.

"Guck!" Isaac's voice screeched as he held

out two jacks. Rhoda's nephew had finally captured two jacks with one bounce of the ball. Arie squealed with delight and clapped her hands. The adults applauded from their spots on the braided rug while the children remained on the hardwood floor nearby so the ball would bounce properly.

Rhoda's gorgeous blue eyes met Samuel's, and his happiness stirred anew, mingling with gratitude. "I have cards to share." She held up a thick fan of them.

"I see that, but I wouldn't want to take your cards" — he cleared his throat, enjoying teasing her — "especially since the purpose of the game is to empty one's hands of all of them."

"But, Samuel, it's Valentine's Day, and you should do something really sweet."

"I should. But I'm not going to."

She laughed before frowning in mock anger.

He couldn't help but think back to this day a year ago. Rhoda had been struggling as false accusations and lies were piling legal evidence against her. Jacob fought to keep his tarnished past from coming to light for fear it would add fuel to the lies and suspicions about Rhoda. So he had gone into hiding and had stayed there way too long, leaving Samuel to take care of his girl. While

Samuel aimed to be the support she needed, he also spent his days fighting against his love for her.

It'd been his goal to hide his love from Rhoda and not betray his brother. In the long run Samuel had lost both battles.

Jacob had yet to forgive him. That weighed heavily, and Samuel prayed for his brother, but he was grateful Rhoda was here with him and able to be herself.

Rhoda's brother Steven nudged her elbow. "Here, let *me* help you with your card situation."

Her eyes grew wide as Steven eased an Uno card from his hand and laid it face up on the discard pile. It was a pick-up-four card.

"What?"

The group broke into laughter. Rhoda's sister-in-law Phoebe stroked her rounded stomach, half laughing and half grimacing from discomfort. After losing a baby last May, Phoebe and Steven had grieved hard. Now they looked forward to welcoming another little one at the end of July.

While Rhoda picked up the four cards, Leah whispered something to Landon, who grinned at her but said nothing. Samuel recognized the looks that ran between them.

If they weren't in love, they weren't far from it.

Was he wrong to allow Landon, an Englisch man four years older than Leah, to share game time with the King and Byler families? Samuel didn't know. Actually, if he'd learned anything in his twenty-six years, it was just how little he actually knew. Experience offered hints and clues, and he tried to use them to figure out the truth about whatever stood before him. But little was clear. He knew Landon was a good worker, one Rhoda had trusted and relied on years before she and Samuel met. Landon was honest and determined. And he cared for Leah. A lot.

But he wasn't Amish. That nagged at Samuel, but what was he supposed to do about it? Be controlled by his fears that Landon's Englisch lifestyle would affect Leah's future? Still, in the long history of the Amish in this country, he doubted any of them had allowed an Englisch man who was romantically interested in a family member to join fellowship time.

Leah tossed a piece of popcorn into Samuel's lap. "Your turn, bro."

"Again?" He needed to pay more attention. "Bro?" Samuel pulled the meanest card he had in his hand and laid it on the

42

discard pile.

"Oh, Samuel," Phoebe gasped through her giggles, "how *could* you?"

"What?" He looked to his left. "Leah needs more cards."

Leah waved her two remaining cards. "Think so?"

"Definitely." Samuel nodded.

"Then why, dear bro, did you use a pick-up-four card on Rhoda?"

"I didn't."

"Oh, but you did," — Rhoda scowled at him, her eyes teasing and flirting as she reached in and began getting cards — *"sweetie."*

She used that term when talking to the children and dogs — and to Samuel when ribbing him. So what had he done?

"Ya, sweetie, it's okay." Steven smirked as he leaned against the couch next to Phoebe and put his arm around her. "We don't mind a bit if you cause Rhoda to lose. Somebody has to do it."

"Wait." Samuel thrust his hand over the pile. "It's Leah's turn."

Phoebe opened her arms as little Arie crawled into her *Mamm*'s lap. "I played a reverse card. That made it go to Landon, then Leah, then you, and now Rhoda. Where were you during all that?"

"Thinking on something else." Rhoda gathered her cards. "But I will get you for this, Samuel King."

Landon chuckled. "Like adding four cards to your hand will make any difference in whether you win or lose."

"True." Rhoda nodded. "What would make a difference is if somebody helped me hold all" — the cards shot from her hands and flew in all directions — "these cards." Her shoulders drooped, but her smile was undeniable.

Even as he tried to keep a straight face, Samuel couldn't stifle his laugh. "Need some help?"

"Not from you." She waggled her head from side to side.

He valued how much she'd healed since Jacob had left. It'd been a slow journey for him too, one with plenty of remorse and grief. They hated that Jacob had been hurt, but now that seven months had passed since his departure, Samuel and Rhoda could talk about everything. As enjoyable as days like this were, he knew there wouldn't be many more this year. Prepping the orchard for springtime, with its long, hectic hours, was right around the corner.

As Samuel was helping Rhoda gather cards, Landon's cell phone buzzed, and he reached into his pocket. He usually glanced at it and slid it back into his pocket unless his grandmother was calling. But this time his smile faded, and he held the phone out toward Samuel. "It's the number from your family's farm in Pennsylvania."

Since the only phone for this place was in the barn office and they spent very little time out there when it was below freezing, Samuel had given Landon's number to his Daed in case of an emergency. The room grew quiet, and all eyes were on Samuel. He took the phone and slid his finger across the screen. *"Hallo."*

"Samuel, what's going on up there?"

His Daed's tone was severe, and a bad feeling washed over Samuel. "Can you hold for a few minutes and let me get elsewhere?"

"Ya."

Samuel got up, hitting the mute button. "I need to talk to him, but apparently there isn't an emergency."

Leah tossed her cards onto the pile. "I'm done."

Landon and Steven nodded and gathered the cards. Clearly, the mood was broken. Samuel had fielded many more calls from his Daed lately, each one less tolerant of this new settlement than the previous call.

Leah moved from the floor to the couch.

"For him to stay this riled, he must be on that Amish chat line again, hearing negative stuff about us." She sighed and rolled her eyes. "They ought to call it what it is — the Amish gossip line."

"Leah, *kumm alleweil.*" Steven's gentle correction was meant to settle her, and as the only church leader for this new settlement, his words carried weight.

While walking into the kitchen, Samuel turned off the mute. "Hey, Daed. I'm surprised you're using Landon's cell when there's no emergency."

"It might be a crisis. What's this rumor I've heard about Leah seeing that Englisch assistant of Rhoda's?"

Samuel pressed his lips together. Which of the new Amish families that had moved here over the last six months had shared that information? Apparently someone intended to end the relationship.

Samuel braced himself for another uncomfortable, difficult conversation with his Daed. It seemed to be the pattern since Jacob had left. Although his Daed apparently didn't know what had caused Jacob to take off, he obviously blamed Samuel. He called regularly these days with a long list of grievances, including Rhoda being allowed to help make decisions about running the orchard and Samuel changing its name from Kings' Orchard Maine to Orchard Bend Farms. His Daed would like the name even less if he knew it'd been Rhoda's idea.

"Leah is in her *rumschpringe,* Daed."

"But I let her leave Pennsylvania under your charge, and I'm not going to put up with these rumors."

Dozens of arguments ran through Samuel's mind. As he opened his mouth to rebut, he saw movement in the living room that caught his attention.

The three women — Rhoda, Leah, and Phoebe — had moved to the couch. Arie was sitting in Leah's lap, and her hair had been taken down from its bun. Leah brushed Arie's hair as the women whispered and giggled. They worked hard and loved deeply. He'd never witnessed the kind of unison they had.

Phoebe's eyes grew wide, and she grabbed Rhoda's hand and placed it on her stomach. Rhoda's smile warmed his heart, and when she looked his way, he grinned. As much as Rhoda rejoiced with Phoebe over the unborn child, Samuel looked forward to the day Rhoda and he would start a family. But since he had stolen his brother's girl, he'd have to wait until Jacob was okay with their marrying. The question was, how many

47

years would they need to wait?

"Samuel," his Daed growled, "are you even listening to me?"

Samuel's mouth went dry as angst grabbed hold of him. He'd been clinging to the hope that if he handled the situation right between his Daed and Leah, he could keep all the relationships intact. Had it been a false hope?

The Amish had ways of applying constant pressure when they disagreed with someone's behavior, and if that failed to change the person's actions, he or she was shunned. Not officially through the church, but through mandatory actions that said you're not welcome here anymore unless you change. How could he possibly shun Leah? Worse, how could Rhoda and Phoebe do so? But if it came to the point of shunning her and they didn't do as told, they would be subject to the same treatment. Besides, Steven was a church leader now. He and Phoebe would have to uphold the *Ordnung,* or the consequences would be unbearable. Maybe Daed just needed a reminder of who was the spiritual head here.

"Steven is working with Leah, praying for her, guiding her as he sees fit."

"He's young, not yet thirty, and some don't think he's handling the Old Ways as carefully as he should. Others doubt he should've been chosen since his sister remains under a shadow of doing witch-craft."

"That's absurd. Rhoda doesn't —"

"Save it, Samuel. I heard on the chat line that a bishop in Berks County is thinking of moving his family to your area. If he docs, he'll outrank Steven and bring the kind of order Orchard Bend Amish should've had all along."

Every Amish person who'd helped estab-lish this new settlement firmly believed in the Amish ways and culture, but they had pushed a lot of lines since arriving here sixteen months ago. Their hearts were in the right place, but sometimes the Amish rules got in the way of believers following their consciences. That's when those on Orchard Bend Farms bent the rules, and Samuel didn't regret doing so.

Somehow Samuel had to stop his Daed from doing anything that would cause the Old Ways to move into this home like a poisonous gas, choking the breath out of the relationships.

But how?

FOUR

While Rhoda scrubbed burned residue from a pot, she looked out the window of the harvest kitchen. Snow danced and twirled, white specks of beauty against the black sky. The white dust insulated the world from sounds, bringing such peacefulness, and she soaked in the lingering quiet.

The farmhouse sat on the same acreage as the harvest kitchen, but even without snow or night hindering one's vision, it couldn't be seen or heard from here. However, she knew it was loud and busy this time of day. If this winter weather continued much longer, her niece and nephew might explode with pent-up energy. But whenever Rhoda came here to work, she enjoyed the blissful silence.

A light scratch on the kitchen door made her heart quicken. That was Samuel's knock, if one could call it that. As she grabbed a hand towel, her chest thudded with anticipation. It didn't matter how much she relished quietness, her heart was far from silent on the topic of Samuel King.

"Kumm." She strode across the room, smiling.

Unlike their first winter in Maine, this one had been a lot of fun. She could still hear her friends' and family members' shouts and laughter and see their beautiful smiles framed by red noses and pink cheeks when they went sledding or ice-skating.

The door handle jiggled but didn't turn. Were Samuel's gloved hands unable to open it, or were his hands full?

Just as she reached for the knob, the door swung open, and a blast of cold air blew snow inside. Samuel entered, and the sight of him — his broad shoulders and expressive brown eyes — made her wonder if he had any idea how much she loved him. They talked about most things but not this. Not yet.

Sure enough, his arms held a large covered basket. She glanced outside. He was by himself? That was odd. By his own rules he was rarely alone with her. She closed the door behind him. As he set the basket on the table, the aroma of chicken and fresh-baked bread mingled with the smell from her burned concoction.

She swiped the towel across the table where flakes of snow had landed and melted. "Hard to believe it'll officially be spring in two days."

"I agree." Samuel removed his snow-covered hat and hung it on a peg. "I'm looking forward to warmer weather." He glanced at the pendulum wall clock. "But that needs winding."

She studied it a moment. It had been stuck on ten minutes after six for quite a while. How had she not noticed that?

He moved to the wood stove and held out his hands. "Do you have any idea what time it is?"

"Time for you to bring me food?"

He shook his head, a trace of a smile showing despite his apparent efforts to subdue it. "If I didn't remind you it was time to eat, how many meals would you miss?"

"Apparently none. Ever again." Her eyes met his, and she could feel how drawn he was to her.

He returned to the table and propped his palms on the edge of the basket, still studying her. "Sustenance. It's what's for dinner. Now go wash your face and whatever else you like to do before you eat."

"I'll hurry." She scurried up the narrow

stairs that led to a small attic.

Rhoda lit a kerosene lamp and pulled the straight pins out of her apron. Despite the really rough start when they had moved to Maine seventeen months ago, she'd still choose to come here and do it all again because it had brought what now existed between Samuel and her.

Thoughts of Jacob tried to push in again, but she said another prayer for him and then refused to ponder where he was or how he was doing. She unpinned her hair and ran a brush through it. With her hair fixed, prayer *Kapp* in place, and a fresh apron on, she blew out the lantern and descended the stairs.

She was on the third-to-the-last step when she stopped cold. Samuel had set up what looked to be new outdoor furniture. And the worktable had been transformed into a kitchen table of sorts with two perfectly arranged place settings, a kerosene lamp, and a small cake . . . with lit candles.

Her birthday! Until this moment it hadn't dawned on her. She was twenty-four.

If she could find her voice, she'd say something. Her family hadn't celebrated birthdays since her sister had been killed on her Daed's birthday, and Rhoda had stopped even thinking about them.

Samuel walked to her. "Now that I know when your birthday is, it's a day I'll always celebrate."

Tears pricked her eyes, and she swallowed hard, emotions carrying her like a snowflake on a strong wind. Her nature was to put on blinders and labor like a workhorse, but Samuel had ways of removing her blinders and causing her to pause so she could take in the beauty of life.

He motioned to her. "Kumm. Make a wish and blow out the candles before all the frosting is covered in wax."

She drew a shaky breath and walked to a barstool. He'd thought of everything, even coffee, and she hoped he'd brought the de-caffeinated kind. If not, after they cleaned up here, they'd move to the farmhouse with its many chaperones and stay up half the night talking.

Hmm. Maybe she did want caffeinated coffee after all.

At the table she paused, closed her eyes, and then blew out the candles, wishing for something silly — for this to be the last snowfall of the spring. If she really wanted something, she'd pray for it.

She opened her eyes, feeling a little awkward about all Samuel had done to honor her. Why had he spent good money to buy outdoor furniture when they had old foldup chairs? Her discomfort grew as she walked over to the all-weather wicker furniture.

"Samuel, it's lovely." Since they liked to end their day sitting outside when weather permitted, it was perfect for them, but how could she accept such a gift? "I . . . know this sounds odd, but it's easier when we argue and yell."

"And I'm all for making your life as easy as possible." He smiled. "You know, through yelling." He pulled out a barstool for her. "Just not today."

But she knew he preferred not to argue. It was just necessary when two strong-willed people with heavy-duty opinions had a relationship. She returned to the table. "I can't believe you did this for me."

"The furniture I ordered via phone and had it delivered. Landon drove me to the store where I bought the cake and candles. And Phoebe made the dinner. So nothing I did was all that remarkable. But you are free to count my actions every bit as amazing as you wish. It is, after all, your birthday."

She laughed. He smiled and bowed his head. She finished her silent prayer before he did, so she waited. When he was done and looked up, she took a bite of the baked chicken and noodles. "I love this dish."

"Ya, Phoebe said it was your favorite." He used a napkin to wipe the Alfredo sauce from his lips. "Did she cook this last year and I had no idea it was your birthday?"

"Ya." Several months ago she'd told him her birth date, explaining that since her sister was killed on their Daed's birthday, her whole family had stopped celebrating those days.

Emma's death had shattered far more than their hearts. It had broken traditions and celebrations. It had stolen sleep and peace. What it didn't steal, it buried under their shock and grief. Her family simply learned how to maneuver with missing limbs.

Her eyes met Samuel's, and sadness and guilt faded as love for him captured every thought. Her heart pounded.

Samuel swiped the back of his thumb across his forehead. "Did you create a new recipe today?"

She laughed. "Only if you count the ones that list what *not* to do."

He smiled. "Life needs those too, doesn't it?"

The conversation moved slowly as they ate. The ends of Samuel's usually straight hair curled into ringlets as it dried from the melted snow. "It's after ten, Rhoda. Once we eat and clean up, you need to call it a night, okay?"

"It's that late?"

He nodded.

She bit her bottom lip, hoping to tease him while keeping a straight face. "Then why didn't you bring me dinner sooner?"

"Because you messed up my plans. *Gross dank.*"

"You're very welcome. Anytime you need anything messed up, I'm your girl."

Amusement danced in his eyes. "How is it that I like the sound of that at the same time I don't like the sound of that?"

"Because you confuse easily." She raised one eyebrow, aiming to look defiant.

"Birthday girl or not, don't give me any lip . . . uh, eyebrow. I had planned this celebration to be at the house, and I kept waiting on you to arrive, but you never came home."

The man was going to drive her crazy, making her feel so unworthy of his kindness, so she decided to do what she did best in these situations — push back. "That's not true. As long as I'm on this farm, I am home."

He grinned, looking as if she'd given *him* a gift. "I apologize for lying."

"And well you should." She waved her

fork in the air. She noticed there was a lumpy blanket over one of the worktables. "Samuel King, have you done something else?"

"Two things, actually."

She pointed at him. "Do not make me yell at you."

Samuel laughed. "But I'm so good at it." His lopsided smile melted her heart. She giggled, nodding in agreement. Thankfully, when they argued, he neither caved because he loved her nor tried to bend her will to his because she was *only* a woman. He fought fair, and she appreciated it . . . eventually.

She eyed the long workbench, noting that whatever was under the king-size blanket was quite bulky. "What is it?"

"Go see if you must."

She crossed the room and removed the blanket. Was she looking at a new kind of apple butter stirrers . . . automatic ones?

Samuel stayed seated. "They're not really a birthday gift, but since they arrived yesterday, I thought I'd surprise you with them."

"Are they automated stirrers?"

"Ya. It'll take some time to set them up, but they'll run off solar power, and you'll be able to set a timer."

"Samuel, this had to cost a fortune."

"It'll save you enough time and backbreaking work to be more than worth it. I would've gotten them in time for last year's harvest, but they had to be specially made to fit our Old Order Amish harvest kitchen."

"Denki."

He nodded, and from seemingly nowhere Samuel slid a gift across the table. "It's not much."

She returned to the table and eased it from him. "Samuel, what else have you done?"

"Open it and find out."

She sat and turned it over, enjoying the beauty and smooth texture of the wrapping paper. It felt like a book of some kind. She wouldn't blame him if it were a cookbook. She could hardly make anything other than recipes to can. At least those came out delicious and sold really well, shoring up her waning confidence when it came to the kitchen.

As Rhoda opened the gift, she realized it was a photo album. "Well, aren't you the bold one? An Amish man giving pictures as a gift."

"I won't tell if you won't."

"Oh, I'm definitely telling." She winked before flipping through it, seeing images Iva had taken — pictures of her niece and nephew; of the orchard; of everyone eating at the table, all except Iva, who was taking the picture. Most were carefully done, showing no one posing and only a few discreet but full faces. What a beautiful treasure.

Her heart jumped when she came across a picture from last fall of Samuel with her niece asleep in his lap and her nephew standing at his knees talking to him. She remembered being in the living room with him when this happened. It was a Saturday evening, and she and Samuel were going over business stuff when Arie climbed into his lap and soon fell sound asleep. It'd stolen her heart that day, but she hadn't realized Iva had taken a picture of it.

When she turned the page and saw a collage of tiny images, an odd sensation skittered through her. The page blurred for a moment. Was it her imagination, or was God trying to share something with her? As she prayed and ran her finger over the collage, she realized someone from the core group was missing. But every one of them was on that page mere moments ago. The blurry images wavered and shifted before being covered with a black veil. She blinked, and nausea churned. Someone in an Amish dress had disappeared from the page, and

60

the rest were fighting to survive without her.

Rhoda's insides quaked, but she wouldn't share her thoughts with Samuel. She searched the image. It seemed that either Phoebe or Leah was gone. Rhoda couldn't tell which, but fear ran cold chills down her spine. The missing one wasn't just living elsewhere. She was beyond being reached by any human method.

Alarm gripped Rhoda, and she couldn't swallow.

Dear God, please let these thoughts just be my imagination.

FIVE

The house seemed unusually quiet for a Sunday evening as Leah tiptoed down the stairs. She didn't have to sneak out, but that was easier than having to meet the eyes of those she shared a home with as she left to attend an Englisch church week after week.

Her brother and the others knew where she went on Sunday evenings — Unity Hill Church.

She pulled her coat and scarf off the wooden pegs. Before she opened the front door, Steven walked out of the kitchen, a small plate of banana pudding in one hand and a spoonful of it on its way to his mouth. He spotted her and lowered the spoon. His gentle smile was outweighed by the concern, maybe also disappointment, in his eyes. "That time again, huh?"

Leah nodded. "I'll be back around ten."

"Okay."

Leah started to open the door.

"Maybe I shouldn't say anything, but then again" — Steven crossed the living room, closing the gap between them — "maybe I should. Would you mind if I share a few thoughts . . . just out of concern?"

"I'm going to church, Steven. Not to some sinful place."

"I know, and I want to like the idea, but it concerns me. We live as we do because we believe it's the community's responsibility to live as close to the ways of the New Testament as possible."

"And it concerns me that the Amish may be seeking a fulfilling life through giving up who God has made us to be so we can serve a man-made community."

"Is Unity Hill less of a man-made community than the Amish community?" Steven stood there, the expression on his face indicating deep humility, but his eyes radiated desperation that she would hear him *this time.* "The Word says to 'lead a quiet and peaceable life' and not to be 'conformed to this world.' "

She had no doubts that his concern was genuine. "We agree on what the Word says, Steven. It's how one accomplishes those goals that divides us. Rather than the Ordnung dictating how I should live, isn't it possible the decision should be between each individual and God, just as salvation is?"

His gentle smile wavered. "Perhaps. But there is strength in numbers, in banding together against the onslaught of worldliness. What are a few rules when one is surrounded by such a rich culture of faith and unbroken families?"

Steven never went for the jugular. He stayed steadfast and gentle. She knew too many church leaders who would point fingers and sling the phrase "you're going to hell for . . ." A lot of things could fill that spot — embracing the Englisch lifestyle or not submitting to her Daed's wishes, just to mention two.

Steven finally took a bite of his pudding. "You stay safe. I think we're supposed to get more snow later tonight."

"We'll drive slowly." She slid into her coat. "Bye."

She scurried to Landon's truck and climbed in. "Sorry." She shivered. "I had almost made it out the door when I got held up by Steven."

"Not a problem." Landon pulled out of the driveway. "Was it?"

"No. Steven's as careful with his words as I'm trying to be with mine."

When time allowed, she and Landon had

attended Unity Hill on Sunday nights for nearly a year and a half. A few months back they sat in his truck in the church parking lot, talking about faith and their hopes until nearly midnight. And then they prayed together, giving their hearts and lives to Christ. The prayer didn't change or solidify anything about their future together. They agreed on that. The prayer meant they were both new creatures in Christ, just as it said in Second Corinthians chapter 5. That night, bathed in the forgiveness and hope of Christ, Leah knew that with a past like hers, she'd already received far more than she deserved.

But she had no clue how to pull away from her family or how to leave the family business when they needed her.

Landon pressed the brakes hard. "Whoa." He pointed out the window at a large moose crossing the road.

"We spot more moose than anyone I know."

They started talking and never paused until they were walking through the church doors. They went to the classroom where the young adults met. The topic for the last six months had been discipleship. After that they listened to the preacher teach from the pulpit on the grace of God. This was her favorite topic: "There is therefore now no condemnation to them . . ." Her heart pounded with excitement. This pastor used numerous historical books and discussed the best translation of words from the original Hebrew and Aramaic. The teachings were so different from those in the Amish church. It fascinated her, and yet she could see how the Word for each — the Amish and the Englisch — was built on faith and had merit.

After the last song they walked to the front steps of the church.

Pastor Weld stood about halfway down the stairs, telling folks good-bye. He held out his hand to Leah. "It's always good to see you two."

Leah shook his weathered hand. "We enjoy coming."

"Good." He shook Landon's hand. "Would you mind if I made a home visit one day?"

Landon hesitated. "You could come to my place anytime."

"Yes, only your place, Landon. I should've thought to clarify my meaning." Pastor Weld lowered his voice. "I understand the complexities of Leah's family being Amish and the need for discretion."

"Exactly." Landon nodded. "Do you need

my address?"

A horse and buggy slowed on the main street right in front of the church. Leah suddenly wished she were invisible. Since she and Landon were under the church's floodlights, whoever was in that rig could see Landon and her clearly. But with it being dark, she couldn't see who was in the rig.

"You filled out a card about a year ago." The pastor pulled a pair of leather gloves out of his pocket and put them on. "Do you still live in the same place?"

"Yeah." Landon glanced at her and then to the road.

The pastor looked in that direction. "Then I'll use that information."

As the horse picked up speed, Leah could see the back of the rig. It had a spot of black paint, a repaired area that she recognized. The buggy belonged to Crist. He was probably joy riding a bit after tonight's singing. Since there were a few new girls in the settlement, he likely had a girl with him.

Would he cause trouble for her and Landon? Those within her household kept her rumschpringe ways quiet. If her parents realized what she was up to, there was no telling what they'd do to stop her.

"We'd better go." Landon nodded to the pastor, and then he put his arm protectively around the waist of her coat as if that would somehow shield her from the firestorm that might come her way. But the gesture was sweet and a first, so she slowed her pace, enjoying feeling loved and cherished.

Once in the truck Landon started the engine. "Any idea who was in the rig?"

"Probably Crist. It was his buggy."

"He might not say anything, but if he does, how much strife will it stir?"

"Hard to tell. I don't know the new families very well, and what happens depends on how angry people get after they learn I dress like the Englisch when I go to church here." If the news got back to her parents, they'd try to pull her home, but it was borrowing trouble to worry about that, so why voice it to Landon?

He leaned back against the headrest. "I suppose we knew someone outside Orchard Bend Farms would find out sooner or later."

"Yeah, but I always opt for later."

"Me too . . . for your sake."

But she knew he also wanted to protect Rhoda. If Leah got in trouble, Landon would too, and Rhoda could be forced to let him go.

There were so many reasons they needed their relationship to remain as private as possible. So many people they both cared about might pay an unfair price. As much as they tried to act as if their future would work itself out, their lives were entangled with the strictness of the Old Ways, and there wasn't anything anyone could do about it.

Six

Jacob's breath formed white clouds as he drove the wagon of lumber through the darkened back streets of town. It wasn't a very big town, and it closed up tight before seven on weeknights. Even the diner served only the breakfast and lunch crowds before locking its doors.

But he had too much restless energy and too little social life to stop work because of nightfall. *Without any family or real friends around . . .* The half thought threw darts at him, and he refused to finish it. But he couldn't get free of how he felt.

Something on the sidewalk more than a block ahead caught his eye. He focused on it and could make out a silhouette of a black bonnet on someone who was crouched, perhaps messing with a crate of some sort on the ground. Other than this woman the streets were empty of cars, rigs, and people.

But even if they were filled with folks, he'd

be just as isolated. Still, the worst of the hurt from the breakup had been behind him for months now. The problem was that, unlike heartache, loneliness couldn't be fixed by time passing. It actually grew wider and deeper and darker — like an unattended sinkhole, he imagined.

Distraction seemed to be the only pardon granted from the depth of his loneliness. So he'd started attending singings a couple of months ago. How else would he find the right person? He'd even gone on a few dates. But —

The shadowy woman stood, grabbed the box, and hurried toward the crosswalk. Apparently she wasn't going to stop at the curb. Couldn't she hear the *clippety-clop* of his horse?

"Whoa." Jacob tugged hard on the reins, trying to halt the rig quickly. The phone in his coat pocket vibrated, but he couldn't look right now to see who was calling.

Maybe the woman's problem was her black bonnet, which seemed to serve like blinders on a horse. The horse whinnied in protest as Jacob pulled the brakes on the rig. The woman looked up and stopped abruptly, remaining on the curb. He motioned for her to go. She nodded and stepped onto the street. Once she was directly in front of him, a nearby siren blasted.

His horse jolted. *"Begreiflich."*

A few seconds later blue strobe lights pierced the darkness, and a police car slowed as it passed him.

His horse lunged forward.

The woman tried to retreat to the curb, but his horse broke into a gallop.

"Whoa!"

Everything blurred. The woman screamed. Metal rattled and plunked. The horse whinnied. Jacob kept yelling *whoa.*

Finally the rig stopped some thirty feet down the road. Complete silence filled the air. Had the horse trampled her? It'd all happened too quickly for him to be sure.

He jumped down and saw the woman sprawled flat on the asphalt, faceup. What appeared to be old doorknobs, handles, and rusty hinges were in disarray around her.

He ran to her. *"Bischt du allrecht?"*

"Ya." She grimaced and blinked. *"Ich bin ganz gut."*

He doubted that she was quite good, as she'd said. But Jacob recognized her. She was the woman who'd come to the construction site four months ago. What was her name? His cell phone buzzed again. "Just stay still. Did the horse trample you?"

"I don't think so." She inhaled deeply, frowning. "I think its shoulder knocked me out of the way and the breath from my lungs. I just need a minute." She placed her hands on her stomach and drummed her fingers. Within seconds her brows knit. "Jacob?"

For four months he'd been glad they weren't in the same church district and relieved they hadn't bumped into each other, in part because he'd been rather abrupt with her and extremely rude to his uncle in front of her. But most of all he did not want to have to turn down her salvaged goods again. And now he'd run over her. "Ya, it's me." Should he assist her in getting up, or should he keep her right here in the road while he waited for help? "I'm going to call for an ambulance."

"Why? So they can help you and the police finish the job?" Her whispery laugh surprised him, and then she gasped as if in pain.

His phone buzzed again. The third call in the last five minutes. He'd like to see who was repeatedly phoning him, but it was probably Sandra having a meltdown for one reason or another. Helping her wasn't much fun, but he had no rocks to throw. What was it like for her to deal with bipolar disorder while being a single parent? "Are you hurt?"

She sat upright. "Only my knee, and it was injured before this."

Jacob remained kneeling beside her. What *was* her name?

She stood up, wobbling a bit, but Jacob didn't offer her a hand. Married women didn't take any man's hand except their husband's.

"She girdeth her loins with strength. . . . She has no fear."

"What?"

"That passage was going through my head when you ran over me with your horse." She shook the dirt off her skirt, standing a little straighter. "Of course the next thing that went through my head was 'Grandma got run over by a reindeer.' "

Did she have a concussion? Why else would she crack jokes? He stayed right beside her as she moved like a snail toward the curb. "How bad do you hurt?"

"About as bad as getting hit by a horse while crossing a street." She paused, looking up at him. "Really? None of my quips even get a smile?"

If his sense of humor hadn't died, it was on life support.

She continued walking. "Apparently you don't understand that being run over is

74

probably the most entertaining event to happen to me in a while."

If she was trying to help him feel better about the incident, it was working.

"I'm Esther Beachy." She sat on the curb, rubbing her knee. "We met a few months back."

"Ya, you had salvaged goods."

She nodded. "Speaking of, while I wait for my head to stop spinning and my knee to feel better, would you mind getting my things?"

"Oh. Sure." He grabbed the wooden crate she'd dropped and gathered the old door-knobs and hardware from the asphalt. Once he had the items in the crate, he set it in the gutter beside her feet and sat next to her. She ran her hands over the items, but despite her sense of humor, she was trembling.

He had no idea where the closest medical facility was. "I still think you need to be seen."

She worked on the kinks in her shoulders. "Relax, I need maybe twenty minutes tops of sitting here, and then I'll be fine."

Jacob propped one elbow on his bent knee. The minutes passed, and only one vehicle drove down this side street. All was quiet except for his phone, which wouldn't stop buzzing. Not only did it seem rude to look at it right now, but the Amish in this area were against using cell phones for any reason.

He stared down the road. What were the odds of the event that had just happened — a police car, an Amish man in a rig, and a pedestrian on a deserted back street at the same time?

There wasn't much excitement happening among the Amish in Virginia. That was for sure. Not that he expected it. At least the Appalachian ridges and valleys were beautiful.

She rubbed the back of her neck before turning to face him. "You okay?"

"Me? Of course. I'm not the one who got hit by a horse."

"Just because a person is fine physically, that doesn't make him fine emotionally."

She'd nailed that truth. He'd walked away from Rhoda without a scratch, and yet his heart had been cut out. But since that day, each time he crammed his belongings into his travel bag and moved to another town, he toted less emotional baggage. His move here had been his best yet. He expected the next one to be even better.

His life felt like a twelve-step program for surviving not being loved enough by Rhoda

76

— and losing her to his brother. He was no longer brokenhearted. Or angry. Or resentful. Except for the restlessness and loneliness, he was somewhat content.

Esther's hands trembled as she rubbed her forehead. "Four months later and now you're not even looking to see who's calling you?"

"I was trying not to be rude."

She chuckled. "Ya, I guess flattening a woman will do that to a man." She rubbed her temples. "Check your phone, Jacob."

Relieved at her insistence, he pulled it from his pocket.

Sandra, just as he'd figured. When she became this desperate for him to answer, he knew he'd better do so — for her sake and Casey's. "Do you mind if I take this?"

"Oh, please." She made a face. "Answer it."

He ran his finger across the screen and put the phone to his ear. "Hey, what's up?"

"I was at a red light, and someone ran into the back of our car!"

"Someone rear-ended your car just now?"

"No. Thirty minutes ago! That's how long I've been trying to reach you!" Her screeching and her exaggeration of time indicated she wasn't far from full panic.

"Is Casey with you?"

77

"Yeah." Sandra sighed. "But I'm important too, you know."

That she was, and she was also difficult,
moody, and high-strung. Still, for reasons
that defied all logic, she mattered. "Of
course you're important to me too. You
know that. Come on, Sandra, just breathe.
Can I speak to Casey?"

"Yeah. Here."

Muffled noises came through the phone
and then, "Jacob?" Casey's little voice
washed over him.

"Hi, doodlebug. You okay?"

"Mama's upset."

"I know, but your mama will feel calm and
happy soon. Are you hurt?"

"It was a big boom, like thunder."

He cradled the phone closer, wishing he
could hug her. They'd talked about noises
several times before. "And thunder doesn't
hurt anybody. It just startles them, right?"

"That's right." Her voice quivered, and he
imagined her eyes getting teary. "You coming home?"

To Casey, wherever she and her mom
lived was Jacob's home. "I can't come home
just yet. But I'll call you before bedtime
tonight, and we'll read *Winnie-the-Pooh*."
They each had a copy of the book, and at
least three times a week, he read while she

looked at the pictures. "Let me talk to your mama again."

"The car," Sandra said. "Do you have any idea what it'll cost to get the lights fixed?" She rushed through explaining the whole scenario again and again.

Jacob stood and meandered down the sidewalk. He probably should've done that as soon as he answered, but he didn't want to go far. Running over Esther was bad enough. He wouldn't leave her sitting on the curb while he looked for a more private place to talk.

Sandra had no one other than him, and he wasn't around a lot. He visited them far more often than was convenient and sent money to help with bills. Last year when he'd learned that she'd lied to him for years in order to keep him in her life, he was really tempted to walk away and not look back. But as out of sorts as Jacob could get at times with life and God, he'd never forgotten the hours that preceded Casey being born. She was nearly four now, and Jacob remained as faithful to the difficult relationship as he could. He was like a brother to Sandra — one she lied to when it suited her and one she needed financial help from regularly.

He whistled, trying to get her to pause.

"Sandra? Helloooo?" She finally hushed. "Come on. You can do this. Get control. Just breathe. Having a fender bender is really upsetting, but you're looping. Do you realize that?" Looping was when she said the same thing over and over. If she didn't gain control, she'd continue doing it until she was so wound up that she couldn't sleep or eat decently for weeks. "Trust me. We'll get the car fixed. The only important part about this incident is that you and Casey are safe, and you're fine, right?"

"When are you coming for another visit?"

"I was there for Christmas."

"And it's now March."

Had three months already passed? "True." She sounded as if she needed a concrete commitment to when he'd visit again. "I have an idea. How about I head to your place the day I wrap it up here? That means I'll arrive in about three weeks, and I'll make the visit as long as I can before I start my next construction job."

"Really?" Her voice changed, the panic already fading. "I thought I wouldn't see you for another six months at the earliest. You promise?"

"I do." He mentally calculated what it'd take to get there. It was the same trip he'd made here, only in reverse, so it'd be a two-hour trip by car to the train station in DC. He needed to hire a driver for that, but he'd rather get to a hub like Union Station than use a little depot in the Charlottesville area. Too many times their limited schedules didn't allow much to choose from. He'd then need to change trains in Boston. "You can mark it down, Sandra. I'll be there around noon on Saturday, April 13."

"You're the best, Jacob."

Doubtful. But he missed Casey. A project he could do for her popped into his head. She needed a play set of some sort, and if he built her one, it'd be a constant reminder of his love, wouldn't it?

"Ya, me and Winnie-the-Pooh are the best."

She chuckled.

"I need to go, Sandra. Give Casey a kiss for me."

"Okay. Talk to you later tonight."

"Sure thing." He disconnected the call and slid the phone into his pocket. He walked the few yards back to Esther. "If you're feeling better, I can give you a lift to wherever you were going."

She stared up at him. "Maybe we should talk first."

He hesitated. It was dark and cold. He just wanted to make sure she was okay, get her somewhere safe, and go on his way.

She nodded to the curb beside her. "Please."

He sat.

"I believe God directs our steps, just like it says in Proverbs, even if that direction knocks us down and sends our treasures flying."

He believed God *could* direct one's steps. God had certainly seemed to direct him away from Rhoda time and again while putting Samuel in her path. Apparently He'd directed Samuel's steps. And Rhoda's. "Is that what you call those old doorknobs, hinges, and handles — treasures?"

She smiled. "They are antiques, but be that as it may, I believe God has caused our paths to cross. Just last week I was thinking that if I could talk with you, I'd ask a favor."

"About showing the owners of the new houses your reclaimed items?"

"No." She elongated the word, making a face. "We had that conversation, and it's over."

He never accepted no as easily as Esther had. Maybe he should. Evidently, holding on to hope only made one try to make relationships work when they should end. "So what did you want to talk about?"

"Dora."

82

Esther wanted to talk about the girl he was dating? "How are you two connected?"

"Sisters."

He rubbed his aching head. How many coincidences could one evening hold? Was there a full moon behind those clouds?

After months of single Amish construction men attending singings, Jacob had started going too. He'd met Dora at a singing a couple of months back, and it didn't take him long to realize that none of the other guys had asked her out. He liked the idea of bringing her out of her shell and opening her mind a bit to the world around her. So he had gone out with her three times since then, which was probably two dates too many, but something about her shy, awkward ways brought out the best in him.

Esther propped her folded arms on her knees. "She seems to think you're a great guy, but based on the phone call you just had, I tend to think you have someone already."

Jacob debated how to answer Esther. He hated questions and people prying, so maybe he should tell her it was none of her business. But rudeness on top of running into her with his horse seemed a bit much. "Sandra is a friend. She's never been more than that."

Esther nodded, but the wariness didn't leave her eyes, and he suspected she didn't believe him. As he recalled the phone conversation, he could see why. But that didn't mean he owed her more than he'd already said.

"Besides, Dora and I are a universe away from serious, so no harm, no foul."

"Perhaps for you."

He shrugged. "She had a nice time. I expanded her small-town thinking. And when I leave here for good the middle of next month, she'll realize I meant what I said — that I was only passing through her life."

"Despite having gone out with her three times, you clearly don't know her *at all.*"

Maybe not, but if Dora was getting serious, he was ready to let her go. All he'd wanted to do was help her overcome her shyness.

Jacob stretched his legs, propping the soles of his boots on the asphalt. "I have three younger sisters, and I can tell you that you're being entirely too overprotective."

"I'll admit I can be unfairly cynical, but I'm not sure it's possible to be overprotective when it comes to innocent girls and handsome young men."

Since she sounded sincere and apparently

meant no insult, he resisted the urge to ask, *Just what are you accusing me of?*

"For my sister's sake, I . . . I'm just trying to figure out your real goal."

He stared into the dark, cloudy sky, struggling with whether to answer. Something about Esther caused him to relax his usual tendency to shut out people, and he longed to be honest. "To forget." The blackness of the sky seemed to go on forever, and he felt lost in it.

Her silence felt appropriate, but as he kept his focus heavenward, he could feel her studying him. "It was a particularly bad breakup, wasn't it?"

He nodded.

Again she waited, and he appreciated that she didn't rush into the topic with silly clichés or empty words of advice as if she had answers.

"I forgot that men can be vulnerable too, and I am sorry for that." After several long moments she softly cleared her throat. "The good part is you're not holed up, licking your wounds. You're getting out and trying to move forward after a painful breakup. But I am concerned for my sister. You and I both have had our hearts broken, and I don't want her to go through that."

"It's been a few dates. The worst that can

happen is she'll be disappointed."

"You're wrong about that. She's been sensitive since our Daed died."

A loss like that changed people — their thinking and their needs. "I didn't realize he'd died. When?"

"Nine years ago. Dora was eleven."

"You must've been a teen."

"Eighteen."

That meant Esther was twenty-seven, two years older than he . . . well, after he turned twenty-five this summer. "I'm sorry for your family's loss."

Her faint smile spoke of genuine peace, and he envied it. "Job said it well: 'Yet man is born unto trouble, as the sparks fly upward.' "

"You think about God a lot."

The sounds of a rig drew closer.

She shrugged, kindness radiating from her smile. "At least I do tonight, which is to be expected, I think."

Interest in what she meant overrode his hesitancy to ask. Besides, she hadn't been reluctant to ask him personal questions. "Tonight?"

She circled her gloved thumbs around each other, looking thoughtful. "It was on this night —"

"Essie." A man yelled from a rig as it came

to a halt near them. A bearded man jumped out. "Are you okay?"

"Ya." She stood, hobbling on one foot.

"When you didn't pick up the phone in the warehouse, I got worried." He rushed to her and took her by the arm.

"I never made it that far. I had a bit of an accident, and this man helped me."

"Did you injure your knee again?"

"Perhaps. Now mind your manners."

"*Ach,* ya." The man looked up and held out his hand. "Ammon, and denki."

"Jacob, and *gern gschehne.*" They'd barely shaken hands when Ammon returned his full attention to guiding Esther to the rig.

"Let's get you home."

Jacob grabbed the crate of *treasures* and set it in the rig.

"Denki, Jacob." Esther waved.

Jacob returned the gesture and headed for his rig. Parts of their conversation had been pretty uncomfortable, yet he was glad they'd talked. He needed to know that Dora might be getting serious, although he wasn't quite sure what to do about it. Should he not call her again, or should he tell her face to face about his plans? Which would be easier on her self-esteem? Based on what Esther had said, he apparently had little understanding of how Dora thought. Or women in general, for that matter.

As he stood in the silence and emptiness of the small town, the encounter began to feel eerie. He felt a weird pulsating sensation in his chest, and his skin tingled. He'd had this feeling once before — the day the tornado came through and God used Rhoda and him to save his family.

Was there something more to this encounter with Esther than he was seeing?

Seven

Sunlight streamed through breaking clouds and glistened off the melting snow in the apple orchard. Leah's homemade work sled jiggled and bounced her as the horse pulled the apparatus between another row of trees. The goal of this device, with its sack of feed for extra weight, was to tamp down vole tunnels.

If one had to work all day — and around here that's about all they did — she figured riding on a sled was the best job currently on the roster. At least now, because of the amazing harvest they'd had last fall, she received good, steady pay for her efforts.

As she came to the end of the row, she made a large loop, turning to the left, and spotted Crist Schrock crossing the field on his horse. He logged about ten hours here a week. It wasn't much compared to what they needed, but as a farmer tending his own land, he couldn't give any more time to this side job.

Before last Sunday, when he saw Landon and her coming out of church together, Crist would grin and wave and go out of his way to speak to her. But he hadn't shown much enthusiasm this week. What was bothering him more — her attending a non-Amish church or her wearing Englisch clothes with her hair down?

"Hi, Leah." He slowed his horse to an amble, probably making sure that the animal didn't kick snow in her face as he approached or, worse, that it didn't step on the back of her sled and break it.

She had to smile. Despite being disappointed in her, he remained polite. But she was especially grateful he'd remained silent about seeing her, never mentioning it to her, Landon, or apparently anyone else. Since he hadn't brought it up, neither would she. If they discussed it, an argument could erupt. Or worse, the news of it could travel throughout the Maine Amish and find its way to her Daed.

Orchard Bend Farms needed Landon far more than it needed her, because his skills and expertise were deeply intertwined with the success of the King-Byler family business. She and Landon had to move forward with great caution and patience. If they

90

didn't, they'd disrupt the stability of this farm more than Jacob had when he left. Jacob worked hard when he was here, but he'd been absent a lot. Landon had been here six days a week, helping Samuel and Rhoda, and when he did go home, he worked on the business end of the orchard through an avenue no one else could: the Internet — buyer connections, website updates, and marketing the products.

He brought his horse to a complete stop mere feet from her.

"Crist, if you didn't tower over me before, you certainly do on that horse with me sitting on this toboggan." She'd never known a man quite as tall or broad shouldered as he was.

He looked around. "You by yourself today?"

She tugged on the horse's reins, trying to keep it still. "Ya. Last I saw, Rhoda was in the third greenhouse, and Samuel was in the barn. You looking for someone in particular?"

He shifted in his saddle. "I just expected to see Landon nearby. Am I wrong to think that?"

She swallowed, wishing he didn't sound so hopeful. Should she tell him that she intended to marry Landon? Probably not.

91

She should simply avoid answering Crist's question directly. "He's not too far, I'm sure, but I haven't seen him yet today." While tugging on her gloves, she shifted the reins from one hand to the other. "I should get back to it."

He nodded. "Me too. I told Rhoda I'd see if I could get the spreader working again. It's gonna be a long spring of spreading mulch by hand if I can't."

"It's still under the lean-to on the east side."

"Okay, thanks." He rode off, going in the opposite direction from her.

Leah jiggled the reins, and the horse soon topped the hill. When she saw Landon several rows down, perched on a ladder, she couldn't help but smile. He was probably cutting scions for grafting. What was it about Landon that always made her heart rate go wild? She clicked her tongue, slapping the reins against the horse's back. Soon she was heading straight for him.

He smiled the moment he spotted her. She came to a halt, and he stepped off the ladder. "Good morning."

She smirked. "It is now. What happened that you weren't around before I had to leave for the field?"

He grinned. "I was running late."

"Uh-huh. Being lazy is more like it. Sleeping in. Meandering into the orchard when it suits you. Right?"

"That's a mighty strong accusation from a woman who's done nothing for two days but sit on a toboggan being pulled by a horse." Landon scooped up a handful of snow and eased toward her. "I think you said you were lazy, right?" He held the snow threateningly above her.

"Wow, so you've recently become lazy *and* hard of hearing." She slapped the reins and yelled for the horse to move before he got too close.

He stopped and shrugged, so Leah brought the rig to a halt. He tucked his hands behind him, meandering toward her while staring into the sky and whistling.

"You're fooling no one. Put down the snow." She tapped the reins against the horse, causing it to move away from Landon.

"What snow?" He moved his hands from behind his back. "This stuff?" He threw the ball he'd made and hit her directly above her coat collar.

"Landon!"

The two-way crackled. "Lunch in thirty." Iva sounded chipper, and Leah imagined she was keeping Phoebe quite entertained.

Leah slowed the horse again. "That's our cue to head for home. Come on."

He looked leery of her offer to wait on him, but he headed for the toboggan anyway.

When he was almost there, she took off again. Then stopped. "Problem, Landon?"

"Problem, thy name is Leah King."

She made a face. "Landon Olson, thy name is not Shakespeare."

Landon walked up and stepped onto the back of the sled.

"Geh!" she hollered, tapping the reins against the horse's back. Her command caused the horse to jolt forward, and Landon started to fall backward but somehow managed to land belly first on the sack of feed behind her.

He crawled to a sitting position and straddled the sack of feed. "Don't you know you can't keep a good man down?"

"I knew that. I just didn't realize you were a good man." She turned, her face inches from his.

He shook his head. "The older you become, Leah King, the meaner you get."

"And yet you fight to ride on my toboggan anyway."

He closed the space between them and reached his arms around each side of her.

94

"Until the day I die," he whispered.

What a rare moment of him being so honest and so close, even though thick coats separated them. Actually, if the coats weren't between them, Landon wouldn't be where he was. She knew that. But he was suddenly more willing to show affection.

He kissed her cheek, bringing added warmth to this cold spring day. "How's your morning been?"

She angled her head so she could see him. "I know how it could be even better." Surely he could see in her eyes what she meant.

He studied her, probably considering the worst-case scenario if he actually kissed her on the lips. How many people dated, albeit secretly, for well more than a year without kissing?

He cradled her face, and soon his lips found hers. It was the best kiss a woman could hope for. Even better than she'd imagined. And she'd done a lot of imagining.

A lot.

When he pulled away, he shook his head, a trace of sadness in his eyes. "I'm a fool to be this far gone over a girl who doesn't know what she wants."

But she did know, didn't she? As much as she loved those she lived with, she became

95

more certain every week that she couldn't remain Amish. But she couldn't leave, not for quite a while yet. Still, there had to be a way for her to extract herself from being Amish without causing Orchard Bend Farms to lose Landon in the process. She simply had no clue yet how that could be done. Not only was it too much for them to talk about, but it was also too much to think about.

Leah covered his lips with her fingers. "Don't ruin the moment."

He nodded, studying her face.

Landon leaned in and kissed her again.

Sunlight streamed from heaven. Birds sang. Snow glistened. And she was in love with a man who was willing to wait for her.

What else could she possibly want?

Samuel dragged two orchard sprayers across the floor of the hayloft. For the third time this year, he slid containers of oil from their storage space. They needed a shed for storing equipment. What they had was half of a hayloft.

He didn't mind. He'd been made keenly aware of what was and wasn't important in life. And he'd been set free. Free to be in love with Rhoda. Free to love her more with each passing month. And what he'd come to accept since Jacob and Rhoda's breakup was that Jacob had been set free too. Samuel continued to pray that Jacob would realize he was free. It would happen . . . eventually.

But until enough time had passed that they could marry, Samuel had to find a way to stop all the can't-think, can't-sleep love nonsense. Had to. Men were supposed to be strong, so why did he feel like an apple in the hands of a woman with a paring knife?

Maybe organizing this area would help clear his mind. He slid canisters of oil out of the way and began moving the mess of equipment they didn't need right now.

Was that a car door he'd just heard? If so, Landon was probably leaving to run another errand or was getting back from one. How would they have managed here without a full-time driver?

"Samuel!" Rhoda's excited voice came from below. "You won't believe this!"

"Ya?" He set down the stuff in his hand and worked his way around the mess.

"Samuel?"

She must not have heard him respond. He went to the opening of the haymow and peered down. "I'm right here."

"I have good news . . . I think. An intuition about finding Camilla's granddaughter came to me."

Her smile ignited fresh love, but he wasn't sure if he should go down the ladder or just listen. Her rare bits of insights were as fragile as a child's sense of safety.

"I was minding my own business, and, *wham,* the name of the town or city or street came to me, and it came without any odd voices of supposedly dead people." She shuddered. "It'd help if the whole incident was clearer." She motioned for him.

"This is great news." He climbed down, and when his feet hit the floor, he turned.

She clutched his shoulders. "Ya, it is, isn't it?" She shook him. "And it's way past time!"

He laughed. "How can it be? You just now got it, didn't you?" But Rhoda had begun receiving tidbits of info concerning Camilla's granddaughter, Sophia, and the child's mother, Jojo, during Rhoda's first night in Maine. At the time Rhoda didn't even know Bob and Camilla Cranford, their Englisch neighbors.

"But I only heard a little, like a whisper on the wind." She pranced her fingers through the air. "I'm almost as confused as I am excited, which is where you come in. You have to help me sort through it." She lowered her hands and began pacing.

He studied the freshly raked dirt under her shoes. Months ago he'd thought he noticed that when the rare insight pressed in, her footsteps, whether in snow or on the soft dirt of the barn floor, were deeper than usual, as if the insight physically weighed on her.

"When I heard a piece of a name of a place — road, town, something — I saw piles and piles of office supplies strewed about as if they'd been hit by a storm. Why?"

She wasn't actually asking him, not yet anyway. Her body language said she was thinking out loud, so he waited. A crackling sound caught his attention, and when he looked in that direction, he saw a shadow moving out of sight. Was someone outside the barn?

She stopped. "Where are you?"

"Right here." He gestured at his body. "See?"

"You seem distracted."

He doubted if that bit of insight was because of her gift. She'd grown to know him, his moods, his thoughts. "*Nee,* I'm focused."

"You sure everything is okay?" Concern tightened her brows.

"Ya. Sorry to be distracted."

She smiled. "Forgiven." She took a breath

and began pacing again. "George Knox or something like that. Do you know a place by that name?"

He glanced out the double-wide doorway of the barn. "I don't think so. We can check the maps I have in the office and see if it's in Maine."

"Ya, let's do that."

They went into the office, and he opened a huge atlas and flipped to the Maine page. With pencils in hand they scanned it. "Here's a Saint George." Samuel cross-referenced it by looking at the listings of counties. Eeriness and excitement churned within him. "Look at this. It's in Knox County."

Rhoda knotted her hands into fists. "Is it possible she lives there?"

Something creaked, causing them both to look in that direction. His father stood in the doorway. Disbelief stole every organized thought from Samuel, and heat flushed his body as anxiety collided with reality. Samuel moved in front of Rhoda, wanting to shield her from what was about to happen. "Daed."

His father stepped to the side and pointed a shaky finger at Rhoda. "How dare you conjure up witchcraft! And *you*" — he pointed at Samuel — "not only allow it, but you encourage it?"

Rhoda closed her eyes, and Samuel knew every bit of her focused energy had just scattered like dust flying from hay during feeding time.

"Daed, stop. Now." Samuel gritted his teeth, trying his best to keep his voice low and calm for Rhoda's sake.

"Benjamin." Rhoda gave a slow nod of acknowledgment. "I didn't realize —"

The man clenched his hands. "If you'd known I was here, I wouldn't have seen for myself what you're dabbling in and how you're dragging my son with you. No wonder Jacob left here."

With her lips pressed together, Rhoda gave an understanding smile. "What I was saying sounded really weird and outside of acceptable. I know that, but —"

"Nee." Daed shook his head. "I'm not discussing this with a woman."

Rhoda's face flushed, but to her credit she simply nodded.

Samuel's hackles rose, and regardless of the consequences he had to speak up. "Daed, you have no call and no right to be rude to anyone on this farm, man or woman."

"I'm not going to stand here and listen to her justify herself."

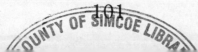

"But you said unfair, insulting things, and then you refused to let her respond because she's a woman."

Daed pointed, his face taut. "While taking on a woman for a business partner, have you forgotten that the man is to lead, that the man is to have final authority and final say?"

Who had been bending his Daed's ear lately? Whoever it was, they had him riled against women — as if his Daed needed those burning embers stirred in him. In the past his Daed had no passionate desire to set women straight. He'd only wanted to be left alone, even when Leah was young and crossing moral lines. Now he wanted to stand his ground and argue?

"I haven't forgotten about the man's authority, Daed." How could he? It was the foundation of the family unit and the Amish culture. "But in those same passages we're told to love as Christ loved the church. I can't see Jesus saying unjust things to people and then refusing to let them speak because of their gender. Can you?"

His Daed's face turned a purplish red. "Whatever darkness she's dabbling in, it's not of God."

Samuel looked to Rhoda. "Maybe you should go into the house."

102

Rhoda glanced from one man to the other. "Ya, okay."

Samuel looked through the office window, waiting until Rhoda was halfway to the house so she wouldn't be within earshot if they started yelling. "You're judging the situation and Rhoda too quickly."

"I don't need time to ponder and listen to know she's wrong. How blind and deaf have you become for us to need to have this conversation?"

"You've never had knowledge come to you from out of the blue? You never knew when a loved one was sick or in danger or had been in an accident? You've never known for sure what you needed to do in a sticky situation and you couldn't explain how you knew it?"

Daed scratched his forehead. "But she said she hears dead people!"

"No. She said she didn't hear from any *supposedly* dead people."

"You are straining at gnats."

Samuel hoped he could find the right words. "She was talking to me, and I understood what she meant."

"And?"

"Have you ever heard a barn cat cry and at first thought it was a baby? Or heard fireworks and thought it was thunder, or a car backfire and believed it was a gun going off? We think we know what a sound is when we first hear it, but with a bit of thought and investigation, it is often revealed to be something else."

"You don't wish to righteously evaluate or judge anything happening on this farm, do you?" Something outside the window caught Daed's attention, and he narrowed his eyes as he moved closer to the glass.

When Samuel looked through it, he saw no one. If someone had been out there, the person had gone around the front or back corner of the barn. "Daed."

His Daed held up his hand. "Sh." A few moments later he left the office and entered the barn.

What now? Samuel followed him.

His sister stood on her tiptoes, her lips on Landon's. *Good grief.*

"Hey." Samuel stepped forward. "Daed's here." Who did he get to drive him here, anyway?

Leah froze.

Stiltedness was about all that had ever existed between Leah and their Daed, but his scowl sent a clear message to his eldest daughter. "Pack your bags. We leave here tomorrow morning."

Leah glanced from Samuel to Landon,

terror filling her eyes. "Daed, please, I can explain."

"I'm sure you and Rhoda can both wrap Samuel and Steven around your fingers, but I won't stand for it. The rumors of what takes place on this farm have motivated a bishop from Pennsylvania to choose to move here. He could be here within a matter of days, and if he'd witnessed what I just did, he'd have everyone on this farm shunned, including Preacher Steven for allowing his sister to practice witchcraft!" His father's face was beet red. "Samuel, do you understand that if that happens, not only will the King name be mud, both here and in Pennsylvania, but everyone who supported this venture will pull out of it, expecting their money back in full? We could lose this farm and the one in Pennsylvania!"

Was that true? Or was his Daed's anger causing him to toss out far-fetched possibilities? Samuel had never heard of anyone being shunned on the grounds of witchcraft. How severe could that shunning be?

Landon and Leah remained quiet, probably in shock. How long before the shock wore off? And when it did, what would his sister and Landon do?

"You've put me in a horrible position."

His Daed grabbed his head with both hands, and his hat tumbled to the ground. "If I don't tell the bishop what I know, and he discovers it later on, I could be disciplined too."

Eight

Jacob fidgeted with the reins as he drove the carriage along the back roads of Virginia. Dora's arms were crossed inside her heavy coat as she stared at the floorboard.

The answer to his question of how to deal with Dora became really clear after he talked to Esther five days ago. He only needed to ask himself how he would want her to treat him if the tables were turned. But now he searched for the words to sum up all he'd said to Dora during this outing. "It's not you." That was completely honest. "You caught my attention, and we enjoyed each outing enough for me to ask for another, but I've decided against dating for a while." That was true too. Unless he met someone he thought he might actually want to build a life with, he wasn't asking anyone else out.

She didn't look at him, but her eyes brimmed with tears as her face twisted. He could see why Esther was concerned for Dora. She didn't handle disappointment well. She should feel only mild disillusionment and annoyance, but she was reacting as if they'd been seeing each other for quite a while.

He'd picked her up about twenty minutes ago, thinking they'd only need to make a loop from her driveway and back again. But she'd gotten overly upset, so he'd meandered down unfamiliar roads, giving them time to talk. He was completely turned around, but it was just as well. She wasn't absorbing anything other than rejection, and he didn't want to drop her off at home in this condition.

Dora wiped at her tears. "So I mean nothing to you?"

"That's just silly. *Nothing* is way too strong a word. But I'm not looking for a girlfriend. It's too soon after my last one."

"Then why did you ask me out . . . *three* times?" Her tiny voice and mumbled words did nothing to endear her to him.

He'd already answered that. "I'm really sorry this hurts your feelings, but I told you the first night I asked you out after the singing that I was leaving in April and wouldn't be back."

"When you said it, I was hoping you'd

take me with you."

"What?" His voice boomed, and he regretted his response, but how could anyone seriously consider marriage *before* a first date?

She covered her face, bright red skin showing around her hands and down her neck. They rode in silence, and she finally got her emotions under control, wiped her tears, and drew a ragged breath.

A colonial style home came into view with a much smaller house next to it, probably the accompanying *Daadi Haus.* A clothesline stood between the two places, and a couple of teenage girls were nearby, wet clothes in hand, one flailing what appeared to be a diaper toward the other. Jacob narrowed his eyes. Most Amish women did laundry on Monday or Tuesday, not Saturday. A moment later one of the girls landed on the ground. Had she simply fallen or been pushed?

The front door of the larger house flew open, and Esther hobbled out of it, the baby on her hip. The little one had grown quite a bit since Jacob first saw him four months ago. He appeared to be ten or eleven months old. Despite all the female turmoil in his life today, he smiled at the scene.

Jacob slowed the rig, his curiosity piqued as he chuckled. "More sisters?"

"What?" Dora jerked a breath in and looked up from the floorboard.

He pointed behind them. "Esther seems to be breaking up a fight between two girls younger than you."

Dora looked offended. "They are *not* my sisters, not related at all."

His interest inched a little higher. "Then who are they?"

Her body tensed into a shrug she didn't release.

He laughed. "Dora . . . who are they?"

She plucked balls of wool from her coat. "You know Esther?"

He hadn't meant to let that slip. "Ya, actually, I do. We sort of bumped into each other in town the other night."

Suspicion hardened Dora's face. "Did she say something that changed your mind about me?"

"No. Of course not." Esther's only influence had been to help Jacob understand that, since he intended to end things with Dora anyway, sooner was better than later, for Dora's sake. "So who are the girls?"

"Esther houses young women from across the states who need a temporary place to live. She's done it for almost six years now."

Was Esther providing a halfway house for those who didn't wish to remain Amish?

That didn't make sense. Those still living Amish didn't help others leave. And when children weren't in a good Amish home, the Amish often had someone go into the home to help set things right. "So the girls are pregnant."

Dora nodded.

That situation didn't happen often among the Amish, but it wasn't exactly rare either. If the girls hadn't had on those bulky coats, he might have seen they were expecting. But when a girl found herself in that predicament, she usually married right away. Even if that didn't happen, parents rarely kicked them out. Did they?

"I love my sister, but how she lives is embarrassing."

If this was what Esther did regularly, some sort of mission outreach to pregnant girls, her suspicion of Jacob's phone conversation and her disbelief about his explanation made perfect sense. But Dora's attitude seemed immature. "I'm sure she's taken plenty of heat over the years for doing this. Maybe you should try being proud of her."

Disbelief filled her eyes. "You have her for a sister and walk in my shoes, and then we'll talk about this. She's relentless in frank discussions about men. It drives me and my sisters crazy."

111

"How many sisters do you have?"

"Three — Esther, who's older, and two younger. Four brothers. Two older and two younger. In Esther's defense she's no easier on my brothers than she is on us girls."

"I can imagine." He came to an intersection that had the name of her road on it. "Right or left?"

"Right."

"So the stuff she salvages to sell — does she do that for herself or to support the home for the girls?"

"The girls. The good news is the bishop's wife has a heart for those girls too. Some of the other families in the community also donate to the cause, but not many. Money is tight for most families, and there's a sense that the girls made their bed, so let them lie in it, which I fully agree with."

Jacob didn't see it as Dora did. Was Esther's financial need for her charity the reason he'd had the same feeling the other night as he'd had the day the tornado came through?

He wasn't sure, but there was only one way to find out: do a little cautious exploring. He had no idea if the owners of the new homes would be interested in her repurposed flooring, and they'd already picked out what they wanted, but it hadn't been installed yet. Maybe Jacob could sell one of the two sets of owners on the idea of using salvaged wood in one room of the house. That should help some, and he could find the extra time to install that flooring in one room and still finish on time, couldn't he?

Within ten minutes he spotted Dora's house and pulled onto her driveway.

Dora turned to him. "How can you tell when someone really cares about you?"

That was a good question. Jacob got out of the rig, went around the carriage, and opened her door. "I don't know, but it seems like one way is to stop wanting the person to love you so much that you make yourself believe things that aren't true."

That's what he'd done with Rhoda. He wanted to marry her so much that, despite the insecurity and jealousy that tormented him where Samuel was concerned, Jacob often saw in her what he wanted to — love for only him. How *did* people tell if someone they loved really loved them back?

Dora stared at the ground. He bent his knees, lowering his body so he could catch her eye. "Remember what I told you. Just because you feel shy at the singings doesn't mean you should act that way. Be a little bold."

In a blur of moments, she slung her arms around his neck and kissed him on the lips. Jacob took a step back, and she released him, looking pleased and maybe terrified he'd be angry. He laughed. "Well, Dora Beachy, I guess I got what I asked for when it comes to boldness, huh?"

She grinned. "And it paid off." She ran her fingers over her lips. "When you're over the former girlfriend, come back. I'll be waiting."

"Dora, no. Don't wait."

Without responding she turned and hurried up the few stairs of the front stoop. Pausing, she turned back. "I meant what I said. I'll wait." She hurried inside and closed the door.

Jacob returned to his rig, fairly baffled. The girl was an immature mess, and her emotions were all over the place, but she was sweet with a good heart. Hopefully time would take care of the rest.

As he started to pull onto the main road, he decided to turn left so he could swing past Esther's place. If she was still outside, he would stop for a minute. Should he simply offer to donate money toward the home? That felt wrong, although he didn't know why. Maybe because she hadn't told him about the place for unwed moms. But his gut said aiming to work out a business deal would be best.

When Esther's place came into sight, he saw her and Ammon and four boys. Four? He thought she had two. The eldest appeared to be around five or six. Esther and Ammon were looking at some old doors propped against the side of a shed near a garden. Ammon scowled as he inspected them.

Jacob pulled onto the shoulder of the road, just past the mailbox that had the street number and the names: Ammon and Esther Beachy. Before now, he hadn't thought of what her last name might be. But this meant Esther's maiden name had been Beachy, and then she married a Beachy. With less than a dozen Amish surnames in these parts, he'd met a few men who'd married women with the same last name as them. The man Jacob lived with had said that over the decades three different families of Beachys had joined one of the two districts in these parts, and none of them were related. He could see that happening in Maine too. At some point a family of Kings or Bylers might move to the area and be completely unrelated to the founding members.

Esther, with a little one in her arms,

looked in his direction, a welcoming smile greeting him before she waved.

She spoke to Ammon, and he glanced up, looking quite solemn. Unless Jacob was mistaken, Esther was nudging him toward Jacob.

Ammon slowly headed his way. Jacob covered far more ground than Ammon.

"Jacob." Ammon reached out, and they shook hands. "It's good to see you again. I appreciate that you stayed with Essie and helped gather up her goodies and such until I arrived." Despite the man's words Ammon didn't look grateful about much of anything.

"It was the least I could do. I hope you don't mind that I stopped by."

"Not at all." Ammon shook his head.

Esther shifted the baby from one hip to the other. "I'm surprised you're in our poor neck of the woods. On a nice day like today, I would've pegged you to be working on those fancy houses."

"I was, and I will again, but I needed to talk to Dora."

Ammon gave Esther a quizzical look. She moved forward. "Jacob met her at a singing, and they've gone out a few times."

Ammon nodded, not looking the least bit interested. He unfolded what looked like a picture from a magazine.

Esther smiled. "I'm sure she was pleased to see you."

Jacob shrugged. But it made little sense to keep the conversation between him and Dora private. She was bound to tell Esther every detail the next time they were together. When Dora explained about the kiss, would she make him out to be the one who pursued it? It didn't matter. If that's what Dora needed to think, then let her.

Ammon turned the image one way and then the other. "Tell me again what you're wanting me to help you do?" A phone rang, and Ammon jolted. Clearly *that* interested him. "Essie, I *have* to catch this."

"I know that. *Geh.*" She shooed him away.

He held the picture toward Jacob. "If you have time, would you help her figure that out? I'm a farmer" — he sighed, tossing a slight smile Esther's way — "not a room designer."

Jacob clutched the paper, and Ammon ran for the phone.

The little one on Esther's hip opened and closed his fist. She kissed his cheek. "*Mach's gut,* Daed." She spoke for the little boy, waving bye to Ammon with his hand. She shifted the boy on her hip. "You don't have to help me. Ammon shouldn't have asked it, and I can figure it out on my own." She gazed into the little one's eyes and smiled. "Isn't that right?"

"I've got a little time."

She looked up, her brown eyes reflecting peace. The little boy he'd first seen at the construction site ran to her and tugged on her dress. *"Mammzu, Ich bin hungerich!"*

His words were a little hard to understand, but Jacob definitely caught "Mamm" and that he was hungry.

Essie rested her hand on his head, telling him that he hadn't eaten his dinner she'd cooked but that if he'd play while she spoke to Jacob for a bit, she'd see to it that his Daed let her warm up that meal for him a little later.

The boy wrapped his arms around her. *"Ich lieb du."*

She tousled his hair and said she loved him too, and then he ran off. Chuckling, she looked at Jacob. "Where were we?"

He studied the picture. It showed six shutters connected through hinges in such a way they folded up like an accordion. "This is ambitious."

"But the real question is, can it be done with the shutters I have?"

He went into the shed. It was filled with old doors and shutters and windows. "More treasures?"

"Ya. If all goes well, we'll have everything ready for the annual City of Chelsea Fire Sale three Saturdays from today."

"Do you still have the pine flooring?"

"Ya, but not here. It's at the warehouse." She shifted the sleepy baby onto her shoulder. "I'll cut up the planks and use them to make tabletops and picture frames."

"Are they still whole?"

"Ya. Why?"

"I'd like to talk to the owners of the houses I'm working on about using it. Could you give me a week before cutting them?" Easing farther into the building, he noticed she had quite a collection of old pieces of junk. He inspected the shutters for dry rot and uniformity.

"Your idea is very kind, but I promise there's no need for favoritism just because you're seeing my sister while you're in the area."

He stood two shutters upright. "It's not favoritism. I . . . would like to do something that would go toward the home you give those girls."

She put her knit neck scarf over the face of the now-sleeping baby. "Dora mentioned the pregnant girls to you? She's mortified by their presence and my connection to them."

"You're right about that, but we passed by here, and I saw you and a couple of young women outside, so I asked questions." Some of the slats in the shutters looked loose, so he jiggled them. They were sound. "With the right tools and hardware, these can be connected like the one in the picture. But I don't know what your skills are, so I can't say whether you can do it or not. The shutters aren't completely symmetrical, so that'll cause a bit of trouble."

"Do you know exactly how I would add the hardware so the shutters would fold like they're supposed to?"

"Sure." He stood two shutters side by side. "The first step would be to stand the pair that will share a hinge, and —"

"Essie!" Ammon bellowed as he charged out of the phone shanty.

"Right here where you left me." Her voice was a gentle melody.

"We've been doing it all wrong. Can you believe it?" He grabbed the little boy who was hungry and hurried toward the house, yelling for the other two children. Ammon motioned at her. "You too. Kumm."

She looked longingly at the shutters. "I guess that's all the work I'll get to do."

A stab of disappointment for her went through Jacob. He put the shutters back and passed her the page from the magazine. "Maybe we could talk about it another day."

"Essie!" Ammon turned and hurried back toward her, scowling as if coming after a disobedient child.

"I'm sorry, Jacob." Esther's cheeks turned pink. "He doesn't mean to be rude. He's under a lot of stress as he tries to take care of his family."

"No need to apologize to me. Go help your husband."

Her gentle brown eyes intensified as if she hadn't understood his words. She shook her head. "My —"

Ammon had put the two- or three-year-old on the porch, and then the man all but ran to Esther. "I forgot about your knee." Ammon cupped his hand under her elbow. "Now will you walk already?"

Esther blinked, pulling her attention from Jacob. "Ya."

Ammon clicked his tongue, hurrying her along. "If you'd stayed home the other night like I said, you wouldn't be injured."

Jacob watched as Ammon helped her hobble up the stairs to the house. The man seemed to be whispering harshly the whole way. The children were already inside when

Esther and Ammon disappeared into the home. Once they were inside, he heard Ammon yelling. A door slammed, and the baby started crying.

What had he just witnessed? He started to walk toward the rig, but as Ammon's outburst kept ringing from inside the house, Jacob couldn't budge. Disheartened for Esther, Jacob shook his head.

It's none of my business.

He sighed. He could barely understand his own actions and reactions to life. But how had she let herself marry someone who seemed like such a bad fit for her?

Look away, Jacob.

But he just stood there. Finally he broke his gaze from the home and strode toward his carriage.

Was any romantic relationship worth it? If someone with Esther's spunk and love for life had known that Ammon was going to treat her like that, would she have married him? Apparently few people ever really knew the person they were dating.

Was he destined to be lonely forever?

NINE

Standing in her bedroom facing her Daed, Leah felt like a defiant toddler — all tantrums and no actual power. "Daed, I won't go." He'd been here twenty-four hours, and whether she tried to be respectful or was defiant, he wouldn't accept her answer of no.

He pointed at her. "I'm still your father."

"That doesn't mean you own me."

"This attitude comes from Landon, doesn't it? No Amish would support such rebellion. I forbid you —"

"I'm nineteen! You can't *forbid* me to do anything!"

His face was so red he looked like an overwatered tomato ready to split. "Is that what you'll do, Leah? Stand on man's law that says you're free of your father's will at eighteen instead of standing on God's?"

"Maybe . . . because I've done nothing wrong, and I'm not leaving here!"

"Leah King, think. The only way this district survived the legal troubles that Rhoda faced is because the Amish in Pennsylvania supported it. If you think Orchard Bend Amish is a self-governing district, free from the opinions and guidance of the Pennsylvania Amish, you're as blind about that as you are about what your future will be like out in the world!"

"I'm not going to the world. I attend church, and I'm in love with Landon."

Her father didn't blink or twitch or breathe, and then Leah realized she'd confessed her Daed's worst nightmare: she was involved with an Englisch man *and* his church. Daed probably could've coped more easily if she'd been drinking or was pregnant. At least in those situations he would have had solid footing to lead her to repent.

"Where's your suitcase?"

"Daed, no!"

He went to the closet, dragged it out, and tossed it onto the bed. "Pack, or I'll do it for you." He waited. When she didn't move, he jerked dresses and aprons off hangers and threw them into the suitcase. "We're leaving. You can tell Landon good-bye, and after that you're not to see him again."

He opened a drawer. Leah hurried across

124

the room and slammed the drawer shut, knocking a kerosene lantern from the dresser. It shattered on the wood floor, the liquid spattering against the wall and bedspread and running until it hit the area rug.

Her father's lips thinned. "Leave it and pack."

"I said no!" Leah jerked items out of her suitcase.

Someone knocked on the door and opened it. Rhoda stood there, looking from Daed to Leah. "I . . . came to see if I could be any help."

"Ya." Leah hung up a dress. "You can help. Tell him that he can't make me go."

Rhoda looked sympathetic, but for which one of them? "Perhaps if we sat and talked this out."

That's when it dawned on Leah where Rhoda stood. She had never agreed with Leah seeing Landon. She'd asked Landon to stay away from her until Samuel had reminded Rhoda that Leah was in her rumschpringe and that they had no right to make decisions for her.

So where was Samuel now?

"You're on *his* side." Leah slung the dress in her hand to the floor. "You made that clear when you tried to do the same thing he's doing." She'd had enough. "Excuse me.

I have work to do."

Rhoda stepped aside, and Leah bolted downstairs and out the door. She bridled a horse and mounted it without a saddle. The need to ride outweighed having a specific destination. Metal pinged against metal, and she spurred the horse toward the sound. She knew where it came from — the compost pile where the now-repaired spreader stood. Within a minute Crist came into view.

Was he the one who had told her Daed?

She squeezed her heels against the horse's belly, hurrying the animal. Crist had a shovel in one hand and a hammer in the other, banging on the hem where the blade connected with the handle.

Leah brought the horse to a stop so quickly her torso thrust against the horse's neck. She clutched its mane and straightened. "Was it you?"

Crist straightened from his bent position, hammer in hand. "What?"

She intertwined her fingers with the horse's mane, steadying herself as the horse shifted from one foot to the other. "Someone got word to my Daed about Landon and me. Was it you?"

He stared into her eyes, saying nothing.

She slid from the horse. "Answer me, Crist!"

"So now you want to talk about this." He shoved the handle of the hammer into his tool belt. "That's real nice of you, Leah. I've asked you out five times since moving here. I thought maybe you were getting over somebody back in Pennsylvania."

"Do you know what you've done?"

He grabbed the shovel and began moving mulch from the pile onto the spreader. "You knew how I felt about you, and you should've told me you were seeing somebody." He jammed the blade of the shovel into the ground and held on to it. "But no. It wasn't me. I've said nothing to no one."

Then who did? Her anger eased. "Oh, uh, I appreciate it. Sorry."

"Don't think I wasn't tempted. Only God knows why I kept my mouth shut because I wanted to call your Daed and tell him." He waved his arm in her direction. "You and an Englisch guy."

As she saw the situation through his eyes, she couldn't believe how blind she'd been. She of all people knew what it was like to care for someone Amish but for that person to have eyes for someone with store-bought clothes, a vehicle, and a higher education. It was like a slap in the face, a rejection that said being Amish wasn't good enough. "I'm sorry."

He removed his gloves and moved in close enough to pat the horse. "I get it." He stroked the animal. "I don't like it, but Landon's a nice guy. I blame Rhoda for bringing him along and Samuel for allowing it."

"Landon was in Rhoda's life long before any of the Kings were. After the tornado destroyed our orchard in Pennsylvania, he's the one who opened our eyes to the amount of affordable farming land in Maine. Without his help I doubt we could've made the transition successfully."

"Maybe we'd all be better off." He removed his hat, taking away the shadow that hid his brilliant blue eyes. "When my folks were considering this move to Maine and joining this district, they asked if I'd move with them. They needed me to get their farm going, but there were plenty of single girls where we lived, and I wasn't sure I liked the idea of leaving there. During our visit here I met you." He stared at the ground. "I agreed to move here because of you, Leah."

Her heart pounded. How could he, someone who barely knew her, consider her that desirable? "I wish I could've been more upfront about seeing Landon."

He put his hat back on. "Me too."

"Any idea who would've told my Daed?"

"Does it even matter?"

"It does to me."

"Three families have moved here since summer, each with single guys who'd like your attention. Iva's too. Any of them, or one of their parents, could have called. I don't know. A better question is, what are you going to do, Leah? Rip out every heart on this farm and the hearts of your family in Pennsylvania so you can marry a man who isn't suited to you?"

Now that she realized how honorable Crist had been, she wouldn't do as she wanted and yell or even sound annoyed at him, not ever again. "How can you say that when you don't know Landon?"

"Because I know what it means to be raised Amish, and you do too. The Englisch don't get it. They can't. But you know the depth of differences between how you and he think, and because of it, you'll never be truly happy with him."

His soft-spoken words cut deeper than all the hurtful demands Daed had made. Without another word she grabbed the horse's mane and tried to pull herself onto the animal's back. But she didn't have mounting steps to help her.

Crist interlaced his fingers and cupped

them for her to use as a stirrup.

She could hardly breathe for all the emotions pounding her, but she stepped into his hands. With a gentle movement upward, Crist boosted her onto the horse.

"Crist —"

"Don't apologize again." He shook his head, backing away from the horse. "Just do one thing for me — think about what I've said."

Despite his staunch opinions grating on her nerves, she kept her resolve not to raise her voice to him again. "Ya, okay."

TEN

Samuel sat in the dark at the kitchen table, staring into the blazing hearth as he waited on his Daed to join him. Anger continued to fester, and Samuel fought to control it. How dare his Daed speak to or about Rhoda as he had! And Leah didn't deserve the wrath or the badgering either.

But Samuel had kept control of his temper and tongue while giving himself more than twenty-four hours to think about what to do. No more pondering. It was time to take a stand.

Unfortunately, he would have to do so on a Sunday morning and a church day. He had no choice. The mood in this home was oppressive, even abusive, but his Daed would see it as holding people accountable. At least the church meeting wasn't being held here.

Underneath all his anger, Samuel grieved. He'd miserably failed to keep the Old Ways

from moving into this home like a poisonous gas. It was doing exactly what he knew
it could — choking the breath out of them.
How could a faith as genuine and temper-
ate as the Amish ways be used against them
like this?

Witchcraft. Daed only called it that because
Rhoda's intuition was stronger than he was
accustomed to. If intuition was wrong, then
let everyone refuse every ounce of it. If it
wasn't wrong, then no one should judge
someone else for having more or less.

The stairs creaked, and he knew it'd be
his Daed. After a night of almost no sleep,
Samuel had tapped on his Daed's door
about twenty minutes ago and told him they
needed to talk.

Daed pushed the swinging door open, carrying a lantern and looking none too
pleased. Samuel rose, poured a cup of coffee, and set it on the table for his Daed. His
Daed put the lantern down and picked up
the mug before he went to the fireplace and
stood with his back to it. The temperature
had dropped to twenty-five degrees last
night, but it would be nearly sixty this
afternoon. Daed sipped his coffee. "What's
so important you needed to wake me?"

Phoebe had told Samuel that while he and
Steven were working in the orchard yester-

day, Samuel's Daed was relentless in hounding Leah, trying to make her go home and giving her ultimatums. Phoebe said he'd also wasted no opportunity to mumble scripture under his breath whenever Rhoda was nearby. Rhoda had said nothing about his Daed's behavior, and Samuel knew she longed to be a peacemaker as much as possible. But harmony wasn't possible with some people.

"I have some things that need to be said before anyone else is up."

"That's fine." His Daed took another sip of coffee. "I have things to say to you too."

"Not today you don't."

"You are to honor your father!"

"I try, Daed. Surely you know that. And I will continue trying to do that, but since you've decided to quote scripture, what about the one that tells you not to provoke your children to wrath?"

"I will *not* be spoken to —"

Samuel smacked the palm of his hand on the table. "You will, and you'll listen." His insides quaked with fury, but so far he'd managed to speak softly. "Despite your financial support of this venture, this isn't your home or property. It's in my name, and if I wish you to leave and you refuse, that's trespassing. Are we clear?" Samuel

133

couldn't imagine escorting his Daed from here or calling the police, but he'd do one or the other if necessary. Boundaries had to be drawn. "As to the money you and the others have invested, I believe all of it can be paid back after this year's harvest."

"This isn't you talking. She's bewitched you."

Samuel sighed. "That's a ridiculous, ignorant statement. When the Word talks about people being involved in divination, they are actively practicing it, seeking knowledge and control, and when they have it, they try to use it to gain what they want, which is most often money or power over someone. Rhoda does none of that, and her only spiritual connection is prayer to God."

"You're in love with her, aren't you?"

"I am."

"You say that without any shame. She was seeing your brother!"

Samuel took a deep breath, praying for wisdom and peace — and, as always, for Jacob. "I'm keenly aware of their past relationship."

"That's wrong of her and of you. Why can't you see that?"

"Whatever is there to see is between Jacob, Rhoda, and me. But I didn't wake you so you could grill and chastise me. I

134

have a couple of ultimatums of my own to share."

"You what?"

Samuel leaned forward and looked his Daed in the eye. "You'll say nothing else to Leah today. It's the Sabbath, and you will let her and everyone else under this roof rest. You will make plans first thing in the morning to leave here. Not only are you to be gone by dark tomorrow, but you are never to return uninvited."

"Which will be never, right?"

"That probably depends on you. See, I understand that I've wounded my relationship with Jacob, and since it couldn't be avoided, I was willing to work to pay for the damage. But you seem clueless as to how much destruction you've caused."

His Daed looked too stunned to respond, and Samuel needed to finish what he had to say before his Daed got his feet under him again — or, more accurately, his words under him again. "If you want to contact the new bishop who's coming to Orchard Bend and tell him that Rhoda is practicing witchcraft, that lie will be on your conscience. But if you ever speak to or about her like that again in her presence or mine, I'll take *you* before your bishop on grounds of lying, gossiping, and slander, and I will be able to prove my accusations quickly."

His Daed's countenance changed, as if his self-righteous anger had drained from him. Anger and disgust were still evident in his eyes and in the set of his jaw, but the haughtiness had deflated. Samuel breathed a sigh of relief. Maybe now his Daed would come back to himself. Wasn't the offended outrage his Daed had heaped on everyone the result of self-righteous people discussing at length other people's wrongs? If so, who was his Daed meeting with to get to this point?

His Daed cleared his throat before he narrowed his eyes. "I will stick by my ultimatum to Leah and Landon. I won't stand for my daughter marrying an outsider while I do nothing."

"Because it's morally wrong, or because of how it will make you look to the church?"

His Daed started to speak, and Samuel held up his hand, halting his retort. "Just consider the question. That's all." Everyone on the farm had deep concerns about Leah leaving the Amish, including Leah, he imagined. But they'd worked to make sure their feelings were based in love and true concern, not fear, pride, and an effort to save face. Samuel drew a deep breath. "We'll discuss the Leah-and-Landon situation tomorrow."

There were areas Samuel could influence, like Daed's behavior while here. But the situation with Landon and Leah was quite sticky, and since Rhoda and he had hired Landon, they would be held accountable for keeping him on once they realized the two were falling in love. "Daed, I want to be reasonable and to work out the issues as peaceably as possible for all our sakes. Perhaps the new bishop will be offended as you said, and he might heap painful edicts on us, but no one has a right to speak or act as you did when you got here."

"I was only trying to warn you about what's coming! You're too young and too inexperienced to understand the trouble that will come to us because of Rhoda. Leah's a teen, and we can manage people's outcry by separating her and Landon, but Rhoda is serious trouble. I've told you that from the start."

"And you've been wrong from the start. Even after all I've explained about divination, you're still set against her?

"I know what I know, and her *gift* isn't of God."

"What makes you so quick to judge? When Mary went to visit Elisabeth, her voice caused Elisabeth to be filled with the Holy

Spirit, and Elisabeth spoke of things that defied what she could possibly know. That tells us gifts of knowing are possible. Because of God's doing, the same Spirit that rested on Elisabeth's child also lives in us."

"What you're talking about is dangerous."

"It can be. You're right about that. But to deny His ability to reach inside us and give us knowledge beyond our understanding is to deny God's right to be God."

His Daed pursed his lips. "You have an answer for everything, don't you?"

"What would you have me do? Simply accept every judgment you speak without giving it another thought?"

His Daed walked out.

Concern for what was ahead for Rhoda, Leah, and Landon wrapped itself around Samuel's throat. If the new bishop was anything like his Daed, Samuel had quite a battle ahead of him. But he wouldn't cave, and he wouldn't walk away from living Amish. It was a faith and a way of life he believed in.

Evening services at Unity Hill would begin in thirty minutes, but Landon had no plans to pick up Leah. He wouldn't attend either. His goal was to stay as close to the farm as he could without causing any trouble for

Leah, and he had the volume on his phone on high. If she called him, he'd do whatever she wanted.

He had hated leaving her there on Friday. What had her weekend been like? Landon couldn't stand imagining it. Her dad's anger kept playing over and over again in his mind. Whatever had caused him to accuse Rhoda of witchcraft, Benjamin was beyond reason by the time he learned how his oldest daughter felt about an English man.

Landon sighed and scrolled through Bible passages on the laptop resting on his legs. When Samuel had asked him to leave the farm until Monday, Landon's temptation to ask Leah to go with him had been unbearable. But he'd fought with himself and walked away. What was the right thing to do? He and Leah could marry and be done with Benjamin King. Only two things stopped him —

His phone rang. It was the number from the barn office! "Leah?"

"It's me," she whispered.

"Are you okay?"

"Yeah. Daed was awful yesterday, but he's not said a word to me today. Last night before I went to bed, he gave us an ultimatum. Either I return to Pennsylvania with him, or you can quit working for Orchard

Bend Farms and give your word you won't see me anymore."

Landon's heart raced, and all he could think of was picking up Leah once everyone was asleep and them running off together. *Think, Landon. Be rational.* But he hated ultimatums. Hated them. The giver of one believed he had all the power. But rarely did one person have *all* the power.

Could he negotiate with Benjamin? It'd be preferable to doing something rash, like breaking ties with all of Leah's family. Maybe he could get Benjamin to put a time frame on what he wanted, something reasonable like separating them for only a few months. He and Leah could weather that, but if her Daed thought that's all it would take to break them up, he might agree to it. "He's actually given us something we can work with."

"How?"

"We'll try to —"

Leah gasped. "Daed's coming this way. I have to go. You're coming to work tomorrow?"

"Nothing could keep me away." Although Benjamin could keep the two apart once Landon was on the property.

He heard the distinct click of a phone being put in its cradle. He put his phone down. What did he possess that would cause Benjamin to negotiate?

The front door opened, and his grandmother's spry steps carried her inside. She tossed in his lap a white bag with a silver apple icon. "Who'd have thought a phone store would be that crowded on a Sunday?"

Landon opened the bag. She'd had to drive more than an hour to get to the phone store. But to get this phone activated today and put on his account, that's where it needed to be bought. "Granny, thank you."

"The man had it at the counter, waiting for me, when I arrived. Is it the one you asked to be set aside when you called them?"

"Yes." He clutched it. "I can breathe again. You did that."

She moved to her recliner. "From your expression I assume there's been no change of heart in Benjamin King."

"He's given Leah an ultimatum. Either she returns to Pennsylvania, or I leave the farm and never see her again."

"What will you do?"

"Not sure, but I never imagined all this drama and the threats. What has me baffled is trying to figure out what's truth and what's overzealous religion. I think I'd rather try to find a needle in a haystack."

"She's his daughter, and you have to respect that."

"I know. But where's the line between godly obedience and using God's Word to get your own way?" Besides, did Benjamin have a clue how much Landon was needed on the farm? Or that Leah was needed just as much? "I gotta figure out what I need to do. Otherwise I'm paralyzed."

"I've yet to hear you say what you want."

"I want to remain faithful to what Rhoda and Orchard Bend Farms need. I want it to be okay with Leah's family that Leah and I love each other. But most of all, I want to marry her."

But none of that addressed the foundational questions: what was right, and what did Leah want? Unfortunately, the priority of those questions came in that order. What was right had to come ahead of what he or Leah wanted.

"What I don't want is for us to have to marry in a hurry. It's ridiculous that we're being forced into a divisive, bridge-burning position."

He turned his focus to his laptop again and decided to check out the verse of the day on Bible Gateway. " 'And not only so, but we glory in tribulations also: knowing that tribulation worketh patience; and

patience, experience; and experience, hope.'
Romans 5:3–4"

He moaned.

Surely God didn't expect him to do as Leah's Daed wanted. How could he walk away from the woman he loved?

Eleven

Gray, murky light began to lessen the darkness as Jacob dressed for the day. The Amish family he lived with — Noah, Barb, and their five children — were still asleep. He usually ate breakfast with them, and she fixed him a sack lunch, so he'd leave them a note before he slipped out. But since he was awake early, he'd get a jump-start on his day.

The lumberyard had delivered wood yesterday for making mantels for the new houses. He wasn't sure why they'd brought it here instead of the construction site, but he needed to get it loaded.

While pulling his suspenders over his shoulders, he knocked a book off the nightstand. He picked it up. A Bible. The tattered leather cover and the coarse, heavy pages indicated it was an old one.

He sat on the edge of the bed and opened it. He couldn't make out the words — the light was too dim — but he caressed the pages. Regardless of how easy it was to go his own way, he did want to find peace. But answering his brother's calls or saying *I forgive you* felt impossible.

Was Jacob now as far from doing what was right as he'd been in his teen years? When he'd left the Amish as a teen to travel and support himself by doing construction work, he had no desire to sin. His scrape with the law was more a matter of being fresh off the farm and not understanding what was legal than anything else. When he realized his actions were illegal, he believed he could set everything right while helping a friend. That was his biggest mistake.

He wasn't the best decision maker, and he was a restless soul, but he wasn't a bad guy. At least he didn't think so. He seemed to fall somewhere between not being bad and not doing as he thought God wanted in every circumstance. Instead of landing at the halfway point, causing him to be balanced, it just left him . . .

Useless.

He laid down the Bible, threw the covers on his bed into place, and left the room. After writing Noah and Barb a note, he grabbed his coat and tool belt and eased out the back door. Cold air and patches of fog welcomed him. With it being the first of April, highs in the midfifties, and lots of sunshine, even the most stubborn mounds of snow had melted.

He hitched the horse to the wagon, and by the time he had it loaded with the wood and fresh supplies, sunlight was streaming through broken, pink clouds with golden linings. He climbed onto the driver's seat and headed through town.

Rhoda had helped him find peace. With God. With himself. She'd been his strength and inspiration to get free of his legal issues. After leaving her behind, he'd finished what he'd begun by using the immunity he'd been given and testifying in court. Every trial — criminal and civil — was now behind him.

Odd really. As unrestricted as his life was — no legal authorities chasing him, no fear of his past pinning him to an orchard, no church ministers watching his every move — he'd never felt more imprisoned. So if freedom didn't make one free, what did? If he knew the answer to that, maybe he wouldn't feel so restless.

Movement up ahead drew him from his thoughts, and he saw an Amish woman walking down the middle of street. He slowed the rig to a crawl, studying her from afar.

The slight limp was a dead giveaway. Esther.

She hobbled near the area where they'd collided last week, apparently looking for something. Had he not gathered up all her scattered treasures?

His horse whinnied. She looked up, and her eyes grew wide as she stuck out her hand and shook her head, clearly asking him not to run over her.

His laughter caused pigeons on the nearby roofs to scatter into the sky.

After stopping the rig a good fifty feet from her, he got down and tied the reins to a hitching post. At the far end of the block stood a horse and wagon, carrying what appeared to be shutters. While approaching her, he began talking. "Seems to me you're just asking to be run over again."

One barely-there dimple deepened with her smile before she returned her attention to the gutters along the curb. "And it seems to me you're just itching to do a repeat performance."

He chuckled. "You did say the accident was the most entertaining event to happen to you in a while, but I thought it best not to indulge you this time."

A smile crossed her lips. "Denki."

"For running over you with my horse the first time or for resisting this time?"

Her laughter welcomed him. But when she turned back to searching the gutters, he felt something stir inside. Something he hadn't felt in a long time. A desire for friendship. It surprised him that he liked her. With the exception of immediate family, he'd never really desired to befriend women. That was part of the reason Rhoda had knocked him off his feet. He'd just turned twenty-three, and she'd been the first woman to hold his interest.

But he was tired of thinking about Rhoda. Tired of rehashing what had once existed between them.

"So just why are we standing in this road looking around?"

With the toe of her shoe, Esther nudged wet leaves out of the gutter. "I'm missing two sets of antique doorknobs."

He saw a slight flinch and heard an almost inaudible sharp breath.

"Does your knee feel *any* better?"

"Not yet." She continued walking along the gutter, kicking debris out of the way as she went.

Jacob went with her. "I hate to keep repeating myself, but if your knee still hurts, you should be seen. I'm the one who ran into you, so the bill will be mine, not yours."

"It's only been a week today. It'll be better in a month."

"Does Ammon realize how much your knee is bothering you?"

She startled, seemingly embarrassed. Was she bothered by the way Ammon treated her in front of Jacob the other day? She shouldn't be. That was Ammon's to own, not hers.

But Jacob wished he hadn't mentioned Ammon's name. "I'll tell you what. Let's not discuss Ammon. I won't ask you what he thinks, and I won't try to force you to go to a doctor. But if you feel you need to see one, the bill is mine to pay, okay?"

She studied him with warm, expressive eyes. "That plan works."

"Gut."

She returned her attention to the gutter while walking. "Look! Isn't that one?"

The sun glinted off something buried under wet leaves. "Let me get that." Jacob grabbed the two connected glass doorknobs, saving her from bending her knee. "Here you go."

Looking pleased, she took it from him and brushed off the grime and rotting leaves.

It couldn't be worth more than thirty dollars, even if she got top price for it. "We're getting too far from the accident. Let's go back, and I'll check the other side of the street." After waiting for a car to pass, he ran across the road, and as he worked his way back to where the accident happened, he spotted the missing doorknobs. "Got 'em."

"Really?"

He held them up. "Ya." He walked to where she was and gave them to her. "I guess if that's all of them, I should be on my way."

"Actually" — she looked at the palm of her hand and then ran it down her coat, wiping off debris from the doorknobs, he guessed — "if you came by the shop, you could show me how to connect the shutters. Ammon's keeping the children until after lunch so I can get some work done, and think of how much more I could get done if I had a clue what I was doing. The warehouse is only a couple of blocks from here."

"Ammon won't mind?"

"Not a bit. If he could, he'd hire you to help me. Now Dora, she would mind. She's asked me more than once if I did anything to sabotage you and her." Esther headed for her wagon. "And I had to admit that we did talk about you two dating. She's really angry with me."

Jacob hated that he'd caused trouble between them. He walked with Esther. "I didn't mean to drag you into the conversation. I barely mentioned your name, and she was immediately suspicious that you may have said something to influence me."

"And did I?"

"No. I'd told her from the start that I was leaving in April, but since she was thinking of things more seriously than I was, it was time to end it. Sorry for my part in causing trouble."

"Completely forgiven. It's not your fault that my relationship with Dora is a bit complicated. I get motherly and smother her at times. Anyway, sibling issues aside . . ." Esther's wry smile hinted of her scheming something, and he was intrigued. "You run over me with your horse, and then you cause my sister to be angry with me."

He could tell by her playful tone where she was headed. "And don't forget your injured knee."

"Ouch." She immediately grabbed her knee and started an exaggerated hobble. "I know how you can make up for it."

"Let me guess. Uh, shutters?"

"The warehouse is really close. I'll lead

the way."

"Go ahead, and I'll catch up." Jacob hurried back to his wagon, wishing he'd eaten breakfast. By the time he got to his rig and started out, he was about a block behind Esther. They continued on for another two blocks, and then she turned onto a driveway next to a large brick building, but it wasn't a warehouse. An electric sign in the window read Hudson's Decorative Ironwork. The sidewalk had a display of tables, chairs, sections of fences, and a piece of a banister. Then it clicked. This was the place that had provided the banisters for the houses he was finishing for Kings' Construction.

As Jacob brought the horse to a stop, a tall, burly black man came out a side door. Jacob recognized him as the man who'd been Esther's driver the day she came to the construction site. "Shark Bait." The man scowled. "I expected you sooner. Where have you been?" He gestured at Jacob. "And why do you have a King of Kings' Construction with you?"

Esther grinned. "He kept trying to run over me with his rig, and I'm trying to rehabilitate his bad behavior by putting him to work."

The man nodded. "I'm Bailey Hudson."

Jacob hopped down. "Jacob King."

"He's going to show me how to put these shutters together." Esther looped the reins around the handle of the brake and scooted across the bench seat toward the step down.

Bailey eyed her. "Knee bothering you again?"

How did the man know that?

Bailey went to the side of the wagon near the bench seat. "You promised me about that knee. Are you keeping your promise this time, or am I calling Ammon?"

Esther shook a doorknob at Bailey. "If you think I'm spending my morning away from the house to go to the doctor's, you've lost your marbles. All they'll say is stay off it, don't tote children, and take ibuprofen."

"That's not all, Miss Essie. They'll also say you need to get an MRI." Bailey scowled, but he held out his hands. "Well, come on."

She set the doorknobs on the bench seat, put her hands on his shoulders, and he eased her to the ground.

Bailey turned to him. "It's nice of you to help our little Shark Bait, Jacob. And for your reward, let me invite you to breakfast."

Esther grabbed the two sets of doorknobs from the bench seat. "Don't let Bailey fool you. He goes by the diner most mornings to buy breakfast for his workers, and he gets too much every single time. If you'll eat, you'll be doing him the favor."

"True enough. Even Shark Bait can't possibly eat all I got today."

Jacob balanced the shutters on one shoulder.

Bailey grabbed several shutters too. "Jacob, you hungry?"

"I am. But I'm more curious — 'Shark Bait' and 'Miss Essie'?"

The man grinned, his white teeth in sharp contrast to his dark skin. "You come inside, and maybe I'll show you why we call her that."

Esther narrowed her eyes at the man.

Bailey shrugged, his eyes mockingly wide, as if he were afraid of her.

Jacob needed to be doing his own work, but he also owed Esther some of his time. That actually just gave him a rationalization for being here. Right now, there was nowhere else he'd rather be. "How many nicknames do you have?"

She sighed. "Too many. My understanding is my Daed started it, but most of them have been given by this one." She gestured from Bailey's head to his toes.

Bailey grinned. "Me and her Daed go way back." He nodded for Jacob to follow him. Esther continued to walk toward the side door while Jacob and Bailey leaned the shutters against the building.

Bailey dusted his hands together as they returned to the wagon for more. "You're probably wondering just who is the boss around here." He smiled, pure joy radiating from his eyes. "It's definitely me. Just keep that under wraps. Okay?"

Jacob laughed. "Sure. But why does she call it a warehouse?"

"There's one out back. She fell in love with it when her Daed started bringing her here before she knew how to speak English."

"You've known her that long?"

"Her Daed was a farmer, but during the late fall and winter months, he'd work in the warehouse for me, and she tagged along when allowed."

"I suppose it was some of your men who put in railings for the porches, staircases, and catwalks, both inside and out, at the new houses."

"Yeah, that's right. They did a good job, right?"

"Excellent."

"Good."

They finished unloading the wagon. When they stepped into the shop, Jacob breathed in the aroma of coffee and breakfast foods. His stomach rumbled as he scanned the place. Five middle-aged men were at workbenches, and a couple of them had on welding helmets and had lit torches in hand.

Bailey pointed. "Breakfast is in the kitchen, and that's at the back of the building. Help yourself to anything that's there." He gestured to some privacy screens toward the front where customers would enter from the sidewalk. "That's Shark Bait's workspace."

Jacob could see her feet underneath the fabric barricade.

"We built the privacy screens for her when she was a teen. That way she didn't need to be self-conscious while concocting weird stuff, as she called it." Bailey chuckled. "See the flooring in the entryway and office areas?"

"Yeah." That flooring covered everything that led up to the cement floors where the workers' shop area began.

"Shark Bait did that — salvaged and laid it. And if it needed sanding, staining, or shellacking, she did that too."

"Really?" Jacob went toward the foyer and office areas. The flooring was laid out in segments of nine square feet, each section showcasing a different type of floor — oak, pine, hickory, brick, and slate. The four corner sectors were a combination of wood and stone. Jacob spied what he assumed were her first stabs at laying flooring. Kneeling, he eyed the floor as the sunlight fell across it, divulging every flaw.

Not bad.

He was no expert when it came to laying flooring. However, it was his job to line up the subcontractors who installed what the buyers ordered, and he had to make sure the owners were pleased. So he inspected a lot of floors before doing a walk-through with the buyers.

"She used this as her practice area, but it also gives potential buyers of the loose boards and bricks a place to get a visual. Not that she has a lot of customers, but she's diligent about the business she does have."

Jacob picked out two favorites and wondered how the owners of the houses Kings' Construction was building would feel if they could see this.

Bailey pointed at a desk. "I'd better get busy."

"Thanks." Jacob stood and walked to the brick-and-wood section. He crouched again and ran his hand along the area where the brick abutted the pine. The repurposed flooring had far more aesthetic appeal than he'd imagined. As a carpenter, he'd always

157

gravitated toward the newest products on the market. Maybe that's what owners wanted because, like him, they didn't realize they had an option or know the aesthetic appeal of old wood and brick.

"Hey." Esther's voice caught his attention.

Jacob remained crouched as he looked her way. "These are beautiful."

She smiled, nodding, as if pleased that he finally got it. "Ya, old wood and stone make for beautiful floors, but there's more to it than that. There's something wonderfully rich about standing on a floor where people stood a hundred or two hundred years ago, isn't there? As if we're touching history while becoming history."

He nodded. "True."

"Some of the sections were my first stabs from five years ago, so I should redo those, but there hasn't been time."

"I can imagine."

She'd had four children within probably six or seven years of marriage. She ran a home for unwed mothers and earned money as a do-it-yourself hobbyist of repurposed goods. He was impressed.

He stood. "Do you install flooring?"

"Not really. I've done a bit of it out of necessity on repairs at home. And I laid this as a display, but I'm not skilled enough to put it in for someone who's paid a premium price for the supplies."

"You could probably get really good at it with a little practice."

"Maybe, but the timing to complete a project on a new house is too precise to fit a schedule like mine."

The word *schedule* hit him hard, and he realized he needed to step up his pace. As interesting as she was and as much as she could use a hand on the shutter contraptions from a carpenter, he had a lot of his own work to get done. He had to finish two houses, including talking to the owners about installing some of her flooring, before he left town in a few weeks.

Still, he could show her how to connect the shutters. Since she could lay flooring, it probably wouldn't take him long to teach her how to put the accordion-style shutters together.

Jacob dusted off his hands. "We should get started."

She pointed a thumb toward the back of the shop. "How about some coffee and breakfast first? If I read you right when Bailey mentioned food, you're hungry."

The aroma of coffee, bacon, and cinnamon wooed him. "I am."

"Kumm."

Once in the kitchen, he couldn't believe the spread of food sitting on warming trays. "I think Bailey wants to own a mom-and-pop diner when he grows up."

"You won't find a nicer guy anywhere."

His phone pinged, indicating he'd received a text message. He pulled the phone from his pocket, touched the screen a few times, and stared at a new image of Casey. He chuckled. "How cute is she?"

Esther held out a plate to him, studying his phone. "Extremely."

Another ping registered, and a private text message from Sandra flashed over the image: *Casey sends her love, and she's counting the minutes until Dad comes home.*

Dad? Casey never called him that, and he didn't recall Sandra ever using that term before, but true to Sandra's nature, her timing couldn't have been worse. Unsure whether to try to clarify it with Esther, he slid his phone into his pocket, and they fixed their plates.

Once across the table from each other, she bowed her head for a few moments of prayer and then looked up. "I understand you've been staying with Noah and his family. Barb is a fantastic cook, isn't she?"

Esther didn't seem a bit put off or uncomfortable with Jacob because of the text mes-

160

sage, but he wanted to explain.

"I didn't lie about Sandra."

Esther studied him. "I appreciate what you're doing for me today. And with you leaving in a few weeks, just let it go at that."

Jacob shrugged. He wasn't very good at building friendships. Even though it was his nature to be warm and friendly, he struggled with his sense of personal privacy. It was easy to help and care for people, but to actually let someone inside his life was hard. That was part of the reason Samuel's betrayal had cut so deep. Jacob had been close to only two people in his life — and they fell in love with each other. Even when sharing with Samuel and later with Rhoda, Jacob had told only what he had to — most often confessing the bare minimum needed to avoid hurting the relationship. "I've never been more than friends with Sandra. Barely even that a lot of the time. But I have been like a dad to Casey, albeit one who doesn't get to visit all that often."

She ate a bite of scrambled eggs. "It's difficult to get a man to own up to the responsibilities of his own child if he doesn't love the mother. Would you mind if I asked what caused you to care enough to stay involved in her life?"

"I can tell you what led up to it" — Jacob

161

dug his fork into the biscuit and gravy, cutting a bite — "but it's a long story." He put a forkful of biscuit into his mouth and then took a sip of coffee. "When I left the Amish at barely nineteen, I worked at various construction jobs until I found this one company and went to work for a man named Blaine. We really hit it off, so I lived with him and his wife, Sandra, and while I was there, she learned she was pregnant. To make a long story short, the night Sandra went into labor, Blaine was nowhere to be found. She didn't want to go to the hospital too early and asked me to stay up with her. We watched a weird movie on TV, one I can't even remember the name of."

Esther set the salt and pepper in front of him. "Go on."

He sprinkled salt on his eggs. "In the movie a guy is able to travel back in time and change what happened. He realizes two of his childhood buddies were traumatized from events when they were young, and as adults, one is suicidal, and the other has become a predator." He ate a few bites of food. "So the guy goes back in time on numerous occasions, changing different events, trying to help both of them have a better future. He finally realizes if he can get them under the influence of one good adult — someone who loves, sacrifices, and makes good decisions — they will grow up to be happy and fulfilled."

"Sounds like a disturbing movie."

He nodded. "Sandra had a really rough childhood, and she deals with bipolar disorder, but she had such high hopes for her baby. When I saw that movie, I felt as if God were saying to me, *With your help Sandra can be the good adult she longs to be.*"

"That was a lot of responsibility to take on."

"I've hardly watched a movie since. I mean, if TV is going to saddle me with lifelong responsibilities, I'd just as soon avoid it."

She stared at him with those expressive brown eyes that he couldn't read.

"That was a joke, Esther. You were supposed to at least smile." But she didn't.

"What happened to her husband?"

"Not long after Casey was born, he disappeared. We're still not sure if he's alive or dead, so I've tried to be there for her — emotionally and financially. But at times I feel like an idiot for going out of my way to try to stabilize a home life for Casey."

"Then, by all means, choose to be an idiot all day long for the rest of your life."

He laughed. "My parents would not appreciate that advice." But he did. "Let's talk about something besides me."

"But I've had one question since you talked to Sandra on the phone the night I was on the curb regaining my wits. Do you mind?"

"Probably not." He hadn't minded anything else she'd asked. "What is it?"

"How do you get away with being gone from home so long and spending Christmas with an Englisch person?"

"Did you overhear the whole conversation?"

"I think so. Sorry, but it was really quiet except for your voice."

"Not a problem. I was just curious. About how I spent Christmas, see . . . I was in the middle of joining the faith when the breakup occurred. I left Maine and went to work for my uncle in Lancaster."

"He's the one I talked to on the job site?"

"That's him. He's a preacher, and he was really worried I wouldn't join the faith or stay connected with my family, so he went to the bishop and got some concessions for me."

"Oh, I'd say he got more than just some."

"True." He ate another bite of eggs. "Your

turn. How did you get into salvaging goods?"

"Ah, I fell in love with it while visiting my Mamm's parents, who live in Lancaster, Pennsylvania."

"Maybe my uncle knows your grand-parents."

"Maybe so. They don't live in his district, though, or I would've seen him at the few Sunday meetings I've been to over the years. So my grandparents were taking down their grandparents' old, abandoned house. It had been considered unsafe, so until a week before the demolition, I hadn't been allowed to step into it. Once I got inside, I begged to be allowed to get the doorknobs and anything else a young girl could dismantle and carry away."

"What is it with you and doorknobs?"

"When one of those knobs is on a door inside a home, and you use it to open a door to a room, it's like using a portal from the past to enter your future. Where was the first house you helped build?"

The conversation never slowed, even when he returned to the warming plates for seconds. It was a complete surprise to discover how much they had to talk about. Apparently there was no end of topics between someone who helped build houses and someone who helped deconstruct them.

He ate the last bite of biscuit and gravy. "So you're contacted by various historical societies to give your opinion on the value of raw materials in old homes?"

"Sometimes they want my thoughts. Mostly I've become friends with people on the committees, and they know I love looking at old houses. So they tell me when one is being assessed, and I get to tag along. It's like offering free drinks to an addict."

He laughed. "That's how I started out feeling about construction work. Then I made some stupid mistakes, and I couldn't pick up a hammer for a long time."

"I could *not* handle losing my love for salvaging goods. Do you mind telling me what happened?"

He took a drink of his coffee before setting the cup on his plate and taking them to the kitchen sink. "I don't mind. We can talk about it while we're working."

Her eyes met his, and she smiled. His heart skipped a beat.

Who was this woman?

Moreover, was he making a mistake to open up to her like this when she was married?

TWELVE

Leah tried to pull air into her lungs, along with some hopeful and fresh perspectives. Her body demanded oxygen, but the simple act of breathing deep seemed too difficult.

Moving like an old woman, she hung another wet dress on the line. It was only Monday midmorning, yet since arriving on Friday, her Daed had somehow, rule by rigid rule, managed to strap three hundred years of the Ordnung onto every part of her: Her limbs. Her back. Her shoulders. Her eyes. Even her skin prickled. All of it was a side effect of what he'd done to her heart — confused her.

Who was God, and what did He expect of her? When she and Landon had prayed together months ago, she'd been so sure she knew Him.

She shoved the basket with the toe of her shoe until it sat under an empty line. How had she so quickly forgotten what it was like to be trapped inside a life she had no control over? Only this time even sleep didn't bring relief. Whispers filled her dreams, saying she'd lose more than a piece of her soul and her self-respect — she'd lose her mind — if she didn't get free. What would she do if her Daed continued to insist she return to Pennsylvania with him?

What *could* she do?

Thoughts of her old life in Pennsylvania haunted her. She used to drink and party, at least until Rhoda found her passed out in her fruit garden. Not long after, at barely seventeen, Leah thought she was pregnant. The memory of that awful time made her cringe. She couldn't tolerate the idea of having to go back. There were too many humiliating memories . . . and people to face.

Dozens of scenarios ran through her mind, but short of breaking all ties and running away, she couldn't come up with one solution. If she did run away, it would allow Landon to continue working the farm, and she could return when things cooled off. Unlike the times she'd thought of running away as a minor, if she chose to leave now, she had money in the bank, job skills, and a reasonable knowledge of how the outside world worked.

What was she thinking? Even she couldn't

be so selfish or rash as to hurt and worry everyone while trying to live without any support system. Not only would she be gone from here, but so would Landon and others who would search for her.

"Hallo." Her father's voice crackled through the two-way. "Meeting in the kitchen in twenty."

Now what? More talk of her returning to Pennsylvania with him?

"Oh." The two-way pulsed again. "The meeting is to include Landon also."

Leah's head spun, and her stomach knotted. Her Daed *wanted* to talk to Landon?

A cold wind made the strings to her prayer Kapp flap across her face. She pulled them away and stared off into the distance. The God her Daed described was very different from the God in the Scriptures she studied while at the local church. Her Daed talked of God as One who criticized how women wore their hair or what color shoes people wore or how they traveled to others' homes, meetings, or stores.

Did God hold people to those things? Her Daed certainly had Bible verses that said He did.

"Leah."

The whisper from somewhere drew her from her thoughts.

She saw Landon slowly walking toward the house. With her Daed staying by her side until she came to hang out laundry, this was her first glimpse of Landon. He held up something shiny for just a moment and nodded toward the front door. She pinned the last garment onto the line and grabbed the laundry basket.

They met on the path to the porch steps, and he slid something into her coat pocket. "This way, no matter what happens, you can text me during the day and call me when you're in your room where no one can see or hear you."

She felt in her pocket. "A phone?"

"Yeah. Granny picked it up for me yesterday."

She and Landon had been trying to respect the rules in this Amish district as long as it didn't clash with their faith, but apparently drastic times called for drastic measures. "Thanks."

Landon grabbed her hand. "Be patient."

The door swung open, making them jolt and separate.

Isaac ran between them. "Daed!"

Iva's eyes moved from their hands to the kitchen. Apparently, Iva had seen them holding hands. She gave Leah a warning look.

"Isaac," Iva called, *"geh zu die Scheier."* After telling Isaac to go to the barn, she hurried Leah inside, putting space between her and Landon. Iva or Phoebe must've seen Steven heading for the barn and was letting Isaac join him there.

Leah's Daed entered the room, studying Leah and then Landon. Daed pursed his lips and nodded at Landon. "There's coffee on the stove."

Leah passed the basket to Iva and scurried into the bathroom. Once the door was locked, she grabbed the phone from her pocket. A quick look through the contacts indicated he'd added several numbers: his, the farm's, his grandmother's, and Jacob's. She went back to the home page and realized there was already a text message from Landon with a time stamp of five that morning. It read: *Good morning, Leah. Your mission, should you choose to accept it, is to respond to this message the moment you read it.*

Should she? She'd messed with his phone enough to know how, but he was in the house with her Daed. One thing she knew about Landon: he was skilled at hiding his phone when he needed to. He'd proved that a few times while they were sitting in Sunday evening class or sharing a meal with

171

everyone in this home — before her Daed arrived, of course. Landon could slide his phone out of hiding, text someone, and make his phone disappear again without anyone seeing him do it.

She smiled and keyed in a response: *Your mission, should you choose to accept it, is to respond while in the house with you know who.* She hit send and waited.

It vibrated. He'd answered already: *One guess. Your dat. Done. Now what?*

She smiled at him spelling *Daed* the way it was pronounced. How many times did she do that with the English language and Landon said nothing? Feeling as if she could breathe again, she typed: *what r we going 2 do?*

A moment later the phone vibrated again. *Seek wisdom. Be patient. Wait on God.*

She typed: *Easier said than done.*

It took longer for him to respond this time. Was her Daed looking right at him or something? Should she continue to wait or rescue him from one of her Daed's lectures? Finally her phone buzzed. *It's not easy, but don't let your emotions lie to you. We can win this.*

She sighed. Landon's life seemed to be built on keeping events in perspective.

Couldn't he just once feel the depth of disappointment in what was happening?

She typed: *Maybe your "look on the bright side" emotions are lying to you.*

She waited, but he didn't respond. She washed her face and brushed her teeth. When he still hadn't answered, she removed her prayer Kapp, unwound her hair, combed it, and pinned it up again. Still no answer.

After taking off her coat, she turned the phone on silent and slid it into the hidden pocket of her apron. She tiptoed out of the bathroom, and her heart skittered when she saw Landon and her Daed in the kitchen talking in low tones.

"Leah." Phoebe was on the couch with Arie in her lap. Phoebe patted the spot next to her.

Leah sat beside her. "What are they talking about?"

"Oh, I think you know."

Fear grabbed her by the throat. "Me. All Daed's done since he arrived is go to each of you, one by one, and share his concerns."

"He's a horrible man." Phoebe pushed her lopsided belly, and Leah assumed the little one needed a bit of repositioning.

"It's not funny."

"I know." Phoebe put her arm around Leah. "And he's been out of sorts and

173

panicked, but he does love you."

"Maybe." Would he care what she did if it didn't have the potential to embarrass him in front of other Amish?

The front door opened, and Samuel and Rhoda walked in. Steven entered behind them, ducking low because Isaac was on his shoulders. Steven put his son's feet on the floor, telling him in Pennsylvania Dutch to go to the playroom with his sister. "Iva?"

A few moments later Leah heard the sound of a door opening upstairs. Then Iva leaned over the rail of the catwalk. "Right here."

Leah didn't blame Iva for hiding in her bedroom, hoping to avoid the meeting. She wasn't a part of the fray, and she didn't want to be.

"Would you stay with the children while the rest of us talk?"

"Ya, sure."

A nervous prickle ran through Leah. Was her Daed going to issue his ultimatum with witnesses who would support him?

"Hey." Samuel motioned to Leah. "Kumm." He started walking toward the kitchen, seemingly uncomfortable, as if he'd rather not stop long enough to look her in the eye. Leah waited for everyone to go ahead of her, including Phoebe, and each one took a seat at the kitchen table. Landon's weak smile made nausea roll through her.

Her Daed patted the table beside him, and she sat.

He clenched his hand around the mug. "I've shared my concerns since arriving three days ago, and I think I've discovered a reasonable solution."

Rhoda stared at the table, and Leah looked at each person, but no one's expression reflected peace, as if Daed's assurance of a *reasonable solution* didn't ring true to them.

Leah's heart pounded in her ears. "I'm listening."

He stared into his cup. "Eli needs more help than I can give. The dairy side of the farm is full-time work, and as the orchard is reestablished after the tornado, he needs good, skilled workers. Leah, I was wrong not to realize what an asset a daughter could be. Samuel saw it before moving to this settlement, and now I do too."

She wasn't fooled. His tone and manner were in sharp contrast to the silent treatment he'd given her yesterday and the fits he'd thrown Friday and Saturday, but all this encouraging chatter wasn't love. It was diplomacy, just a matter of Daed trying to keep peace while he got his way.

"Leah," — Daed turned his mug around several times — "I know you like it here, but it's time you come home to live with Mamm and me, at least for a while."

"No. I won't go." Where was everyone's determination? Did that exist only when fighting to make this farm a success?

Daed cleared his throat. "You will, and we leave at two this afternoon."

"Today?" This couldn't be happening!

Rhoda shook her head. "Whatever else is agreed upon, that's too soon, Benjamin."

Daed looked at Samuel, eyebrows raised.

Samuel nodded. "It's too soon. You can stay another night and let Leah say proper good-byes."

"Wait." Leah splayed her fingers. "I've agreed to nothing. How long do I have to stay in Pennsylvania?"

Samuel reached across the table and clutched her hand. "There's good news. If you'll follow all Daed's saying, when you return, you'll do so with his blessing."

Was it possible her Daed would do that? "When can I return?"

No one answered, but the look in Landon's eyes indicated that he knew.

"Daed, answer me!" Her scream pierced the somber tone of the meeting.

He pursed his lips. "A year."

"A year!" Leah jumped up, knocking over her chair. "No. Absolutely not!"

Anger etched her Daed's face, but he closed his eyes. "Do not tell me no again, Leah." He drew a deep breath and opened his eyes. "Samuel's right. I don't like it, but I've agreed you can return after that. In order for me to allow that, though, you and Landon must give your word that there will be no contact between you two during that time."

"I won't agree to it!"

Resolve filled her Daed's face. "Trust me, I don't think a year is nearly enough. I wanted at least two years, preferably five."

Rhoda flicked her pinkie nail against her thumbnail in quick succession. "Landon helped your Daed understand that if he asked . . . demanded too much, your Daed could end up walking away with nothing, so he has agreed to a year."

"But" — Daed pushed his index finger against the table — "once we leave here, there can be no contact between you and Landon."

"That's absurd! I won't agree to it!" She looked at each person, and not one of them was taking up for her. "Landon, why would you think that's reasonable?"

Landon's face was taut as he fidgeted with his fingers. "Leah."

She heard it in his voice. He'd caved, just like everyone else. She swallowed hard. "This farm and canning business need me too!" She slammed the chair into an upright position.

"It does." Steven rubbed his forehead. "And we're plenty upset that the situation has come to this, but we can't lose another man from this venture, especially not one who knows every side to the business, like Landon does. Right now, I can't see how Orchard Bend Farms can thrive without his involvement."

So because she didn't rank high enough, everyone in this room was willing to cut her loose? "This is just wrong, and every one of you knows it!"

Steven pinched the bridge of his nose. "There is more going on than meets the eye, Leah. A bishop is moving here from Pennsylvania. He and his family arrive next week. He's been told about you and Landon, and if we don't separate you two, *we,* every church member under this roof, will be held accountable."

"I'm in my rumschpringe!"

Her Daed crossed his arms. "It's clear you're not using it to find a suitable Amish mate. That is its intended purpose. The church leaders draw a line for anyone caught misusing the rumschpringe. And you've been caught."

"That's not true!" she hissed. "Unless someone is breaking the law or stumbling home drunk, the ministers leave those in their rumschpringe alone."

"You can believe what you will, Leah. You seem to be good at that. But the last time we had communion at home, Arlan's parents weren't allowed to participate because he and his friends were playing musical instruments in their home."

She didn't know that. She hadn't seen Arlan since he'd visited here more than a year ago. How long had it been since she'd even talked to him — three or four months?

She looked at Samuel. Arlan used to be her closest friend, and his sister, Catherine, used to be Samuel's girlfriend. Catherine and Leah never got along, but Leah wouldn't wish the embarrassment of what was equal to a public flogging on anyone. She should contact Arlan and see how he and Catherine were faring, but now wasn't the time to think about that.

Leah buried her forehead in the palm of her hand. "Why am I being targeted like this?"

"You need to ask?" Confusion flickered across her Daed's face. "Fine, I'll tell you. It's because word got out that you're seeing Landon — an outsider whose employment should've been terminated *before* you grew to care for him. The fact that your brother and even the preacher you live with have not put a stop to it has angered a lot of people." Daed pushed back from the table. "Do you want Steven, Samuel, and Rhoda punished in worse ways than being excluded from a communion? If you do, keep being stubborn, and the new bishop will take matters into his hands when he arrives."

"What I want is to be left alone!" Despite having been raised Amish, she still didn't understand how the Amish did everything. "So because the man is a bishop elsewhere, he gets to step into this district as the bishop here?"

Steven nodded. "Since we don't have one, and he has a good reputation where he is, the answer is ya. Every preacher, deacon, and bishop in Pennsylvania who knows him supports him. That means he not only enters as the bishop, but he also comes wielding the power and support of numerous Amish churches."

Leah had known that untangling from the Amish would be difficult, especially as the daughter of a King and the granddaughter of Apple Sam King. Her grandfather's name had a power and influence that he'd passed on to his sons, including her Daed. "He's moving here to help Daed get his way!"

"No." Samuel reached for her hand, but she pulled away from him. "At least I don't think that's it. Who uproots from one state to move to another in order to fill a church role that receives no pay?"

"Someone who owes Daed or the Kings a huge favor!"

"I've spoken to him," Steven said. "And I truly believe it's just a set of coincidences that are working against us. He's spent years looking for a suitable place to purchase a lot of affordable farming land for future generations of his family. He's been interested in moving here since we arrived, but too many Amish settlements that are in a new region of the country fail, so he was waiting. He feels this one is sustainable as long as all the members strive to keep the Old Ways, and he intends to make sure we're doing that."

Her Daed clutched his suspenders. "This farm needs Landon, so it would be best if you come home with me."

Her father's even tone angered her. He was banking that either Landon or she would find someone else while they were separated. They wouldn't, but it'd be a year of torment.

"Samuel." Leah turned to her brother, hoping against hope he'd tell her what she longed to hear. "This compromise is asking too much, and you have nothing to say about it?"

"Don't look at the time apart. Look at all he's offering you. After the year he won't say or do anything else to keep you two apart."

"A year in exile! Will none of you tell him no?"

The room was deathly silent. She bolted, heading for her bedroom.

"Leah," — Landon hurried after her — "I'll wait for you. I promise."

"What is *wrong* with you? Why are you negotiating with Daed when you should be standing up to him?"

"Because we can't win this argument. Were you able to hear anything that was said?"

She moved closer. "If we ran off together right now while Daed is here and while Samuel, Rhoda, and Steven are trying to get me to return with him, it'd protect them from being responsible for my actions."

"If you leave the Amish like this and I help

you, we'll both lose our jobs. Rhoda and Samuel won't have a choice about letting us go, or they'll be shunned. Can you imagine the scandal it would cause Steven as a preacher?"

"But I know the Amish, and the outrage of us running off will blow over in a year. They'll see that we love each other and attend church together. They won't welcome what we've done, but their hearts will soften, and Samuel can hire us again."

"We can survive a year apart, Leah. Besides, hurting your family and our not having jobs is no way to start a marriage. You haven't even met my parents, but we might need their support. Come on. Our families deserve better. *We* deserve better."

Their lives and jobs were intertwined with those who were dead set against them marrying. Would Landon ever be willing to do what it'd take to marry her? The answer that welled within her gut made her sick. She was such a fool for sweet talkers. "You don't want to marry me, not really."

"Of course I do, when the time's right."

"You mean *if* the time is ever right?"

"Until your Daed showed up to take you home, you weren't one hundred percent positive you wanted to leave the Amish."

"Yes, I was! I just didn't know how I

would do it! Or how long it would take to untangle from the Amish."

He stared at her. This revelation should be joyous news, but he simply nodded. "Okay." He drew a heavy breath. "Here's the good news. Now we know the answers to those questions. Your Daed has asked for a year."

"You actually think that in a year Daed will suddenly set me free? He's stalling for time! And the bishop who's moving here will have a year to make plans and rally others to help him stand in our way!"

Why didn't Landon just say what he really meant? His first loyalty was in the same place it had been when they'd met: with Rhoda. He'd been her assistant and friend far longer than he'd known Leah. The second item on his list of loyalties was this orchard. He wanted to be a partner, and he wasn't giving that up to marry Leah.

Warm tears slid down her cheeks, and she headed for the stairs.

Landon moved ahead of her and turned to face her. "Leah, your Daed will stick to his word, and we'll get through this. He's agreed to let you return in a year. Just a year. We can do this. Okay?"

More tears threatened. "Could you do me a favor?"

"Sure." He took her hand into his. "Anything."

"No more lies between us." She pulled away from him, determined to speak as calmly as he was. "Daed's not going to let me return, but it doesn't really matter, because you're never going to be ready to do what it will take for me to sever ties with Rhoda. And you don't intend to jeopardize your chance of becoming a partner." She stared at him through watery eyes. "I refuse to be the one to get in your way, so I'll go back to Pennsylvania." She sidestepped him and ran up the stairs.

"Leah, please. It's not like that. You know —"

She slammed the door to her bedroom and locked it. Her heart throbbed beyond any hurt she'd ever known before. All of them were against her and Landon, even Landon!

She threw herself onto the bed, buried her head between two pillows, and sobbed.

Landon stared at the closed door. He wanted to climb the stairs and pound on it, demanding she apologize. How could she believe he was trying to guard his position on this farm?

She knew it'd be tough to get free of her

185

family. They'd discussed it. A lot. But she turned on him the first time her Daed put pressure on them?

"Seriously, Leah?" he yelled at her closed door from his spot on the stairs. He waited, but she didn't open it. If staying in Maine was *that* important, she could stay. He turned toward the kitchen.

Don't do this! The warning inside him only irritated him more. He was done being patient and reasonable. Since he'd begun to care for her, back when they were still in Pennsylvania, he'd tried to do what was best for her. Look where it'd gotten him! Leah thought he cared for his job more than her. He'd set that straight right now.

He went into the kitchen, where the group was still sitting at the table as if it were a normal meeting.

Rhoda looked at him, and her eyes widened, apparently reading his anger. "Landon, we were just discussing —"

"Benjamin." Landon straightened his ball cap. He didn't want to hear what else they were discussing. He'd had enough. "What will it take for you to allow Leah to stay here?"

The man interlaced his fingers. "I doubt you understand the gravity of —"

"I understand plenty." Landon gritted his

teeth, keeping his tone as even as possible. "And I'm sick of you thinking outsiders are too stupid to comprehend what's important in life and too evil to be allowed to infiltrate your camps of great holiness." He clenched his jaw. "What will it take?"

"You leave Orchard Bend Farms today, now actually, and give your word you'll not see or contact Leah for a year, and you turn in your phone so she can't contact you."

"Landon," — Rhoda came to him — "you're angry. Don't agree to leave here like this. What he's asking is ridiculous."

The voice inside him kept saying, *Don't. Don't give in to your anger.*

"It's done." Landon held out his phone. "How different is this plan from him taking Leah to Pennsylvania tomorrow?"

"A good bit," she whispered. "Trust me."

But Leah's accusation kept pelting him like a winter ice storm, snatching his breath and all ability to see beyond a few feet. When Rhoda didn't accept his phone, he took her by the wrist, turned her hand palm up, and placed his phone in it. "I really don't want to hear from anyone, and I have to put some distance between me and this farm."

He turned and walked out.

■ ■ ■ ■

When Leah's tears finally subsided, she pulled free of the pillows and sat up. She wiped her face and straightened her crumpled clothes before going to the closet to find her suitcase. Fresh tears welled, but she put the traveling bag on her bed and opened it.

She heard a car door slam and went to the window. Landon was leaving? How much time had passed since she locked herself in her bedroom? Surely it wasn't even lunchtime yet. Had someone sent him home, or was he leaving because he was sick of the drama — her drama?

They still had a little time. It sounded as if Rhoda and Samuel would fight for her to have an evening of talking with Landon and saying good-byes. Surely he'd return in an hour or two, and they'd spend the rest of the time talking — even if her Daed insisted a chaperone go along.

Her complaint that he didn't want to marry her wasn't true, was it? She could hardly blame him if it was. Time and again her emotions built up inside her like a thunderstorm. When they did, she lashed out with what she felt at that moment, not necessarily what she really believed or thought.

While she was staring at the yard and driveway, Samuel, Steven, and her Daed emerged from under the roof of the porch and traipsed to the barn. Had Rhoda and Samuel helped her Daed make plans to take her home, or were they honestly just as caught by the circumstances as she was?

She sighed. Her Daed had left her no choice. Either she went home with him, or Landon had to leave, and Landon was needed around here more than she was. Actually, everyone else, including Steven and even Jacob when he was here, fell into place somewhere below the anchor of the trio of Rhoda, Samuel, and Landon.

But before she finished packing to return to Pennsylvania, she had to talk to Landon. She grabbed the phone out of her pocket and texted him: *What just happened? How did we end up arguing as if we're enemies?*

Surely he'd respond in typical Landon form — understanding and unwavering in his love.

While waiting on him to answer, she watched as Steven drove a wagon carrying large cans of oil mixture out of the barn and into the orchard. Since her grandfather Apple Sam was a young man, the Kings had

189

taken great care of their apple orchards, tending to them organically regardless of the amount of work that required. The Amish were often good stewards of the land, but they'd break her heart and dismantle her future because she didn't view life as they did?

Samuel and Daed rode out of the barn on horseback, going a different direction than Steven. Where was Rhoda?

At least they were leaving Leah alone for a bit. But their goal was no secret — to give her space to make the *right* decision to obey her father.

She clutched the phone. Why hadn't Landon answered her? She texted him again: *Hello?* She waited. Had he turned off his phone?

Or was he simply through responding to her at all?

Someone tapped on the door. "Leah, may I come in?" Rhoda's voice trembled.

Leah turned the lock, and when she opened the door, she saw a rarity — Rhoda's eyes glistening with tears.

Rhoda forced a smile. "I'm sorry." A sob broke from her before she pursed her lips and drew a deep breath. "I never thought . . ."

Leah went to the closet and pulled three

dresses off the hangers at one time. She didn't want to hear anyone's apology. "I'm packing now so that when Landon returns, I have nothing else to do but spend time with him." She grabbed a stack of underwear out of a drawer. "What time do Daed and I leave here tomorrow?"

Rhoda moved in closer. "Leah . . . honey, you can stay."

Leah dropped the underwear, and her puny strength seemed to melt like wax. "What do you mean?"

Rhoda took her by the shoulders and helped her sit on the bed. She knelt beside her. "I . . . I think it's Landon's gift to you."

"A gift?" As realization dawned, Leah ran from the room, down the stairs, and to the front yard. What was she searching for? She'd seen Landon leave! But her head was spinning, and she couldn't make out one clear thought.

Rhoda followed her.

"Where is he?"

Rhoda pulled his phone out of her hidden pocket. "He's gone."

Leah snatched his cell from Rhoda and ran for the barn. He'd be at his granny's. She knew he would. She jerked the landline out of its cradle and dialed Erlene's house. But no one picked up.

Rhoda came to the doorway of the office.

"Why?" Leah knocked a container of pencils off the desk. "Tell me why he would do this."

Rhoda shrugged one shoulder. "He got really angry with all of us."

"What was said after I went to my room?"

Rhoda shrugged again but said nothing.

Leah plunked into the office chair. "It was me, wasn't it? I'm the one who said something that made him leave like this." She tried to think of all she'd screamed at him before slamming the door and locking it.

Her heart pounded, and the room continued to spin as fragments of complaints against him returned to her. She couldn't recall her exact words, but she remembered the essence of what she'd said — that she believed he didn't love her and that he was unwilling to jeopardize his chance of becoming a partner.

Along with her heartache, shame engulfed her, and she longed to turn back the hands of time.

What had she done?

THIRTEEN

Early morning light streamed through the clouds as Jacob drove the wagon toward Esther's. The sunshine breaking through the white billows looked as hopeful as he felt of late. He had a second wind. A new optimism. Maybe because April began a couple of days ago and the air was filled with sunlight and promises of spring. Or maybe he felt great because of opening up with Esther as they worked side by side for hours on Monday. If talking to someone made a person feel this much better, he shouldn't have spent his life avoiding it.

He pulled into her driveway and saw her through the double-wide doors of the shed — coatless and with the littlest one strapped to her back. Even though it'd warm up to near sixty later today, right now it had to be close to forty degrees. But she tended to move quickly, and the cool temperature probably felt just right. Her little boy appeared bundled up enough for both of them.

An old door rested on two sawhorses, and it had various crates on it, as if the door was being used for a workbench or desk. She appeared to be looking through one of the crates for something when she glanced up. Coming to the door of the shed, she motioned to him with one hand and pointed with the other, directing him to the right spot to park. He saw the stack of wood flooring and made a wide loop with the horse, aiming to get the wagon directly in front of the wood.

After seeing the wood floors at Bailey's ironwork shop a couple of days ago, he had an opportunity to talk to the owners of the homes later that day. One owner wasn't interested in anything old, but the other one had already planned to use a turn-of-the-century country look in her décor. So the woman jumped at the chance to have re-purposed flooring installed. She also wanted to know if he could get hold of antique hearths for the two fireplaces and something she called pilaster doorways.

He didn't know what that was, but since he had the roster of all the contractors who'd worked on the houses, he'd called Bailey's shop. Esther was gone for the day, but Bailey gave him the number to Esther's phone shanty. Jacob left a message, and thankfully she returned his call within a few hours.

Although Esther kept most of her wood flooring at the warehouse, she'd told him to meet her at the shed this morning, and she'd have the needed supplies. They discussed everything the homebuyer was interested in except the pilasters. He wasn't even sure he was pronouncing it right, so he figured a face-to-face with Esther about it would be best.

He had six days to get the houses ready for the owners to do a walkthrough. Then he'd need a couple of days to work the punch lists that delineated what still had to be done before the final inspection. After that he would turn over the keys and the responsibilities of the houses to the Realtor and head for Sandra's place.

With the wagon in place, he set the brake and hopped down. "Morning."

Esther looked up, a welcoming smile gracing her face. The little one on her back grinned at him, opening and shutting his mittened hand.

"Hi." Still favoring her knee, Esther moved a crate from the workbench door to a shelf. She dug through the container in search of something. "I've gathered all the hard pine I could since we talked, but I'm not sure it'll be enough to do all the homeowner wants."

Jacob eyed the pile. She must have collected more since they first talked in November, or she'd been mistaken about how much she had. The stack was enough to cover three to four hundred square feet, and if he got the contractors to patchwork brick around the edges, he might be able to do the foyer also. "It'll do. Maybe the owner will like the idea of supplementing with brick. I'll check, but I can't get brick in this load." The horse would struggle under that added weight.

"This is quite exciting." Her brown eyes sparkled. "You should've come through town and run over me years ago."

Jacob laughed. "My apologies." He started loading the wagon. "You have more flooring than I expected."

"Ya." She began looking through the crates again, shifting items from one container to another. "But you should see the bathrooms in the Daadi Haus where the girls live and the front hall of my Mamm's house."

"You stripped the floors of their covering?"

"I did."

He imagined the subflooring looked pretty rough where she'd pulled up the hardwood, but linoleum was an inexpensive fix, and if she could lay the hardwood, she could certainly lay linoleum. He wasn't sure how he felt about her making that sacrifice in order to earn money, but the concept itself was amusing. "Is that sort of like pulling a rug out from underneath someone's feet?"

"Worse. I pulled the floor out from underneath pregnant women and my aging, widowed mom." She gave an evil laugh.

He chuckled. "Do me a favor and remind me to watch where I'm standing when I'm around you."

When he slowed down enough to realize how much he liked her, it scared him. The connection between them was different from anything he'd experienced before. Not only was he able to open up to her, but he didn't feel compelled to be funny or entertaining. They were relaxed, and yet they got a lot done. He glanced her way. "What are you searching for?"

"One guess."

"You've lost more doorknobs?"

She nodded.

He nailed a red handkerchief to the end of the wood to alert cars that the load extended beyond the wagon bed. "Is that similar to losing your marbles?"

"Definitely. And they aren't just any doorknobs, either. They're perhaps the best I've ever collected. I've had them for more than ten years, and I thought they were stored with the other really great ones — in individual, labeled boxes in my bedroom closet — but I can't locate a particular set."

"You have some that you keep in their own boxes with labels? Did you surround them in bubble wrap to boot?"

"Tissue paper."

He stopped and stared at her, shaking his head. "You're serious?"

"Go ahead, laugh. As Ammon always says, I'm about a set of doorknobs off-center of normal." Her eyes widened. "Dora."

Jacob looked behind him, thinking she was heading his way. He hated to admit it even to himself, but he liked Esther so much more than her younger, *single* sister.

Esther put both hands on the sides of a crate, staring into the box. "Several years ago Dora helped me box up my favorite doorknobs to store, and I forgot that we stored some in her closet." Esther moved the crate to a shelf. "Maybe that's where they are." She turned to him. "When are you leaving town again?"

"That was a quick change in the subject.

Nine days from today." He put the last board on the wagon. "I need to look at the old hearths we talked about Monday and take some pictures of them. If they aren't what the owner is looking for, I'll build them myself."

"A cell-phone picture won't show your buyer the beauty of the wood grain or the intricacies of the carvings. I'll get Bailey or one of his deliverymen to haul them to the house. If she doesn't like them, we'll bring them back. I'll send the brick at the same time. Tomorrow around noon?"

"Sounds like a great plan." Since her suggestion would give the best chance of selling the hearths, he wouldn't object, but it did seem to be a lot of trouble. "She also asked if you have something called a pilaster doorway. Any idea what that is?"

"Pilaster doorway?" Esther finally stopped what she was doing and looked at him. "A pilaster is a faux column that projects a few inches from a wall. It's for aesthetics only, but why would someone using country or colonial décor want fake columns?"

"Maybe she said the wrong term." Jacob went to the opening of the shed and gestured at the frame. "When she started describing it, I thought she wanted it to fit an open doorway, maybe like a molding of sorts, but she said what she wanted was much more ornate and covered some of the actual entryway."

"Oh!" Esther's eyes lit up, and she went to a dusty file cabinet that sat on a dirt floor in the mostly open shed. "I'm not sure what the unit as a whole is called, but the base is a plinth, and the top is an arched entablature with fretwork, spindles, or scrolled brackets." She pulled paper from a folder and held it out. "*If* this is what she described." It was another ripped page from a magazine.

"That is simply a very fancy door molding." But the image Esther held up actually made sense. "Do you have one?"

"No." She looked at the page from the magazine. "I have two." She smiled. "But they have a Victorian look, not country, and even if it's what she wants, the dimensions won't work. It's a whole structure, like a doorframe."

"I can make it fit."

"Without ruining the authenticity of the piece?"

"I think so. Got paper?" Jacob retrieved a carpentry pencil from his pants pocket.

She pulled out several sheets of paper from the file cabinet, and Jacob laid them on top of the door that served as a workbench. He sketched his ideas, and they discussed possibilities for an hour. He proposed splitting the top center of the entablature and filling the void with ornate antique wood from a different piece, making it look as if the piece hadn't been cut. As they stood there discussing ideas, he knew that this time would be the best part of his day. Of his week.

Did she know the little one on her back had fallen asleep?

Esther studied his crude drawings. "Your idea for making it fit while keeping most of its integrity borders on brilliant."

He chuckled. "I'm glad you think so." He got his phone from his pocket. "I'll send the homebuyer a few snapshots of the magazine picture." But he'd wait until later in the day in case she was still asleep. "How much is each piece?"

"When I salvaged it, I was hoping to get two hundred. But that was a few years back, so I'd go as low as half that."

He passed the magazine page back to her. "I'll aim for two hundred. That sounds like a very fair price."

She put the page back in the file cabinet. "I can't get free until Saturday, but would you mind if I came to the houses just to see them now that they're almost finished?"

Mind? If she were single, he'd already have asked her to come. "Saturday would be perfect. I'll be there working, and your hardwood floors should be installed by then." As they talked for a few minutes, he remembered some items of carpentry work that still needed to be done, and he typed notes into his phone. "I have a few ideas about trim work and such. Do you mind if I look through the warehouse when I have a chance?"

"You're welcome to whatever is there."

"Denki. And one last thing . . ." He finished typing and shoved the phone into his pocket. "Your knee is still hurting you all the time, isn't it?"

"I really don't —"

"I know. You've made yourself clear." He held up his hand. "You don't want to have it seen. Everyone else's needs are more important, and there is no time to deal with it, but answer one question, okay?"

"I'll try."

"Of all the people you know, who else would you treat this way?"

Her brows knit. "I don't understand."

"Is there anyone you would ask to be sick or in pain for even a week so that *your* day wasn't interrupted?"

She blinked, her face blank. "Jacob," —

the tremor in her whisper indicated he'd hit his intended target — "you're completely right."

He'd been pondering for days how to make her see the situation as she needed to, so this felt really good. He got his billfold and pulled out all the cash he had. "Take this." He counted it — $300. He also had a paycheck back at Noah's house that he'd not cashed. "Whatever it doesn't cover, I'll give you soon."

"I can't. My knee was injured before our incident."

"It was healing, and I injured it again." He held out the money. "Please. It would mean a lot to me."

She reluctantly took it, her eyes expressing gratitude and admiration. "You're one of the good ones, Jacob."

"Some days. Not so much on others."

The sound of a rig made them both look up. Dora drove a carriage onto the driveway. She hopped out, carrying a white plastic bowl with a lid. Despite her smile the taut look on her face indicated she felt awkward. "I was afraid I'd missed you, but you got the wood for the floors all loaded up, I see."

Jacob nodded. Esther had to have told her they were doing business, especially when she stole the floors from the home Dora shared with her Mamm and siblings.

Jacob jiggled the strips of wood, making sure they were settled into place. "I did. So what kind of floor do you have in your bedroom, Dora?"

"Red oak."

"How large is the room?"

Esther chuckled. "Don't answer that, Dora."

Dora shrugged. "About a third the size of that shed, I suppose."

"So it's about a hundred and twenty square feet." He turned to Esther. "I need a hundred and twenty square feet of red oak by tomorrow."

Esther broke into laughter. "I'm not stealing the floor from under my little sister, even for you."

Dora seemed oblivious to Jacob's stab at teasing. "You can have it. I don't mind."

"See." Esther winked at her sister. "She's nicer than I am."

"Esther?" Ammon's voice surrounded them, and Esther stepped outside the shed, looking toward the house.

"Ya?"

Jacob didn't hear another word, and he couldn't see Ammon, but Esther nodded. "Ya, be right there." She turned to Jacob. "I need to go. Did we cover everything?"

"Ya."

Esther folded the cash into her palm and put her free hand on Dora's arm. "You coming up to the house?"

"I came to lend a hand — whatever you need."

Esther grinned. "Denki." She hobbled toward the house.

Hoping not to get caught in a conversation, Jacob climbed into his wagon. "You have a good one, Dora. And don't let your sister steal the floor out from under you."

Dora held the bowl up to him. "I made you some cookies."

"Well, that was nice of you." He took the container.

"I wasn't sure what kind you like, so I made a variety — peanut butter, sugar, and oatmeal–chocolate chip."

"My favorite cookie in the world is oatmeal–chocolate chip. Denki." He set the container on the seat beside him. "I'll have contact with deliverymen from Bailey's shop, so I'll be sure your container gets to the shop, okay?"

"You can keep it if you like. I don't mind. Or bring it by the house."

Wow. She was hoping he'd change his mind about dating her again. "I'll be sure it gets to the shop. Bye, Dora." He released the brake and tapped the reins on the horse's back.

When he left here in less than two weeks, he'd miss having someone to relate to the way he did Esther. Did Ammon have a clue how blessed he was?

With Jacob's heart mended and his feeling more optimistic about life, he would try to find a woman who had some of Esther's qualities. He watched as she climbed the stairs. Ammon held the screen door open for her, and then he glanced up and waved at Jacob.

FOURTEEN

From behind the desk, Rhoda picked up the phone to dial Landon's grandmother. She punched a few numbers before hanging up. He'd left here two days ago, and he'd made it clear he wanted to be left alone. After her lack of support about Leah, he at least deserved for her to respect his request. Besides, she doubted he was there.

She picked up the spring work schedule. It had seemed doable only days ago. But now? Samuel and Steven were in the field, trusting her to figure out what was absolutely necessary over the next few months and what could be cut from the schedule with minimal damage to the orchard.

But she couldn't concentrate. She released the paper, and it floated to the desk. After only a couple of days, she already ached to see Landon. If she hurt this bad, what must Leah be feeling? She had walked through the last two days much as Rhoda had after losing her sister — present in body only. Unfortunately, this was only the start of a very long grieving process.

Could Rhoda do anything to fix the situation? Even if she could, should she? If nothing had separated Landon and Leah and they chose to marry one day, they would face significant and difficult problems. Leah and Landon would raise their children with modern technology, and Samuel and Rhoda would have to put distance between their homes while raising their children without those things. The Amish ways weren't easy, and Rhoda's children would long for all that Landon and Leah's children would be allowed to have — television, Christmas trees, computer games, and fancy clothes. Later it would be phones, cars, jewelry, makeup, music, and . . . Well, the list was endless. It'd be painful to raise one's children always seeing how their cousins had what was forbidden for them. It was a large part of why those who left the Amish were seldom able to keep a healthy relationship with those who stayed.

An odd noise radiated from the desk, and the old wood seemed to vibrate. What would cause that? Wait . . . the one new item in the desk. She opened the drawer. Landon's cell phone shimmied across a stack of papers. Leah had left it here the other day, and later Rhoda had shoved it into a drawer.

She picked up his cell and tried to figure out how to turn it off. While doing so, she saw a text message from Leah. Leah had a cell phone?

Rhoda's heart clenched. Why was she texting Landon if she knew he didn't have his phone? Then something Landon once explained to Rhoda came back to her. Leah was hoping Landon had gotten another cell phone and had moved his cell number to the new phone. Rhoda turned off the phone and put it back in the drawer. She was useless in this office, and Samuel was bound to need help in the field.

Rhoda left the barn and was headed toward the orchard when she heard a car on the driveway. She turned and saw Camilla getting out of her vehicle.

"Camilla." Rhoda waved and hurried to the driveway.

Camilla met her halfway and gave her a hug. "We finally found her!" Camilla squeezed Rhoda tightly before backing away, her face radiating excitement. "The private investigator used the information about Saint George that you shared with me, and he called just a few minutes ago to tell me where Jojo works! And she's there right now. Could you find the time to go with me?"

Now? "That's great, Camilla." Rhoda embraced her again. But with all that had been going on around here and with so much work to do, she couldn't imagine going with her today. "I'm really sorry, but it's not a good time."

"Oh." Her smile fell, as did her whole countenance. "Okay. Tomorrow, maybe?"

Rhoda doubted it'd get any better around here for a long time. "Could you go by yourself?"

"Rhoda, think of all she's done to keep me out of her life. Without you I wouldn't even know she'd had a child. She changed her last name a year ago, and it's possible she did that so I couldn't find her. She believes I'm a detriment to my grandchild." Camilla put an arm around Rhoda's shoulders. "I think my only chance of connecting with her is you. Why else would you be the one to get the insights that led us to her?"

"Are you sure she'll be at work when we get there?"

Hope filled Camilla's eyes. "The private detective believes she'll be there for at least another three hours. After that, he's not sure what her schedule is, and he doesn't know where she lives. If she's renting a place, it'll

210

be hard for him to discover her address."

Rhoda's pulse quickened. Hadn't she botched the whole ordeal of finding Jojo enough already? Even though she wasn't sure what God intended for her to do now that Jojo and Sophia were located, she knew she needed to be there. But what would Samuel think of her leaving when there was so much work to do with Landon gone and Leah too grieved to be much help? Rhoda pulled the two-way off the bib of her apron. "Samuel."

"Ya?"

"Camilla's here, and . . ." Rhoda released the talk button, unsure what to say if Steven was within hearing range. He didn't really know about her intuitions concerning Camilla's granddaughter.

"You need me to come in?" Samuel asked.

"No." At least a few people should get some work done today. "But they've located where Jojo works, and Camilla's asked if I'll go with her now."

There was silence, and she knew he was weighing everything. "Is that what you think you need to do?"

Could Samuel own any more of her heart? With all that was going on, he responded as if the only thing that mattered was what she thought about going with Camilla.

"I think I should go, ya."

"Then do so, and I'll be praying for you."

Her nagging guilt eased. "Denki."

"Gern gschehne. All the time. You'll be amazing. How far?"

Rhoda turned to Camilla.

Camilla scrolled through a couple of screens on her phone. "It's outside of Saint George, about sixty miles from here, but it'll take about ninety minutes travel time each way."

"Samuel, it sounds as if it could be dark, maybe bedtime, before I'm back."

"Okay, if it gets too late, use Camilla's phone to call the barn office. I'll wait up for you."

"Will do." With anxiety making her chest tingle, Rhoda climbed into the passenger's seat. She had no real sense of why God had dropped tidbits of information into her heart and mind about Sophia and Jojo. It'd been almost a year and a half since Rhoda had heard music and a child's voice riding on the wind. She'd felt at times that Jojo was in danger, but she had no idea why.

Was she ready to finally connect with this woman?

Landon pushed the green beans around on his plate, unable to find one clear thought to hold on to.

Granny's fork clinked against her plate as she stabbed several beans. "I'm glad you came back to see me. The way you packed your bags and left here on Monday, I was really worried."

He'd stayed away for only two nights, but they were the two longest of his life. "I'm sorry about that, Granny. I had to get away and think." And he couldn't stay here for more than a night. The temptation to try to sneak visits with Leah would be too great.

"Leah came by here yesterday. I told her you'd thrown a suitcase into your truck, and I didn't know when or even if you'd be back."

As much as he longed for a decent good-bye with her, he knew talking to her would only make the inevitable harder to deal with. It could cause both of them to hold on to hope, and there just wasn't any. "Maybe it's for the best that she thinks I'm already gone."

"If it helps, I agree with what you did. You sacrificed your job and the freedom to see your girl so her dad has no reason to insist she return with him. Leah told me more than once that she'd never been as excited as the day she got to leave Harvest Mills, Pennsylvania." She took a drink of her soda.

"It took guts, Landon, and I'm proud of you."

Landon cut the beans into tiny pieces with no intention of eating them. "There is nothing to be proud of. I lost my temper with Leah's dad and gave him what he wanted. And that's just a piece of the story."

"Do you want to tell me the whole thing?"

"I need to."

Her sunken eyes peered out from almost transparent, wrinkled skin. "I like listenin' to you."

He had a good family. Since he was the only child of an only child, they were a small family, but he couldn't imagine marrying someone his family feared was wrong for him. Should he ask that of Leah even a year from now?

He told his grandmother the complete story of Leah and him, including the argument that took place before he unloaded on her dad. "Granny, she believes what she said — that my loyalty to Rhoda comes ahead of her and that I'm more interested in holding on to my job than to her. She thinks the reason I'm not standing up to her dad is because I want to be a partner at the farm."

"She was upset."

"Leah often says what she truly means when she's upset. And if I discount what she really thinks, it would come between us years from now." He stood and raked the scraps from Granny's plate onto his.

Granny put leftovers into a plastic container. "Her dad can't expect you not to contact her for a year. You agreed to that in the heat of the moment."

Landon grabbed the washrag and began scrubbing the plate as if force could remove the dark blue flowers. "I've known for a long time that loving Leah would probably mean letting her go. I don't blame her." He turned on the hot water, put the stopper in the sink, and squirted in dish-washing liquid. "I just didn't realize that one push from her dad would do the trick. But maybe he's given us both the out we needed."

Granny set two dirty pans beside the sink and grabbed a drying towel. "I think you were and are still way too upset to make decisions about your future."

"Maybe. But it's done."

"What are you going to do for a job?"

"After I left here Monday, I contacted some friends, and I have a couple of leads."

"You've really enjoyed working on the farm."

"Yeah, I like being outdoors."

"And the horses."

Landon couldn't manage a smile, but he

appreciated the fact that Granny didn't forget much of anything he told her about himself. "True."

"You're not staying around these parts, are you?"

He rinsed his hands and dried them, leaving the pots to soak. "No."

Her chin quivered, and she put her arms around his waist and rested her head on his chest. "It's not the ending we were hoping for."

Tears pricked Landon's eyes. "That it's not."

FIFTEEN

The glass double doors swooshed open, and Rhoda followed Camilla into new territory: an office supply store. Rhoda wasn't sure what she expected to see in a store like this, but the white lights reminded her of snow reflecting the sun, and aisle after aisle was packed with items she'd never thought of anyone needing.

Throughout the drive here, Camilla had clung to the steering wheel as if it were trying to get away, and now she looked stiff and pale. Maybe the electric lights were washing out her color. Rhoda touched her shoulder. "You okay?"

Rather than answering, Camilla stared at a young woman behind a long counter with a sign that said Print Shop. "That's her. That's Jojo."

Rhoda cupped Camilla's elbow. "Just keep moving." She didn't know what the next move should be, but they needed a moment to think and settle their emotions. If they handled this opportunity with Jojo wrong, they might never get another. Rhoda guided Camilla to the computer-paper aisle where they could still see Jojo. Rhoda picked up a package of pink computer paper, trying to look like a customer.

Father, please. Give us wisdom.

Camilla kept her eye on the young woman. "I've aged a lifetime since my son died . . ." Her words were low and mumbled. "And she looks as young as the day I first saw her."

Rhoda glanced at Jojo. She'd been a teenager coming out of an abortion clinic the last time Camilla saw her. The current Jojo looked healthy and vibrant, but it was clear she wasn't a teen. Actually, she looked her age, early to mid twenties.

Camilla nudged Rhoda with her elbow. "You doing okay?"

"Nervous, like you, and I have no idea what to do now."

Even after months of praying regularly about this reunion, Rhoda had no idea what to say to Jojo, not even how to approach her. What kind of opening line could they use? *"Hi, I know you've changed your name, trying to hide for some reason, but I've brought your child's grandmother to you."* Or *"Remember Camilla? Her son was the one who got you pregnant."*

Rhoda shook her head. "I thought . . . I'd hoped God would tell me something by now."

"She's still with a customer. Better to wait until he leaves before we approach her."

Rhoda looked back at Jojo. A man about ten years older than Rhoda stood at the L-shaped counter Jojo worked behind. But Rhoda's gut said he wasn't a customer. Despite their businesslike behavior, she felt a vibe coming from both him and Jojo that said they cared for each other.

Camilla was breathing in short, labored puffs. "Look, he's counting and stacking papers. Maybe he works here, but he doesn't have on a uniform or a nametag."

"He works here." Rhoda was sure of it, but she kept stalling, hoping for wisdom to drop from heaven before she approached the counter.

Here's some wisdom for you, Rhoda. Do something before Camilla passes out and you're stranded without a driver in a town somewhere outside of Saint George, Maine!

Right. Time to act. But she should approach Jojo without Camilla beside her. Rhoda pinned Camilla with a stare. "Stay here."

Camilla nodded.

Rhoda walked to the counter. The workspace was on one side of the double-wide entrance-and-exit doors. On the other side were several clerks at checkout counters. Rhoda moved close enough to read Jojo's nametag: Joella.

Jojo was talking to the man about when she got off, and as she did, she extracted papers from a huge copier and stacked them. The man had on a wedding ring. Rhoda moved to the farthest spot from where he stood.

Jojo glanced at her and froze for a moment before offering a polite smile. "Be right with you."

Amish dress caught a lot of people off guard. How ironic. What had originally been intended to make the Amish so bland that no one paid them any mind now caused them to stick out like a sore thumb. "Take your time."

Jojo stacked the items as she got them out of the copier. The man remained at the counter, counting the papers and putting them in a line in front of him. Rhoda's heart pounded as her intuition told her that Jojo was in some sort of danger.

Jojo put a large stack in front of him and came to Rhoda. "May I help you?"

Had Rhoda ever felt this nervous before?

Was it because she feared letting God down *again*? Or did she fear Jojo's reaction? "I hope so . . . or maybe I can help you."

"Excuse me?" Jojo studied her, a crease between her brows.

Think, Rhoda. "I have the strangest story you've ever heard, but you need to hear it. Could we talk?"

"Pictures, copies, or notary issues?"

Rhoda ducked her head. "It's personal."

"Personal?" Unlike Rhoda, Jojo didn't rein in her voice.

The man looked up, studying them. He appeared to be a protector, and indeed he wanted to be, but some dark secret shadowed him.

Rhoda tried to swallow. Maybe explaining too much was a mistake. Should she simply start with provable facts and leave out how intuition had gotten them here? "My name is Rhoda Byler, and I'm a neighbor of Camilla Dumont."

Jojo's eyes narrowed, but she tilted her head, looking as if she may have misheard Rhoda. "You're who?"

"Rhoda Byler. And your late husband's mom is my neighbor."

Jojo didn't blink, didn't appear able to take a breath. Then she broke free, shaking her head. "No." Alarm registered in her voice, and her breathing intensified. "Is sh . . . she with you?"

"Ya." Rhoda nodded.

Jojo searched the surrounding area and spotted Camilla. "Great." She huffed and turned to the man at the counter. "Hey, Cody. Would you take over for me while I go on break?"

He looked at his watch. "Deliveries are due any minute. You know I have to be at the loading dock when they get here."

"I need this."

He nodded. "Okay, go."

Jojo raised a section of the countertop and escaped her large enclosure. Without a word she motioned to Camilla and walked out the front door of the store. Rhoda and Camilla followed her.

Jojo turned. "Mrs. Dumont, I don't know what's going on here or why you've asked a stranger to get involved, but —"

"It wasn't like that." Rhoda shoved her hands into her coat pockets. "*I* got *her* involved."

"Why?"

"I . . . I'm not sure. I only know that you and Zachary have a child, and —"

Jojo's face flushed. Was that fury or panic in her eyes? Or both? "I should've known better than to return to this area." She paced, a hand pressing her forehead. "I did all I could. I changed my last name, left without a forwarding address. I don't even post images online." She stopped pacing. "How did you find me?" Her tone didn't sound at all like the professional woman she'd been only minutes ago. "Better yet, why?"

What was Jojo hiding from? Camilla? Or did something — or some*one* — else frighten her?

Then Rhoda knew part of the answer. Jojo hid because she fully believed a lie about Camilla. "Jojo, Camilla isn't who you think she is."

Camilla stepped forward. "I know I looked like a horrible person, one who'd be detrimental to your daughter. But if you'd give me a chance, you'd see —"

"A chance at what, being a part of Sophia's life? Not happening. Not after what you put Zachary through."

"I'm not married to his father anymore."

"But that doesn't change the legacy, does it? Sophia has an abusive grandfather and a grandmother who let him destroy her father's life."

Camilla didn't flinch. "I was wrong, and I've paid a higher price than I even imagined, but I never abused Zachary in any way. I never hit him or screamed at him. And I never let his father hit him. Didn't Zachary tell you —"

"Stop, Camilla. Just be quiet already." Jojo looked over her shoulder and then moved closer and lowered her head. "You think what you did wasn't abusive, didn't leave scars, simply because it was passive?" She whispered, "You should go to a meeting of adult survivors of child abuse and listen. From the abusive parents who did physical harm to the addicts and lazy good-for-nothings who destroyed all chance for healthy emotional survival — all were guilty of deplorable treatment of their children. Neglect can be just as dangerous as a beating."

Understanding of Jojo's past washed over Rhoda. "You were abused."

"Mind your own business!" Jojo spat.

But in that moment Rhoda saw what Jojo didn't want seen. Zachary wasn't the only one who'd survived an abusive childhood. He had witnessed his dad beating his mom, but Jojo had felt the physical sting of every blow.

Most couples were drawn together by an unseen force. Was that the hidden connection between Zachary and Jojo as teens — wounded spirits recognizing each other, looking for each other even before they met?

Rhoda could see Jojo as a child, could see the many years she'd spent crying out to God to protect her. Jojo thought her prayers had gone unheeded, but He had worked in the hearts of people, and when a parent chose to use his or her God-given authority for evil, He had brought help and justice through other means.

Was Camilla that very belated means?

Chills engulfed Rhoda. She didn't know if Jojo was a believer, but God was on a mission, and Rhoda was merely a messenger who'd garbled the message.

"Jojo." Camilla's voice caught Rhoda's attention. Rhoda blinked. Had she missed some of the conversation?

Camilla grabbed the straps of her purse and shifted them higher on her shoulder. "I know now that I couldn't have been more wrong to raise a child in that environment. I thought it was the only way I could provide for Zachary. Can't you give me a chance to be in Sophia's life?"

Jojo shook her head. "You raised your child as you saw fit. Now leave me alone to raise mine."

Jojo wasn't anything like Rhoda had imagined. She struggled as a single mom, and she longed to be all Sophia needed her to be, but Jojo was jaded beyond her years.

God, why? Why was it so important for me to find Jojo? What do You want her daughter protected from?

Rhoda put her hand on Camilla's back. "Would you wait for me in the car? I'll be right there."

Camilla nodded, dug a piece of paper out of her coat pocket, and then turned to Jojo. "If you don't want me in your life or Sophia's, I will accept that. You didn't need to take a new last name to avoid me. But if you ever change your mind, any kind of contact you make will be more than welcome. Come for a short visit, or come if you need a place to live. And if you discover tomorrow — or years from now — that you want a family for Sophia, please don't hesitate to knock on my door. You'll always be welcome." She held out the paper. "This has my address and phone numbers. I'm there for you anytime."

Rhoda squeezed Camilla's hand, so pleased at how careful and encouraging she had been. "I won't be long."

As Camilla left, Rhoda cleared her throat, unsure what she needed to say. "You don't know me, but the night I moved to Maine, I heard a child's voice and then a man's voice, both saying, *'Tell them.'*"

Jojo backed away from Rhoda. Was that fear creasing Jojo's features? Or . . . maybe . . . a trace of hope?

"Does that mean something to you, Jojo?"

She shook her head, but Rhoda wasn't sure she was telling the truth. "I didn't even know who to tell what, but as time passed, piece by piece I realized Camilla had a grandchild. I knew it before she was willing to let me know she had a son. She had kept his memory locked away for only herself. It took great effort to convince her she had a grandchild. She had never considered the possibility that the day you left the clinic, you'd refused the abortion."

"Why would those things about me come to you out of thin air?"

"I wish I knew." Although she was clueless what else to say, she could ask a few questions, couldn't she? "Do you have any idea why it would be so important for us to find you?"

"No." Jojo looked at Camilla's car. "Did you know that Zachary and his mother hadn't been close for a couple of years?"

"She told me, but two years apart isn't much when one gives birth to a child and raises him for sixteen or seventeen years. Did you know that Zachary contacted her months before he was killed and that at his

227

request the two of them were going to family counseling together?"

Jojo shook her head. "No."

"Joella!" The man from the counter stepped outside. "I'm needed out back on the dock."

"Coming." Joella shoved her hands into her coat pockets. "I gotta go."

As Rhoda prayed for what she should say, one word came to mine — *honesty.* "He cares about you, doesn't he?"

Jojo nodded.

"And he's married?"

"Lots of people marry the wrong person."

"You've gone out of your way to avoid Camilla because you fear she'll be a bad influence, but you wait for a married man? You're waiting for a man to untangle his life from his wife. Won't that legacy harm your daughter far more than Camilla's influence ever could? And what will the upcoming battle do to their children?" She was guessing the man had children, because he appeared to be a good ten years older than Jojo.

Jojo stared into the distance, and Rhoda hoped she hadn't come across as judgmental. Facts and judgment were two different things, but they often appeared to be the same.

"You don't know what it's like to try to survive on your own."

"I don't. I imagine it's terrifying and lonely and filled with hardships." Rhoda put together little snippets from past intuitions and the info the private investigator had uncovered. Jojo had been evicted from a run-down mobile home, but she did all she could to provide music lessons for her daughter. Jojo hadn't been given the opportunities afforded by loving parents. Her view of family — of Camilla — was skewed. "It's easy to make poor decisions but hard to set them right again." Would she understand Rhoda thought that pushing Camilla away was the wrong decision, that waiting for a married man was a wrong decision, but that Jojo could still make them right? "Thank you for talking with me. I'll let you get back to work." Rhoda headed for the curb.

"Wait." Jojo held out the paper Camilla had given her.

Was she refusing to keep Camilla's contact information?

Jojo shook it at her. "Write your info on that too. But don't get your hopes up. And don't contact me again. If I change my mind, I'll contact you."

Relief hit so fully that Rhoda's knees

shook. She hadn't offended Jojo? Rhoda's hands trembled as she scribbled her info. "I hope you can read it." She passed the note to Jojo.

"Yeah, I think I can."

"Bye, Jojo. I hope . . . I pray you contact us." As Rhoda walked off, she realized that while she had ignored the prompting of her intuition, Jojo's heart and life had become more intertwined with a man who was married and had children.

But was that the danger Rhoda had sensed?

Sixteen

When no one was looking, Leah hurried across the yard, heading for an escape. How often had she hidden in a loft while growing up? Countless times. Landon had left here five days ago, and every hour had felt like a week at least. She wouldn't talk to him for a year?

A year . . .

It already had been too long to be apart. But the scariest question was, would she and Landon be separated forever? Was he so angry because of what she'd said that he wouldn't return even when he was allowed to?

Leah hadn't felt this undone since she'd met Landon. Somehow when her Daed had arrived here treating her as he did, she'd been hurtled back to her childhood, to a time of powerlessness and quiet agony. But the situation with Landon made everything so much worse — as did knowing she'd said things that had hurt him, things she didn't mean.

She climbed the familiar rungs to the loft. Everyone had yielded to Daed: Landon, Steven, Rhoda, and Samuel. She should've known Rhoda would vote against her if it meant keeping her Amish.

Leah climbed into the haymow and began to search for the boxes of books she'd moved to Maine. She found several and realized she'd opened them at one time or another while taking chosen books to her small bedroom. But for some reason she'd never unpacked a lot of her favorites. As she removed a few from their box, the dusty books felt like old friends — the only ones she'd been able to rely on while growing up. They'd been her escape from a life she'd never wanted.

Catherine, Samuel's former girlfriend, used to disapprove of Leah reading fiction — and just about anything else she did. Leah had called Arlan the other day, just to see how he and his sister were doing. Arlan was concerned that he'd caused trouble for his parents, but he didn't blame himself. He blamed the strictness of the Ordnung. Still, until he could move out of his parents' home, he wouldn't do anything else that would get them in trouble. He'd said Catherine was doing well. She had a new boy-friend and was so focused on her future that she ignored the constant whispering about Arlan's more liberal and embarrassing ways. Apparently, like Leah, Catherine was finally growing up.

Focusing on the books, Leah continued searching through the boxes. The books were organized into favorites and least favorites by a system that would have made no sense to anyone else. Like most things it barely made sense to her now. She picked up a copy of *The Quiet Man* by Maurice Walsh, one of the few novels she'd enjoyed that wasn't a mystery. Landon once told her it'd been adapted into a famous movie in the early fifties, starring a man who typi-cally portrayed Western American cowboys. Seemed to her that a man known for being a cowboy shouldn't be cast in a comedy-drama. It didn't fit. Just like she didn't fit in Landon's world.

And he didn't fit in hers.

With or without her, he would find his place in his world, and he'd eventually be happy. But she would never fit into hers. Not really. She never had.

Landon.

All her thoughts seemed to lead back to him and their would-be life together. If only she could change something, *anything,* she'd said or done before he left, but life didn't allow for — what did Landon call them? — do-overs. Those were for games and rehearsals of school plays. Of the many things she'd learned during her rumschpringe, the most important was that life was not a game.

A loud voice resonated through the barn. Leah jumped, nearly dropping the book she was holding, before she realized it was Crist talking to someone in the office below. She could only hear every fourth or fifth word, but it sounded as if he was teasing someone. Leah sat and opened the book, remembering how difficult a time the characters had getting along. They'd argued profusely even after they were married. It'd been a fun read, especially knowing that the story would work out for the best.

But reality was far more daunting.

She pulled out her phone and looked again at the text she'd sent him hours ago. Under it in small letters were the words *Text delivery failed.*

He'd had his old number disconnected. Every time she read that, she felt numb. Landon must have gotten a new phone. She'd hoped he had transferred his old number to it, but apparently not. She couldn't even tell him how much this hurt.

"Leah?" Crist called. "Are you up there?"

She didn't respond, hoping he would leave her alone.

"Leah?" His voice was louder, as if he was below the opening.

She sighed. "Ya, I'm here."

His head peeked through the opening. "Hi. We've been looking for you." He climbed into the loft.

"We?"

Iva entered the loft behind him, her camera strap around her neck as she held the camera close to her body. "I know you want to be left alone, but here we are anyway." She smiled and sat. "Phoebe gave me a list of items to get at the grocery store. Without a driver it's gonna take hours, so I enlisted Crist, and we think you need to get off the farm for a bit."

Since Landon wasn't there, he couldn't chauffeur them around at the drop of a hat. "Did you try to call Camilla or another driver?"

"No. Do you really want me to?" Iva wiggled her eyebrows as fast as a rabbit twitched its whiskers. "It's a beautiful day, and I think all three of us should get away. I mentioned it to Steven, and he agreed. Of course I didn't have my camera in hand at the time, but" — she shoved Crist's shoulder, and he barely moved — "ol' Crist here is itching to learn to use my camera."

Crist scowled. "That's not even a little true."

Iva laughed. "Well, it should be, and while we're out, I'll show you why." Iva reached over and shook Leah's leg. "No one expects you to be good company."

"Speak for yourself, Iva." Crist frowned, looking heavenward, clearly teasing. "I expect it. Why drag Leah along if she's not going to be any fun? I have *you* for that."

The misery surrounding Leah lifted a little, and she did want to get away for a bit.

Iva pointed her camera out the open door of the loft, taking snapshots of a barren orchard. "You be you, and we'll be us. If you don't wish to talk, don't. If you wish to scream or hit something, I volunteer Crist."

Crist smiled. "I knew she was going to drag me into that somehow."

Leah rose, straightened her dress, and tucked the book under her arm. "I hope that list is worth all this."

Crist stood. "We need to go by the supply store too."

Since she wanted time off the farm, it didn't matter how far away the store was, so Leah wouldn't complain. But what this farm and growing district needed was a dry goods store that stocked groceries, some farming supplies, kerosene for lamps, and fabric for making Amish clothes.

Iva lowered her camera, wrinkling her nose as if something stank. "Do we have to do that this trip? I'd wanted us to get out at a few fun places between here and the grocery store so I could get some pictures. If we have to go to the supply store, there won't be any time to lollygag."

"Samuel said we need a dozen codling moth traps."

Iva took a picture of the far end of the loft, and Leah wondered what she possibly saw in bales of hay and stored boxes. "Seems like we could find old plastic pickle jugs or something similar around here without having to go to the supply store and pay for actual traps. And I could get more pictures. It'd be a win-win situation."

Hadn't Leah seen empty containers similar to what they needed in the old storage building between here and Landon's grandmother's house? "Landon and I used to look through an old building that belongs to his grandmother. It used to be a gas station and store combined, I think. But it's been used for storage for a lot of years. Since I loved going through it, he gave me a key, and . . ."

Iva lowered her camera, grinning. "It'd be an excellent place to snap pictures — I mean, to look for the much-needed items so we don't have to pay for them or go out of our way to get them."

"Ya, we hear you." Crist headed for the ladder. "Stopping at that old building has absolutely nothing to do with you photographing more nonsense."

Leah didn't know when these two had started playfully sniping at each other, but her dark mood would hardly be noticed amid their banter.

Even though her heart was crushed and her future was in limbo, Leah could see that finding the strength to get through this would come, in part, by letting her friends help her.

Jacob clicked his tongue and tapped the reins against the horse's back. "Geh."

He had a few hours before he'd meet a driver at Noah's and head for the train station. At the end of his journey, Sandra and Casey waited for him. He looked forward to a couple of weeks with Casey, but ignoring his better judgment, right now he had hammered out a bit of time to say good-bye to Esther. Unless something had changed her plans, she should be at the shop.

He hadn't talked to her since she and Bailey came to look through the new houses a week ago. Jacob had given Esther and Bailey a tour, and as she oohed and aahed over Jacob's work, they talked about construction as if it was her favorite topic. Later the three of them had sat on the floor and eaten the sandwiches Bailey's wife had made for them. It was then that Jacob realized he liked her a little too much. So he'd decided to put distance between them.

He hadn't seen or spoken to her since.

The houses were done. The buyers would close on them next week, but Jacob had nothing to do with that part. His job was finished, and later today he'd put this little town behind him . . . forever. So what could it possibly hurt to say good-bye? He pulled into the parking lot and tethered his horse to a hitching rail.

Jacob went in the side door and saw numerous men, some wearing welding helmets. Unfamiliar music played in the background as he received nods and waves. He glanced to Esther's workspace, hoping to see her.

Bailey sat behind the desk and had the phone to his ear. He waved, gesturing that he'd be with Jacob in a minute.

While Bailey and Esther were at the new

239

houses, Jacob had learned a few things about the connection between them. Bailey and his wife had five grown children, all sons. When his wife was seriously injured, breaking her neck and back, he'd hired Esther to be full-time help for her. Esther was thirteen at the time, and his wife had needed her constant help for two years. Esther had stopped working for Bailey when her father became ill, but a few months after he died, Bailey hired Esther to help his wife again, especially when the Hudson family traveled on vacations. And that seemed to be a source of joy for Esther — traveling, all expenses paid. Jacob found it really odd that the church ministers would continue to let a married woman and mom travel with Bailey and his wife.

Bailey put the corded phone into its cradle and stood. "Jacob."

"I'm leaving in a few hours, and I haven't seen Esther since you two came to the new houses last week. I thought if she was around, I'd say bye."

Bailey's brows furrowed. "I suppose it is that time, isn't it?"

"It is."

"Shark Bait is running late, but she should be on her way. With the town fire sale next week, she's finishing items to sell at her booth. I'm sure she could use another hand if you have time."

"I can't stay long, but I'll do what I can." He could handle working by her side. But if she didn't show up, could he go by her house without it seeming improper? It wasn't as if he was planning a rendezvous — although wanting to speak to her this much did seem to cross a line.

He shouldn't like her as much as he did. She was married, for Pete's sake. But that didn't keep her from being an unexpected ray of light for him at the end of what'd been a really long, dark tunnel — a black passageway he'd entered when he lived with the Englisch. That tunnel had almost caved in on him when he and Rhoda broke up.

Bailey rapped his fingers on the arms of his chair. "You coming back this way at any point?"

"Maybe." Jacob shrugged and then re-thought his answer. The only draw to this place was a married woman. "Actually, no chance."

"I hate to hear that." Bailey rubbed the back of his neck. "For several years now I've wanted to build a kitchen in my backyard, and after seeing your work and the diligence you give to detail, I'd like you to build it."

"I appreciate it, but it's time for me to go."

"But you could come back this way after you finish whatever you're leaving to do. I pay top dollar for work on my place." He grabbed the mouse and made a few clicks, and an outdoor kitchen showed up on the screen. "This is what I have in mind. Esther could be a lot of help on the details I'd like added. Then I'd like the cement around the pool redone so that it matches the new that will be poured for the outdoor kitchen. Can you do that too?"

"I'm capable but not when in another state, Bailey."

"Hey, boss." One of the men held up a set of blueprints, motioning for Bailey.

"Hang on." He gestured at the man first and then at his computer. "Care to see why we call her Shark Bait?"

"Sure."

"You know she's not going to like me showing you."

"Yeah." Jacob chuckled. The man had mentioned the clip several times while at the new house. "But you've been wanting to show me anyway, right?"

"True." Bailey moved the mouse, clicking on this and that until footage of a skinny girl with a ponytail appeared. She was wearing a baseball cap and Capri pants while standing in ocean water halfway to her knees. She had a fishing pole in her hands as she fought to reel in whatever was on her line. "Recognize her?"

Jacob studied the screen. "No." All he could see was a wobbly video of the back of an underweight girl as she fought to stay standing. "You're saying that's Esther?"

"When she was nineteen."

"She was a rail."

"Yeah, she got that way while caring for her Daed for three years before he died. It scared my wife and me. She got worse after . . ." He shook his head. "It's not my story to tell. I reckon if you want to know more, you'll have to ask her." Bailey stood. "I gotta check on what Charlie needs. I'll be back."

First there was the offer to work with Esther on a construction project and now this? Why would Bailey encourage Jacob in any way concerning Esther? With the question still ringing inside him, he watched the clip. She must've been walking deeper into the ocean, because the water was now almost to her knees. Her voice and the sound of seagulls and the ocean came through the monitor: "I've never fished . . . for striper from shore . . ." She was out of breath and talking to the camera. "But Travis bet me I couldn't catch one, and, as always, I'm here to prove him wrong. I put squid on my line, and I've hooked something. Now to reel it in . . ."

Who was Travis? The camera turned in jerky movements to give a shot of the shoreline behind the beach area. A piercing scream made Jacob want to grab the camera and focus it on Esther again. The lens jerked back to her. She was hurrying back to dry sand, toting the fishing pole while screaming. "Shark!" She looked back. "He's coming at me!"

"Essie, drop the fishing pole!" Bailey's voice was undeniable. "You're reeling in its supper!"

Bailey ran into the scene. So who was doing the filming?

"Drop the pole!" Bailey screamed, running for her.

She flung it onto the shore, with about a two-pound fish on the line, flopping in the ebb and flow of the water. Then a small shark, weighing maybe a hundred pounds, dove out of the water and toward Esther's legs.

Esther jumped and fell on dry sand. Voices clamored as she backed up on shore, walking much like a crab and pointing as the shark wriggled away from shore and into deeper water.

She broke into laughter and turned, smiling directly into the camera. "And that's how to catch a striper. Apparently striper is also known as shark bait."

The camera moved to the striper.

Bailey grabbed her off the sand and engulfed her in a hug. "*You* were the shark bait."

The footage faded into a series of stills. Jacob watched as strangers popped up on screen in various destinations — a beach, the mountains, the Grand Canyon, New York City. Apparently Bailey enjoyed traveling, taking along friends and family. Some of the images included a woman in a wheelchair, and Esther was often the only white face in the crowd, but her smile radiated joy.

"Sorry." Bailey set a notepad on his desk. "I didn't mean to be gone that long."

Jacob got up from Bailey's office chair, and Bailey sat and rocked back. "You know what I find interesting about that whole shark scenario?"

Jacob looped a thumb through one suspender. "That the moment the danger was over, she found the situation funny?"

"That too, but she automatically calls the

shark a he. I've not pointed it out to her, but she's never referred to it as an it or a she."

Jacob could see that in her. How much of it was compounded by helping pregnant girls? "What I thought was the most interesting is that the cameraman never set the camera down to try to help her."

"Travis, my son. He knew trying to help her would only make the situation worse." Bailey turned off the monitor. "Will you keep in contact?"

What an odd question. "I hadn't planned on it. Do you need me to?"

"No, not for me, but maybe . . . someone."

"Am I missing something? Because I can't see where anyone in this area needs me to stay in contact."

Bailey clenched his lips, nodding. "I guess you're right."

"You guess? Bailey, what is it you're not saying?"

He shook his head. "Nothing."

Jacob had never considered himself insightful when it came to people. Many lied, and he was rarely aware of it until he'd been hooked into helping or was hurt by it, but he had a definite feeling that Bailey was covering up something.

"Is Esther sick or something?"

"No. She's fine."

So what did Bailey want him to know but wasn't free to say? "I mean no disrespect, but this conversation is really confusing."

Bailey sighed. "Yeah, I can see where it would be puzzling. I usually find the answer is to ask questions. Lots of them. To the right people."

The screen door jerked open, and Esther walked in, carrying a basket. Someone turned the volume way up on the music.

Esther smiled. "Ya, ya, ya, I'm here. And look" — she bent her knee and stretched her leg straight a few times — "it works without pain."

The men applauded.

Bailey leaned in. "Don't know why, but she finally went to see a specialist, and she's been doing what he said."

"Good for her." Jacob knew why.

She headed for her workspace behind the privacy screens. The men started clapping to the beat of the music, and the music blared even louder. She rolled her eyes, set the basket down, and immediately made moves like a dancing robot — smooth, to the beat, and funny. Jacob suppressed laughter, but the men didn't, and they applauded.

He knew why she did the little dance —

because in her father's final days, he told her a lot of things that didn't necessarily line up with the Ordnung. She told Jacob that one day he clutched her hand and said, *"Always remember to dance."* He hadn't needed to clarify what kind of dancing he was referring to. Esther had told Jacob she would often do an innocent jig throughout the house when she was young, but he'd punished her for it time and again, even sending her to bed without dinner a couple of nights when she was twelve. But as her father's physical strength drained, he saw life differently, and when he whispered the insights, she took them to heart.

After a final move she stopped and waved her hand under her neck, giving the cut-the-noise motion, and someone turned down the music.

"The wagon is loaded. Could someone give Ammon a hand?" Without looking at Bailey or noticing Jacob, she went to her workspace.

Bailey stood. "She's not supposed to lift anything for a while."

Jacob wished he hadn't seen the video clip or watched her respond to the music. It only made him like her more. He shouldn't have come. "I could use some air, so I'll do it." He strode out the door.

SEVENTEEN

Landon led the last three horses into the barn for the night. He stopped near the saddle racks and dropped the reins. When bridled, these horses wouldn't budge until told. They were too well trained. He unfastened the breast collar from the D-rings and began removing the latigo from its ring. Because he'd learned to ride, feed, and work with horses while on the farm in Maine, he'd applied for work on this guest ranch. After all, he knew plenty about horses. Or so he'd thought.

He'd been wrong.

Alec strode into the barn, his cowboy hat in place and his spurs jingling. Odd sight, really. One that would take as much getting used to as Amish attire had when he began working for Rhoda years ago.

Thing was, Landon didn't look much different from Alec. He'd had to trade in his work boots and baseball cap for cowboy boots and a hat, but he didn't wear spurs. One thing for sure, no one wearing spurs could sneak up on anybody. Landon figured he could put bells on his boots and have the same effect for a lot less money, and since no one used spurs on the horses, the bells would be just as useful.

Aside from this guest ranch, he didn't recall ever seeing cowboys in Pennsylvania, even in the Poconos. But it was beautiful here — mountains, valleys, lakes, and wild-life.

"How's the new guy tonight?"

Landon pulled the blanket and saddle off the horse in one swoop and set the saddle on a rack. "Same as yesterday. Tired of being called the new guy."

Alec cracked his knuckles. "It stops when someone else is hired, which could be a year from now."

Would Landon be here that long? Most of the workers were nice, but the hardest part of this job was living in a bunkhouse. He'd never had to share a room in his life, and now he had three other guys in there with him.

"Test time." Alec let the horse nuzzle against him before he moved to its side. "This one's been on the trail all day, ridden by a woman who is no featherweight, and"

— he ran his hands over the horse's back and girth on one side and then moved to the other — "it's apparent the horse sweated as she needed to. No cowlicks where the saddle was on wrong, no cinch marks, no evidence the pad slipped back and caused the saddle to rub against her." He lifted her mane near her shoulders, still inspecting her. "I'd say you saddled her right this morning."

Having worked here only a week, Landon was still learning all the dos and don'ts of how to treat horses. A horse that stayed on the trail all day, with a different rider every few days, needed attentive care, starting with preventive measures — equipment that fit and proper saddling. A horse in pain spooked easily, and part of Landon's job was to make sure the horses were never in pain.

Alec removed the horse's bridle, adjusted her halter, and grabbed a brush. "After we get these three taken care of, we're off for the evening. Since the guests leave in the morning and no others arrive until the following day, we've been given off until noon tomorrow."

Landon glanced outside. It was pitch black. "I guess that means some extra sleep."

"Where *is* your partying spirit, dude? I've

been looking for it since you got here." Alec made short, fast strokes with the brush. "We go into NYC during breaks like this. Since you didn't go with us last time, I'll ask again, you got somebody?"

Landon wished he knew. Would Leah wait? Did he even want her to? Maybe she'd be better off finding an Amish guy and building a life with him.

Alec stood straight, peering over the horse's back. "Gabi's got her eye on you. Any interest?"

Landon shook his head as he unsaddled the last horse.

"She's cute. Nice. Enjoys having fun."

"I appreciate it, but I have someone. Maybe . . . probably." Heat flushed his body. How had he let things happen in such a way that he didn't even know? Is that what he and Leah needed in order to go their separate ways — no real breakup, no set plans to reunite, just a fading away of who they'd once been?

He'd given his word to stay away from her, no communication whatsoever, for a year. It was her chance to find peace with being Amish. Her opportunity to discover if an Amish man was a better choice than he was. In that sense he was grateful he'd walked off without a way for her to contact him.

Maybe they needed that.

Alec leaned back against a wall and folded his arms. "Go with us. We'll eat out, catch a movie, walk through Times Square — nothing big or expensive, just different. Sounds to me as if you need a break from thinking about Miss Maybe-Probably. True?"

Actually, he did. If his heart didn't stop aching, even if only for a few hours, Landon might just become an irrational lunatic while working with ranch guests.

"Sure, why not."

Jacob finished helping Ammon unload the wagon. Since they were stacking the goods outside Esther's privacy screen, she'd yet to realize Jacob was there. He put the last of the shutters on the pile. He'd worked with her on hinging one set, and she seemed to understand how to do it, but it had taken her a lot of time to get it right. He hadn't realized she had this many left to do.

When he stepped back outside, Ammon was coming toward him.

"Denki, Jacob."

"Glad to do it."

"All that's left is what's under the wagon bench." Ammon disappeared into the building, carrying two old windowpanes without glass in them.

Jacob went to the wagon, reached under the bench seat, and pulled out a crate of junk.

Ammon hurried out of the shop, dusting off his hands. "Essie told me you stayed and helped her for nearly five hours a couple of weeks ago."

"I did." Jacob spotted a rusty door hinge under the wagon seat and grabbed it. Ammon certainly didn't sound as if he minded. "I thought I might stay for a bit today, just until I need to leave to catch the bus. Unless you'd rather I didn't." He put the hinge inside the crate he held.

"If Esther doesn't mind, I don't."

Interesting and odd, but . . . "Gut. So where are your boys today?"

"Dora's at the house, baby-sitting." Ammon propped his forearms on the top of the wagon side. "Listen, Essie said I don't need to bring this up, but I disagree. I probably shoulda come to you and said my piece before now. Since we're together, can I get something off my chest?"

"Sure." Jacob set the wooden crate on the ground and leaned against the wagon.

Ammon shifted from one foot to the other. "I . . . I shouldn't have spoken to Essie the way I did when you were at the house. She said I embarrassed her. It took me a while to see what she was saying, but she's right. I'd be humiliated if anyone treated me like that."

"It was disturbing to witness."

His brows narrowed. "That bad?"

"Every bit and worse."

"I feel so much pressure concerning . . . stuff going on in my life. I'm sure a single man can't imagine. Did Essie ever tell you the situation?"

"She mentioned you were under stress but nothing else."

Ammon removed his hat and scratched his head. "Anyway, the bottom line is, I should've been much calmer that day and certainly nicer to her, whether you were there or not. Even when I'm at my best, and that's been a while, she deserves better than I can give."

This was a welcome side to Ammon, and the relief Jacob felt for Esther surprised him. "You want to talk about what has you under such pressure?"

"It'd be nice, but I can't, not if Essie hasn't talked about the situation."

"Not a problem. I forgive your outburst, Ammon."

"Gut." He scratched his beard. "She said you've been traveling since you were a teen."

"At times. I settled down for a while, but

it didn't work out too well."

"So you've seen and heard things people like me never will."

"Maybe. What's on your mind?"

"My troubles."

Jacob chuckled. "Of course. That's nearly all we think about when they're screaming at us. Ya?"

Ammon nodded, and his smile erased some of his usual solemnness. "Do you think God controls every bit of our lives?"

"It's what we've been taught, but I wonder about it sometimes."

"Me too. I want to believe it. But if it's true, doesn't that take the responsibility for our actions right off our shoulders and put it on God's?"

"That's a good question, and I've asked it a time or two myself." Jacob would like to know what Esther thought about that. "What does your wife say?"

"She believes everything is His perfect plan."

"Really? That doesn't seem to line up with her fighting so hard for young people to make the right decisions, does it?"

"Oh, you meant Ess . . ." Ammon stopped cold. Was that guilt on his face?

Jacob motioned. "Go on."

Ammon shook his head. "I was up with

the baby half the night, and it's all" — he pointed at his head — "fuzzy and confused in there today."

Jacob wasn't good at sizing up situations because all too often he took what people said at face value. The trouble was that some people lied, a lot. Hadn't he had some of these same troubling thoughts when talking to Bailey only minutes ago? He doubted that either man would tell outright lies. Still, it seemed both were hiding something.

He pondered again the strange conversation he'd had with Bailey. It was as if the man wanted Jacob to have a reason to return and work on a project with Esther. And Ammon didn't appear to mind Jacob spending time with his wife.

The name bobble was huge. He and Ammon were talking about his wife, and suddenly Ammon got confused as to the name of the person they were talking about?

If Jacob didn't get this cleared up, it would nag at him for years. Was Ammon not married to Esther? A lie like that made no sense. But he wouldn't put Ammon on the spot. He seemed really nervous, and if someone was lying to Jacob, it was Esther.

Ammon grabbed the reins. "I need to go."

"Bye."

Ammon paused. "You know about the

situation, don't you?"

Jacob's chest pounded. "You could clarify it." Jacob didn't really know, and he hated the idea of asking directly, are you and Esther married? Jacob had known her for nearly six months, but he wasn't sure Ammon and the Esther inside the shop were married. They were together a lot, and Jacob had never seen Ammon with any other woman. She took care of his children, or maybe they were hers. They did call her Mamm.

His head ached from the confusion, or more likely it ached from his pounding pulse and rising anger. If his suspicions were correct, what would be her point in tricking him? He'd relaxed with her and opened up to her.

Ammon stared at the sky before he released a slow sigh. "She gives all the time and asks almost nothing of me, but she wanted this. You'll be gone in a few hours. Could you leave well enough alone?"

Jacob's skin pricked up and down his body as his ire grew. He wanted answers, but he wanted them from the person lying to him!

"It was nice meeting you, Jacob."

Jacob gave a halfhearted nod, and Ammon drove the rig out of the parking lot. How could Jacob let this go? He grabbed the crate of junk and went into the shop. When he set it on the counter inside Esther's cubicle, she turned.

Her eyes grew wide, and she grinned before shaking a putty knife at him. "This is a nice surprise. When we were at the new houses last week, you said I wouldn't see you again."

That's when it occurred to him. Even though her smile and words welcomed him, it wasn't the same vibe single girls gave off. Whenever he and Esther were alone, she talked to him and carried herself like a . . . He wanted to say *married woman,* but that wasn't quite right either.

She used the putty knife to flick loose paint off an old windowpane. A moment later she stopped and studied him. "You're angry."

He wouldn't raise his voice much above a whisper, but he wasn't leaving here until he understood. "Who is Ammon to you?"

He wasn't prepared for the depth of disappointment that etched itself on her face. She closed her eyes. "Jacob —"

"Who is he?"

"My brother."

"Why would you let me believe you're married? It doesn't add up, Esther."

She drew a deep breath and lifted her eyes

to meet his. "Please don't let this ruin our friendship. I didn't realize that's what you thought until Ammon was upset and you told me to go help my husband. I was too surprised and in too much of a hurry, so I dropped it. When we saw each other two days later and his name came up, you could see I was uncomfortable, and you said we didn't have to talk about Ammon. Remember?"

"Of course. I thought you were embarrassed because he'd yelled at you in front of me. I had no clue your secret was that you weren't a wife at all. The children call you Mamm. Are they yours?"

She fidgeted with the putty knife, scraping flecks of paint from the dull blade, but she finally shook her head. "They call me *Mamm zwee,* only they make it one word that sounds like *Mammzu.*"

"Mamm two." He shook his head.

"Esther Mae, Ammon's wife and my good friend, needs a lot of help when she's pregnant, and I'm the one who meets that need. She came up with that name. But she's not pregnant right now, just hurt from a bad fall."

Jacob didn't want to hear about Ammon and his wife. "When you realized what I thought, why not tell me the truth?"

"A lot of reasons, and, believe me or not, all of them centered on us being able to simply be friends while you were here."

Did she actually think any type of real friendship was built on lies? "You've yet to give me even one reason."

"You'd dated my sister, and she was so angry with me when you stopped seeing her. Dora thought it was my fault, and when she realized we were seeing each other some — in town, here at the shop, at my property — it was easy to reassure her through the simple words *he thinks I'm married.*" Esther focused on the old, weather-beaten window-pane, and as she scraped off loose paint, her fingers trembled. "There was something enjoyable and exceptional between us *be-cause* you thought I was married. I didn't want to ruin that." She looked up at him, her eyes asking for understanding. "I'm twenty-seven years old, and I like my life as it is, Jacob. But no one Amish, especially a man, believes a woman wants to be single. If you'd known the truth, you would've avoided me like you have Dora. I . . . I just wanted us to be able to be friends."

"I don't want a friendship based on lies." He had issues — plenty of them — but he saw himself as a patient man. But women could be so wearying. First Sandra. Then

Rhoda. Now Esther. For Casey's sake he dealt with whatever lies Sandra dished out. But he didn't put up with that from anyone else. "I told you things about my life. I talked to you about the construction company I went to work for and the legal troubles and Sandra and returning home injured, and the list goes on. You should've stopped me."

Concern and self-doubt radiated from her. "I . . . I thought I was giving you the chance to be yourself. I would never tell anyone a word of it, but I really, really needed to hear what you had to say."

"You needed to hear it?" What she must really think of him seared like a hot iron. "Why, so you could be assured of what you already believed? That men are reckless and senseless?"

"Jacob." Disbelief echoed inside her whisper. She held her forehead. "Okay, maybe this will help." She lowered her hand, studying him. "You understand riptides. For a lot of reasons, we were caught in one from the first night we met in town. You know that the best thing people can do to free themselves of a riptide is to relax and let it carry them to the end of it. That's their best chance of having the stamina to swim to shore."

He resented her using that analogy. She wouldn't know to say that to him if they hadn't swapped stories of learning to snorkel and swim in the ocean.

She fidgeted with the scraper. "Can you understand?"

Underneath his anger he realized a part of him was relieved that she wasn't married and that he wouldn't have to feel concerned over her being married to Ammon. But he no longer liked her the way he had before. She was like too many others he'd known — willing to trick him because it suited her needs.

"That's just it. I *don't* understand. How foolish did you make me look to the men in this shop and to your brother? Whispers must be making the rounds to plenty of folks I've never even met."

"I doubt anyone knows you think I'm married except Bailey, Dora, and Ammon." She stared at the buttons on his shirt. "I only wanted to give us the chance of being a friend to each other — no strings or fears or expectations."

"A friend," he mumbled, remembering when he considered Sandra and her husband his friends. In the name of friendship, he had done things that could have landed him in jail. And then there were Samuel and

Rhoda, who had been among his closest friends. "The older I get, the more I find the whole *friend* concept a myth. I thought you — *we* — were different than that. How would you feel if a guy lied to you and brought others in on it too? You wouldn't be that desperate for a friend, and surely you didn't think I was either."

Her shoulders slumped, and she kept her eyes focused on the work station. "I'm sorry. I just . . ." She shook her head. "I'm sorry." She ran the scraper down the sides of the old windowpane. "Forgive me?" Her hoarse voice sparked a sense of eeriness, but why?

Of course he forgave her, and not because he'd been taught relentlessly that Scripture was clear about having to forgive others in order to be forgiven by God. He had no desire to punish her or imprison her inside his disappointment. But even so, he was done here. She'd proved who she was. The tunnel around him — the one he'd thought he would soon walk out of, the one she'd brought light into — seemed to lengthen, and the light at the end of it faded until darkness surrounded him again.

She stood there, staring at him, waiting for his final verdict, the one that would define who they'd be from now on. "Can you forgive me?"

"Ya. I forgive you." But he wasn't hanging around. "I need to go."

Eighteen

Samuel's stomach growled as he parked the wagon near the barn. Phoebe had called him to eat lunch more than three hours ago, but he'd stayed in the orchard until all the oil tanks in his wagon were empty. He got down and unhitched the horse. Walking the animal into the barn, Samuel heard Rhoda talking on the phone, and despite how hungry and tired he was, he'd rather have some time with her before getting a fresh horse and reloading the wagon with oil.

While he put the horse in a stall, filled its water trough, and fed it, he listened to her doing some type of business. She could make reading a grocery list sound interesting.

Wind whipped through the barn, playing with the fabric of his lightweight jacket. Strong winds this time of year seemed to be normal. April had only four more days left, and the snows had not only stopped, but most of it was melted. The ice in the rivers had broken up enough to be whisked toward the ocean, and he'd read in the newspaper this morning that the first canoeists of the season were getting on the water today.

Despite the great springtime thaw, Samuel had to admit this business venture had an odd wintry feel to it of late. Could they move past the weight they seemed trapped under without Landon? He doubted it. Landon had left a hole no one else could fill — not just in the field, although that alone might sink them, but also as a friend. Leah's grief had buried her, and no one knew how to help ease that. Well, they didn't know how to do it *and* remain in the good graces of the Amish. Landon had been gone for more than three weeks, and it felt as if it'd been three months.

"That's fine. I can wait." Rhoda's voice drifted into his awareness.

Samuel smiled, wondering who she had on the line. True to form, she showed strength and determination despite the situation they were in. But when he looked in her eyes, he saw the hurt. He didn't want her life mired in difficulty and pain. He longed to give her everything — love, joy, peace, and help for the house and office duties. His goal was, by this time next year, for her to tend the orchard as it suited her, not as the orchard demanded. Then she'd enjoy the canning season even more.

But the truth was, all his hopes could be dashed if they didn't catch a break. They'd come to Maine with four men and three women — Steven, Landon, Jacob, and Samuel; Rhoda, Phoebe, and Leah. That wasn't enough full-time workers. Iva then joined them, and that had helped. But then they lost Jacob. Now Landon. And the part-time help from the other families who had moved here fell far short of compensating for their losses.

Sometimes Samuel wanted to pound his head against a wall. If it'd help anything, he would.

When it came to making the farm profitable, losing Jacob and Landon had been a huge blow. If one more thing went wrong, he doubted Orchard Bend Farms could survive. Who was he kidding? They might not make it as it was — even if everything went right from here on.

Once the horse was taken care of, he pulled off his dirty, oil-covered jacket. It'd been a bit warm today to wear it while working, but it kept his clothes from getting a layer of oily mist. He tucked the hose between his arm and body and used the flowing water to rinse his hands and face. He turned off the water and hung the hose on its hook.

While wiping water from his face and slinging it from his hands, he went into the office. Rhoda had the phone to her ear and papers spread out on the desk, looking studious. "Could you run those numbers again, please? One of us is mistaken."

She glanced up and waved, a gorgeous smile on her lips.

"Yes, that matches my figures." She scribbled on a notepad. "You get it in on Monday, but you can't deliver it before the following week?" She paused, listening while taking notes. "Yes, I remember. Landon picked it up for us before, but he's no longer with us, and . . ." She cradled the phone between her head and shoulder and motioned for Samuel to take a seat. "Okay, I'll call you back about whether you need to deliver it or we can pick it up. Sure, I'll call Monday. Thank you." She hung up. "The good news is they can have the oil in the store by Monday. The bad news is they can't deliver it until the following Monday. And if we have to get it by wagon, the round trip will take most of a day."

"We need a driver with a truck."

"What we have is a wagon with a team of

horses. Is there enough oil to last until they can make a delivery?"

"Doubtful. My guess is I'll be out by Tuesday."

She opened a drawer and slid the notes inside. "I put an ad for help in Amish newspapers across the states. Maybe we'll get a few nibbles soon."

He hoped so. "That'd be nice." Thus far the Amish who'd moved here were farmers, and they were busy with their own spring-time work — plowing fields with a team of horses. Crist was good, stout help, but his first priority was his parents' farm, so he had only a day now and then when he could work here.

She frowned and set her two-way on the desk. "I didn't hear much of anything you said today through that radio, including when you told Phoebe you weren't coming in for lunch. I learned about that when I went to lunch and you weren't there."

He put his radio on the desk and took the one she'd laid down. "I'll work with it later."

She rose. "You're not fooling me, Samuel King. Every tenth word someone says is more than you care to hear most of the time anyway." She paused, looking up at him. "True?"

"Only when it's someone else on the two-way radio. I want to hear every word you say on the radio or in person." He longed to kiss her, but if he did, he'd only want more. He shoved his hands into his pants pockets.

She giggled. "I didn't realize you were such a smooth liar."

"Now you know."

She let loose a full-fledged laugh. "You realize you just told me you love listening to every word I say and then admitted you're a good liar?"

He smiled down at her. "I did, didn't I?" He scratched the side of his face. "Did you know it's almost too warm for a jacket today?"

"Was that supposed to be a smooth change of subject? And fifty degrees is not that warm." She put her cold hands on his face.

He gasped. "Tell me the saying is cold hands, warm heart and not cold hands, cold heart."

"What I'll tell you is that you're a good hand warmer." She moved her still cool hands to his neck.

Since their lives had taken such a hard hit because of his Daed, they'd become even closer and were more demonstrative with their feelings. On the one hand, he appreciated that. On the other, it only made him crazy with desire to court her, kiss her, marry her. He cleared his throat. "How about joining me for lunch?"

She removed her hands. "Sounds good, although lunch wasn't the usual fare. It was sandwiches and canned soup. Phoebe's under the weather."

They left the barn and started across the yard. "She seemed fine this morning."

"It hit fast and hard. Sore throat, head congestion, and currently in bed with a fever."

"I'm sorry to hear that. You know, one of us may need to learn to cook just for such an occasion."

"About all I can do is scramble eggs, but you don't care for them."

He turned up his lip. "You are right about that."

Once they were at the house, he opened the door for Rhoda, and when he stepped inside, Arie ran to him, holding up her arms. "Samuel *iss Heemet!*" She danced around, singing about Samuel being home.

Rhoda turned to him. "I guess that makes me scrambled eggs in her sight."

He laughed while picking up Arie. *"Du hungerich?"*

Arie hugged him before nodding. "Ya. Du?"

"Ya. I'm *very* hungry." He rubbed his belly and set her feet on the floor. "I need to wash up with soap." As Samuel crossed the living room, Phoebe came down the stairs, wearing a bathrobe, her cheeks flushed.

"Phoebe," — Steven came out of the kitchen, a dishtowel on his shoulder — "to bed."

"Samuel hasn't eaten since breakfast."

Steven gestured. "We'll handle it. To bed."

"Did anyone get a chance to go to the grocery store with the list I made?"

Getting to the store had become really problematic without Landon. Paying a driver to go that far was like paying for a taxi, and coordinating with a paid driver when most had full-time jobs was even harder. Camilla and her husband, Bob, refused to be paid for such trips, which meant they didn't call her or him unless they had no other choice. Landon's grandmother was retired and had the vehicle and time, but since they felt as if they'd run off Landon for not being Amish, they didn't want to ask his grandmother for help.

Steven headed for the steps. "No one has gone yet, but I'll get Leah and Iva to do so in the next few days. They seem to enjoy that outing. Now, go to bed."

"Goodness, it's just a cold."

"It hit so fast and hard, it may be the flu." Steven hurried up the stairs. "To bed or to the doctor, your choice."

"I'm fine," Phoebe protested as they disappeared into their suite.

Samuel looked around. "Where's Isaac?"

He heard giggles from behind or under the couch.

"No earthly idea." Rhoda wiggled her eyebrows at Arie. Isaac understood and spoke English fairly well these days, and Arie even understood a few words and seemed to put together the rest by observation.

Samuel saw Isaac's fingertips reaching from under the couch. "That's a shame, because I was thinking of us taking a buggy ride into town to get some pizza."

"Ich bin do!" Isaac thrust half of his body out from under the couch as he shouted *I am here.* But then he stopped cold, chortling and flailing his arms, obviously stuck.

"Somebody help the boy." Samuel lifted the couch. It felt so good to laugh. He watched Rhoda and smiled. Thank God for a woman as determined as he not to let heartache over the situation with Landon and Leah steal more of their joy than necessary.

Rhoda lifted the thick wooden spoon to her mouth, smelling her latest batch of the new recipe. "Please be as good as you smell." She blew on the bits of apple salsa, cooling it. She'd been in her harvest kitchen all day, working on recipe after recipe. She eased the spoon past her lips. Her mouth instantly watered as the scrumptious flavor burst on her taste buds. *Finally!*

Oh, how she wished Landon were here. He'd been rejoicing with her over recipes since she was a teen. He'd tease her, saying that despite her being a horrible cook, she concocted great canning recipes.

No one was around. Samuel was in the orchard, miles from here. Even Leah, Iva, and Crist were gone today — on another grocery-shopping trip and whatever else they were up to. They always managed to take hours longer than they should. At least it seemed to help lift Leah's spirits a bit.

"I did it, guys!" Rhoda's skin tingled. She talked as if they were here, but joy bubbled up, and she knocked the oversize wooden spoon against the side of the pan, freeing it of salsa before she marched outside.

Even out here no one was within hearing

range. She couldn't wait to tell everyone, but for now she whooped a good holler, filling the air with the shrill sound. This new apple salsa recipe with several unique herbs she'd grown herself was sure to please buyers. "I did it! Oh yes, I *did*!" She danced a little jig before laughing at herself.

When only the hills echoed back at her, she wondered if she should've stayed at the house to work today. But Steven had banned everyone from making any noise while Phoebe rested. So she and Samuel had packed their lunches and parted ways. She'd offered to take the children with her, but Steven had said they would be fine staying with him as he worked the fields. He did, however, ask to keep the dogs with him to help the children enjoy their day while he worked. Rhoda had to admit that it was a particularly glorious spring day to be outside. Sunlight filled a cloudless, sixty-degree day.

She returned to the stove, still smiling. Peering into the pan, she stirred it once more. "You're tasty enough to make people who've never cared for or tried apple salsa to totally change their minds."

"Rhoda!" Samuel's voice tore through the open windows. She scooped up a bit of salsa and took it with her as she headed for the door. She wasn't waiting one minute longer for Samuel to taste this.

The door flung open, and Samuel filled the entryway. "Are you okay?" He rushed to her, his brows knit as he studied her. "I heard screaming, and the two-way kept cutting out." His breaths were short and intense. "Bleeding? Bruised?"

What had she done? And where was her two-way? Unable to speak, she simply shook her head.

"Oh, thank God." He pulled her to him, embracing her as a drowning man might his next breath. "I thought . . ." He took her by the shoulders and backed her away from him, still scrutinizing her. His gaze met hers, and he cradled her face. He kissed her forehead and worked his way to her cheeks, each kiss becoming more intense. "Rhoda . . ."

His lips found hers.

The spoon slipped from her fingers and thudded on the wood floor. Rhoda wrapped her arms around him and forgot everything except this moment and how much she loved this man.

When he lifted his lips from hers, he stared into her eyes. "I shouldn't have done that, but I thought the worst, and I can't imagine living without you." His hoarse voice cracked, and his eyes misted. His strong arms held her, one hand on her back and one caressing her face.

"I'm fine, Samuel. You heard me on the porch yelling a victory whoop." She snuggled in closer, smiling up at him. "Although if this is the end result, you haven't heard my last performance."

He took a deep breath, and everything reflected in his eyes spoke of loving her. "From where I was, I had to pass by here to get to the house, and when I saw smoke rising from the chimney, I took a chance you'd be here." His relief faded a bit. "Right after the scream, your brother" — Samuel pulled the two-way out of his pocket — "said your name, and then the last words I could make out were 'can't breathe' and 'ambulance.' I thought you were hurt, but . . ." He raised his eyes from the radio to hers, and a bolt of lightning shot through her.

"Phoebe!"

They took off running, and by the time she was outside, Samuel had already mounted his horse. He grabbed her arm, and when he hooked his foot, she used it as a stirrup.

"Hold on tight." Samuel urged the horse into a full gallop, going faster than she'd ever ridden a horse, and soon the house came into sight. An ambulance sat near the front porch, and men were guiding a stretcher out of the house.

Samuel brought the horse to a stop and helped Rhoda down before dismounting. He grabbed her hand, and they hurried toward the house. The dogs barked furiously, sounding as if they were pinned somewhere.

"What's wrong?" Rhoda caught a glimpse of Phoebe's bluish skin around the breathing mask she wore. Her chest heaved, but her body was limp and her eyes closed.

"I . . . I . . ." Steven's eyes were huge, and he seemed dazed. "I came back with the children to check on her, and she was in the yard, trying to get to the phone. She said she couldn't breathe and needed help, so after I got her back inside, I called an ambulance. But a few minutes later she lost consciousness." He flailed his arms while talking as if he were a rag doll in someone's hand. "Why couldn't I reach either of —"

"Sir? You going?" An EMT stood at the back of the ambulance. One was in the vehicle with Phoebe.

"Ya." Steven descended the steps, looking at Rhoda. "When I couldn't reach you, I thought I was going to have to stay here, because the children can't ride in the ambulance. Watch them."

"Of course."

Steven got in the ambulance, and one of the medics quickly closed the doors. Rhoda peered through the window "Call us."

Steven nodded, clutching Phoebe's hand. The man who'd just closed the doors went to the driver's seat and got in. As the ambulance pulled onto the road, the sirens rang out. Wherever the dogs were, they were ceaseless in their protest.

Rhoda blinked. "The children." She hurried into the house. "Arie! Isaac!" She turned, silently asking Samuel where they could be. Something pulled her attention to a door upstairs, and she ran up the steps, Samuel right behind her.

Rhoda tried to open the door.

"No! *Du muscht net kumm im!*"

She mustn't come in? "Isaac, honey, I'm here to help." Could he think clearly enough to trust her? "Isaac, what's wrong?"

The lock clicked, and he opened the door less than a third of an inch and peeked out. Rhoda's heart broke for them. She knelt. "Du allrecht?"

He was crying, which told her that, no, he wasn't okay. When she tried to ease open the door, he pushed back.

"Stop!" He sounded panicked. "You don't

280

understand!"

The dogs continued to howl. "Samuel, could you find the dogs and make them hush? They're only frightening the children more."

He hurried off, and she turned back to the door. "Isaac, you're safe. I promise you are. Would you let me in?"

His tears slowed. "Daed said, 'Lock the door and do not come out!'" He sobbed. "I don't want Mamm to die."

Tears blurred her vision. He thought disobeying his Daed could kill his mother. "Isaac, you can trust me. Your Daed is ready for you to come out now." It would take hours to convince him and Arie that their obedience wasn't connected to all that had taken place over the last hour.

The dogs finally hushed, and Rhoda whispered to Isaac in Pennsylvania Dutch, speaking the only language that really mattered — that of love, trust, and understanding.

Isaac finally stepped back, and she eased open the door. He stood there, stoic and stiff, tears staining his cheeks. Arie rose from the corner and flew into Rhoda's arms, weeping.

Samuel returned, and the four of them sat on the floor as the two adults comforted the distraught children. Within twenty minutes the children were at the kitchen table, using crayons to express themselves while they talked and sipped on a favorite drink they didn't get to have often — lemonade.

"Samuel," — Rhoda pulled him to the side — "do you think you could handle the children and I could slip out? I'm sure Camilla or Bob or Erlene could give me a ride to the hospital."

Samuel nodded. "We'll be fine. Go."

He didn't have to say it twice. She called Camilla, and within forty minutes Rhoda was walking down the halls of the hospital while Camilla parked the car. As Rhoda stepped off the elevator and onto the floor she'd been directed to, she saw something out of her peripheral vision. Chills ran down her arms, and she refused to look, but she knew . . .

It was someone not really there.

Someone wearing an Amish dress.

She went to the waiting room and found her brother in a chair, hunched over and staring at the floor. Before she called to him, movement rustled behind him, and before Rhoda could divert her eyes, Phoebe stood before her.

Rhoda closed her eyes. Was there a bundle in Phoebe's arms? *Stop, Rhoda.* Phoebe wasn't there. It was just her imagination. That's all. The stress had her imagination running wild, and she hadn't realized it until now.

Pulling her focus from the vision, she looked at her brother. "Steven."

He rose and engulfed her in a hug. "It's viral pneumonia, brought on by some strain of H1N1. They don't know if she or the baby will make it."

Rhoda closed her eyes. She wouldn't open them, would not look at the vision. She was too afraid of what she might see.

NINETEEN

Groceries and plastic bags rattled in the back of the wagon as Leah kept a steady eye on the horizon. Erlene's old store was just over the next knoll, and for some reason the sight of it eased some of her heartache. Was it because she'd really enjoyed rummaging around in it with Landon a few times? Or maybe it was because the Olson family had used the building for storage, and some of the items in it were from the Great Depression. It was comforting to touch things that had once belonged to others who'd been through really tough times too.

Crist tapped the reins against the two horses' backs and made a tsking sound numerous times, encouraging the team to pick up speed as they approached a hill. Iva and Crist sat next to each other on the wooden bench with Leah. The two of them moved from one conversation to another like a gentle river, but Leah found it impossible to stay tuned in to the discussions. Still, getting off the farm with friends brought her a little peace.

How could Landon have agreed to leave and not speak to her for a year? Who did that?

Iva looped her arm through Leah's. "Spring brings such lovely weather."

Did it?

Leah pulled from her gray, cloudy thoughts and noticed the crisp air and golden sunlight. But it was like being hungry and homeless and looking through a window into a well-stocked, warm home.

She'd brought some of this on herself by accusing Landon of caring more for his job and potential promotion than her. As rash and wrong as that had been, she'd said it in the heat of the moment. Landon should have known not to give in to her Daed's demands . . . unless he was fed up with her as well as her family. Did he agree to her Daed's terms because it gave him the out he wanted?

She reached into her coat pocket and felt the phone he'd given her. If he'd wanted free of her, he wouldn't have given her a phone earlier that same day. Maybe her Daed had said something to him that made him realize just how impossible it'd be to free her from her family and the Amish community. Or maybe he realized what it would mean to marry someone whose family could never embrace him and could never be part of a support system for him and Leah and their children.

They topped the hill, and Erlene's old store came into sight. Thoughts of past years and all the heartache people had survived came to her again, and she could feel hope for her future begin to stir.

Crist peered around Iva. "You want to stop by it again?"

Leah shook her head. She didn't need to go in again. They'd gone through it once today already before going to the grocery store.

Iva squeezed her arm. "Sure she does. During our two visits thus far, she's yet to have time to go into the attic." Iva lifted the camera from her lap. "And *Leah* wants to see the attic and take more pictures."

Crist chuckled. "Having trouble separating what you want, Iva, from what Leah wants? Last time we were there, I told you to go up to the attic, but, no, you were too busy staging items on the first floor for good snapshots."

A few weeks ago Crist would have nothing to do with Iva's camera or her taking pictures, but now he helped her stage inanimate objects, and after she took a few shots, he looked at the LCD panel with her to see if they needed better lighting or needed to add different objects to the scene.

Iva jabbed Crist with her elbow. "Just hush it and stop at the store."

"Oh, I'll pull in at the store, but I'm not hushing. And you can't make me." Crist smiled as he continued prattling, and he didn't get quiet until he'd pulled onto the driveway.

Once he was parked, Leah did what she did best of late — moved like a snail. Iva and Crist hurried into the building while Leah meandered around outside. She pulled the cell phone from her pocket and took a few images, although she had no idea why.

A car slowed as it passed by, and the driver, an Englisch man, craned his neck to look at her. Was that Pastor Weld? He came to a stop, put the car into reverse, and then pulled in behind the wagon. He rolled down his window. "Hi, Leah. I thought that was you. I'm actually coming from a visit to Landon's." He searched her eyes. "Erlene said he didn't live there or in the area anymore. I don't need to know anything other than are you okay?"

Leah's eyes filled with tears, and she shrugged. "My Daed found out I was seeing Landon, and" — she blew out a long stream of air — "that's that . . . for now. Maybe for forever."

"I don't want to instigate any trouble between you and your family, but if you need anything, you're welcome to reach out to me. If you want to talk or want someone to pick you up for church, you call me."

"Thanks."

He gave a nod and started to back out but stopped again. "Listen, Leah, I need to be sure you feel safe at home. If you don't, there are people at the church who can offer assistance."

"It's not like that. My Daed yelled a lot at first, but the real issue is my family doesn't understand how I feel, and it leaves me so isolated from them."

"I know about being an outcast in a family. My family believes in academia and not much else. To say they were humiliated when I came to Christ is an understatement, and they were mortified when I gave up the family wealth and status and went into the ministry. Family often tries to control us for reasons that make perfect sense from their point of view."

He understood? Even if it was just a

breadcrumb of understanding being tossed her way, she deeply appreciated it.

"Leah?" Crist called as he and Iva came out of the old store. "Is everything okay?"

Pastor Weld looked from them to Leah, his face taut with concern.

"It's okay, Pastor. These are friends." She gestured for Crist and Iva. "I'm fine. This is the pastor from the church Landon and I went to. Can we have a minute?"

They nodded and disappeared into the store.

Pastor Weld breathed a sigh of relief. "I thought I'd gotten you into trouble. Remember, Leah, you have the right to follow your conscience — in church attendance, your future spouse, and just about anything else you can think of. It really comes down to only a few things, and I think the most important of those is, Do you have the strength to set aside what everyone else wants — Landon, your family, or even people like me — to discover what's in your heart and follow it?"

"I'm not sure. I keep getting stuck before I can get that far."

He smiled. "I like your answer of not being sure. It shows careful forethought. What are you getting stuck on?"

"For years I've gone round and round

about what to do, most of my life actually. The one thing I can't figure out is what happens if I burn a bridge with Landon or my family and then I regret my choice?"

"That's a great question. Again, it speaks of your wise caution. But everyone has regrets. Whatever you choose, you will have to accept your regrets and commit to staying faithful to your decision. I regret that my relationship with my parents and siblings hasn't been good since I chose to become a pastor. I regret that they're so uncomfortable with my choice we can't enjoy a meal or a family discussion around a fire in winter. But I do not regret following my heart. It led to my finding the real me — not the one my family wanted, but the person I was born to be. So the first question you need to ask isn't which path you will regret, but which path you are willing to commit to."

"Shouldn't the first question be, what does God want?"

"Some would say so. But in a situation like yours, where it's not a matter of sin drawing or tempting you, you need to trust that your heart's desire is His heart's desire. The latter part of Psalm 37:4 says He will give you the desires of *your* heart. If you want to discuss that further, I can give you other scriptures to back up what I've said."

She had so many questions for him, but it would be dusk soon, and the wagon didn't have any lights, only reflective strips, so they needed to get home. "Another time. We really need to go before the others start to worry." As he pulled out, Leah called to Crist and Iva.

They loaded into the wagon and headed to the farm. Leah kept mulling over all the pastor had said, and she longed to latch on to it. Was it possible that her future was already written on her heart and she just needed to follow her heart?

The thought caused fresh peace to mix with hope. Maybe she would survive this time after all.

As they pulled into the driveway, Samuel came to the door of the barn, carrying Arie. Isaac was at his feet. Crist brought the rig to a stop.

"Hi." Samuel waved, but he looked upset with them. "Crist, I need to talk to Leah and Iva. Could the children help you take groceries into the house?"

Crist paused, glancing at Leah and then Iva. "I know we've been gone most of today, but that is my fault."

Leah didn't see how he was to blame, but she appreciated his willingness to say so.

Samuel carried Arie closer to the wagon. "It's not about your lengthy trip to get groceries. Phoebe's in the hospital."

Leah's heart began to soar. A new baby! But her next thought stole her excitement. It was too early for the baby to come. Way, way too early.

Samuel was pale, and his hands trembled. She'd rarely seen him look this way. Fear gripped her heart, and she got out of the rig. "What's wrong with her?"

Iva got down, and Samuel set Arie on the seat next to Crist. Isaac climbed into the back of the wagon and made a place among the grocery bags. Crist drove the rig to the house.

Samuel put his hands into his pants pockets. "I just got off the phone with Rhoda. Phoebe has a strain of the H1N1 virus." He lowered his head. "She might not make it."

"No!" Leah turned to Iva, who had her hand over her mouth, her eyes large.

Leah turned back to her brother. "That's not possible!"

"I know it's hard to believe, especially since she goes almost nowhere."

"But she got Camilla to take her to town a few days ago." Iva sighed, shaking her head. "They went to half a dozen stores looking for fabric and acceptable shoes for the children and even went to the pharmacy to stock up on over-the-counter stuff. Maybe she picked it up then."

"Maybe." Samuel shrugged. "Regardless of where she came in contact with it, the doctors have put her in what's called a medically induced coma, hoping to give her and the baby a fighting chance."

Leah couldn't see for the tears, and the barn seemed to be spinning. "If I'd been more help lately . . ."

Iva took her by the hands. "It's a virus, Leah. She would be in the same place no matter how much work we'd done."

Leah stood there staring at Samuel as he choked back emotions.

Samuel was normally a nose-to-the-grindstone man, and Leah had convinced herself that he could shoulder the weight of the world. But seeing him like this . . .

She opened her mouth to speak, but no words came out. Her mouth was dry, and her face burned with an embarrassment she didn't understand. As dizziness caused the world to sway, she realized why she felt the sting of shame.

Here she'd been lamenting that she wouldn't speak to or see Landon for a year, and Steven could be facing a lifetime without his wife and the mother of his children. What must it be like to think you might not ever see your wife and baby again? Or that you'd raise the little ones without the person who helped create them?

"It's a boy, they said. Phoebe's child." Samuel smiled weakly. "The doctors did a sonogram."

"Oh." Leah couldn't manage to say anything else. A baby boy. It somehow felt more real knowing what that beautiful protruding belly held. Phoebe was having a boy.

At least Leah prayed she would have the baby.

"I want to check something in the office." Samuel went into the barn office, and they followed.

He made sure the phone was securely in its cradle before he sat on the front edge of the desk. "Steven and Rhoda are staying at the hospital. Phoebe's parents will arrive tomorrow. Steven and Rhoda's parents too. Hopefully she'll get better and there won't be a reason for more relatives and loved ones to come to Maine." His voice returned to its usual timbre, although Leah suddenly heard his voice differently than ever before. The harsher tone he used at times wasn't because he was trying to be tough or cold. He was trying to be strong, to be what other people expected or perhaps even needed him to be: a rock of leadership. The one who would do whatever was necessary without complaint.

Samuel stared at the floor. "Phoebe also has pneumonia."

Iva sat quietly, but Leah remained standing, longing to throw things and scream until this problem with Phoebe went away.

"Samuel," — Iva angled her head — "I know pneumonia is really bad, especially for a pregnant woman, but they have antibiotics to help, right?"

"It's viral pneumonia. There is nothing to do for a virus but let it run its course. The doctor explained that it's like having a really bad head cold, one where you need to blow your nose a half-dozen times in an hour, but in her case all the congestion is filling her lungs."

Leah's knees threatened to give way. "Samuel." She couldn't catch her breath, and when he moved to hold her, she didn't back away. "Why Phoebe? She honors God with every move she makes. She works hard, never raises her voice or complains." And she loved Steven and her children with a purity Leah had never known. Her mind jumped. "Jacob. He needs to know."

"I've tried to call him." Samuel's shoulders slumped a bit. "I haven't had any luck getting hold of him in a long time, but I left him a message. Hopefully he'll listen to it."

Leah fully met her brother's gaze for the first time in weeks — for the first time since he'd let Landon walk out of here. "We'll get through this."

"Ya. We will."

But Leah knew that neither of them believed what they'd said. They only hoped.

"Iva, I'll distract the children so they aren't hearing the bad news time and again. You should tell Crist." Samuel started for the door and paused. "Leah, you coming?"

Her mind and heart raced. *Jacob.* "In a minute."

They left, and she snatched the cell phone out of her pocket, flipped through her small contact list, and typed in a text message to Jacob: *This is Leah. SOS! Now!* She hit send, praying he'd answer. Her phone rang before she finished her prayer, and the name Jacob came across the screen. Had he even had time to get or read her message?

"Jacob?"

"I'm here. What's going on?" His voice was filled with concern and the brotherly affection she so missed from him. She nearly burst into tears as she launched into clusters of explanations and fears. She fumbled through some of the events since he'd left, realizing just how long he'd been out of contact. Still, he listened, never once venturing a question or needing additional information to piece together what all had happened.

"So who's left to work the orchard?"

She grimaced at her next words. "With Steven, Landon, and you gone? The only man left is Samuel. Crist helps a day or two a week." When she wasn't busy pulling him and Iva to go with her on outings. Leah had been nearly useless since Landon had left, but no one had corrected her. "We need you now more than ever."

He was silent. Had he hung up? She frowned and looked at the phone for hints of what was going on.

"Okay . . ." He finally said what she had been silently and desperately hoping he would say. "I'll head for Maine in a few days."

"Jacob . . . denki."

"It's fine." He didn't sound like it was, but he'd agreed to come, and that was the most important thing.

They said their good-byes and hung up. When she exited the barn, she stopped and gazed at the orchard. She'd grown up seeing an orchard every day. That orchard represented what the Kings always stood for: hope.

Perhaps it was time for Leah to embrace hope like that too — a hope that didn't look at what was but what could be through prayer, work, and patience.

TWENTY

Jacob pushed the swing, and Casey gave a delighted squeal. Was he really heading back to the farm later today? He wanted Phoebe well, but, man, everything in him rebelled against the idea of returning.

Casey giggled. "Higher!"

"To the moon, little one." Jacob responded as if there weren't a miserable weight sitting on his chest.

If Esther had been who she'd pretended to be, he might consider calling her. He certainly needed to talk about having to return to the farm and what was happening with Phoebe. But he wasn't so desperate for a friend that she could lie to him and he'd come back for more. Besides, friendships weren't really all that important. He knew lots of men who had no real friendships, only coworkers. What was so bad about that?

He took a deep breath of the crisp spring air.

Sandra sat in a lounge chair nearby, watching Casey and sipping on hot tea. She caught Jacob's eye and smiled. Her regimen of meds seemed to be working well, and she had a steady job as a receptionist at a medical office. When Casey started preschool this fall, Sandra was going to enroll in classes to get certified in medical billing and coding. If she passed, she'd almost double her current hourly wage. Moreover, it'd be a good boost to her morale.

At least he'd done one thing right lately. Sandra had needed this extended visit. While he was working on the play set, she had spent time outside helping him and had met several neighbors.

How different the past two weeks had been, him meeting neighbors and being able to hold conversations with them without fearing they'd learn his secrets. But as long ago as his secretive days felt, they'd been behind him for just a little more than a year.

Jacob continued pushing Casey.

"Jacob, I want down now!"

Jacob didn't flinch. "Casey, doodlebug, I want to be asked nicely."

"Mom!" Casey yelled.

Jacob held up his index finger, telling Sandra to stay where she was. He pushed the swing again. "If you're too tired to be nice, you can go inside and sit. No toys, no television."

Casey didn't say anything while Jacob continued to push her. She finally glanced over her shoulder. "Dear Uncle Jacob, would you help me stop swinging now, please?"

Okay, so it was overkill laced with teasing, but he slowed the swing. "Why, yes, little doodlebug."

Despite having referred to him as *dad,* according to Sandra's text message, Casey was now calling Jacob *uncle,* thanks to Sandra's prompting. Casey managed to say the word *uncle* only some of the time, but the title had been necessary as he and Sandra met her neighbors. Everyone used a specific connection when introducing one another: spouse, partner, roommate, son, daughter, or, in his case, uncle.

Visitor. Stranger. Those were the words that described him to the people he lived with when moving from one Amish community to the next to work. But he enjoyed going up and down the East Coast, even when traveling by bus and train. Where others found it exhausting, he found it invigorating.

Casey jumped down from the swing. "Thanks!"

"Hey," Jacob called as she ran toward the ladder he'd built to a raised walkway with rails. "We have to go in five minutes."

She held up her hand, splaying her five fingers. "Got it."

He moved to the chair next to Sandra and sat. Regardless of how he usually felt about traveling, he wasn't looking forward to the bus ride to Orchard Bend Farms. If it wasn't for what had befallen Phoebe, he wouldn't be going back.

She is going to get better, isn't she, God?

Sandra put her hand over his. "You've been quiet this visit."

He shrugged. "Just thinking." He wanted to ask, what is it about me that makes women lie? But Sandra had lied to him longer than anyone, so he couldn't ask her. He wasn't sure whether Rhoda had lied to him or to herself until the truth of her love for Samuel was too strong for Jacob or Rhoda to deny.

Sandra watched Casey, smiling the way she used to when Jacob had first met her. "If you weren't leaving, *this* would be a perfect day."

"May first, and it is a beauty." All except the black cloud of reuniting with Samuel and Rhoda. "You ready?"

"As ready as I get when you leave." She

302

stood. "I wish we lived closer to you."

"That would be easier to do if I actually lived somewhere." He called to Casey, giving her a one-minute reminder. She did best when she received ample notice. After the three of them ate out, Sandra would take him to the bus station. At the end of the bus trip, a driver would pick him up, although he didn't know who, and take him to the farm.

"Where would you like to have that late lunch we talked about?"

She frowned. "I miss you already."

"Neither of us likes me having to leave this time."

Sandra drove them to a restaurant. As they ate and she took him to the bus stop, Jacob soaked in his last hours with Casey. Actually, now that Sandra was more stable, he enjoyed her too, which was a welcome relief.

Once at the bus station, he lifted Casey into his arms. "You be good for your mama."

She put her arms around his neck and held tight. "You be good too."

He passed her to Sandra. "Bye."

Sandra waved, and Casey followed suit. They continued standing outside, waving as he rode off. The bus ride would take only three hours. Could he have himself emotionally ready to see Samuel or Rhoda by then? He rocked back, wishing he could slow his mind and heart enough to doze off.

What had him so edgy about returning, anyway? It wasn't as if he still loved Rhoda. He wasn't afraid that seeing her would rekindle old feelings — unless those feelings included fresh disappointment and anger.

When the bus pulled up to his stop, it felt as if the trip had taken only a few minutes. He grabbed his travel bag and stepped off the bus. Camilla stood on the sidewalk, waiting for him.

Great. They'd sent a driver who loved Rhoda and thought Samuel had hung the moon. Couldn't they have asked Erlene to come? She at least seemed neutral in the great divide between Samuel and Rhoda and him. Camilla and her husband had even invited Rhoda and Samuel to their home one night and excluded Jacob.

Was he seeing the situation wrong? Man, he needed someone to talk to. "Hi, Camilla."

"Jacob, you're looking as robust as ever." She smiled before turning the other direction and leading the way to her car.

He tossed his traveling bag into the backseat and got in. They made small talk as Camilla drove the winding roads, each of them seeming determined to keep the conversation going.

Jacob fidgeted with the door handle. "Any updates on Phoebe?"

"Not that I know of. I drove her parents and Steven's to the farm Sunday. I sort of expected you then too."

"I was in the middle of a project I couldn't drop." He'd made too many promises to Casey about them building the play set to leave without finishing it. She'd gone with him to buy the wood, and she had been so excited throughout each step.

Camilla nodded, and they fell into talk about the weather. It was dusk by the time she dropped him off at the farm. He simply stood in the yard, staring at the house.

Leah eased out the door, moving as cautiously and respectfully as one did at a funeral. Her eyes met his, and he ached for his little sister. Making sense of life, especially as an Amish woman, was never easy.

"Hi." She stopped in front of him, staring straight ahead at the third button on his shirt.

Had he expected more of a welcome from her? He'd walked away and not stayed in contact, and he of all people understood there was a price to pay for that. His thoughts jumped to Esther. There wouldn't be a price where she was concerned. Unlike his family, she wasn't a person he would need to reconnect with again. So why was he even thinking about her?

Like a hundred times before, Jacob did his best to push Esther out of his mind. "Leah, I'm so sorry." There was so much to express sorrow for — Landon, Leah, Phoebe, Steven, and their children. He saw it in her eyes — confusion, loneliness, and turmoil.

She nodded. "It's ridiculous." Her eyes misted. "I feel so many things that I think I'm going to burst. I'm so scared for Phoebe and her unborn child. I hurt for Rhoda because she loves Phoebe so much, and yet when it comes to Landon, I'm so angry with her I can't stand it. She never liked me seeing him, and once Daed added pressure, she did nothing to defend Landon or me or to keep either of us on this farm."

He looked at the house. There were too many emotions to sort everything out right now, but a couple of thoughts were clear. "Well, I guess you and I can vent to and console each other during all this. But you're angry with Rhoda for being cautious and unsure about an Amish girl giving up everything to try to fit into an Englisch man's world? Didn't you feel the same way at times?"

"I deserved her support!"

The last thing he wanted was to defend Rhoda, but reason demanded he look past his own emotions. Back when he'd thought it was impossible to find peace with God and himself, Rhoda had been the only one who could see the roadblocks for what they were. She'd stood with him and never once stopped believing in him and wanting what was best for him.

Jacob opened his arms, and Leah slid into them. "At the risk of sounding as if I'm not mad at her, I know she believes in and supports you as a person, and Landon too. But maybe she's just as confused and unsure of what's right concerning your relationship as you and Landon have been at times."

Leah backed away. "Boy, do you have a lot to learn about holding a grudge."

He chuckled. "Think so?" He didn't. He just held on to them differently from his sister. If Leah could understand people's reasons for doing something, she could forgive them. Jacob couldn't. Even when he appreciated the best in the person, he could still hold on to his personal grudge. One day he'd like to wake up a fully mature person, able to handle life as he knew he should.

Esther came to mind to again. Was it immature to be unwilling to have anything else to do with her, or was it an acceptable boundary against someone who'd tried to deceive him and would still be deceiving him if he hadn't figured it out?

The front door opened, and Iva walked out, smiling. "Hey, I know you!"

Leah backed away and turned, motioning for Iva.

Iva held out her hand, and Jacob took it. She squeezed it. "I know it was hard to come back here, but I never doubted you'd do it."

"How're you doing, Iva?"

"Not bad. It's good to see you again."

Ziggy and Zara charged at him out of nowhere, barking, and when Jacob looked beyond them, he saw Samuel driving the wagon to the barn. Jacob whistled for the dogs and made a kissing sound. They slowed, bristled, and then inched forward to sniff his hand. He wasn't one of their favorite people, but they recognized him. Samuel stopped at the hitching post outside the barn, apparently not even noticing him or the girls in the front yard.

Jacob drew a breath. He had an awkward greeting to get through. At least Rhoda wasn't with Samuel right now. It'd be nice to know where she was so her sudden appearance didn't startle him, but he wouldn't ask.

"Leah, Iva, I'll see you in a bit."

Both glanced at Samuel and nodded. He strode to the barn.

Samuel removed the rigging without looking up. Jacob imagined his brother spent untold hours working this orchard. He and Rhoda loved tending God's land. It made them feel connected to its Creator.

Jacob had never felt that way about it, but he hadn't minded the work when he'd had no other choice. "Hey."

Samuel turned, and they stared at each other. Jacob wondered what his eyes said to his brother. Samuel's reflected both a welcome and sorrow. *Willkumm. Es iss gut du kumm.*"

Jacob only managed a nod in response to Samuel's welcome. Jacob shoved his hands into his pockets. "I heard it's been bad around here."

Samuel nodded. "Times of it."

"But there is nowhere else you'd rather be, right?"

Regardless of the weight on his shoulders or the sadness in his heart, Samuel's lopsided smile said it all. "Nowhere." He held out his hand.

Jacob was torn between the desire to embrace his brother and the desire to punish him. Would it always be this awkward between them? Memories of the friendship they'd had while growing up mocked him. Jacob put his hand in his brother's. "We can't let nature take over the orchard. It's the family's best source of income, and by *family* I mean my best source."

"You liked the cut you received after the harvest, did you?"

At the time, receiving it had only saddened and annoyed him. But now that he no longer fought to let go of Rhoda, he saw it for what it was: a sacrifice to give Jacob his portion. Samuel had sent it to their uncle, who got it to Jacob.

"It wasn't bad." Jacob went to the horse, grabbed her by the halter, and headed into the barn. "It paid off almost half my legal fees."

His brother fell into step with him, looking fully exhausted, but it was dark now, and nothing else could be done in the orchard. Jacob put the horse in its stall. "What's on the schedule for tomorrow?"

Samuel hung the rigging over a half wall. "One guess."

"Spraying the trees." Jacob put oats in the horse's trough. It was time they put the niceties to rest and got down to business. Samuel wouldn't speak about the real situation unless Jacob asked directly. "How behind are you?"

Samuel shook his head. "There's no way to get caught up, not after all this. After you left, we hired Crist to work whatever time he could spare from his family's farm, which is only a day or two each week. Then we lost Landon. Now Phoebe and Steven. And right now Steven wants Rhoda to stay with him."

So that's where Rhoda was, at the hospital. "So it's just you?"

"For now."

Jacob searched for the right words. "You've gotten through worse."

Samuel's brows knit. "This is different."

Jacob waited, but Samuel added nothing to his brief statement. It seemed the Kings had been battling one huge issue after another for several years. Had Samuel lost his heart to fight, or was he simply overwhelmed with exhaustion?

"How bad is Phoebe?"

Samuel turned a bucket upside down and sat. "Bad." He propped his forearms on his legs and studied hay-strewn dirt on the floor under his feet. "Steven is beside himself. Phoebe is connected to wires and tubing, and a machine is breathing for her." Samuel's slow, heavy speech weighed on Jacob. "The doctors called a meeting with the immediate family today, saying decisions have to be made."

Jacob's mouth went dry. "What kind of decisions?"

Samuel hesitated, shaking his head. "I'm not sure." The sound of tires on gravel caused Samuel to jump up. "They're back."

Jacob peered through the open barn door and saw a vanload of Amish streaming out of the vehicle. First he saw Steven, followed by his and Rhoda's parents. Another middle-aged couple emerged, probably Phoebe's parents.

Then . . . Rhoda.

His pulse raced, and his head spun. He hadn't expected seeing her to do this to his insides. Had he been wrong all these months?

Was he still in love with her?

TWENTY-ONE

Rhoda sat on the floor of the bathroom, hugging her knees as she watched the second hand on the clock make another slow circle, tick by tick. Desperate for time alone, she'd hurried from the van directly into the bathroom, seeing and speaking to no one.

Even now, with her eyes wide open, she saw Phoebe's limp body on a hospital bed with a ventilator connected to her mouth, blowing extra oxygen into her lungs. Decisions had to be made, but the wrong one could cost Phoebe and her unborn child their lives.

"Father, please." Rhoda pressed her lips against the dress covering her knees. "What should we do?"

She couldn't keep hiding in this bathroom, hoping for answers. She rose and turned on the water in the sink. She splashed water on her face, rinsing away her tears, but water couldn't wash away the sorrow. Or fear. With the doctor's words ringing in her ears, she stared at herself in the mirror. Dishes clanged. The women were getting food on the table. The inevitable family meeting had to take place.

Would Steven begin the discussion before, during, or after the meal? The idea of food made her sick. She dried her face and left the bathroom. She glanced into the living room. The men were there, staying out of the way until they were called for supper — her Daed, and Phoebe's, Steven, Isaac, Samuel, and . . . her heart skipped a beat.

Jacob.

Their eyes met. When had he arrived? Had someone told her he was coming and it didn't register? After months of praying for him, she couldn't budge to welcome him. He stayed put too.

Her Mamm stepped into the living room with Arie on her hip. Having turned four recently, Arie was really too big for her grandmother to carry her. Mamm glanced into the kitchen. *"Es iss Zeit esse."* When the men continued talking without responding to Mamm's call to eat, she motioned. "Kumm."

Samuel rose, gesturing for the older men to go ahead of him. Rhoda unglued her feet and went to Jacob. "Denki." Would he understand that *thank you* covered everything from coming here now to being gracious when he'd told others why he'd left Orchard Bend Farms?

He shifted, looking as uncomfortable as she felt. "I'm sorry about Phoebe."

"Denki." Rhoda bit back tears, her mind too blank to think of anything else to say. She went into the kitchen. After the prayer, dishes were passed around, but few words were spoken. Despite the sting of nausea in her throat, Rhoda ate the roast beef sandwich made from leftovers. She didn't doubt the food was tasty, although it felt like cardboard in her mouth, but if she didn't eat, her parents would worry.

Samuel pulled a piece of notebook paper from his pocket. "All of Phoebe's and Steven's siblings have called today and left voice mails, hoping for an update and assuring us of their prayers and willingness to come here if we want them to. I wrote all the messages down."

An update. Rhoda lowered her fork of sliced apples and bananas. She and Steven had an update to share, but it held as much grief as it did hope.

"Could you read what they said?" Mamm poured fresh water into Steven's glass.

Steven nodded, giving Samuel the go-ahead to do as Mamm asked. He read the messages, and they jumbled together, each one unique and each one the same. "The most pressing message, Steven, is from your brother John. He asked again if he should leave Lydia and the children and come here."

Steven tossed his napkin onto his plate of half-eaten food. "He can't do that. Daed's here, and John needs to work. I told him that yesterday. He needs to stop asking me if I want him to come."

"We can fix that for you." Samuel turned to Rhoda's Daed. "Karl, do you want to call John with clarification, or would you like me to do it?"

"I'll do it. Denki." Her Daed laid his roast beef sandwich on his plate. "Son," — he looked to Steven — "can you tell us now what the doctor said?"

Rhoda hated that every sentence spoken at this table sounded as stiff as the men's starched Sunday shirts.

Her Mamm wiped her mouth with a napkin. "Or let Rhoda tell us what he said."

The doctor would have given the report to all of them, but Steven wanted only him and Rhoda present, feeling that too many ears would hear too many different things, adding to the confusion.

Steven blew a stream of air from his lips. "Rhoda."

"Ya, sure." She glanced at Phoebe's children, wishing they understood even less English. "We were told that this case is unusual, that not many doctors in the US have a lot of experience with this strain of H1N1. So as Phoebe progresses, the doctors are learning how this strain affects the body, especially one that is pregnant. But her primary doctor believes Phoebe is fighting with all she has to get better." Rhoda's tears tried to break free, and she took a deep breath. "Although I have no idea what would make him think that when she's in a coma."

Shaking, she took a sip of her water. "But even when the virus has run its course, and that could be another week, she'll continue to deal with the life-threatening side effects of the viral pneumonia. That battle could last a month. So it's easier on her body, and it's her best chance of getting better, if she remains in a medically induced coma. It also gives the baby the best chance of survival. Barring a turn for the worse, she'll be in this condition for five to ten weeks."

"Five to ten weeks?" Her Daed gestured with one hand, almost knocking over his glass of water. "A month to almost three months? Why so long?"

"The baby needs at least four more weeks in the womb to have a good chance of survival. If the baby comes before the thirtieth week of pregnancy, there could be serious, lifelong issues. Even after that there are many dangers, so the doctor wants as much time as he can get. If Phoebe can carry the child for eleven more weeks, she'll deliver on the early side of full term."

Phoebe's Daed held Rhoda's gaze. "Maybe we need a different opinion."

Rhoda had met this man when Steven and Phoebe were dating, and he used to remind her of the friendly-looking Santa she'd seen on billboards: bright eyes, jolly laugh, and joy shimmering off him like magic sparkles. Right now, though, his gray hair, long beard, and drawn features made him look like old man winter.

Steven pushed his plate toward the center of the table. "There is a team of doctors meeting daily about her. Keeping Phoebe in a coma is the team's opinion, not just one doctor's opinion, of what's best."

"Steven," — Daed played with condensation on his glass — "I overheard the doctor say that decisions have to be made. What decisions?"

318

"The doctors feel she should be moved to a different hospital, one better suited for handling preemie babies. The ambulance driver was aiming to keep her alive that day, so he went to the closest hospital."

"But their plan is for her to carry to full term," Mamm said. "Then the baby won't be premature, right? And moving her must have some measure of risk, so why chance it?"

Steven put his head in his hands. "I wish I knew."

The doctors had explained this to him half a dozen times. Rhoda ran her fingers across the table, swiping up crumbs she hadn't realized were there. "Phoebe's situation is filled with unknowns, and they want to be ready for whatever may come. The doctor said the risks of moving her should be minimal."

"Should be?" Mamm covered her mouth, her skin almost as white as her hair. When had her mother turned so gray? Rhoda looked across the table at Samuel, wishing he would sit next to her and hold her hand. But with Jacob there, they wouldn't let their guard down and possibly rub salt into his wounds. "If Steven doesn't wish to move her, he doesn't have to."

Daed leveled a look at Steven. "Maybe

I'm too tired or too dumb to hear what you're saying, but if they're waiting to take the baby until he's full term, why move her?"

"You" — Steven briefly pointed at Rhoda — "explain it."

Could she make herself say the words? Rhoda's hands trembled as she took a drink of her water, praying. "If Phoebe . . . doesn't survive, they'll have to take the baby right then. There won't be a minute to spare as they try to save him."

Him. They hadn't even chosen possible names yet.

Daed rubbed his forehead, looking from one person to the other. "When we saw her at the hospital, she looked peaceful and safe, as if she only needs time to get better. Are you saying she could slip from this world at any minute between now and three months from now?"

"Apparently." Rhoda nodded. "I don't understand the difference between the life-support system she's on now and what they would do if she dies, but if she passes, her body won't be able to keep the baby growing and thriving. They would have to take the baby immediately."

She glanced at Jacob. He had his chin propped in his hand and sat staring at the table. He hadn't said a word since sitting down.

Iva rubbed her shoulders as if they ached. "Is there nothing we know for sure?"

"She asks a good question." Steven's eyes filled with tears as he stared at Rhoda. "You have a gift of seeing. Where is it?"

"Steven, I —"

He raised his hand and let it plunk to the table, rattling the flatware. "What good is a gift if you can't use it when it's needed most."

"Steven." Samuel's calm voice held complete authority. "Enough."

Steven stared at her, waiting, wanting her to know without any doubt what needed to be done. Her brother wasn't himself. Tomorrow would he even remember badgering her? She doubted it. How much had he slept or eaten since Phoebe took sick on Saturday?

Rhoda fidgeted with the strings to her prayer Kapp. "I've told you already. On this I have neither a woman's intuition nor a God-given one." At least not yet. Maybe she never would. Seeing Phoebe as she had a few days ago, standing in the hospital near her husband and holding their baby, might be nothing more than the trauma of the events stirring Rhoda's imagination.

Jacob scooted back his chair and propped an ankle on his knee. "If you're not careful, Steven, Rhoda will use her most powerful gift of all. When Phoebe is home months from now, irritable from all she's been through and from being up all night with an infant, Rhoda will tell on you."

Steven stared at Jacob. Then he laughed. Softly at first, and then it was as though the dam broke, and tears, laughter, and chuckles rippled through the weary group. It was a couple of minutes before the room grew quiet again, and Rhoda was grateful Jacob had come.

Steven sighed. "Sorry, Rhodes." He forced a smile, and she saw true remorse for his outburst. "It won't happen again."

"Don't buy it, Rhodes. He just doesn't want you tattling to his wife." This was the Jacob she'd met long ago — all jokes and cutting up. She hoped it was a sign that his heart had healed from the breakup as hers had.

"I won't tell, Steven. And you're forgiven."

Rhoda's Mamm bounced Arie on her lap. "If you need to move Phoebe anyway, why not bring her closer to home?"

Rhoda and Steven had talked about that. It would give the children two sets of grandparents they could stay with. Rhoda, Leah, and Iva loved his children, but they had work to do, and his children needed the stability of grandparents. If something were to happen to either child because their caregivers were spread too thin and were too distracted, Steven wouldn't be able to live with himself.

Besides, Mamm would focus all her attention on making things as easy as possible on Steven and her grandchildren. She'd provide meals and child-care, and they'd take turns staying by Phoebe's side. "They have good hospitals in Lancaster. And Hershey Medical is supposed to be one of the best, isn't it?" Mamm asked.

Daed angled his head, his faint smile wavering. "I don't mean to throw a monkey wrench into this difficult situation, but Samuel and the girls can't stay here without Steven and Phoebe. There has to be a married couple in with single people."

Steven rapped his fingers on the table. "It's not something I've talked to them about yet, but what you're saying is true."

"What if Samuel slept in the harvest kitchen?" Iva asked.

Rhoda's Daed pressed his fingertips against his chest. "I wish that would work. But there are too many rumors circling about this settlement as it is." He gestured at her Mamm and himself. "We don't believe them, Rhodes. But you have to be careful."

Even her Daed had heard the same things Samuel's Daed had? Suddenly she was pretty confident who was stirring rumors — Rueben Glick, the man who'd ripped out her herb and fruit garden years ago. She doubted he was the one voicing the strife, not after Samuel had put his lies into perspective in front of her church leaders and district before the move to Maine. Rueben had probably misled someone into doing the dirty work for him, someone who would sow strife through the most anonymous venue available — the Amish chat line.

"Rumors aside," Steven said. "We're on thin ice with the new bishop as it is."

She supposed the Amish who'd supported their move here had been as patient with their nonconformity as they were going to be, which helped explain why Samuel's father had been so difficult about the situation with Leah and Landon.

"What about Camilla?" Iva asked. "You were living with her when I moved here. Samuel could stay there."

"Not a good idea." Daed shrugged. "Rhoda got away with living at Camilla's house because no one outside this home realized it was happening, but Samuel can't live with an Englisch family and stay in the good graces of the new bishop. Every Amish community needs to be as self-sufficient from the Englisch world as possible. We may need to hire drivers and use hospitals, but surely we don't need to rely on outsiders for a place to sleep."

Leah got up and started stacking plates. "Couldn't he move in with one of the new members of this community? I can't think of an extra room in anyone's house, but surely someone would sleep on the couch for a while and give him a room."

Steven pushed back from the table. "We can't solve this tonight." He stood, his countenance that of a man on the brink of losing the wife he adored.

"Steven." As weariness set in, Rhoda struggled to find the strength to voice her question. She was positive that before Benjamin King left here, he'd extracted some sort of promise from her brother about making sure Landon kept his word and stayed away from Leah. But he deserved the opportunity to visit Phoebe. "I'd like to contact Landon." He'd been Rhoda's assistant long before she partnered with Kings' Orchard, and Phoebe had often invited him to have dinner with the Byler family. Besides, this wasn't about Landon and Leah. Would Steven set aside his position as an Amish preacher long enough to give her permission to try to reach him?

Steven studied the table for several long moments, and then he nodded. "Phoebe would want him included. Do you know how to reach him?"

"Not directly, but his granny will."

Steven nodded. "*You* make the call."

As he left the room, Rhoda saw movement from her peripheral vision, and she shut her eyes tight, praying the image would disappear. Phoebe's voice echoed in her ears, calling her name. *Rhoda . . .*

Rhoda refused to look. *No. No. No!*

Someone touched her shoulder, and she jolted with a gasp. Every eye in the room was on her.

Leah pulled back her hand. "Samuel was talking to you."

Samuel was beside her chair, looking down at her, and his effort to smile didn't hide his concern. "Feel like getting your coat and going for a walk?"

An odd, sickening feeling stirred. She should want to go with him, but anxiety held her captive. Between the emotional upheavals concerning Phoebe and the mounting work load of the farm, Samuel

326

was under enough pressure. She wouldn't tax him by sharing her visions of Phoebe.

"After I call Erlene, I . . . I think I'll turn in for the night."

Maybe a good night's sleep would clear her mind and spirit.

TWENTY-TWO

Rhoda dialed the number Erlene had given her moments ago. Would Landon answer a call from this number?

"Hello?" Landon's familiar voice stole her ability to speak.

Did he have any idea how much she wanted to invite him back, how much she missed him? She couldn't voice it. Neither he nor Leah needed any more mixed messages than they'd already received.

"Leah?" The concern in his voice over the woman he loved made Rhoda fight against tears.

She cleared her throat, determined to find her voice. "It's me, Rhoda. Leah's fine." Well, that was an exaggeration. Leah was probably about the same as Landon — confused and grieved. "There's a problem with Phoebe, and I wanted you to know." She explained the situation as best she knew how. He asked a lot of questions about

Phoebe's prognosis that she didn't know the answer to.

"Landon, I . . . I'm really sorry . . . for how everything played out. Are you okay?"

"I regret giving my word to leave without talking to Leah and agreeing to no contact for a year. But there are days when I think maybe it had to go this way to give her and me perspective on what it would mean for both of us if she were to leave the Amish."

Rhoda soaked in every word as he shared a few things about his new life, but she heard in his voice that he was struggling with anger. Before they let the conversation take them to places they shouldn't go, they said their good-byes. She lowered the phone into its cradle, but she couldn't pull her hand away.

Surely he understood that she could've given the message to Erlene to pass to him, but Rhoda needed to hear his voice. And he needed to be reminded that she valued him as much as always, even though he had the power to whisk Leah away to a life she, her children, and many generations after her might regret.

She propped her elbows on the desk, folded her hands, and covered her mouth. "Father, what is right concerning them? After all we've been through this week, I no longer care what anyone else thinks or fears, including me. I only want to stand on the side of right. Show me, please."

She could hear a couple of people tending to the livestock. When she looked through the office door into the barn, someone in an Amish dress passed by. Was it Leah? Rhoda stood.

Rhoda . . . kumm. Phoebe's voice, as clear as if she were standing in the same room, echoed inside Rhoda.

She walked out of the office, searching for . . . something.

Jacob, Leah, and Samuel were in various places in the barn, each doing some chore.

Samuel came out of a horse's stall and locked it. "Something wrong?" He strode to her, his brown eyes begging her to talk to him.

"No." She hated lying, but she wouldn't put her burden on him, not when he was doing all he could to keep his family together, the reputation of this settlement intact, and the farm running. "I talked to Landon."

Leah tossed the hay in her hands back onto the bale and inched toward Rhoda. "Did he say anything . . . about me?"

"His first concerns were how you're faring. He's struggling too — with hurt, anger, and confusion, much like you are, but he's trying to do what's right. He's got a new job at a guest ranch in Pennsylvania, and that's where he's living."

Leah put her hand on her chest, patting it as she breathed deeply. She had to be greatly relieved to hear — even indirectly — at least this much from him. "How'd he take the news?"

"Hard. He likes Phoebe. When I first hired him, the rest of my family was leery of the trouble it'd cause for me to have an Englisch assistant, especially a young man about my age, but Phoebe invited him to eat with my folks and siblings and won his heart right then." Rhoda looked past Leah, seeing a misty-colored Phoebe. She closed her eyes for a moment. "He's concerned about you and said to let you know he's praying." When had Landon gone from a skeptic to one who prayed? "I'm going to bed."

Samuel stepped in front of her, blocking her way. "We need to talk."

His gentle voice warmed her, but she shook her head. "Not tonight." She went around him, but he moved, blocking her again.

"Rhoda." He stayed put, and when she tried to step around him, he stopped her. "I know you're exhausted, but I know what

331

else I know too." His voice raised several notches. "It's never good when you try to squelch your fears. They then mix with your faith until you can't tell one from the other."

What was he thinking to voice her most private struggles in front of others? Rhoda glanced behind her at Leah and Jacob doing their chores and acting as if they weren't witnessing Samuel being difficult. "Don't do this." Rhoda balled her fists, warring with whether to shove him or burst into tears and run.

Samuel looked at her hands and then his eyes met hers. "You planning on hitting me?"

"The thought crossed my mind."

He postured himself, puffing out his chest and daring her to do it, an understanding smile in place. "When you're done, will you talk to me?"

Tears welled, and she shoved him. "You're a pain. You know that?" A bit of laughter escaped her.

He stepped back on impact, grinning. "Is that it?"

"Just let me pass. Okay?"

He waggled two fingers in front of her eyes. "I see what's going on with you, Rhoda Byler. Make no mistake about that. And things have been building inside you since

Landon left. The situation with Phoebe is a lot, but you keep shoving me away." Anger flashed in his eyes, overtaking his effort to remain gentle.

She knew that right then he didn't care who thought what. He wanted what he wanted. "You have enough to deal with."

"I don't *deal* with you!" Samuel glanced up and seemed to realize what she'd thought was obvious — that Jacob and Leah could hear them. He gestured for her to follow him, and they stepped out of the barn far enough that their voices wouldn't echo off the barn walls. "I'm privileged to be someone you trust." The sincerity in his brown eyes assured her he meant what he said.

"But you're tired, and . . ."

"We've traveled a long, difficult journey to have the freedom to be here for each other. Ya?"

She nodded.

"Don't take that from us, Rhoda. Not ever."

She wanted to melt into his arms for a long, warm hug. But she wouldn't with Jacob here.

She swallowed. "I'm seeing Phoebe . . ."

The argument between Samuel and Rhoda rang in Jacob's ears as he finished filling the water troughs, wound the hose, and put it on the hook. His brother and Rhoda had gone from view, leaving Jacob baffled and raw. At the end of their short but passionate disagreement, he couldn't resist looking up from his chores, and he realized that whether they were enjoying the best life had to give or enduring the worst, Rhoda and Samuel knew and loved each other beyond what made logical sense.

He realized something else too. He often fought for what he shouldn't, like when he kept trying to dig that Englisch construction company out of the mess they were in and when he fought to get Sandra's husband free of his gambling debts. But Jacob often gave up when he should fight, like when he ran from the law instead of trying to clear his name and get his freedom back. Of all the things he gave up on, he worried that giving up on friendships was one of the easiest.

Samuel entered the barn, and Jacob lost his train of thought.

His brother took one of the lit kerosene lanterns off its peg. "You're about done, right?"

"Ya, why?" Leah leaned a pitchfork against the wall.

"I think all of us should call it a day."

"Uh. You're not thinking about this right." Jacob had known before coming here that he'd be offended by Samuel at the slightest thing, and he'd been right. What was his brother thinking? "I'm going to the hospital tomorrow morning, so I won't be around to help. We could get a jump on your work load by mixing the oily concoction and filling the tanks tonight."

"I appreciate that a lot, Jacob. But I'll get an early start on it tomorrow. Okay?"

Jacob grit his teeth. Samuel wanted time with Rhoda, probably to talk for hours. Jacob didn't come here to lend a helping hand so his brother could stay up all night talking to *his* ex-girlfriend. Besides, why now? Weren't there already enough raw emotions without Samuel and Rhoda needing to talk about their feelings? Sometimes love seemed the stupidest thing on the planet.

Yet love is all that really matters. The thought struck him cold, and he immediately wondered what Leah might need from him to help her cope better with Landon being run off and Phoebe being in the hospital.

The thoughts cooled his offense. "I guess I could use some time with my little sister, if she's game." The house didn't have a

335

quiet or private space. "Maybe a walk in the orchard or sitting in the loft."

Leah studied Jacob, looking interested in what he might want. She motioned toward the ladder that led to the hayloft, and Jacob nodded before reaching for a lantern.

"Oh." Samuel's voice made them pause. "There's been an issue with restocking our oil supply. I'd originally thought we'd be out before now, but since Steven hasn't been in the field at all due to Phoebe's illness, we still have some left. However, we only have enough to work the field tomorrow. The order is waiting at the supply store. We just haven't been able to get it."

Jacob wondered what else they were behind on. Getting the oil would take a while, but it was necessary. "I'll return from the hospital before the others, and I'll be sure the driver takes me by the place to get it."

As he and Leah took lanterns with them and climbed into the hayloft, he wrestled with his feelings toward Samuel and Rhoda. Maybe it was jealousy. Or maybe it was just weird being around the girl he'd intended to marry. How soon could he get off this farm and return to . . . to . . . a different kind of loneliness?

While he hung the lanterns, Leah grabbed several old blankets out of a box. She walked to the end of the hayloft that faced the orchard and put several on the floor like a mat. Then she tossed one to Jacob. "When are you leaving?"

"I was just asking myself the same thing. I should go see Phoebe and assure Steven he can call me anytime."

"And help Samuel finish covering the trees in oil before the insects hatch — so at least a week or two? Right?"

That had been his plan before he saw Samuel and Rhoda interact, but Leah was right of course. He nodded. "I guess I'll be here a week." And hopefully not two.

They sat, and through the open door he saw Rhoda and Samuel carrying chairs and lanterns toward the orchard. A silvery, thin fog rested on rows and rows of scraggly-looking trees. They were healthy, of that he had no doubt, but apple trees without leaves reminded him of a haunted forest. He assumed this view appeared completely different to Samuel and Rhoda. They set their chairs at the edge of the orchard.

Samuel and Rhoda — he sighed — there had to be a better topic. "So, how are you really doing?"

Leah talked about Landon and missing him while being angry with him.

Jacob shifted, leaning his back against the

frame of the door. "You don't seem as upset as I thought you'd be."

She tucked one of the blankets over her legs. "I'm plenty stressed, and my heart feels as if someone ran it through a blender."

The last time Leah was really stressed over a breakup, she couldn't keep food down, her stomach hurt all the time, and she lost a lot of weight. Of course, she added to the problems by drinking on the weekends. Leah gave up her willful ways, and Rhoda provided her with a lot of herbal tea concoctions that seemed to help. "How's your stomach?"

"Good. I don't have much appetite these days, but even with all this stress, I'm not having any serious problems." She propped her hands behind her. "A couple of things have given me a few smidgens of peace. One is that whatever happens to us, I know Landon loved me, and I know he's not out trying to erase my memory with some other woman." She looked out the open door. "Despite the agreement Landon made with Daed, when the dust settles, I'll see if I can get his new phone number."

"Leah King."

A sheepish smile shined bright. "I know, I'm a horrible person, right? So tell me where you were when I texted you."

"New Hampshire, building a play set for Casey."

The conversation meandered for nearly an hour before neither one seemed able to think of anything else to say. He'd been gone nine months, and they were finished talking in an hour?

"I'm lying down." She snuggled under a blanket, facing him and using her arm as a pillow. "You haven't told me anything about you, not really." She yawned.

"And yet you're bored already."

She smiled. "I've missed you."

"Good to know someone has."

"Are you serious?" She stifled another yawn. "We all have, and I mean *all* of us. Grief hung in the air for months after you left. Did you think otherwise?"

He didn't know what he'd thought.

"And" — Leah freed one hand from a blanket and shook a finger at him — "I'd bet a year's salary that Rhoda and Samuel have spent more time praying for you and grieving over hurting you than anything or anyone."

"I don't like that."

"Why?"

"It makes it harder to plot against them."

Leah chuckled. "I guess so."

But the earlier argument between Rhoda

and Samuel had made one thing really clear: he didn't understand her, not where it counted most. Not where her greatest strengths crashed head-on into her greatest weaknesses. He could never deny that she was kindhearted, gorgeous, and a gifted horticulturist who worked really hard. And she had a head for business. Nor could he deny that she'd been really good for him from the day they met until the last few months they were together, which was only a year from start to finish, much of which he spent elsewhere, dealing with his past.

"I see they still argue pretty easily."

"Less and less, actually. But one of them will get stubborn about something, and they'll butt heads until they work it out." Her words dragged as her eyes became heavy with sleep.

"You ready to go in?"

"No. I hate the idea of going to my room. Every weight and fear seem to crash in on me once I lie down on my bed. Is it okay if we stay here instead?"

"I doubt I can sleep anyway." Jacob picked up a piece of straw and twiddled it. And twiddled it. And twiddled it. As the minutes ticked by, he mulled over every conversation he'd had with Esther.

What was *wrong* with him tonight? Did

he miss her? He stared skyward, seeing nothing but fog. Seemed fitting somehow. Why would Esther lie? What was the point?

If he knew her better, maybe he'd have the answers he was looking for. That night in town when they sat on the curb talking, she'd said, "It was on this night . . ." But then Ammon interrupted them, and she never finished her sentence. What was she going to say? Would it have helped him know the real Esther Beachy? And on the last evening Jacob was in Virginia, Ammon seemed to be searching for answers of his own, but to what?

Leah took a deep breath. "Hey." She stretched. "I dozed off. How long did I sleep?"

"About an hour. Maybe." He tossed the straw out the hayloft door. Apparently he and Leah didn't have all that much to talk about. He and Rhoda used to talk, but they talked about little things, memories, and events. They also covered some serious stuff but only when she insisted. He'd helped her navigate a few rough patches, like when she didn't want to move here. He listened and helped her because *he* wanted something from her — for her to agree to move.

"We needed you, and you came." Sitting

up, Leah stretched. "You're a good guy, Jacob."

It struck him a little funny that Esther had said something similar not all that long ago.

Leah yawned. "You know that, right?"

"That's not what I was sitting here thinking, but okay." Sure, he was amicable enough, but the longer he thought about who Esther was to him and how quickly he'd given up and walked away, the more he understood why he struggled with loneliness. Leaving people behind that he cared about seemed to be who he was. He gestured toward Rhoda and Samuel. "Did you and Landon talk until the cows came home?"

"Sometimes. Nobody talks like that all the time." She removed her prayer Kapp. "You okay?"

"Would you say we're close?"

"You and me? Sure. As close as you let someone get."

"What does that mean? I've been there for you every time you've asked it of me. We talk. We laugh. Not on this trip, but you know what I mean."

"I agree with everything you just said. You were the only person I trusted at times, no matter what was going on in my life. You even came this time, despite that you're here

342

to help your former girlfriend and Samuel. You're a great guy. Seriously."

"But?"

"You sure?"

"Please."

"Okay. You've seen some Spiderman or Superman movies, right?" She pulled the pins out of her hair, releasing a ponytail that went halfway down her back.

"I've watched pieces of a lot of things on television at Sandra's, so I've probably seen enough. Go ahead."

"You're a superhero. You swoop in, help, and disappear. But the thing about superheroes is people love and admire them and even need them, but no one really knows them. They keep too many secrets."

Is that who he was? "Seems to me most have one girl who finally figures it out, or the hero tells her."

"Exactly, Jacob."

He'd tried that with Rhoda. Of course he was also gone, elusive with details when he returned, and rarely around to help her with whatever was going on in her life.

"It comes natural to hide." He'd been hiding something as far back as he could remember. His first memories of hiding things were at his parents' insistence, because he was gifted at math, and that ability wasn't Plain enough. Then he hid how he detested working the family orchard until he was fourteen, when he convinced his parents to let him move in with his uncle and apprentice as a carpenter. His next secret was that he longed to leave the Amish and practice his math and carpentry skills among the Englisch. At nineteen, living among the Englisch, he hid his eighth-grade education and his ultraconservative roots, embarrassed to be himself. By the time he returned home, he was hiding from the law and hiding from everyone around him what he'd done. "I'm still hiding."

"My secrets were recently exposed to everyone, or I could say 'you and me both.' " She shrugged. "Landon says it's not really our fault. The Old Ways make secrecy a necessary evil for those of us who don't fit the social mores of Old Order Amish. We bring shame to our parents if we comb our hair differently. But you joined the faith, so you've accepted the Old Ways, right?"

"I have. I choose being Amish. I agree with far more than I disagree with. Rather than fighting against the Old Ways, I tend to fight with myself, and I've done that all my life, whether I'm in the Amish world or the Englisch one."

"Sounds to me as if you need to stop being a superhero and find someone to talk to." She tugged the blanket, snuggling against its warmth. "No one got me like Landon, and if his leaving as he did wasn't bad enough, now my heart is broken because of Phoebe, and I can't even talk to the one person who listens in just the right way."

Her words "listens in just the right way" struck him. He'd never opened up to anyone the way he had to Esther, and her drawing force for him was more than her sense of humor and interesting ways. No one listened the way she did. "I met an Amish woman in Virginia, and I came clean about lots of things just because I wanted to."

"Ohhhhh." She leaned toward him. "Do tell."

"I really liked her."

"Did you go out?"

"I thought she was married, so no."

"But if she's not married, why not ask her out?"

"She wanted me to believe she was married. Why?"

"Absolutely no clue. She doesn't really sound like the kind of person you'd want to be friends with."

"The situation is different than it sounds." Esther was a better person than it sounded.

Wasn't she? Why was he defending her? He studied the orchard. It went through so much change with each season, and right now it seemed that people went through drastic changes too.

As he watched Samuel and Rhoda sit in the cold so they could hash out what was troubling her without anyone hearing them, Jacob realized that despite the work load and grievous circumstances, Samuel was content — a kind of contentment a man couldn't get by hiding who he was. Or letting others hide. Why hadn't Jacob known who the real Esther was? She hadn't clarified his misconceptions, but why had he made deceiving him so easy for her when one or two simple, natural questions would have revealed everything?

TWENTY-THREE

Snores and heavy breathing assured Landon his bunkmates were still asleep as he dressed for the day. The sun had yet to rise, but after talking to Rhoda last night, he needed to get some chores done so he could meet with his supervisor as soon as possible.

He went to the barn, flicked on the lights, and began tending the horses. He moved some from their stalls and fed them elsewhere so he could clean their stalls and spread fresh straw ahead of schedule. When the man who'd hired him asked what he'd done this morning, and he would ask, Landon wanted to give an answer that would cause the man to understand he'd work hard to make up for every day he asked off.

He *hated* this with Phoebe. Hated it. But despite his sorrow, his heart pounded with the hope of seeing Leah, of having a chance to talk with her. Since he'd never been in a relationship before, he hadn't known that a bitter argument lasting for weeks was a world better than stone-cold silence. As long as words were flying, there was hope of a breakthrough. But complete stillness between two loves was a telltale sign of death.

Maybe his and Leah's relationship was in a medically induced coma. Or maybe it had died and no one had told Leah and him yet.

With the stalls clean and the horses tended to, he saddled six of them, matching each one's personality and strength with a specific rider. Daylight filled the barn, and Landon turned off the lights. The aroma of coffee brewing wafted through the air, and he knew the smells of bacon and pancakes would soon follow. The hired help would eat breakfast first, giving the guests plenty of time to sleep in and move slowly through the early morning hours. But the hired help ate lunch and dinner after the guests.

He followed the dirt trail to the supervisor's office and tapped on the door.

"Enter." The burly man behind the desk didn't look up as he studied a calendar with the day's events.

Landon removed his cowboy hat. "Sir, I've had a situation come up."

The man made several red marks, checking some items, scratching out others. "It's supposed to rain this afternoon. That'll put a kink in our day." He sighed and looked up. "Landon, right?"

"Yes, sir."

He pointed to a chair. "Tell me what you've done so far today."

Landon reeled off the list.

"Well." The man tossed his pen onto the desk. "You have my attention. So what kind of situation has come up?"

How did one explain who Phoebe was? She wasn't exactly a friend, but she was more than just the sister-in-law of the woman he worked for. She wasn't even a relative of his girlfriend . . . if Leah was still his.

"Someone I worked with for a lot of years is pregnant and in a medically induced coma. She may not survive, and she's a relative and good friend of people I care about. I know I haven't built up any time off yet, but I need to go there."

The man rubbed his clean-shaven face. "You intend to quit so you can go there full-time?"

"No. I need this job." He made enough to cover his truck payment and health insurance. Plus this job included room and board. "I don't know much yet. I should get a call later today or early tomorrow that

349

will clear up a few things — like what hospital they'll move her to and when."

He nodded. "We hired you over others because you seemed stable. But things like this can't be scheduled. When you know more, come back and see me. I'll do what I can to swap your workdays and to help you get consecutive days off so you can visit. But you have to make up any lost time, and when you're here, you'll be expected to work really hard."

Landon stood and held out his hand. "Thank you." With that weight lifted off him, he left the office. When he stepped outside, Gabi stopped him.

She smiled, her cowgirl hat unable to hide the curiosity in her eyes. "There you are." She looked behind him. "Coming out of the boss's office. You quitting?"

"No. Just need a few concessions to my schedule due to a friend having health issues." It was easy to call Phoebe a friend when not trying to be super aboveboard with a boss.

"A girlfriend?"

That was typical of Gabi. She didn't mind asking questions most would consider too personal. But her forwardness seemed to be the worst thing about her, and he answered her questions when it suited him and ignored her when it didn't. "A work-acquaintance friend. She has two little children and is pregnant, and no one is sure if she'll survive."

"That's awful. If you need to swap days with me, just say the word. Some of the others will feel that way too." She nodded toward the mess hall. "Hungry?"

"Actually, yeah." He put his hat on and fell into step beside her.

Jacob's knees weakened at the sight of Phoebe, and his eyes stung with unshed tears. He sat before he toppled. Her pale body lay unconscious. Her rounded belly bulged from under the sheets. She'd always been so kind to him. No matter what, she never said a discouraging word or gave off a negative vibe, even when Steven was frustrated with how often Jacob had needed to disappear, sometimes for months.

Heart monitors beeped, one for her and one for the baby. Despite the grating sound that indicated beating hearts and a machine that pushed oxygen into Phoebe's lungs, she didn't appear to be in this world any longer.

Medical personnel came in and out, milling about her as if she were no more than a piece of furniture that needed dusting or rearranging. Jacob longed to ask one of them what Phoebe's chances were, but he didn't dare, not with other family members in the room. Maybe the family knew and wasn't talking about it, or maybe if they learned the truth, they couldn't hold up under the cold facts of stats. When Phoebe's mom tried to pass a Dixie Cup across the bed to her husband, she dropped it, spilling its contents on her daughter.

Phoebe never once moved, not when the cold water hit her or when they dried her off with a towel and covered the wet sheet with a thick blanket. It didn't matter to Phoebe if she was wet or dry or warm or cold or if people were there or still at the farm working. None of it mattered, and yet she continued to breathe.

Steven escorted the family out of the room, giving Jacob some time alone with her. At first he sat there in silence. When a nurse came in to change her IV bag, Jacob asked about Phoebe's chance of survival.

"Hard to tell."

"But you have an idea, and I'd appreciate a gut-honest answer."

She watched him for a minute before shrugging. "Her body will be worn out before the battle is over. If I were you, I'd brace the family for the strong possibility they won't see her conscious again." She continued adjusting Phoebe's monitors. "Right before losing consciousness the last time and before the doctor put her in a coma, she grabbed his arm and pulled him close, begging him to do whatever it took to save the baby." The nurse lifted her head, appearing truly touched by the situation. "We see all kinds here, but her words . . . Well, we're hoping to give her what she asked. I understand that her husband is talking to the doctors right now, trying to decide what to do about moving her. The doctors are clear on their goal — to keep her alive for as long as possible so the baby can have the best chance of surviving and thriving outside the womb." After the nurse gathered the empty IV bag and other paraphernalia, she paused. "If you want to comfort her, talk to her. We don't know if people in her condition can understand the words, but they seem to respond to the love being shared."

We probably won't see her conscious again?

Jacob tried to think of something to say to her. After lying there hearing all those hospital noises, she would probably appreciate a familiar voice. "Hey, Phoebe." He couldn't remember the last time he felt this uncomfortable. "I . . . saw Arie and Isaac yesterday. Since I was here last, they've grown like apples in summertime." His words began to pour out as he told Phoebe all that was special about her and how Kings' Orchard couldn't have survived in Maine without her, let alone thrived and made a profit.

As he talked, he realized she'd rarely stepped into the orchard, but she was as much a part of making the farm and new settlement a success as anyone.

When Jacob heard Steven coming down the hall talking, he put his hand in hers and told her a final good-bye.

TWENTY-FOUR

Winds played across the orchard, and Leah took a deep breath of the crisp evening air. Despite Jacob and her spending most of last night in the loft talking, she didn't feel exhausted today. With every move she made, she prayed for Phoebe, and she knew many Amish were doing the same.

Crist was just over the hill at the start of several mounds, setting rodent traps. Leah tugged on the ropes attached to each end of a three-by-three-foot board. Holding on to the ropes the way someone would clutch the chains of a playground swing, she put the board on a fresh piece of ground at the base of the tree and stood on it. This crushed rodent mounds, the ones closest to the tree, which she'd been unable to reach while riding on a toboggan.

She wished Phoebe were here, in the house doing what she did best — making it a home for all of them. The few who weren't at the hospital were in the fields working again. They had little choice. Could Phoebe sense how much everyone loved her? It all felt unreal. Steven, the children, and the parents were at the hospital. Jacob had gone too. Like her and Iva, he needed to see Phoebe . . . although it didn't make a lot of sense. She certainly wasn't aware of who was or wasn't there.

"Leah." Crist topped the knoll, driving the wagon. "I'm really hungry. You about ready to head back?" Rhoda's Mamm had packed sandwiches for everyone to eat while working, but it had to be nearly five by now.

Ever since he'd said he came to Maine because of her, the vibes between them had been a bit awkward, but their conversations flowed more easily now that they'd spent a few outings with Iva. Since almost every relationship she had was negatively impacted by the storm surrounding her and Landon, she was grateful that she and Crist were getting along.

After talking to Pastor Weld last week, she'd spent a lot of time thinking about what he'd said, and now she was certain of one thing — to find her heart's desire, she had to embrace the possibilities beyond the Amish faith. When everyone's nerves weren't so raw, she'd return to attending the local church. Her family could keep her from Landon, but they couldn't keep her from going to an Englisch church or seeking to discover what her true heart's desire was.

Crist brought the rig to a stop. "Aren't you hungry?"

Now that he mentioned it, she realized how hungry she was. "Ya. I wonder if the Mamms have returned." She tossed the homemade mound smasher into the back of the wagon and climbed onto the bench seat next to Crist.

"They must have, because I definitely smell food cooking." He whistled softly as he drove.

The cool air rippled past her face as the rig ambled among the trees. It was the kind of weather that made the traditional Amish clothing feel cozy and comfy.

Crist sighed contentedly, and they rode in silence until they reached the driveway. With the reins in hand, he gestured ahead of them. "Iva seems to want us."

Iva stood halfway between the house and the barn, motioning for them to come to her. Crist stopped a few feet away, and they jumped down.

"Hey! I was hoping to catch you two before you went into the house." Iva strode toward them. Was that a mischievous grin on her face? "I'm afraid I bear terrible, awful, horrific news of the worst kind."

"About Phoebe?" Crist's eyes grew intense.

"No." Leah swatted at him, some three feet from where he stood. "Have you even met Iva?" Rolling her eyes at him, Leah frowned. Didn't he know Iva at all? "Can't you read her body language?"

Iva bit her bottom lip, acting playfully hush-hush. "Rhoda's in the kitchen . . . cooking."

Leah covered her mouth, stifling a snorting laugh. "Iva." Her correcting tone only caused Iva to shrug, grinning.

Crist sniffed the air. "Something smells pretty good to me."

"Oh, poor Crist." Leah patted his arm in mock comfort. "He hasn't yet realized that aromas can be deceiving."

"It's an important lesson, Crist." Iva nodded. "But I haven't had anything except a sandwich at eleven this morning, and I'm *so* hungry." Iva grimaced as she looked at the house.

Leah chuckled. "With Steven's and Phoebe's Mamms here, I was hoping they'd returned from the hospital and cooked."

Iva shook her head. "Didn't happen. Any

chance of us getting out of this?"

"Oh, come on." Crist sounded genuinely confused. "Rhoda makes the best canned goods I've ever had, and they sell like hotcakes, so I'm not the only one who thinks so. I hear that Orchard Bend Farms can't keep up with demand from the stores and shops it supplies."

Leah interlaced her fingers, amused at Iva's humor and embellishment of the situation. "We do not deny that. Rhoda's amazing at plenty of other things too, but, trust us, cooking dinner is *not* on the list."

"What list is it on, then?" Crist seemed to be coming around to the joke.

"Nausea," Iva offered.

They all laughed, but Leah tried to think of possible options. "If we figure out something else to do about dinner — maybe eat at Crist's — do you think Rhoda and Samuel will care that we're not eating with them?"

"Are you kidding? They're so lost in each other's world, they won't even notice we didn't join them." Iva was enjoying her exaggeration, but there was a bit of truth to it.

"Well," — Crist reached into his back pocket and pulled out his wallet — "we could always take a ride into town and get some pizza." He searched through his billfold. "I have forty-two dollars on me. That should be plenty, right?"

Iva grabbed his shoulders and shook him. "You are my hero!" She released him, straightening the sleeves of his shirt where she'd crumpled them. "Leah?"

"Ya, that's a good plan. I just need to leave a note on the desk in the barn in case they start to wonder where everyone is."

"Hurry, Leah." Iva headed for the wagon. "Crist, kumm. Take us away so we may dine *without* fear of what we put in our mouths and bodies!"

Iva was remarkably good at helping Leah find something to enjoy about each day, despite how much she missed Landon.

Landon.

Fresh ache flooded her, but she refused to dwell on him. All her energy to muster hope and prayers would stay focused on Phoebe for now. She missed him. Needed him. But Landon had chosen to leave.

Samuel picked up the calendar from the kitchen table and compared it to the to-do list.

If Jacob would stay for a few more days, and if Landon could return —

"Ow!" Rhoda dropped a Pyrex dish onto

the open door of the stove.

"Did you burn yourself?" Samuel set down the calendar.

She waved her hand through the air, trying to cool it. "Not too bad."

He rose. "Let me see." He took her wrist. The pads of her thumb and index finger were fiercely red. "Kumm." He led her to the sink and turned on the cold water.

"What is it about getting a meal on the table without a catastrophe that escapes me?"

"Don't know." He left her at the sink and got some ice out of the freezer. Once he had the ice in a sandwich bag and wrapped in a dishtowel, he returned to where she stood. He brushed stray hairs from her face, longing to kiss her. "But the dinner looks and smells great, so you're getting the hang of it, right?"

She narrowed her eyes. "Are you babying me? If you are, you need to stop. Now. And forever."

He rattled the ice compress and tossed it at her. Just as he'd known last night that they needed to talk, he knew this side of her too — the one that became defensive after being vulnerable. The first time he saw it, Jacob was in hiding, and Rhoda appeared to be on the edge of going to jail for a crime she didn't commit. She'd finally given in to her fears and cried while Samuel held her. A few days later when he tried to bring a little reprieve to her life with a trip to look at dogs they might buy, she'd accused him of mollycoddling her.

He knew her better than he knew himself, and he would love her entirely too much for the rest of his life. If right here, right now he asked her to marry him, would she say yes?

If they were married, he could stay on the farm when Steven left with Phoebe. But the living arrangements would be a perk, an opportunity to sidestep waiting another agonizing year and a half — if not longer — before they could marry. Since the Amish were allowed to marry only during the wedding season, which was in the fall, that created a problem for orchard owners. How could they marry while they worked day and night harvesting and canning apples? So they'd have to wait until winter, and since Jacob wouldn't truly be ready to see them marry during the next wedding season, they'd have to wait at least until the following one. If they waited until Jacob was truly ready to see Rhoda marry, it might be almost three years.

But if Samuel just forgot about waiting, if

he told her how he felt and asked her to be his, how would she react? Would she see a proposal as him looking out for the farm and the fledgling district? He wouldn't deny that played a part. How could it not? But more than that, the need to do what was right for the farm also provided him an excuse to do what he longed to do: ask the woman he loved to marry him.

"Samuel," — she snapped her fingers — "get back to work, or I'll have to send you to your office." She smiled. "Or maybe to the doghouse."

"You'd send me to the doghouse for trying to be nice?"

She frowned, but it didn't hide the gleam of a teasing dare in her eyes. "Quite possibly, ya."

"Fine." He returned to the table and picked up the farmer's almanac and a pencil. He should be in the barn office, close to the phone and more focused on work, but he much preferred being near Rhoda. The deeper bond he'd felt since last night seemed odd. They'd discussed nothing romantic, no dreams of the future. They'd talked about her seeing Phoebe and the trauma of her little sister's murder and dozens of memories and wounds she'd suffered due to her intuition.

Samuel tapped the pencil's eraser on the table. "Last night helped you, right?"

Rhoda set aside the ice compress and spooned up a good helping of the casserole on a plate. "More than I knew was possible."

He pushed his work stuff out of the way, making room for the plate.

She dipped up stir-fry vegetables. "You gonna use last night as your get-out-of-the-doghouse-free card for years to come?"

"I don't know. Can I get away with it?"

Her pursed lips didn't hide her grin as she set his plate on the table. "My fear, Mr. King," — she sat in the chair nearest him — "is that you can and will get away with far more than is wise for a headstrong man such as yourself."

If that was true, could he convince her they should marry? "Aren't you eating?"

"Later." She picked up his notes. "I'm not hungry. You said you were. And I want to be sure there's plenty for others."

He bowed his head, but his silent prayer wasn't about blessing the food. What did God think of him setting aside how Jacob might feel so he could ask Rhoda to marry him? Was Samuel wrong to want to end the slow progression of their relationship with a quick wedding?

She cleared her throat, and he raised his head. In an Amish home it was the man's place to clear his throat and end the prayer. How long had he been praying?

"Beseeching God for a meal that is edible and safe?"

"What? No." Samuel took a forkful of food and blew on it. "It smells and looks amazing." He took a bite.

Oh. He tried to swallow without making a face, and he prayed he didn't gag. Thankfully, Rhoda was looking over the work schedule. Realizing he didn't have a drink, he rose and got a glass of water. Could he spit the bite out in the sink without her realizing it?

He washed it down with several gulps.

She flipped through some of the notes he'd made. "How is it?"

What could he say?

She turned, and her quizzical look was soon replaced by a knowing one. "It can't be that bad."

He wanted to defend himself, to assure her that he hadn't said it was bad, but instead he stayed by the sink, drinking more water.

"Fine." She rose and whistled for the dogs. "So the only thing I'm able to cook is scrambled eggs." She paused, studying him.

"A person could live off eggs and apples."

Her disappointment crept into disbelief. "You *hate* eggs."

"I may have discovered something I hate more." He gave an apologetic shrug. What did she do to food? "But I love *you.*"

She narrowed her eyes, thrusting the plate toward him. "Keep being overly nice to me, and you'll be wearing this food."

The dogs danced at her feet, ready to eat the leftovers — all ninety-nine-point-nine percent of the food he hadn't eaten. His stomach growled.

"This is another reason to have dogs, I suppose." She set the plate on the floor. The dogs rushed forward, took a lick, and backed away. They looked up at Rhoda as if to say, *You're kidding, right?*

Rhoda gasped. Samuel tried to stifle the laughter bubbling within, but it broke loose, and Rhoda joined him. He came up behind her and wrapped his arms around hers as they peered down at the dogs. Their laughter faded, and he propped his chin on her shoulder. "Yum. Eggs. Right?" He kissed her cheek before he returned to the sink to get more water.

"There's no telling what spice or spices I added too much of." Rhoda sat and picked up the almanac. "The humor of this incident aside, apparently I'm fairly incompetent at everything but tending the orchard and canning the harvest."

"It won't cause me to love you any less."

The first time Rhoda and he met, he'd thought she was married. He was concerned that she spent all her time tending her fruit garden and canning and didn't take good care of her family. He'd been ready to correct her, and when he learned she was single, he'd been relieved for her nonexistent husband's and children's sakes. Now he didn't care that she wasn't a traditional Amish woman. Or that she might never be a skilled *Hausfraa*. Now he was ever so grateful for exactly who she was.

He crouched beside her chair. "Rhoda, I know what we could do." Though he knew it wasn't customary for Amish men, he eased onto one knee. "You could marry me." He took her soft hand into his. "Please."

She didn't blink, and her breathing seemed to stop. A few moments later her utter shock faded. "Samuel," she whispered, caressing his cheek. Her eyes misted, but her warm smile defied all the pressure of what was happening around them. She lowered her lips to his. "With my whole heart . . . ya."

TWENTY-FIVE

After Jacob ate with Steven at the hospital, he got in the van with the driver. The man didn't own a typical family van but a work van, which was good for carrying a lot of folks *and* hauling supplies. They went to the supply store and picked up the oil before heading back to the farm. Jacob rode, looking out the passenger's window, lost in dozens of thoughts.

He couldn't recall the driver's name. He'd met him this morning while climbing into the van with Steven and both sets of parents, and he knew he'd been one of two drivers shuttling the family back and forth to the hospital since Monday.

Had it really been only five days since Phoebe had entered the hospital?

The driver pulled into the farm, and he even helped Jacob unload the drums of oil.

Jacob looked around. Where was everyone? The dogs weren't even barking. A carriage and one horse were gone. He paid the driver and headed for the barn office. As he suspected, a note was taped to the phone. *Gone into town to get pizza. Crist, Leah, and Iva.*

The dogs barked then, and Jacob looked out the office window. Samuel and Rhoda came out of the house, holding hands. But within a few seconds, they released their grip and put distance between them.

Disappointment waged war with acceptance. Would he ever be able to see them together without feeling as if he'd been sucker-punched? He believed they were meant to be together, and his feelings for her had faded greatly, but how could they expect him to stay here and help?

Jacob drew a deep breath and left the barn. The last thing he needed right now was to get caught in an enclosed space with those two. That would be too many emotions colliding.

"Hey." Samuel strode across the lawn, putting more distance between him and Rhoda. "You're back."

"I am." Jacob held up the note. "Leah, Iva, and Crist went to get pizza."

Samuel glanced at Rhoda as she continued walking their way. Was he concerned how she'd take that news? After all, she was supposed to fix dinner tonight.

Rhoda closed the gap between them. "You hungry, Jacob?"

"I ate at the hospital."

"Gut." Rhoda held out her hand for the note. "It's dangerous to be hungry around here." She glanced at the note. "It's Leah's handwriting, but she didn't jot down the time they left. Samuel, if you call the pizza place, you may catch them, and they could bring you pizza."

"Not a bad idea." Samuel started to leave and then paused.

Rhoda shooed him. "Go. I haven't had a moment alone with Jacob."

Samuel disappeared, and Rhoda rolled gravel around under one foot. "How are you? Really?"

He wasn't sure how he felt about her asking. "Fine."

She gazed up at him with her piercing eyes, and he was sure she knew every truth he'd ever hid from anyone. "I am sorry. Painfully. Awfully. Terribly so. I should've been the one to let you go."

"You're kidding. Would you have taken *that* away from me too? I saw what I needed to, and I had the strength to walk away. It let me be a hero of sorts, making a clean cut for all our sakes." Although now that

Leah had given him her description of a hero, Jacob wasn't so sure he wanted to be one anymore.

"I hadn't thought of it that way."

"I let go for both of us to find happiness, Rhoda. Not just for you." It would simply take him longer to find that joy, in part because he had to figure out who he was all over again — not because he'd lost her, but because he was free from his legal mess and free to pursue his dreams as a skilled, joined-the-faith Amish man.

She stared at the barn. "I didn't know how I felt about Samuel, not until the day it came to me that we needed to build a harvest kitchen on this property. Revelation hit, and I realized how I felt. In turn, I immediately agreed with what you had been telling me — that you and I needed to leave here together."

"It doesn't matter."

"Of course it does. I don't want you to think Samuel and I were sneaking around. The three of us are connected. We own a business together. And we'll be family once . . ."

"You marry Samuel."

"Ya."

"When?"

She searched his eyes. "With Phoebe and

the situation as it —"

"Soon, then." He didn't need her to finish the sentence, but his heart pounded as he faced the choices in front of him. He could react with the offense he felt, or he could respond in a way he'd be pleased with years from now.

"If things were different, we'd wait until you had someone and no longer minded." She turned toward the orchard as if it called to her even now. "That will happen, you know. You'll look at me and think, *I thank God I'm not with* her."

"I've had days of that already."

"I'm sure you have." She smiled, gentle understanding radiating from her. "If you'd tried the dinner I just fixed Samuel, you'd be laughing at him for thinking he wants to marry me."

"That bad?"

"The dogs turned up their noses."

Laughter burst from him. "You're kidding."

She shook her head, her cheeks a pink glow. "I wish."

Her body language said she wanted to walk, so he ambled toward the orchard. Jacob took a cleansing breath. "He always planned on marrying the perfect Hausfraa."

She fell into step beside him. "Ya, well,

you can marry her and wag it in his face."

Her humility and the hope she gave him about his future eased the offense he wrestled with when it came to Samuel and her. "We had some good times, didn't we?"

"Don't ever doubt that. You taught me to laugh again, Jacob. You brought me hope and love. You lifted unbearable guilt off me by making it clear there was no way I could have saved Emma. And my heart broke with yours the day you left here. It didn't really start to mend until I knew in my soul that you'd weathered the worst."

Why did it feel as if they were able to talk more openly and honestly now than when they were together? "We don't have much of anything left to hide from each other. Do we?"

"Not much."

"I can't come to the wedding, not this soon." Amish tradition said any single sibling of marrying age was to be in the wedding party and celebrate with the couple all day and into the night.

"I understand. We'll make some excuse as to why you're out of town. Maybe even a few people will choose to believe it since we'll have to get a special exemption to be allowed a quickly planned wedding. But" — she poked his shoulder — "when you find

373

the best woman for you and get married, I'm going to come up to you throughout your wedding day and whisper, 'I told you so.' "

He liked the idea of falling in love and being loved above all others by a woman he couldn't even imagine yet. "You do that."

"How are Sandra and Casey?"

Her genuine concern touched him, now as always. He'd put his sense of duty to Sandra and Casey ahead of Rhoda so many times, and yet she'd never doubted that he was faithful to her or that he was doing the right thing by his friends.

"Good. I was with them when I got word about Phoebe."

"I'm glad they have you."

"Sometimes, when I'm really weary of dealing with Sandra, I wonder if I've just convinced myself how important it is I stay connected."

"Then I'll pray about that too, that it becomes clearer in your heart why God's asked this of you."

Such kindness and sincerity. No wonder he'd fallen in love with her. But as they talked, he realized something. He wasn't in love with her anymore.

Rhoda was too complicated, which was why Samuel had stayed up most of last night talking to her, and when her gift stirred, she grew restless and difficult and became a target of those who feared her intuition wasn't of God. "Can I ask you something?"

"Anything."

"Suppose a new guy shows up in town, and he meets a really interesting woman, and they work on projects together, but she lets him believe she's married when she isn't. Why would she do that?"

"How old is she?"

"Does it matter?"

"Definitely. The thinking and rationale of a teen or a twenty-year-old is totally different from that of a woman in her mid-twenties."

"She's about two years older than he is."

"Older?" Rhoda's eyebrows arched.

"Hey, watch the tone."

"No, I didn't mean anything by that. I just caught a glimpse that put everything into perspective."

"How?"

"You said the guy is new in town, so anyone who sees them together thinks she believes she's snagged a man."

"No one saw."

"Jacob, someone always sees, especially among the Amish. *You* just didn't notice them. But she knew people were whispering about her, saying the old maid thinks she's snagged a catch. She risked her reputation."

Could she be right about that? "Are the Amish that rough on single women?"

"I don't think they mean to be, but ya. Some started calling me an old maid at twenty, and they meant it." Exasperation filled her face. "They earnestly warned me that I'd better get busy trying to hook a man. At twenty! Anyway, she must have strength of character to put herself in that position. And a strong desire not to marry. So the question is, how do you . . . I mean, how does the man feel about just being her friend?"

"It's not an unappealing idea."

"Is she interesting?"

"Yes, and witty and unconventional and mysterious." A horn tooted, and Jacob turned, realizing how far they'd walked. "Must be another family meeting."

"Just when it was getting really interesting."

"Any chance this could stay between us?"

"No chance. It's an absolute." She made the motion of zipping her lips and throwing away the key. "Maybe one day, Jacob, you and I can be friends again."

He doubted it. His self-esteem, or maybe

just his ego, had taken a beating to have once loved her and then lost her to his brother. Even though Jacob could see they'd never been the good match he'd once thought, he still felt he was doing well simply to be here and behave like a gentleman.

While he and Rhoda walked back to where Phoebe's and Steven's parents stood, Crist drove the carriage onto the driveway. Soon they all stood in a group. Leah had two boxes of pizza in her arms, and Jacob saw Samuel eye them. A desire to tease his brother tugged on Jacob, but he just wasn't ready.

Steven slid his hands into his pants pockets. "She's weak, and her oxygen levels aren't good, but keeping her fever down is no longer a constant battle, and the flu will have run its course by tomorrow. That's our good news. The battle with the viral pneumonia is another story. Now that she's survived the flu, the doctors think her best chance of beating the viral pneumonia is to be in a hospital that specializes in pulmonary conditions. One of the best facilities is in Boston, but that's hours from here and from Daed's place in Pennsylvania. She needs to be where family can visit, and I need to be able to visit her every day and still have time for the children. I've chosen Lancaster Medical." He looked at Rhoda. "Does anyone disagree with that?"

Rhoda lowered her head and shrugged. "It sounds fine."

Jacob felt bad for her. She'd made it clear she had no more insight than anyone else on what to do, but Steven kept hoping.

Leah passed the pizza boxes to Crist. "When, Steven?"

"Monday. I'll go with her in the medical transport vehicle." He focused on his sister. "Rhoda, I'm sorry, but when I leave, I'm taking the children and their grandparents, and I'm not coming back until Phoebe is with me." Steven closed his eyes. "If God wills it and she survives all this, she'll need at least a month of rest and physical therapy."

Samuel shifted. "Listen, we need help. Everyone leaves on Monday, but that gives us two days, three if we work on Sunday, to get the trees covered in oil. If we have enough hands in the orchard, we can do this, especially if the women are here to cook and bring food to the field."

"He's right." Steven nodded. "If all the trees are coated with the oil mixture before everyone leaves on Monday, then, barring an untimely frost, Samuel has a fighting chance of the crop being healthy enough to keep the bills paid with the harvest. Any volunteers?"

The group gave their consensus, and Jacob managed to nod his head. Orchard Bend Farms needed him beyond Monday. More than likely Samuel and Rhoda would be married by the end of next week so they could stay on the farm and keep working it. "I'll stay until the trees are sprayed. Then it's time for me to go."

Rhoda's pursed lips formed a sad but encouraging smile. "That's plenty to give, Jacob. Denki."

When would Samuel and Rhoda share their news about their plan to marry? Now wasn't the time. Jacob understood that. He only hoped he would be gone when the announcement was made.

Emotions piled on top of him, as numerous as dust particles and as heavy as gold. Was he wrong to leave when so much rested on Samuel's and Rhoda's shoulders? Was he letting his family down?

He had to talk to someone, and he knew exactly who that someone was.

But would Esther even speak to him after the way he left?

TWENTY-SIX

Rhoda leisurely paced the hospital room, Bible in hand, reading Phoebe's favorite passages of Scripture — the book of Ephesians. She paused and watched Phoebe. What was the saying, "So close and yet so far"? That's how it felt with Phoebe. Rhoda moved to the chair and took her by the hand.

"You have to keep fighting. We're praying, just like I've been praying out loud since I arrived hours ago. I . . . I wish you were going to be at the wedding. You'll be moved Monday to a hospital close to our parents, and everyone will leave the farm together. Samuel and I will marry on Thursday and return to the farm Friday. It's all happening so fast."

Was it right to get married while Phoebe's life hung in the balance? All of life seemed upside down. Everything except her and Samuel.

"I've been seeing visions of you, and I heard you call to me." Just like Rhoda had heard Emma's voice after she'd died. "But Samuel helped me understand what was happening and why." Rhoda ran her thumb over the back of Phoebe's hand. "I should start calling him Stonewall Samuel." She laughed. "When I try to run from all that frightens me, he won't let me. He insists I dump all my fears and visions and pieces of intuition onto him. We talk until I have peace. I think I understand myself and my gift better now. It wasn't really your voice or Emma's. It was my own recollections mixing with trauma that taunted me."

Even now warm peace surrounded her, but one thing troubled her. Phoebe had spent years looking forward to the day Rhoda would marry. She'd prayed for the right man long before Rhoda even admitted to herself that she might want to marry one day.

"You'd be proud of Steven. He's making hard decisions, good ones, I think. No one knows for sure, not even the best doctors." The men were in the orchard spraying the trees. Rhoda's and Phoebe's Mamms were cooking while Leah and Iva watched the children, did laundry, and delivered drinks and food to the men. "And I'm here with you because Steven wanted someone with you, and I won't get much time with you after today." Rhoda squeezed her hand. "The idea of marriage is terrifying. What if I can't keep his love? Do men think of such things?"

Rhoda longed for Phoebe to open her eyes, to talk with her. Without Phoebe who would she ask such things? Rhoda took a sip of water and cleared her throat. "I know you want the baby to live, and you know everyone who loves you will do their best to help raise him right, but he needs his Mamm."

I need you.

"Steven won't be the same great dad without you. Did he tell you that you're having a boy?"

The sheet over Phoebe's belly moved. Rhoda's pulse quickened, and she lifted the sheet out of the way, revealing Phoebe's rounded stomach. Sensors on her taut skin were connected to a monitor that showed the baby's heart rate. Phoebe had on a hospital gown, but her stomach was bare, probably to make the wires attached to it more easily accessible. Phoebe's stomach seemed to wad on one side, and then her skin quivered in that very spot.

"The baby's moving." Rhoda glanced at

Phoebe's face. "Can you feel him?" She placed her hand on Phoebe's belly. "Little one." Chill bumps ran from Rhoda's head to her feet as she realized he missed hearing his mother's voice. Rhoda had to tell her brother to keep talking to the baby, to read aloud and make sure his son knew his Daed was still here. "We're here for you, little one. You stay strong and fight. Do you hear your aunt? You fight."

This planet needs you.

It felt as if God was speaking the words inside her. Rhoda took Phoebe's hand in one hand, rested her other hand over the baby, and prayed as she'd never done before. As real as the living, moving baby inside Phoebe, Rhoda felt faith and hope move inside her.

A thought of Jojo and her daughter washed over her, and she went to the phone and dialed 411. In less than a minute, Rhoda had the store number and was dialing. She hoped Jojo was at work. A voice came on the line, and despite a slight tug of anxiety, Rhoda asked for Joella and waited as they connected her.

"This is Joella. How may I help you?"

"Jojo, it's Rhoda Byler, and I had an encouraging thought about you and your daughter. I'm hoping you'll let me share it."

Jojo clicked her tongue. "Am I supposed to say no after some premonition led you to Camilla?"

"Do you believe in the forces of good and evil?"

"I'd be an idiot not to, but what controls those forces is anybody's guess."

That was enough to build on. "Darkness tried to extinguish the light in you. But you held on to all of it you could, and now you're doing all you can to protect the light in Sophia. I think that's remarkable. And as a believer in God, I think He's very pleased with you."

"I can't say I return the favor to God."

"No. How could you? You prayed for help as a child, and none came."

"How . . . do you know that?"

Rhoda hadn't meant to let that slip. "Probably the same way you look at Sophia and know things. Maybe it was your body language when you tried to hold back your years of anger while telling Camilla how you felt about her keeping Zachary in an abusive home. I really don't know. Sometimes love just knows."

She scoffed, and Rhoda knew she didn't believe anyone cared except the married guy. "Anyway, I'll let you get back to work. I just needed to let you know that I believe you've done a great job protecting Sophia so far."

"I know I haven't done great. I . . . I try, though."

"It's remarkable that you have it in you to try as hard as you do. We don't all start at the same place. With a home like you grew up in, you began life in the negative numbers. But you're not there anymore."

"But you think that I'll get there again and that I'll drag Sophia with me. Isn't that what this call is about?"

Rhoda hadn't realized how difficult it would be to encourage someone who was jaded. "I think you're being tempted to make an unhealthy choice and God is giving you an out."

"And that *out* is Camilla?"

Rhoda hoped Samuel would agree with what she was going to say. "It can be me if you like. We'll make room for you and Sophia on the farm. It's not ideal, but it's a start."

Stony silence. Had she hung up? "Jojo?"

"I'm here." But she said nothing else for more than a minute. "I didn't want any parents in our lives, and Zachary, Sophia's dad, disagreed with me. When I was pregnant, he'd say, 'We should tell them about the baby. Sometimes he'd cup his hands around my fat belly and speak as if he were Sophia and say, 'Tell them, Mommy. Tell them.' So, yeah, I believe there's a higher power involved here." Jojo grew quiet. "Why would God let me be beaten and then fight so hard for Sophia?"

"I can only guess at what happened. Parents are meant to be our first protection, and yours were tempted to be horrible people, and they gave into it. Maybe because of their own childhood. I don't know. But you're fighting for good in Sophia's life, and God has joined you in that fight."

"Why me?"

"It's not just you. God is light, and light slips through every cranny and crevice it can."

"If He's God, He doesn't have to wait for a crevice to open."

"Jojo, we barely understand ourselves." Rhoda had made her life, and the lives of the people she cared about, so much harder because she didn't know half of what went on inside her, much less the hows and whys of God's actions. "We see our world every day, and we're still stumped by our actions and reactions. How can we possibly grasp God?"

"Yeah. I can see that. I . . . I need to go."

Rhoda hung up. As unexpected as it was,

she felt as if she'd made some progress, but a few questions pressed in. Should she call Camilla and tell her, or would that just get her hopes up?

She decided against telling Camilla, but she had something she and Camilla could do — study the affects of childhood abuse on adults. If Rhoda understood more, she'd have a better chance of saying the right thing the next time they talked . . . if there was a next time.

And on the off chance that Jojo accepted her invitation to move in with them, how would Samuel feel about that?

Twenty-Seven

A woman in her midthirties, wearing a white lab coat, stood beside Phoebe, mashing buttons on a machine that dispensed liquid medicine into one of the tubes. Leah could barely keep her eyes open. Everyone in the family had been scurrying in all directions since Phoebe had collapsed more than a week ago.

Steven had everyone pack and leave the farm that morning, including Iva. Since she wasn't family, she didn't need to be here for Phoebe or Samuel and Rhoda's wedding. But Iva was reluctant to stay there by herself, and Steven saw no reason for it. He'd said that by herself she couldn't get much done except office work — mostly bookkeeping — and she could bring that with her. Besides, she didn't want to be the only one there when Samuel and Rhoda returned after the wedding to spend a few days alone. So Crist was taking care of the farm and feeding the horses and dogs.

Leah found it hard to believe she was sitting in a different hospital. Everything was similar — super-bright hallways and dimly lit patient rooms; a stale, morning-breath smell lingering in the air; and the same constant interruptions that left everyone feeling exposed and uncomfortable. And the same gnawing anxiety in the pit of her stomach.

"Did you have any other questions or concerns about her medications?" The woman's tone was almost robotic as she glanced at Steven. He didn't take his eyes off his wife but watched her every breath. Is that what he'd done the whole way while riding in the medical transport vehicle?

During Leah's forty minutes in this room with Phoebe, she'd seen four hospital staff members barge in after a warning knock on the door.

"Do you think the move here from Maine set her back any?" Steven had asked this same question to each one who'd entered the room.

"I'm sorry, but only her doctor can make that assessment." The woman didn't *sound* sorry.

Steven shifted. "But didn't you introduce yourself as Dr. Meeks?"

"Yes, I'm a hospital pharmacist."

"And the man who was in here earlier, who gave the same basic answer as you, didn't he introduce himself as a doctor?"

"He did. He's the pulmonary specialist. When he gets the test results back, he'll have more answers for you. Your primary doctor will be able to answer your questions, probably first thing tomorrow."

"Tomorrow?"

"We each have a job, Mr. Byler. And your wife just arrived here today." She took notes on a computer that sat on a contraption they'd rolled in. "Any other questions I can answer about her current drug regimen?"

"None. Thank you." Steven's shoulders slumped a bit more.

Leah remained silent. Time seemed to pass all too slowly here. Other family members were in a nearby waiting room, because only two visitors were allowed at a time.

Phoebe's Mamm came to the doorway. "Steven, I think the children need to see you. I'll stay for a while." Steven shook his head, but she went to his side. "Geh. You need to eat and rest."

He clutched Phoebe's hand, pausing for several long moments before he slowly stood. He motioned for Leah to go with him. She trailed behind him. *What must it be like for Steven to go through this day after day?*

He slowed his steps. "I'm sure other people want to visit her too."

Leah nodded. After a few twists and turns of the hallways, she was almost certain they had gone in a loop because the hallway looked exactly like the one they had just left.

A woman in scrubs spoke from behind a nurse's station. "Down this hall and to your left."

Leah looked at her. "The waiting room?"

She nodded, smiling. How many times had Leah and Steven passed this same nurses' station? Following her instructions, they found the waiting room full of Amish. A quick nod from Steven was all Phoebe's Daed required to brush past them and head for Phoebe.

Steven eyed a vending machine. "Where're the children?"

They weren't allowed on this floor, so various people took turns walking them around the grounds, to a nearby playground, or to the cafeteria. Everyone simply shrugged.

"The cafeteria."

Leah's heart jolted at the quiet voice. *Landon!*

She searched for him and peered around a small group of Amish standing nearby.

Landon sat in a chair, his fingers interlaced in his lap, looking as peaceful as ever. His eyes met hers, and her knees trembled. He then looked to Steven. "Iva has the children."

Steven moved forward, and Landon stood. Tears pricked Leah's eyes as they embraced. "Steven, I can't tell you how sorry I am to hear about Phoebe."

Steven backed away. "Thank you."

"Your driver's van was full, so Rhoda called, asking if I was in the area and if I could help drive folks as needed. I hope you don't mind after everything . . ."

"No." Steven clutched Landon's shoulder. "Thank you."

When Landon's eyes met Leah's again, she suddenly found herself biting back tears, rage, and laughter. She wanted to hug him as much as she wanted to scream at him for abandoning her. But most of all she wanted the truth of where they stood.

Landon's attention returned to Steven. "You may not be interested, but with the wedding coming up and all, if you need someone to stay here with Phoebe, I'd be more than happy to do that."

What a shame that after years of friendship, Rhoda couldn't invite Landon to her wedding without causing a ripple of anger through the community. If Leah hadn't been seeing Landon, Rhoda could invite him, and no one would mind.

"I appreciate that, Landon. We're keeping people she loves talking, singing, or reading to her round the clock, and it would ease my anxiety a good bit if you were here doing that during the wedding."

"I'll be here then."

Steven took a step toward the door. "Would you mind showing me where that cafeteria is?" Steven nodded to the hallway. "After I arrived with the transport team, I followed the aides to this floor as they got Phoebe situated, and I haven't left it since."

"Yeah, sure." Landon glanced at Leah, and she saw the same questions and doubts in his eyes that weighed down her heart.

Leah's heart sank as they left the room, but every Amish eye was watching her, so she stayed put.

Steven turned back. "Leah, didn't you say you were hungry too?"

Leah glanced at the disapproving faces, but Steven, her preacher and a man under the stress of possibly losing his wife, had invited her to go with Landon and him. The others made way for her as she walked

393

toward the hallway. Once she was within steps of them, Steven and Landon went ahead, leading the way down another hall of endless fluorescent lights.

Why would Steven ask her to go with them? Was it absent-mindedness, or did he intend to let them speak for a few minutes?

After an elevator ride and more hallways, she saw Iva coming toward them, holding the children's hands. Isaac and Arie spotted their Daed, and their little faces lit up as they pulled free from Iva's grip. Isaac appeared to have orange juice pulp on his chin, and Arie's green lips indicated she'd had a Popsicle. They rushed down the hall, and Steven scooped them up in one swift motion, asking them what they had been up to.

How could Steven change from mourning husband to heroic dad in the short distance between walking down a hall and seeing his children?

Iva welcomed Landon and then turned to Steven. "They've eaten really well and been very good . . . until they spotted you."

Steven hugged the children again, kissing them, and then he balanced one child on each hip. "Landon, do you mind making sure Leah eats? I'd like to take my children outside for a bit."

"Uh." Landon's hesitancy was far from the hopeful, leaping-at-the-opportunity reaction Leah would've liked.

"I need this," Steven assured him. "I'll let Leah's Daed know it was my request."

Without another word Steven went down the hall, his children in his arms, Iva following. She turned, shooing them and mouthing the word *go*.

Landon watched the retreating family.

His lips formed a smile, but his eyes reflected sadness. "It's good to see you."

Her heart pounded. "I . . . I don't understand, Landon. How could you turn in your phone and just leave me like that? Why would you agree to Daed's demands and choose to leave in a way that didn't even include us getting some sort of final conversation?"

His hands remained in his pockets as he stared at the floor. "I regret that." He looked up. "I'm truly sorry for it."

Despite his words the apology felt empty, as if he didn't really get what he'd done.

Leah hoped they were able to finish this conversation before someone pulled them apart. "I didn't even realize what I'd said until after you'd left, and I shouldn't have said it. I was upset, and I overreacted, but, Landon, you abandoned me."

The elevator bell sounded, and he looked that way as strangers left it. "If any part of you believed that I cared more about my loyalties to Rhoda or keeping that job, I had to prove to you that you were wrong."

"Had to prove me wrong?" Was he serious? "That's why you left without any way for me to contact you?"

"You don't know what it's like to be the outsider, to know that most of your community and relatives look at me as if I'm some sort of lowlife drug dealer."

"I don't get what it's like for you? How can you say that? I'm the outsider, Landon. I sit in church and wonder what the pastor just said. Was it a reference to a sitcom or a sports team? Everyone laughs, and I'm completely lost!"

Landon slumped, looking weary. "Regardless of where we are, your world or mine, we can't fix the issues the other one is having."

What was wrong with them? Why weren't they making plans to survive the next year rather than arguing like children?

He lifted his ball cap, scratched his head, and put his cap on again. "The pressure on us is ridiculous." Landon rested his palm on his chest. "I love you, Leah . . ." His eyes misted.

He didn't need to say the word *but.* She'd heard it loud and clear. There were too many people against them. If she left her family, Landon would carry the weight of that responsibility. He'd always wonder if her Englisch life was worth the sacrifice of severing all ties and enduring the continual disapproval and wrath of her Daed and her community.

He brushed his fingers along her jaw line. "Our love is good and strong, but it just isn't enough to win the war, not without leaving us too injured to pick up the pieces."

Her heart broke. Was she still standing here? It felt as if she'd melted into the floor, as detached from her surroundings as Phoebe was.

Leah longed to say all the great speeches she'd imagined, explaining how they could make the relationship work. But she couldn't find any words. *This* was the talk she'd been waiting for?

She choked back tears. Her Daed had won. "This isn't at all how I thought a conversation with you would go."

"Me either. But seeing your family and understanding all that is against us . . ." He fidgeted with a string to her prayer Kapp. "I never imagined we'd land here."

She brushed a tear from her face. "So this

is it, then?"

Landon cleared his throat, apparently fighting with his own overwhelmed emotions. "I will love you all my life."

She sobbed, and he drew her into his arms. "Me too." He backed up and lifted her chin, gazing into her eyes. "You stay at Orchard Bend Farms. I know how much you wanted to get out of Pennsylvania. Maine is freedom for you."

"But —"

He covered her lips with his fingers. "Let me do this."

She nodded. "Okay." Her heart broke, not just for today or tomorrow, but for all the years ahead.

She knew she'd never love or be loved like this again.

Twenty-Eight

Jacob stretched in the carriage seat, trying to relieve the stiffness in his back. Days in the orchard working. Then twelve hours traveling by train, car, and bus. And now sitting in a carriage that rode like flattened cardboard being pulled across a gravel driveway. All to reach Virginia. And on top of that was the nagging sentiment that he could really regret coming here.

No wonder his whole body ached.

How would Esther react to the U-turn he'd made concerning their relationship? He wished he knew.

He'd gone by Bailey's ironwork shop first, but it was locked up tight. Now as Jacob pulled the carriage onto Esther's driveway, he frowned. Which of the two houses did she live in — the main house with her brother or the Daadi Haus with the unmarried, expectant girls? How could he not know this about her? She'd volunteered no information, but, then, he'd never asked her anything, either. It had made their friendship seem easy and uncomplicated at the time, but evidently easy and uncomplicated also meant without roots and easily withered.

A young woman opened the front door of the Daadi Haus, laughing as she waited for a cat to scoot outdoors. The woman, maybe twenty-two, spotted Jacob and stared for a moment before walking toward him. She appeared possibly nine months pregnant. *"Kann Ich helfe?"*

"Esther Beachy?"

"You want Esther Mae." She gestured. "In the big house."

"Nee. Essie."

She narrowed her eyes as if she didn't believe he was asking for the right Esther Beachy.

"Shark Bait."

The term seemed to make her even more leery. "Why?"

"To talk."

"What's your name?"

Had Esther taught the women to question all strangers like this? Seemed to him this woman could be a little warmer. "Jacob King."

She eyed him. "No guys allowed beyond

400

the doorway. Standing rule." With that, she motioned for him to follow her.

He got down, tied the horse to a hitching post, and went inside, stopping just inside the door. The home seemed to be brimming with young women. A delicious aroma of food — some spicy concoction and freshly baked bread — filled the air. Despite the scant furniture he realized his assumptions about what a place for unwed mothers would feel like didn't match reality. He'd imagined it would be cold and oppressive with guilt and shame. But the girls here were talkative and cheery.

He spotted Esther, and hope of patching things up mingled with raw nerves. She sat at a beat-up old kitchen table. She had one bare foot resting in the chair and her chin on her knee. She looked utterly content. But was he about to embarrass himself in front of her and the roomful of women?

Esther and a girl were playing checkers, and several other girls were watching and talking while eating popcorn. He hoped the girl who sat across from Esther was one of her sisters and not someone expecting a child, because she couldn't be more than sixteen.

"*Eens. Zwee. Drei.*" Esther hopped three

pieces, counting each time and taking each piece.

The girl broke into laughter, scooped up popcorn, and tossed it on Esther, who laughed in response. Her laugh was contagious, and the girls broke into loud chatter.

"Bad sportsmanship." Esther giggled, picking up a couple of kernels and leaving the rest of the popcorn on her wherever it lay. "But good game." She ate the popcorn she'd plucked from her dress. When she spotted Jacob in the doorway, she paused for barely a moment before gathering the checker pieces. "We have a guest."

The women turned.

Esther swooped her hand through the air. "This is Jacob King." Seemed odd she didn't clarify that he was a friend, an acquaintance, or a one-time coworker on projects. "Jacob, this is Fanny, Dorothy, Annie, Malinda, Florence, and Ruth." She pointed to each one as she said their names. Florence seemed to be the oldest of the young women, probably five years younger than Esther, and she was the one who'd led him inside.

He removed his hat. "Hallo."

Esther studied him, tapping one of the game pieces on the table. Then she glanced at Florence and barely nodded.

Florence blinked and turned back to Jacob, staring at him as if he had two heads. "Apparently you're an exception." She held out her hand. "Give me your coat."

Jacob did so but held on to his hat as he walked toward the table, mostly so he'd have something to do with his hands. Every eye was on him.

Except Esther's.

She dusted at her dress, picking popcorn off it. Without getting up she dumped the handful into a nearby trash can and then stacked checker pieces in her hand. She seemed rather unenthusiastic that he was here. "Do you play checkers, Jacob?"

That seemed like a good start to this visit. "It's been a while." He felt as if every woman in this room was judging him for all they'd suffered from men — fathers, brothers, classmates, and lovers. Was that his imagination?

Esther put the pieces in place, and Jacob hung his hat on the spindle of a chair before he sat across from her. Florence whispered to one of the girls, and she whispered to the next one. After a few tugs on sleeves, one after another left the kitchen, until the last one eased out, closing the door, giving them a bit of privacy.

Esther skimmed her index finger from the

base of her neck to her chin. "Guests first."

He slid a checker into a new spot.

She moved a checker piece. "Does this visit mean you truly forgive me?"

"Actually," — he slid a piece into place — "I've come to ask your forgiveness."

The coolness in her manner seemed to melt, and she smiled. "Thank you, Jacob."

He looked into her eyes, seeing someone worthy of his trip here. "Same to you, Shark Bait. But I have to warn you that I'll probably need to ask for forgiveness again. I'm coming to realize that I can be really dense at times."

"Dense?" Her eyebrows and voice rose. "You?" She laughed while moving another piece. "Hardly."

He studied the board. She was good. He slid another piece into place.

Esther jumped two of his men and gathered the pieces. "In hindsight, Jacob, I know I was quite wrong to lie to you as I did."

"I've been there more than once."

"On the bright side, it seems apparent that your friendship is worth having, or I wouldn't have lied to keep it, right?"

Jacob liked this woman. She had flaws same as he and everyone else did, but her heart seemed to be in the right place. So why was she so set against dating?

A click and a creak, as if a door had opened, came from somewhere.

He moved another game piece. "You play a mean game of checkers, and I'm out of practice."

She nodded.

"Esther plays a mean game of volleyball too," one of the girls whispered. He looked to the door the girls had gone through and saw it was open less than an inch but had a few eyes, ears, and one set of lips in the narrow space.

"Girls." Esther's motherly tone surprised him, but it probably shouldn't have. The door slammed shut.

He eyed her. "So tell me about yourself. Do you enjoy volleyball?"

"I do. But not quite as much as I once did. I used to get quite vocal at those things."

"Used to?" The loud, girlish whisper from the doorway was followed by giggles and shushes from the other room.

The door was ajar again, with pairs of eyes and ears in the gap.

Esther smiled, shaking her head. "They have a valid point. I'm *still* loud while playing." She turned toward the door. "If you're only going to pretend to give us privacy, please come sit with us. At least that way you'll hear correctly, and we'll be aware of what's being heard." How did she manage to sound like both a mother hen bent on teaching her baby chicks and a dear friend who was simply one of the brood?

"Sorry," one girl said, and the door slammed shut.

Jacob imagined this home was a handful day and night. Why would she take on being a housemother to pregnant Amish girls? He jumped one of Esther's pieces.

Chatter and laughter rose in the other room, which told him no one could overhear them now.

"I've been wondering a couple of things, Esther."

"Like?"

"The afternoon I realized you weren't married, I was talking to Ammon, and he asked whether I believe God controls every bit of our lives. He seemed weighed down with the worry of it."

She stayed focused on the board. "I know what that was about. The church believes in having all the children God chooses to give, and the deacon's been preaching that hard lately, but I told Ammon it wasn't God causing Esther Mae to conceive. Ammon's twenty-six with four children. He might consider using a little abstinence, but he has to figure out what *he* believes — whether it's all in God's control or he should take personal responsibility." She finally moved a piece. "What else have you been wondering about?"

He started to make a move and changed his mind. "That night in town when we were sitting on the curb talking, you said, 'It was on this night,' but then Ammon arrived, and you never finished your thought."

"Ah. It was the anniversary of my Daed's death. He was both difficult and good, so losing him was heartbreaking but also freeing."

Her words were matter of fact, but he sensed a depth of emotion that she was holding back.

She pointed at the board. "It's still your turn."

He slid a piece into place. "Thanks for the answers."

She smiled. "Anytime."

At the sight of Esther's wry smile, he thought of the first time he went to Bailey's to help her. "I am glad to see that you still have your ears."

"Me too." She made a face and touched each ear. "Were they in jeopardy?"

"I about talked them off that first day we worked together at Bailey's."

She chuckled. "That was a good day." She moved a checker piece.

"All you ever wanted to know about one Amish man's journey into the world and back again." He countered her move.

"You didn't cover everything." She studied the board before making another move. "Was the outside what you'd thought it would be?"

"It was better in some ways, worse in others. But you travel with Bailey and his family. You see what it's like."

"Vacations are insulated from real life."

"I can understand how they would be." He moved another checker piece. "Our preachers warn us what it's like out there, but despite their description, the reality is very different."

"Like reading about a place in a brochure, and then when you get there, its cultural feel is not at all what you'd expected." She moved another checker piece into place.

"I wouldn't have thought of it like that, but ya." He jumped another man of hers. "The problem isn't sin staring you in the face. It's the real people with real hurts and problems, and when you try to help them, they grab you and pull you under with them while hoping you're strong enough to keep them afloat."

She studied the board and frowned. "I'm losing."

"You are." He slid the bowl of popcorn out of her reach. "Just in case the winner always wears popcorn."

She smiled, her eyes reflecting such calmness. "So other than a desire to forgive and be forgiven, which you could have expressed by phone, why are you here?"

An image of Phoebe lying in the hospital sent fresh grief through him. Followed by thoughts of Steven beside her, hoping against hope that she'd recover . . . of Leah's and Landon's broken hearts . . . of Rhoda's and Samuel's love and their fight to keep Orchard Bend Farms well tended. Fresh hurts and turmoil churned within him, and he was surprised to realize his eyes were misting. "I need a friend."

"Ah." She studied him. "Friendship I can do. But at the risk of sounding both conceited and motherly, I will confess that single men aren't particularly good at being just friends with single women."

Which had to be why she wanted him to think she was married. "You know yourself well, Esther, Essie, Shark Bait Beachy. You definitely sounded conceited and motherly."

"I know. Sickening, isn't it?"

"I've never before met a single girl who

wanted to stay that way."

"My poor Mamm still struggles with it. It was about her undoing when I was younger. I almost have her calm about it these days. Give her three more years, once I cross that thirty-year-old threshold, and she'll come to terms with who I am . . . maybe." Her eyes lit up with a hint of surprise.

"New thought?"

"Dora." She tossed her pieces onto the board. "I'm not sure what to tell her."

"I get the feeling if she thought I was here right now, she'd be in a chair beside me. Am I wrong?"

"No. I don't mean to share too much, and I feel guilty for what I need to say."

"But I have to know the straight of it if we're to avoid conflict or misunderstandings with her."

"If she knows you're coming to our district at times and don't have houses to build, she'll believe that her prayers are being answered and that you are warming up to the idea of happily-ever-after with her."

"Could you and she be any more different?"

"Doubtful. But if she thinks there's a chance with you, she won't move on."

"I definitely want her to move on."

"And without us working on projects,

please don't get caught being around me. She'll blame me for you not dating her, and like I said, our relationship is complicated enough as it is."

"Sounds like you two have had guy trouble before."

Esther nodded. "About a year ago a nephew of one of our members moved here. I thought he was trouble the moment I saw him. He dated a few girls in the area before he set his sights on Dora. Rumors were swirling that he was going to ask her out, and she was so excited. I didn't handle it well."

"You came between them before their first date?"

"I know what I saw, Jacob."

"She might have seen it too if you'd given her the chance."

"For almost nine years I've housed girls who've given some Casanova a chance."

Jacob could see why the relationship between Esther and Dora was complicated. Esther loved her sister, and Dora desperately wanted to find romantic love.

"So what do we do about your sister?"

"You are careful not to be seen coming here or hanging out near me for a year, maybe two. After that, Dora will find someone, and you won't ever matter again."

411

"Thanks."

"Anytime. What are friends for?" Her smile faded. "Do you think that's a reasonable plan?"

"Sure. I doubt I have much reason to be in Virginia very often anyway."

She held out her hand. "Phone."

He gave it to her.

She touched various buttons, clearly comfortable with the forbidden item. Bailey's influence, he guessed. "I'm sharing phone numbers where I can be reached. You may call, or don't call. I don't care. But unless you say it's an emergency, I probably won't return the call in less than three to four days. However, if I call you, you'd better pick up."

Once again she had stirred humor within him, and he was glad he'd come. "You're demanding *and* have a double standard."

"What was your first clue?"

"When you opened your mouth."

She laughed. "Hey, you'll be the one with a cell phone in your pocket. There's no excuse for not answering." She touched another button and listened to a salsa ring tone. "That'll do for now." She looked up from his phone. "Amish in these parts don't cotton to keeping a phone in their pockets."

"They may not, but you should."

"You take that up with the bishop. If he says yes, you can buy me one. Until then, I gave you the numbers to the phone shanty and Bailey's shop."

Her sassy attitude deserved a little harassing. "What if I prefer to text?"

"Then text. Neither number gets text messages, but if you need to vent, and I'm not available, text away, my friend." She slid the phone across the table, and her smile faded as she studied him. "Tell me, Jacob, what's so heavy that you came all this way to talk?"

"It's a lot to unload."

She leaned in. "I live with pregnant teens. I dare say we have more drama between waking and eating breakfast than you could share if you took all night."

"You're sure?"

She went to the oven and opened it. "For now and future reference, could you not ask me if I meant what I've already said? Trust me, unless I'm teasing, I mean what I say, every time." She turned off the oven and pulled out four loaves of bread.

"Good to know."

She sat back down at the table. "What's going on?"

He drew a deep breath, hoping to steady the pounding grief and confusion, and told

Esther about Phoebe. He paused and then said, "And the girl I told you I hoped to forget — she's marrying my brother . . . in two days."

"Jacob." Her shocked tone resonated as a victory. He'd found someone he could tell the hardest parts of his life to and feel better afterward. That was rare.

"And as much as I can't stand the idea of returning to Orchard Bend Farms to help out, especially during the first few months of their wedded bliss, the family business desperately needs me." As he continued to list everything on his mind, including Leah's woes, all he could think was, *I can't return to the farm. I can't.*

She returned to the oven and dumped each loaf of bread onto a cooling rack. "What a mess."

"Tell me something I don't know."

"I can't. You're a man, and men know everything."

He chuckled. "Not this one."

She snapped her fingers. "That must be why I like you." She glanced at the clock, and her eyes widened for just a second. "So the original Orchard Bend crew is now down three men — you, Steven, and Leah's Landon, leaving only Samuel?"

"Ya."

"That's tough." She glanced at the clock again. "We need to leave. Dora's coming by with a donation from a local grocery store. I prefer to keep this home for unwed girls as private as possible, but the store manager is one of Bailey's good friends who knows about the girls and helps out whenever he can."

"You have things to do, and I should just go." Disappointment wrapped around his shoulders. "I've said what I needed to."

She made a face. "Do you actually believe that giving an outline of the issues is equal to finding some peace with them?"

He couldn't imagine what else there was to say on the topics, and he felt better for having shared his burdens, but he didn't want to part ways just yet. "Where can we go?"

She wrapped a loaf of bread in a kitchen towel. "A back way to Bailey's. During your rare trips here, his place will be the best spot to meet. No one will think anything about a rig or two being there, and yet few Amish ever have a need to go there, and Dora never has."

"Why not?"

"Bailey likes to tease, and she has no sense of humor whatsoever."

An idea hit. Bailey had asked Jacob to

build an outdoor kitchen. If he returned to help on the farm in Maine the way he should, he'd need an escape — an excuse to pull away and find a refuge of sorts. This seemed like a good solution. He and Esther could visit at Bailey's without Dora discovering their friendship too soon.

Esther went to the door of the room where the girls were and knocked while opening it. "I'm going to Bailey's. Dora will be here shortly. I expect each of you to help her unload the groceries. The stew and bread are ready. No arguments and no leaving the kitchen a mess. Okay?"

The young women stared at him and nodded.

Jacob grabbed his hat and coat. She passed the bread to him, put on a heavy sweater, and went down the steps with only a hint of a limp.

They crossed the lawn toward the hitching post. "What if they mention to Dora that I was here?"

"Then we deal with it, but they won't. We have a code: no lying but no volunteering information about someone else's life." She held up her hand. "I know, you seem to have gotten caught in some version of that yourself, and that's my fault. I absolutely, positively . . ."

Even though she'd already apologized, he expected her to finish her sentence with another one.

She raised one eyebrow. ". . . should not have let you near Ammon."

"What?" He laughed.

"Did I mumble?"

He started toward her door to open it for her, and she shooed him away. "Much appreciated, but I'm not your date, so get."

He did as requested and went to his side. As he worked to turn the horse and rig in the right direction, he looked forward to talking about the serious things and getting perspective. But he also hoped to find out things about her — like why she felt so strong about not marrying, why she began helping unwed expectant moms, how Esther Mae was these days, whether Esther lived in the Daadi Haus with the girls, and dozens of other questions.

"Go right."

"Right it is." He pulled onto the road, and another question popped into his mind. "How's your knee these days?"

"Gut. A doctor injected steroids into it. If the pain returns, I'll get another injection. But all tests indicate that there's no permanent damage and that it simply needs time to heal. I appreciate the nudge to have it seen and the money to cover the cost."

"Anytime. So how did you originally hurt your knee?"

"In the same accident where Esther Mae was injured."

"Were you two in a buggy accident or something?"

"No, that would be you and me, remember?"

He'd never forget the awful feeling when he hit her with his horse. But would he have gotten to know her otherwise? "That will stick with me forever. So how did you hurt your knee?".

She straightened. "I was at Ammon and Esther's home, on the stairs, and had paused while talking to Ammon. Esther Mae was at the top of the steps, carrying a riding horse for one of the children, when she tripped over a piece of loose carpeting and fell."

"Wait." Jacob needed a moment to absorb this. So Esther was in her brother's house when her sister-in-law ran over her with a horse — a toy one but still a horse. He pulled off the road onto the empty parking area. "Could you get out now?"

"Why?"

"Safety precaution. For me. The way I figure it, it's about time for you to get hit with another horse, and I'd rather not be sitting next to you when it happens."

Her eyes reflected shock. Apparently she hadn't thought of the connection. Then she broke into laughter.

When their laughter quieted, he felt refreshed and strong and whole again.

And for the first time in a long time, he knew what he had to do.

TWENTY-NINE

A loud thud ricocheted against Rhoda's nerves, and the plates slipped from her hands and crashed onto the hardwood floor. A quick glance told her that her uncle had just dropped two benches. The poor man. Everyone was exhausted.

Trembling, she knelt inside her childhood home, separating broken plates from whole ones. At least a few had survived. As if Phoebe's illness weren't stressful enough, her family now had to deal with a wedding. If only there had been a better way for her and Samuel to marry, but Amish girls married in their parents' home, and the parents provided two meals to the guests.

Warm hands covered hers, and she looked up. Samuel crouched near her, wearing newly made black pants and a well-ironed new white shirt. His silky blond hair shone like a halo that emphasized his dark brown eyes. "Hi." He paused. She wasn't surprised he'd seen her drop the plates. How many times had one of them been caught admiring the other from across the room or the yard today?

Her cheeks warmed. "Hi."

He helped gather the broken pieces into a mound.

She and Samuel had left Maine three days ago, along with everyone else, and they'd needed every minute of those days to get ready for this small, simple wedding. He'd been tempted to stay at the farm to work an extra day or two, but at the last minute they decided against that. Good thing too. Otherwise, there might not *be* a wedding today. Getting an expedited marriage license had proved to be quite the task, and it'd taken both of them to accomplish it. Before they left Maine, they'd written and overnighted a letter asking for a waiver of the three-day wait for a license, explaining their reasons and need. Even so, they'd spent most of Tuesday at the courthouse getting their license. Yesterday the men had moved furniture out of the house and replaced it with tables and benches while the women cleaned and prepared food.

Rhoda bit her lip. She must have been out of her mind to think she could pull off even the smallest of Amish weddings in three and a half days. Feeding a wedding feast to sixty-three guests on Thursday when they hadn't arrived here until late Monday afternoon was nearly impossible.

Another plate slipped from her shaky hands and bounced against the floor.

Samuel grabbed it, stopping its whirling vibration. "It's still whole." He angled his head, catching her eye. "Just breathe, Rhoda."

She swallowed and nodded. Would her wedding day be the final straw for her? She'd wanted it to be simple, but Samuel was the first inside his nuclear family to marry, and he was a King of Kings' Orchard. They had to provide a wedding his family could accept — one with family, close friends, and a day of feasting and fellowship.

Iva brought a trash can, and they discarded the broken pieces. Samuel passed the stack of rescued plates to Rhoda's Mamm and gave Rhoda a hand as she stood.

Leah arrived with a broom and dustpan in hand. "I'll get it."

Samuel tugged on Rhoda's hand, and she followed him, snaking around tables and people to wherever he was leading her.

With Phoebe and Steven having to leave the home they all shared, she and Samuel had easily received permission from the church leaders to marry immediately. The wedding festivities and number in attendance would be similar to that of a widow's or widower's second marriage. Of course, with the circumstances as they were, Rhoda and Samuel's wedding was painfully more somber.

Samuel paused at the foot of the stairway that led to Rhoda's bedroom. He wrapped her hands in his, and her heart pounded. Regardless of all else, she wanted to be his for the rest of her life.

He'd arrived at the house this morning around seven, his family in tow. That was probably about four hours ago now. He'd barely said *hello* before she was pulled in one direction and he in another. They'd managed to brush fingers before parting ways.

He gently squeezed her hands. "It's hard to believe that the start of the best thing to ever happen to me will take place today."

The twinkle in his eyes was undeniable. It was these moments that she'd cherish about today — the looks shared across the room, the deep rumble of his quiet voice as he spoke words meant only for her, the happiness of their love that squeezed past the grief and held on tight to hope.

She freed a hand and eased her fingers to his hair, pretending to straighten a few misplaced strands. How many times had she wanted to run her fingers through it? "And the amount of stress and labor?"

"Should such a remarkable event happen without effort?"

She lowered her hand to his crisp starched shirt, admiring everything about him. Where was the new black dress coat his Mamm had made for him? "I wish Phoebe were here."

He kissed her cheek. "I know." His love and assurance caused her to take the first full breath in hours. "Go on and change clothes."

She glanced at the clock. *What?* "We should've started twenty minutes ago."

"Almost everyone invited has been working to help us get ready, and, trust me, we all needed the extra time. The few *real* guests have been seated and are chatting." His eyes bore into hers, and she knew he longed to kiss her, but parents and relatives were everywhere. "The ceremony will be the start of our life together. It doesn't matter whether it begins precisely on time. Only that it begins."

She loved this about him too. He tended to think in terms of the big picture and posterity, where she focused on to-do lists for the day or week. He saw beyond all that to what would be accomplished through their efforts. Together they could weather any storm and would bask in every ray of sunshine.

She straightened his shirt collar, picturing him walking her down the aisle. "I'll meet you right here in twenty."

"I'll be waiting." He winked.

She scurried up the steps and into her bedroom. Without wasting a moment, she slid into the teal-blue dress her Mamm had made Tuesday and then pinned her white organdy apron into place. She'd worn a white apron like this to the meetinghouse every church Sunday since she was a baby. But today would be her last time to wear a white apron . . . until she was buried in this same wedding apron. She hoped they would have many, many decades filled with love and children and grandchildren before she — or Phoebe — needed to wear the aprons they'd been married in.

With her hair in place and her new prayer Kapp on, she stood in front of the mirror. How had she, a misfit, been so blessed to have Samuel fall in love with her? Could she keep his love throughout the years?

Someone tapped on the door. "Rhodes,"

Daed called.

"Kumm."

He opened the door, a tender smile in place. "You look like a woman in love."

She laughed. "More than I ever knew was possible."

"Your Mamm and I are so happy for you."

"Denki."

"Samuel is a good fit." He kissed her cheek. "He'll be good for you, and you for him."

"Ya. Like you and Mamm."

But she and Samuel had made mistakes already. It was so hard to let go of how they'd hurt Jacob. And was she mishandling the situation between Landon and Leah? What should she think or feel about them? She shook her head. Those thoughts needed to wait for another time. Right now she needed to focus on the wedding.

"I should go. Your Mamm is probably waiting on me so we can take our place."

"I'll be down in just a minute."

He left, and she straightened her prayer Kapp and tucked a few wisps of hair in place. Her heart overflowed with every good gift from God. Despite how many mistakes people made, He never stopped being generous. She prayed for Phoebe, and with the hope of today flooding her, peace rushed in, washing away all anxiety.

She heard a car door shut and looked out the window — and couldn't hold back a smile. There stood another gift for today.

Jacob.

Samuel strode toward the paddock beside the barn. He thought the rhythm inside him seemed a little odd for someone Amish, but it was as if trumpets were resounding inside his chest. Night had fallen. Cicadas and crickets sang. The bonfire was fading, but it still crackled and popped.

He held out a carrot, wooing the final horse belonging to a guest. Once he had a grip on the halter, he went toward its buggy near the house. Rhoda stood in the doorway of her home, talking to an aunt and hugging a final good-bye. He'd never celebrated life in all its wonder as he had today.

The fact that Jacob had come, making today even better, was a good indication of how much his little brother was changing. He no longer seemed to run from the awkward and uncomfortable. Samuel passed the horse to Rhoda's uncle, and they worked together to hitch it to the buggy.

Steven had returned to the hospital almost eight hours ago. He had stayed only through the ceremony and the meal. Arie and Isaac were spending the night with Phoebe's parents. Samuel's family, including Leah, had headed home about twenty minutes ago. Iva went with them. At the side of the house, Jacob filled two buckets with water. No doubt he was going to douse what was left of the bonfire. Samuel waved as Rhoda's aunt and uncle left, but he didn't see Rhoda.

Jacob came around the corner of the house. "My driver should've been here hours ago."

"It's meant to be." Samuel clasped his shoulder. "Kumm." He didn't know where Jacob was going after this. Jacob had always been a private person, and from childhood Samuel had known that keeping their relationship healthy meant he didn't ask many questions.

They went inside, where Rhoda's Mamm and her sister-in-law Lydia were still washing dishes.

"She just now took a seat." Rhoda's mother nodded toward the sitting room.

Samuel and Jacob joined Rhoda there, each taking a wingback chair.

"I just need to catch a second wind." Rhoda yawned and shifted to lie down on the couch. "So, Jacob, tell us about this construction job you mentioned earlier."

"It's in Virginia."

It had been a long time since Samuel had seen this kind of excitement in Jacob's eyes.

Rhoda put her hands under her cheek, looking even sleepier. Even now she was radiant. "You'll be part of a construction crew?"

"No." Jacob drummed his thumb and index finger on the arm of the chair. "It's for a man who owns an ironwork shop. He asked me about a month ago if I'd consider building him an outdoor kitchen and resurface his pool deck. He asked again a few days ago."

"Have you ever done either of those things?" Rhoda had chosen a good topic. Jacob didn't mind talking about construction work.

"Nee." Jacob propped his feet on an ottoman. "I know what you're thinking. Why would I agree to do something that will require a learning curve when I could do what I know and make easier and better money?" He interlaced his fingers. "But it's not about the money. It'll be different, and it's what I want to do."

Hope sprang forth. Did his brother have someone special in Virginia? "You'll never know what it meant to me for you to come today."

"It wasn't so bad, and it's getting even better."

"Ya? How so?"

Jacob leaned in. "Because it's your wedding night, and your wife is sound asleep on the couch."

Samuel glanced at Rhoda and laughed. It was tradition for Amish couples to spend their wedding night in the bride's home, mostly so they could help clean up the following day. But it wasn't exactly a comfortable situation for the newlyweds.

Of all the things he and Rhoda had discussed in the last week, sharing a bed wasn't one of them. But he'd not expected them to sleep together tonight. He knew her too well. When she was really tired, all it took was her relaxing a bit, and she was out cold, like a candle being snuffed. He rose and grabbed a quilt to cover her. "I doubt she budges even to roll over before daylight tomorrow."

Car lights reflected off the wall, and Jacob rose. "My ride's here."

Samuel walked out with him. He'd hoped to embrace his brother before they parted, but Jacob hopped in the car.

"Thanks for coming." Samuel held up his hand.

Jacob waved as the car drove off. Samuel

went inside and talked to Rhoda's family for a bit before telling them good night. He climbed the stairs to Rhoda's bedroom and stripped down to his T-shirt and boxers. The bed was a welcome relief from the last few days. The sounds of springtime at night echoed through the open windows as hope continued to beat its rhythm inside him. As tired and sore as he was, would he be able to sleep tonight?

"Samuel."

Rhoda's whisper stirred him from the dark place filled with dreams, and he tried to open his eyes. Daylight stretched its golden arms across the room, and birds were singing loudly. He blinked.

"Hi." She stood next to his bed, a cup of coffee in hand.

"Morning." He sat up, and she placed an extra pillow behind him. A sweet, girly scent surrounded her every move. "You smell nice."

"I've showered and done my hair."

He took the coffee from her. "What time is it?"

"Late for you." She picked up a plate from the side table. It had two bacon-filled biscuits and a large side of fresh fruit. "It's eight. You have about forty minutes before the driver arrives to take us to see Phoebe and then to the train station."

Unable to take his eyes off his wife, he sipped the coffee. "I look forward to our lifetime together."

She caressed his face. "Me too."

"Rhodes?" Daed called from the foot of the steps.

"I'd better go. You eat and shower, and I'll meet you downstairs."

"Okay." He ate his breakfast, enjoying the slower pace, but soon enough the day became a blur of getting ready and packing, visiting Phoebe, saying good-bye to Steven, Arie, and Isaac, as well as the rest of Rhoda's family. And Landon. He didn't see Leah or Iva today. They were at his folks' place, but they'd return to the farm in a few days.

Once they were on the train, Samuel felt like a newlywed again and held Rhoda's hand as they whispered to each other and enjoyed the view while the train sped them homeward.

Camilla picked them up at the station in Boston because the train schedule for Bangor was too limited. Rhoda sat in the backseat with Samuel. After riding with Camilla for three hours to reach the farm, he couldn't get his mind around the fact that Jacob enjoyed traveling on a regular basis.

Today was a joy because he was taking his bride home. They would try to make the trip back to Pennsylvania once each winter, but that was more than enough for him. Rhoda's family could come as often and stay for as long as they liked. He enjoyed their visits. But his Daed was another story.

Camilla pulled onto the driveway. "Welcome home."

"Thank you for doing this for us, Camilla."

"Glad to. You know that."

The dogs rushed from the barn, barking.

Rhoda clutched the handle of her traveling bag. "We'll visit soon. Okay?"

"Not this week. It's your honeymoon, but if you need anything — a ride into town or whatever — you holler."

"Thanks." Samuel slid money across the seat.

She shook her head. "Put that away."

"Thank you."

"Don't mention it. As I understand it, you two are going to have your hands full tending the orchard from now through the harvest and canning season, and I just want you to know you're welcome to bring laundry to my place anytime. We can wash and

433

dry it in no time."

Rhoda glanced at Samuel, and he saw her insecurity about her homemaking abilities.

He squeezed her hand. "Thanks. We'll keep it in mind, but I'm sure we can manage somehow." He'd need to help wash dishes, cook, and do laundry, even though he would be worse at those things than Rhoda. But they couldn't start relying on Englisch ways for everyday chores. If they did, how would they hold on to the Old Ways for themselves and their children and grandchildren?

Rhoda got out and petted Ziggy and Zara while walking toward the barn. "I want to check the messages."

"Sure." Samuel unloaded their stuff and waved good-bye to Camilla.

When she drove off, he felt the weight of the oddity of being here alone with Rhoda. A new thought struck him. They'd accomplished their goal — they could share the same home, neither having to live elsewhere. But with Phoebe in the hospital fighting for her life, did Rhoda find the idea of possibly conceiving a child unnerving?

A chill ran down his spine. Did he? Until this moment he hadn't thought about it. They were going to have to talk about the most uncomfortable subject of all — the marriage bed. He set the luggage outside the barn and tended to the livestock for the evening. When he was finished, he went to the office door.

While listening to a message from someone about codling moth traps, Rhoda took notes, and then she clicked a button, making the machine go silent. "All done."

Samuel shifted. "I should probably clean the stalls."

She sat back in the chair, studying him. "Are we avoiding going inside?"

His heart pounding, he moved to her side of the desk and sat on the edge. "Maybe."

Her eyes held a smile that tipped her lips.

He shrugged. "We need to talk."

She raised an eyebrow. "Okay."

"We rushed into this —"

Rhoda stood, a hint of amusement dancing in her eyes. "Having second thoughts?"

"What? Of course not. But I wasn't sure what you wanted . . . I mean —"

Her hand covered his mouth, silencing him. "You're overthinking. If you want to know what I want, you can't find out by staying in this barn."

He kissed her neck, mesmerized by how soft her skin was. "No?" He kissed her neck again. "It seems to be working really well so far."

She chuckled. "True."

"What do you want, Rhoda?"

"To be yours and to forget about heartaches and harvests and all that can go wrong in this world."

Samuel stood, sliding his hand around the small of her back. He remembered being right here with her once before, a little more than a year ago, longing, thirsting for the moment to last forever and for her heart to turn toward him.

And here he stood again, every hope and dream his. His eyes met hers.

No matter what the future held, he knew one thing would always remain true.

"I love you, Rhoda."

THIRTY

The dueling beeps from monitors were ceaseless, grating on Landon's nerves as he talked to Steven. With the wedding over yesterday, Landon needed to head back to the guest ranch. It'd take him the better part of three hours to get there, and he was scheduled to work in four hours, but right now Steven seemed to want to talk.

Landon repositioned his aching body against the chair. He didn't recall these seats being this uncomfortable yesterday when he stayed with Phoebe during the wedding. Had someone swapped them with chairs from another room?

Steven was on the other side of Phoebe's bed, and Landon tried to think of another round of simple things to talk about, subjects that would be easy for Steven to discuss while getting through another long day. "So what made you willing to change from being a handyman in Byler and Sons to becoming a trainee in a huge orchard?"

"Ah, I've asked myself that same question. What makes a man throw away years of apprenticeship and honing one set of skills to learn a new vocation?" Steven leaned forward and sandwiched his wife's hand between his. "The simple answer is love." He paused, staring at Phoebe's still face. "I knew firsthand there wasn't enough land or affordable housing in Lancaster or the surrounding areas to support future generations. So my love of the Amish ways nudged me to be a part of establishing a new settlement in an affordable place with lots of land. Phoebe loved Rhoda too much to simply let her go, as did I, and the farmhouse had to have a married couple. Since we didn't have a home in Pennsylvania to sell or children who were in school yet, I figured, what did I have to lose?" He patted his sleeping wife's hand. "As fraught with troubles as our time in Maine has been, Phoebe's never been happier." He shrugged. "Maybe *happy* isn't the right word. Fulfilled? As if what we're doing really matters, not only to everyone in that home and to Orchard Bend Farms, but for future generations." He chuckled. "After being one of three cooks in my parents' home, she loved . . . *loves* being the head cook and running the home."

"Good thing, because there was lots of that going on." Landon leaned his head from one side to the other, working out the kinks as his mind meandered to and fro.

"Do you mind if I ask" — Steven slid the chair to the right, more directly in Landon's view — "where things are between you and Leah?"

Landon tapped the ends of his fingers together, taking time to gather his thoughts. His first reaction to that question was to be miffed. He and Leah had landed exactly where Steven and every other Amish person wanted them to. But could he blame anyone for how things had ended for Leah and him? It'd been clear from the start that no Amish person would approve or support their love for each other. Some — like Samuel, Rhoda, Phoebe, Steven, Jacob, and Iva — wouldn't fight them, but he'd known the majority would silence them. He'd had a view inside the Amish world for too long not to know where everyone stood. The Amish were their own culture, with their own thoughts and values that were completely separate from his viewpoints. He couldn't blame Steven or anyone else at Orchard Bend Farms for that.

He interlaced his fingers and stared at his

439

hands. "We've agreed to go our separate ways. It stinks, but how I ever thought Leah would really want to leave her roots is beyond me. I guess I looked at all the trouble Rhoda had in her district with a few Amish people being set against her, including that jerk who ripped up her fruit patch, and I got it in my head that it wasn't worth what it took to live the Plain life. But I didn't see all the invisible and unbreakable threads that bind Leah to the Amish."

"I have to say it sounds like a good, solid decision, Landon."

"Not sure we had a choice. She would have to leave, or I'd have to join, and as much as I respect what it takes to live as you do, I simply don't agree with man — whether that's church leaders or the rules of the Ordnung — deciding how others should live. I mean, what if your people are missing their calling because it's outside acceptable Amish vocations?"

Steven nodded, unperturbed by Landon's question. "How many of your people are missing their calling because they follow wherever their flesh leads, no boundaries concerning anything, only doing what they want?"

And there was the dilemma — no guarantee of either lifestyle yielding a good harvest.

"I still believe it's the individual's responsibility to follow God as he or she believes is right. But we both lose out if we focus only on what separates us."

"You're completely right about that." Steven scratched his jaw line where his beard was thickest, looking as kind and thoughtful as ever. "I am truly sorry for the hurt you and Leah feel."

"I appreciate it. But she needs to find someone who can give her everything — like Rhoda found in Samuel." Landon had to fight a snort. He had little doubt that Crist would be happy to try to be that person. The thought of it made his heart blister, but at least Crist seemed to be a really good guy.

Steven ran his fingers over Phoebe's hand. "Everyone is returning to their normal lives as much as possible. Do you think she'll miss hearing their voices?"

"I don't know, but I could pick up a few recorders and get them mailed with return envelopes. That way people can talk to her, and you can play it for her as often as you need to."

"It's not something Amish do, but this could be the exception. If she can hear anything, I know it'd help her to hear the children talking to her."

"Her and them."

The children had come to the hospital to be near their dad and to understand where their mom was, but hospital policy didn't allow them to visit their mom.

Landon glanced at his watch. He needed more time, but he'd have to make do with what he had. "I'll run to the store and get a few recorders. When I return with them, we won't have much time to get the hang of using them before I have to head out. I'll take one with me to send to those in Maine."

Landon had a lot of thoughts on how he could keep the recordings circulating from others to Phoebe. The need was there, and he knew how to do it.

He just had to find the time to execute it without losing his job.

Leah walked beside Iva, toting both of their bags as Iva took pictures while they made their way through the Boston train station. She could feel the phone Landon had given her bouncing around in her hidden pocket. It made no sense, but it helped her feel less isolated and alone. "Rhoda and Samuel have been on their own for six days. Think they've lost weight?"

Iva paused, lining up something in her

viewfinder. Leah waited while Iva snapped several images. "No, but I imagine they're tired of pizza."

They started walking again, and Leah kept an eye out for Bob Cranford, hoping to remember what he looked like. Rhoda had lived with Bob and Camilla for months, and Samuel knew them well, but Leah remembered seeing Bob only a couple of times. And that was from a distance.

While she was grateful to be returning to the farm, she couldn't help but wonder, would it ever carry the sense of freedom it once had? When she'd moved to Maine about twenty months ago, she had set aside her daydreams of leaving the Amish in order to help her family. Now she returned to the same basic situation — here to help in their time of need.

But this time was different. She understood life and love and herself better. As much as she longed for Landon and would for a very long time, she also felt a little freer. She no longer was torn between his wants and her family's. He'd tried so hard to assure her the decision was fully hers — and it was — yet she knew what he wanted.

Now —

Someone tapped on her shoulder. "Excuse me, miss."

Recognizing the voice, Leah dropped the luggage and wheeled around. "Jacob!"

His open arms welcomed her. "Wow, little sis, that's quite a bit of excitement coming from you when we saw each other just a week ago."

"You came." She held him tight. "You're going to the farm, right?"

He seemed just shy of rolling his eyes. Even so, his face held plenty of disapproval. "Seems so."

She didn't blame him for being frustrated by having to return to the farm after Rhoda and Samuel were married. "You're the best, Jacob."

He turned his attention to Iva, who stood mere feet away, snapping pictures of their reunion. How many pictures had she taken since arriving in Pennsylvania for Rhoda and Samuel's wedding?

Iva released her camera, letting it hang from her neck, and nodded to Jacob. "Have you been waiting for us to arrive for the last week?"

"Nope, I spent a few days in New Hampshire with Sandra and Casey, who send a warm hello, and then I went to Virginia to see a friend." Jacob picked up their hefty bags.

Leah grabbed his featherweight bag. "So

how did you know when and where to find us?"

"You said plenty in those numerous texts you sent me, including what day you were arriving at this train station. So who's picking us up?"

"Bob. Does anyone know you're coming?"

"Not yet."

When Leah was young, she admired Jacob as if he hung the moon. Then all his troubles hit, and he had to go into hiding every time she turned around. She had lost a lot of respect for him during that time. Right now, though, she saw a rare and strong man. What made him willing to come back to help Samuel and Rhoda? Had he finally figured out who he was and how he wanted to live? If so, she wanted to know how he'd done it. "How long will you stay?"

"I don't know. Long enough and not a day more . . . provided I can stand it that long."

"Look." Leah pointed. "Isn't that Bob?"

The man waved.

It was so good to be back in Maine, to be reunited with Jacob and Iva. That time with her parents had been more than enough, although she and Iva had enjoyed spending time with Leah's younger sisters.

But when would she get a break from the

pain of losing Landon?

Jacob chatted as if his stomach wasn't in a knot. Had he tricked himself into believing he could live with the newlyweds for the sake of the family business?

It'd seemed doable when he was with Esther. She had a way of making life feel new again. The days they'd spent planning Bailey's outdoor kitchen and shopping for needed items, he'd felt solid. Ready to tackle whatever needed to be done.

Right now he felt like an idiot.

Bob slowed the vehicle as he rounded a curve, and the house came into sight.

Leah poked Jacob's shoulder. "Won't it be an extra surprise for Rhoda and Samuel when they see you're with us?"

"Extra?" He turned from the front seat to look at his sister. "They don't know you and Iva are coming in today?"

"They think we're arriving tomorrow."

Jacob turned to Bob. "Did you mention to them that you were picking up Leah and Iva?"

Bob turned onto the driveway. "Leah contacted me and said it was a secret." He put the car into park.

Jacob's concern melted when he saw Samuel in the front yard. Jacob squinted. He couldn't actually be seeing what he thought he saw! He got out and strode toward his brother. Apparently Samuel hadn't heard the car. He was too focused on grabbing a wet dress out of the laundry basket and putting it on the line.

Jacob broke into laughter.

Samuel dropped the dress and turned, eyes wide. "Jacob."

"This is priceless." Jacob pointed from his brother to the laundry basket.

"Hey." Samuel's sheepish grin was worth coming here. "You tease all you want. If she can work in the field beside me all day, I can do laundry."

Jacob picked up the dress and held it out on one finger. "Drop something, miss?"

Samuel laughed and snatched it from him. "Mess with me, and *I'll* cook for you."

"So she sleeps on your wedding night and has you doing laundry during the honeymoon. My, weren't you a fine catch?"

Samuel's face turned red from laughing. When they were children, they used to tease by finding fault in each other and then saying, "My, won't you be a fine catch?" Jacob hadn't thought of that in years, and based on Samuel's laughter, he hadn't either.

A bit more of the ice that still hung in the air between them melted. Jacob stared at the old house. "We've traveled ten thousand miles since we met Rhodes, ya?"

And he realized that he was grateful for every step he'd taken.

Was it possible that the contentment within him meant he actually looked forward to the next ten thousand miles?

THIRTY-ONE

Rhoda stirred from her sleep, feeling Samuel's arms around her. But the room didn't feel familiar. Before she could open her eyes, she basked in the joy of being in his arms as he slept. Was there a better feeling in the world than to wake beside one's best friend? They'd been married for four weeks, and it'd been a beautiful beginning — even in the face of Phoebe's tragedy.

Unable to place the room, she opened her eyes. It was daylight, a delicious between Sunday, and with no church today, they could sleep in and move as slowly as they wanted. They were in Phoebe and Steven's suite. She and Samuel had moved out of her bedroom and into here after Leah, Iva, and Jacob had arrived. At first it seemed irreverent to take over someone's living quarters while she fought for her life. But the room had a separate bath, and the door off the hallway led into a living room area, so it gave Samuel and Rhoda some much-appreciated privacy. This suite was comparable to living in a separate home — until one went to the shared kitchen.

She kissed Samuel's arm and snuggled her face against his biceps. After their late night of talking, she wasn't surprised when he didn't stir.

Despite the windows being open only a couple of inches, Rhoda inhaled the orchard's sweet aroma riding on crisp air. June had been a long time in coming. Phoebe had been in the hospital for six weeks. The doctors had told them if she lived to June, her chances for survival increased. And even if they had to take the baby as early as tomorrow, he stood a fighting chance of surviving now. Despite this milestone and all their encouragement by taking turns using a recorder and sending the tapes to Steven, the doctor said that Phoebe's heart seemed worn out from the fight.

Rhoda closed her eyes for a moment. They wouldn't slow their prayers or falter in their hope. A feeling of static electricity ran down her arms. It was one of the many feelings that accompanied a sense of intuition, but unlike in the past, it didn't make her fret or set her imagination into motion. Whatever it was, she'd neither ignore it nor pursue understanding it. Much like the weather of the day, she'd simply adjust to it as needed. She glanced at the clock. Eight-thirty.

That was quite late for this household. The dogs were probably hungry and maybe wondering where everyone was. They watched the fields at night to keep deer and moose away, and they came to the porch at daylight, wanting to come inside for food and sleep. She smiled and eased from Samuel's arms.

She slid her feet into the large red house shoes Camilla had given her. Iva called them her clown shoes, but they were comfortable and warm when she first got out of bed. She grabbed her housecoat, pulling it on as she moved to the window. Unlike her bedroom window, this one looked out over the back of the house, her greenhouses, and the orchard.

The apple trees' thick foliage swayed in the breeze, proclaiming health. With the temperature hovering in the low seventies, the late spring days were perfect weather for working. But right now the air pouring in from outside had to be near fifty degrees.

"Rhoda?" Samuel ran his hand across the bed, searching for her. He took a deep breath, opening his eyes. "Hey." The sleepy smile on his handsome face was the same one that greeted her each day. Did he know an endearing welcome graced his face every morning when he looked at her?

The dogs barked, a few familiar let-me-in demands. They'd wait maybe five minutes and bark again.

"Good morning." She went to the side of the bed and ran her fingers through his blond hair. "If you can go back to sleep, you should."

He reached for her hand and drew it to his lips, kissing it twice before he rose and slid into his pants. He settled the suspenders over his T-shirt. "I'll deal with the dogs." He peered down at her, looking pleased. "What's for breakfast?"

"Pancakes and bacon." She'd gotten the hang of cooking a few things, even for supper and dinners. But she had a long way to go yet. Iva, who'd honed her skills under Phoebe, was an encouraging and good teacher.

A strange jolt ran through Rhoda. Jojo came to mind, and Rhoda had a feeling . . . "I . . . I think Jojo's on her way here." She wasn't sure whether to dress and pin up her hair or head for the door as is.

A sense of urgency gave her chills, and she ran down the steps and out the front door. Just as she stepped onto the porch, the dogs howled, notifying her someone was here. But where? Rhoda scanned the driveway and saw no one. An overzealous white spruce blocked her view, but was there a car near the mailbox? She hurried down the driveway and spotted Jojo retreating from the mailbox and returning to her car. The woman was wasting no time, and Rhoda was sure she was in a hurry to leave.

She started running. "Jojo! Wait!" How foolish did she look in a housecoat and clown shoes with her long, braided hair bouncing wildly? "Wait, please."

The dogs bristled, barking furiously at Jojo.

"Ziggy! Zara! No!" Samuel's strong voice came from behind her as he clapped his hands. "Kumm!"

The dogs stopped barking and ran toward Samuel, but they paused when they came to Rhoda. She pointed toward the house. "Go." She turned, seeing Samuel on the porch. The dogs obeyed, and she was sure Samuel would put them inside.

Jojo opened her car door, ready to get in. "I didn't mean for anyone to see me."

Rhoda could see her seven- or eight-year-old daughter asleep in the backseat of the car. "I'm glad I did. Would you come in?"

She eased the door shut and left the car

idling. "No. I'm leaving . . . starting over." The look in Jojo's eyes was haunting, so lost and yet so filled with animosity. "It's taken me two months to see for myself the concerns you shared at the store that day." She shuddered. "But I see it now."

Rhoda wondered what had happened that would shake Jojo like this.

Jojo looked at her daughter. "I was a fool to put Sophia in harm's way as he and his wife battle over a marriage he'd told me had died long ago." Her blue eyes were chilling. "But I would still be blind to it if you hadn't forced me to look."

"Do you know where you're headed?"

"Not yet. I'll know when I get there."

"Jojo." Rhoda couldn't manage more than a whisper. What was Jojo thinking? More important, how could Rhoda reach past all the voices and panic of Jojo's childhood and say something that would matter to her?

Jojo returned to the mailbox and got out the letter she'd apparently put there when Rhoda spotted her. Jojo held it out to her. "You've been nice to me, and I didn't want some cosmic knowledge haunting you again, so I left an explanation rather than just disappearing."

Rhoda took the feathery light envelope, and maybe it was the look of desperation in

Jojo's eyes, but Rhoda understood a little more. "I know you feel there is no other choice than running. There's an alarm inside you, warning you to flee while you still have a chance." She paused, trying to piece together her limited understanding with what she'd been reading about survivors of child abuse. "That warning saved you from beatings as a child, helped you know what to do and where to hide, didn't it?"

The hint of tenderness Rhoda had seen on Jojo's face as she passed her the letter turned stone hard, but she nodded. Chills flooded Rhoda's skin as she felt some of the terror and knew some of the thoughts Jojo had dealt with most of her life. All the confusing, misguided messages and feelings Rhoda had sensed about Jojo and Sophia since moving here — strong danger, abandonment, and a need to flee — were only partially true. The rest was God allowing Rhoda to sense the misery and unrest inside the adult heart of a once-abused child. The depth of pain and anxiety . . . the inability to trust . . . the fear of people warring with the need for people . . . the moments of feeling good about oneself being buried under an avalanche of horrible memories, self-loathing, and doubt. As the realizations battered Rhoda, she could've crumbled right there under the weight of it.

"Jojo." Rhoda held out her trembling hand. She wanted to hug her, but instead she stood there with her hand out.

Jojo stared at her. "You're just weird."

Rhoda laughed and lowered her arm. Perhaps hoping Jojo would take her hand was a bit too much. "The alarm going off inside you, urging you to run, is stuck. You need someone to help you dismantle it or tune it out or something. Fleeing into the unknown isn't the only way to cope with it. I'll help you . . . if you'll let me."

"You can't, because I want as far from Camilla as possible."

"Why?"

"You know why. She's a horrible person."

Rhoda wanted to correct her about that, but she remembered something Samuel had said the night they sat in lawn chairs in an open field and talked. "Is she?"

"Absolutely! I'd never let her get near Sophia. She stood there and let the beatings happen!"

Confused, Rhoda did as Samuel had suggested — if a question came to her, ask it. He thought that if the person didn't answer, her intuition might. "She did?" And then she knew . . . "Or your mother did?"

Jojo got into her car and pulled the gear-shift down several notches.

"She's not your mother, Jojo." Rhoda spoke loud enough to be heard through the closed window.

Rather than pulling off, Jojo clutched the top of the steering wheel and lowered her forehead onto the back of her hands.

Rhoda opened the car door. "She never stood by and watched Zachary be beaten." She kept her voice soft so she wouldn't wake Sophia. "Camilla took the blows. She should've gotten out. But the past can't be changed. *Your future* can be." But then Rhoda realized that Jojo didn't care about her future. She felt used up, like discarded junk no one had wanted in the first place.

"Jojo, think what it could mean for Sophia's future if you didn't keep responding to that false alarm. In ten years when your daughter is a teenager, she's going to look at you on her way out the door, bags packed with bitterness and disappointment because of your addiction to fleeing and your inability to dare to trust the right people, and she'll say *you* should've stayed."

Jojo lifted her head. "Are you sure? Is it the same cosmic voice that said 'tell them'?"

Temptation to lie tugged at Rhoda. If she said yes, Jojo would probably stay, but she shook her head. "No. It's just what I think could happen. But if you stayed here for a few days or weeks, we could think and pray until we knew for sure what you should do. Doesn't Sophia's future deserve at least a pause to ponder your next move?"

Jojo leaned against the headrest. "*If* I do this, I don't want Camilla to know."

Rhoda wanted to dance and holler for joy, but she simply nodded. "Just pull in front of the barn."

Rhoda looked again at Sophia, and that's when she noticed a violin case in the car. How many times had Rhoda heard violin music riding on the wind, coming from nowhere, when she first moved to Maine? "Sophia plays that, doesn't she?"

Jojo nodded. "She seems gifted. At least that's what a music teacher said one time, but I can rarely afford lessons for her. Getting lessons was part of why I made my last move." She shrugged. "But it didn't work out . . . at all."

Camilla could give Sophia all the lessons she needed, at least for a really long time before Sophia outgrew Camilla's abilities. But Rhoda wouldn't mention that until the time was right. Jojo closed the door and backed up the car before pulling onto the driveway.

As Rhoda followed them, her heart sang a song of victory while she prayed desperately about Jojo's next decision.

But for now Rhoda was above all else simply grateful.

THIRTY-TWO

Sunlight as clear and seamless as Jacob had ever seen caused the temperature to climb a little past comfortable. Teams — Iva with Crist, Samuel with Rhoda, Leah with him — worked the orchard like bees during pollination. Even Jojo and Sophia, who'd joined them only four days ago, were helping. Well, mostly Jojo. Sophia helped a little before she played with the dogs or dolls or practiced her violin.

Orchard Bend Farms was thriving, perhaps almost as much as his relationship with Esther. Even though he didn't get to Virginia as often as he'd like, when he did, he spent a lot of time with Esther. She helped work on the kitchen project at Bailey's, which was his whole purpose in building it. He'd discovered that Saturday was her freest day, and if he was there Friday night, she spent the whole day Saturday and into the evening at Bailey's home. Bailey and his wife,

Althea, welcomed him, inviting him to eat with them or just sit and chat.

Several apples fell from the surrounding trees.

"June drop." Jacob knew it well and hated it. "If we had a dollar for every fruitlet dropping to the ground or being pruned, we wouldn't need to harvest a crop of eating and canning apples." He moved the ladder to a different spot on the tree and climbed it, searching for signs of fire blight or wormy or unpollinated fruitlets to prune.

Leah sprayed a rag with rubbing alcohol and scrubbed the blades of the long-handled shears. "Now where would be the fun in not needing a harvest?"

"Where would I be without your sarcasm?"

She shook his ladder. "Up a tree without one of these?"

He chuckled. There wasn't much sense in thinking where he might be if they didn't need a good harvest. He had to be here, dealing with the June drop. Every tree was doing its fair share of getting rid of unwanted fruit on its own, but, as always, for the best yield they needed to help mother nature.

"The shears clean?" He looked at his sister below. She hardly reminded him of the girl he'd grown up with. If she was still broken-hearted, and he believed she was, she didn't show it. When had such maturity set in?

"Ya." Leah held the very end of them, reaching the five-foot pruning shears as high as she could. "Do you really think they need this much cleaning between every cutting of fire blight?"

He grabbed them. "Yep. If we didn't clean them well, rather than bringing the disease under control, we'd actually help spread it."

For some reason he glanced a few trees down. Samuel was animated as he and Rhoda talked. His brother flirted with her, and then they burst into laughter for some reason. Jacob chuckled . . . and then blinked, staring at them.

Could it be? Had he finally found complete peace with Rhoda marrying Samuel? He focused on his feelings and thoughts . . . and smiled. Not only that, but he'd gone beyond it. He was *grateful* to be free to explore a relationship with Esther.

His phone buzzed, and he tried to free his hands, hoping it'd be Esther. Whether together or talking on the phone, he and Esther enjoyed each other. There was something about having a guy-girl relationship with neither one being interested in courting or marriage that was totally refreshing.

But if things kept going as they were, he could see where the relationship might lead to something more . . . if she was interested.

Ach, his hands were full. He tossed the weak or damaged fruitlets he'd been collecting onto the sheet below. "Leah, take these, please." He waited until she grabbed the pruning shears.

With his hands finally free, he dug for his phone. But the call had ended. He pressed icons, trying to see who'd called. *Lancaster Medical.* Jacob's heart jolted.

"You gonna keep playing with that thing or what?" Leah asked.

"I got a call from the hospital." He climbed down the ladder.

Leah froze. "Steven calls the barn office with routine updates. He's never called your cell, has he?"

"No. But if he's trying to reach us while we're in the field, this is how he'd do it." Jacob hit redial, but before anyone picked up, he had an incoming call. The hospital. He pressed accept. "Hello."

"Jacob. Steven here. We finally have a bit of good news! Phoebe's lungs are clear! Her heart rate, blood pressure, and oxygen levels started improving yesterday. She's doing well enough that they're no longer looking at taking the baby this week. She's thirty-two weeks, and they're hoping to get her as close to thirty-four weeks as possible, which is really important for lung maturity and improves the baby's chances of thriving."

"That's great!" Jacob raised the phone, waving his arms. "Guys, kumm. Good news!" Joy danced through him, and he saw it in the steps and faces of everyone hurrying toward him. He returned the phone to his ear. "I'm putting you on speaker. Say it again, Steven."

As Steven repeated the good news, they whooped and hollered and hugged one another — though Jacob avoided an awkward hug with Rhoda. But his brother grabbed him by the shoulders, and Jacob embraced him. Their joy for the Bylers seemed beyond what could be expressed.

They said their good-byes to Steven, and Jacob disconnected the call. While the others discussed the good news, he walked off, touching the number to Esther's phone shanty. On the seventh ring someone out of breath picked up. "Hallo?"

"This is Jacob King. Is Esther around?"

"It's me." The whispered pant didn't sound like her. "Give me a sec." He heard muffled sounds, as if she'd placed her hand over the receiver. A few seconds later there was a change in the background noise.

"Okay, I can breathe again. I thought you would be Bailey." She drew a long breath, her voice returning to normal. "He's checking on an old house that I've been trying to buy the rights to strip before it's demolished. It's a wreck, but it's part of an estate, and the lawyers have been sticklers. Bailey came up with a plan a few days ago. He's offering to save the estate money by demolishing it himself and hauling off the debris free of charge if I can have a week to gut it. The lawyers are balking, but the beneficiaries of the estate like the plan. So what's up with you?"

"I have good news about Phoebe."

"Jacob, that's wonderful and about time. Let's hear it!"

He briefed her and enjoyed her excited response. Soon they were talking about the progress in the orchard and how he was coping with being here. "So how are things there?"

"Two of the pregnant girls — Fanny and Malinda — have moved back home with their parents, one to Ohio and one to Indiana."

"Esther, that's great news."

"Isn't it? Watching the reunion between the parents and their daughters, stilted and awkward as it is each time, chokes me up.

It's really just a matter of giving room for cooling off. Once parents are given a little time, their warmer, loving hearts always prevail over the anger and disappointment."

"Always?"

"Parents love their children even when the offspring have disappointed and embarrassed them beyond what they think they can tolerate. Some families need only a couple of weeks. Some need until the baby is a few months old. But they come around, and when they do, it melts my heart and makes it worth housing the girls."

A beep interrupted them.

"Jacob, hang on. Maybe this is Bailey."

"Sure." He sat on a hill and waited. The others had spread out a blanket and were eating sandwiches. His stomach growled, but he'd talk as long as Esther had time. Then he'd eat.

"You there?"

"I am. Do you get to gut the house?"

"I do!"

"How long do you have to strip what you can?"

"Until Monday."

It was Thursday afternoon, and she wouldn't work on Sunday. "Are you free to start on it tomorrow?"

"I wish." Esther detailed the constraints

on her time and the lack of assistance she'd have for the weekend, but it didn't dampen her enthusiasm. Would she have time to harvest even an eighth of it? Not only would he like to help her, but he'd like to witness her pleasure. He imagined she would radiate joy like a woman fulfilled with good fortune.

"Jacob, hold on."

It sounded as if she'd covered the phone again, but he could hear a woman in the background talking to her. An idea came to him, and he headed for the blanket where everyone sat. Before he got there, Esther called his name.

"Ya. I'm here."

"Sorry, but I need to go. If I can borrow Bailey's cell on Saturday, I'll snap a few pictures and send them."

She wasn't too much of a stickler for rules. Abiding by the spirit of the Ordnung was important to her, but not the letter of it, and like other young Amish women, she saw nothing wrong with taking images of old houses and such. "I'd like that, Esther." They said their good-byes as he reached the group. Iva passed him a plate with two sandwiches and some chips.

"I know there's a ton of work to be done, but if I can find a driver to get me to the station in Boston, I'm leaving for Virginia tonight." If he took the Northeast Regional, he could board around nine o'clock, sleep until daylight, transfer to a bus in DC, and arrive at his destination in Virginia around lunchtime. He wasn't as familiar with bus routes, so maybe he could locate one closer to where Esther lived. "I'll aim to be home late Sunday or by midmorning on Monday."

Samuel nodded. "Sounds like a good plan."

If his brother felt the sting of losing Jacob's help for the next two days, Jacob didn't hear it in Samuel's voice or see a hint of it on his face. All he saw was a brother who wanted him to be happy. And Jacob was very happy.

Jojo got up. "I could drive you to the train station." She set down the trash bag. "I have one problem, though. Sophia won't travel well for that long to simply turn around and return here."

"I'd be happy to watch her," Iva offered, grinning.

He took a bite of his sandwich. "Wipe that look off your face, Iva. I've told you before . . ."

"We know." She held up her hands, her palms facing him. "We got it. She's not a girlfriend." She grinned again. "So, Jacob, where'd you meet this girl?"

"If you must know, I ran into her . . . with my horse as she was trying to cross the street. I knocked her flat on her back."

"Oh, honey," Leah mocked, shaking her head. "That's not what women mean when we say we want a man to sweep us off our feet."

"Not so fast, Leah," Iva said. "Just because we haven't heard of this technique before doesn't mean it didn't work." She held her hand over her eyes, peering at Jacob. "Did it do the job?"

"Women." Jacob sighed. "You imagine romance out of thin air."

Still, even as he discounted their teasing, he knew there was something magical about Esther and him. Wasn't there?

THIRTY-THREE

It was the first day of summer, and Leah had a job to do, but focusing on cleaning and preparing codling moth traps seemed impossible. She set the container on the back of the wagon she was using as a workbench and took in the view around her. The rich green leaves of the trees swayed in the warm wind, the branches teeming with fruit.

Was *teeming* the right word to use on something like this? Landon would know. But she hadn't seen or talked to him in six weeks and four days. That was entirely too long to go without having any communication with him.

What would a decade be like? Would it always hurt like this? Maybe it would even grow worse before it started getting better, but she knew from watching Rhoda, Samuel, and Jacob that healing did come.

"Leah." A man's voice echoed around her,

and she searched for the source. Crist was riding bareback across the field, waving. She waved in return. He'd recently increased his hours on this farm while keeping long hours on his folks' farm.

With a clean, old rag in hand, she wiped the sticky goo from the sides of a trap. The conversation she'd had with Landon at the hospital had made the situation really clear to her. He wanted *and* deserved a whole girl, one who was his peer and came with a family who would love and respect him. He needed in-laws who would not only welcome his future children into their lives but would gratefully shift their schedules for the privilege of spending time with him and his children.

Even if Leah could give him the best possible scenario of her leaving the Amish, it would never include those things. So she had set her will to getting used to missing him.

Crist slowed his horse. "I was heading to the barn to get a fresh horse and wagon when I caught a glimpse of you. Need a hand?"

Her horse shook its head and shifted forward, causing the wagon in front of her to move. "I'm gut, denki." She took a few steps, catching up to the back of the wagon.

Crist dismounted. "You're short some traps, aren't you?" He towered over her, more than Landon did by a good three inches, and Landon was six feet tall.

Holding a codling moth trap in one arm, she quickly counted the number of unbroken containers in the wagon and then the number of trees that still needed traps. How'd he figure that out so fast? She sighed. "It doesn't matter. I'm almost out of molasses too. I'll do what I can. Maybe Jojo can take me to the supply store later today."

Several traps had broken as she'd removed them from the trees, and there weren't enough new ones to replace all of them. Her chore today was to scrape out the dead bugs along with the molasses, water, and yeast mixture; add the fresh mixture; and rehang the traps in at least two dozen more trees before sunset, which would be in less than two hours.

Crist grabbed an empty container and poured in water, molasses, and yeast. He stuck a large wooden spoon into it and stirred. "Where is everyone?"

"Jojo is probably still doing laundry and washing dishes after that huge lunch she fixed. Rhoda and Samuel are on the east side, doing the same thing as me. Jacob's starting another spraying in the southern section. Iva should be back soon. She went to the house to get fresh rags." Leah slung a gooey, insect-covered rag into the laundry barrel in the back of the wagon. "Clearly I didn't prepare well for today."

"I'm surprised Rhoda didn't help you pack the wagon for the day."

"She volunteered to, and I should've let her." At the time Leah had just wanted Iva and her to get into the wagon and head out, thinking the sooner they started, the sooner they'd be done.

Crist easily lifted the huge container with the mixture and carefully poured some into the first trap in the row that lined the back of the wagon. Leah held a towel under the drip line between the two containers — the one in Crist's hand and the empty one in the wagon. It wouldn't do to get the mixture on the ground. That would only attract insects and undermine their efforts.

He moved to the next empty trap. "I got something on my mind."

His statement made her heart shiver. Was he going to ask her out again, as he had before he'd realized she was seeing Landon? As nice and handsome as Crist was, he wasn't the man for her. And Leah wasn't the woman for him — even if she'd never met Landon Olson.

"But before I say anything else, are you doing okay these days?" Crist got in the wagon and shifted the empty molasses jug out of the way and replaced it with one that still had some in it.

Leah exhaled slowly, intending to steady her emotions. He was fishing for answers she didn't want to give, but she was doing better than she had expected. Actually, as strange as it seemed, Landon's absence had a surprising upside to it. Without him waiting in the wings for her, without his love beckoning her and causing her to question whether she wanted to leave the Amish for him or for herself, she'd come to an absolute, peaceful conclusion.

It wasn't based on some huge revelation. At no point did she think, *Now I know the answer!* Her understanding and decision had come to her like a gentle snowfall, answers floating from the sky like feathery white flakes, one by one, until now, months later, everything in her life was covered in a pristine layer of answers.

Since he'd asked her an honest question and she'd been rude not to answer, she set down everything and focused on him. "I'm good. What's on your mind?"

He got out of the wagon. "I don't want to

stir anything negative between us, but I need to clear the air. I don't want to be rude or cruel, but I was wrong when I said I came to Maine for you."

Leah relaxed, her shoulders tingling as stress drained from her. "I'm relieved, not insulted."

"Gut." He pushed a few items back, making room for them to sit on the wagon. "Because you only appeared to be who I was looking for."

Leah sat. "Are you telling me this for the fun of it, or is there a point?"

"Iva. She's the point."

"Ah." Leah's heart jittered with excitement. They just might be really happy together, but she would keep those thoughts to herself. It wasn't wise to influence someone when it came to matchmaking. "Does she know how you feel?"

"She knows I'd like for us to date. I asked if she'd let me take her home after the singing this Sunday night."

"Today's Friday" — Leah crinkled her nose — "and she hasn't answered you yet?"

"She's thinking on it, which means a lot because there's a guy in Indiana who's been writing to her. She's known him for a while, and he moved out of the way when her Daed wanted her to marry someone else.

But now he's letting his interest be known."

"She's been living here more than a year. I'd say it took him a while."

"He works for the man her Daed wanted her to marry. You know how complicated these things can get. Anyway, if she says yes, it means she told him she's decided to see someone else." He grinned. "Me."

"I definitely could see you two together." But what did Iva want?

Leah knew what she wanted for herself — a very plain and simple life guided by her own sense of what God wanted, not one guided by the written and unwritten rules of the Ordnung. She longed to move and breathe without feeling dirty if she let her hair down or wore a flowery dress. Or jeans.

What she didn't know was how she'd make a living. But she would figure that out too, and by the time she left in a year or so, she'd have a good savings from all her time working the orchard.

"Iva's really great." Crist rubbed his hands together, trying to get the sticky goo off. "When I first came here, all I saw was my offense that an Amish girl had a camera."

"And now?"

"She's made me stop being afraid of picture taking as if it's a graven image I'm going to fall down and worship. She's capturing creation in images that say, isn't God amazing?"

Leah gestured toward the knoll that Iva had topped, riding a horse. "I'm not sure she'll be willing to give it up to join the church."

He spotted her and smiled. "Ah, but is she the kind of girl who'd not join a faith she believes in simply because she doesn't agree with every facet of it? Or will she accept the greater good of the faith and put the camera away or use it only when no one is around who would be offended by it?"

"I don't know."

He stood and smiled at Leah. "Neither do I, but I intend to find out." He strode to where Iva had stopped the horse and held it steady while she got down.

"Rags and lots of them." Iva removed the saddlebags and passed them to Crist.

"Denki. But half of the last twenty codling moth traps I've removed since you left have been broken, so we don't have enough traps . . . or molasses." Leah reconnected the thick wire to one of the traps that was ready to be hung in its tree. "What took you so long anyway?"

Iva shrugged. "I had a call to make, and it took longer than I expected."

Crist definitely looked uncomfortable, and

when he turned to put a stack of rags into the wagon, Iva grabbed him by his shirt sleeve.

He paused.

Iva smiled. "The answer is ya. I'll ride home from the singing with you."

All discomfort faded from Crist's face as he smiled, showing a beautiful row of straight, white teeth. "Gut. *Wunderbaar* gut."

"I thought so. Actually, you should pick me up and take me there too." Iva took a stack of rags from Crist. "What will we do about the broken traps?"

Leah shrugged. "Get Jojo to take someone to the supply store tomorrow. She's not going to live here forever, though. What Englisch person would want to stay in a home without a radio or television? Her daughter keeps asking to watch some favorite show of hers."

"It's more than just that. They're ready to feel a part of the Englisch world again. Did you hear Jojo at breakfast this morning?"

"I left early to grab a shower. What'd I miss?"

"Jojo is thinking about visiting Camilla later this week."

"Oh, that's good."

Crist frowned. "You said it's good, but

you look as if it's not."

"Without her here to drive us, getting to the grocery and supply store becomes an all-day event."

"Ya." Iva nodded. "But I enjoy the outings, and you know that with more Amish moving here, someone will eventually open a store closer to this area."

Leah's heart about stopped. Wasn't this the answer she'd been looking for? "That's it!" She grabbed Iva by the shoulders. "A store! A general store right here in this area." Chills exploded over her body.

Iva shook the rags, looking amused and confused. "What are you talking about?"

"We need a store in this area, ya?"

Iva nodded. "Badly. We spend half our time ordering by phone or hiring drivers or traveling too far by horse and buggy."

"And it needs to be one that caters to the needs of the Amish, with farming supplies, fabric for making clothes, oil, candles, kerosene lamps, and everything else — even some basic grocery items."

Crist finished filling the last container and set the barrel in the back of the wagon. "But we're all farmers thus far. Who'd run it?"

Leah's heart turned the biggest flip of her life. "I would." Could she rent the abandoned store from Erlene, maybe doing housework and laundry for her in exchange for living there? Her skin tingled with excitement. It was a perfect idea, wasn't it? An Amish person who was willing to open that kind of store would eventually move to Maine, but if Leah got one started first . . .

Her heart went wild. *That* she could do. No one would know what to stock in that kind of store better than she would, and it'd be worth it to Samuel and Rhoda not to have to spend so much time ordering and trying to get the goods here. Leah could make a profit *and* save them money!

Crist looked hopeful. "My Daed says there's a group of twenty Amish who hope to purchase four hundred acres not too far from here come winter."

Erlene would work with her, and Leah could live there while she built up the business. If she'd learned one thing from her years of living Amish, it was how to sacrifice comforts while building a successful business.

But if Leah's Daed had any power to wield, and he did, he'd see to it that not one Amish in this area bought anything from Leah.

Would everyone go along with that? Would they have a choice?

THIRTY-FOUR

As the rain made a steady pitter-patter on the tin roof, Samuel shuffled papers inside the barn office, catching up on bills and inventory and enjoying the slower pace of a rainy day. He'd let too many supplies run out while keeping up with the demands of the orchard. There had been other rainy days, but those were spent readying the harvest kitchen for the mass production of canning that would begin next month.

He pulled the calendar in front of him. July 6. They had about six weeks, maybe less, to get the harvest kitchen organized to run from sunup to sundown six days a week for a month or more after the last apples were picked. After this harvest they should have the money to buy more land and invest in full-time, year-round help. Lots of workers.

Something pulled his thoughts from the paperwork in front of him. Was someone else in the barn? He left the office, scanning the area.

His wife.

She stood in the open doorway at the back of the building, gazing at the steady, welcome rain that soaked the orchard. If he made a guess, he'd say she was praying and thinking.

He crossed the dirt floor. "Hi."

She glanced back, a tranquil smile welcoming him. "Hallo."

He joined her in watching the rain cover the orchard and wrapped his arms around her shoulders and across her chest.

She rested against him, and he felt bathed in contentment. He kissed her neck, enjoying this rare moment of not having to watch their every move. When Jacob had realized rain was moving in, he made plans to go to Virginia. According to the weatherman the skies there were clear. "In three days we will have our two-month anniversary."

"Do you think it's possible to keep falling deeper in love?"

"It doesn't feel as if it's possible, but I think Steven and Phoebe are proof that no matter how boundless love is, it can grow as the years pass."

Rhoda drew a deep breath and nodded.

She seemed serene and yet deep in

thought. "Something on your mind?" He brushed his fingers along her neck.

"She's not going to stay, Samuel."

"Leah?"

She nodded.

"My sister said that?"

"No. But I know it's true. What if we've been wrong about Landon and her?"

"We did our best neither to condone nor condemn their relationship. They've broken up, and I think it'd be a mistake to do anything that would encourage them to get back together."

She eased from him and leaned against the rough wood wall. "But we allowed them to see each other, knowing they were falling in love. We may not have encouraged it, but we didn't try to stop it. Yet when the pressure from the community hit, we did nothing as they were pulled apart. I've wavered like a woman without faith, and I've done so because in this I've not had faith — only fear. Well, that and selfishness. I don't want to lose her from being in our lives in ways she can only be if she remains Amish. But what about what she and Landon wanted?"

"There were lots of factors, but they decided to break up. Not every relationship is meant to be. Aren't you and Jacob proof of that?"

"Jacob and I imploded because of who we were together and because you and I fell in love. But Leah and Landon were strong together until people hit them with religious prejudices and fears. I've been trying to figure it out," — she touched her temple and then the center of her chest — "and all I can come up with is a question. How are our actions any different than the way Jojo treated Camilla — mistrusting, assuming, fearful, and controlling?"

After living here a couple of weeks, Jojo had come up with a plan to meet with Camilla and the same family counselor that Camilla and her son had been going to before he was killed. Jojo and Camilla had gone to see the counselor three times, and now Jojo was thinking of introducing Sophia to her Grandmamma. It was a good start. But it wouldn't have happened if Rhoda had kept fighting God about the intuitions or if Jojo had refused to compromise by meeting Camilla at a family counselor.

Is that what he and Rhoda were doing concerning Leah — fighting against what they should be fighting for?

Samuel placed a hand on the wall on each side of Rhoda, distracted by her closeness. "What you're saying is against all the Amish believe."

Her eyes were locked on his, and he knew she was looking to him for confirmation and leadership. Was she right?

The phone rang, jolting both of them. Samuel bent and kissed her on the lips, lingering longer than he should have. "Hold that thought." He hurried into the next room. Caller ID said it was the hospital, and he grabbed the receiver. "Hello."

Samuel listened as Steven stumbled through the latest happenings. Phoebe's condition had changed for the worse, and she had a long list of issues going on, including an erratic heart rate they couldn't control. The doctors were going to take the baby, hoping that brought the needed changes in Phoebe's health.

Rhoda came to the door, and when she saw the look on his face, intensity pierced her eyes, and she moved in closer.

"Do you need us to come?"

"Not immediately. She started struggling during the night, and the doctor said if she didn't improve by noon, they'd take the baby today. After letting Phoebe's parents and my parents know, I called Landon. We're at this hospital so the children and I have parents and grandparents and such, and yet I wanted Landon here. Makes little sense, but he arrived about four hours later.

I knew he would. He's been . . ." Steven's voice cracked, and he cleared it. "Anyway, maybe in my exhaustion I'm just making weird and bad decisions, but I feel with such a scant crew, you all need to keep working the farm as much as possible. Besides, they'll take the baby before you could get here. He's only two weeks shy of being full term. If Phoebe improves as they expect, they'll bring her out of the coma two to four days after the C-section. The doctors think her heart rate will stabilize once the baby is delivered. One of their main goals is to get her breathing on her own so they can remove the trach tube. It's a breeding ground for bacteria, and antibiotics can do only so much."

Steven had obviously learned a lot during his lengthy stay.

"So when do you want us to come?"

"Stay there until I call back, but start making plans to come in about four days."

"You're sure?"

"We're taking this by faith and trusting that Phoebe will improve. But it would be good if you were here when they bring her out of the coma, so I'll let you know. If things change, I'll call." Someone spoke to Steven. "I have to go."

"Okay. Bye." He hung up the phone and

told Rhoda all that her brother had said. He remained in the chair, and she stayed on the edge of his desk, facing him. She seemed as lost in thought as he.

Life was so fragile. If something happened to Phoebe, Rhoda and he would be devastated, but they were at peace with their relationship with her. But if something were to happen to Leah, he couldn't say the same thing. That thought made his mind spin with questions. Would defying the church to support Leah be morally wrong? Would he answer to God for not using tough love with his sister?

Why did life have to raise so many more questions than it answered?

He took Rhoda's hands into his. "The questions never end, and seldom can we be completely sure of the choices we make." He squeezed her hands and took a deep breath. "But come what may, and what may come is us being shunned, we'll let Leah know we support whatever decisions she makes. We'll apologize to her and support her, but we won't interfere between her and Landon. That's theirs to work out or not. Still, from here on out, she makes her own decisions, and we back her."

Rhoda studied him, not a trace of a smile on her beautiful face, and he knew she had the same question as he did — what if they were wrong to support her and Landon?

Landon watched from his chair in the overcrowded waiting room as Amish greeted one another with kisses and hugs. They talked in hushed tones, speaking in Pennsylvanian Dutch.

Phoebe had been wheeled into the operating room about five minutes ago. His nerves were stretched tight. Most in this room didn't know about the daily battle that was waged for Phoebe's survival. Doctors changed her medications, altered how they administered the nutrients and oxygen, and combated constant antibiotic-resistant infections, as they fought swelling, bedsores, and more. And yet, for all the struggles, Phoebe seemed to want to live as desperately as Steven wanted her to.

With working full-time, coming here the minute he was off, being a driver for Phoebe's loved ones, and ensuring everyone made fresh recordings for Phoebe to listen to, Landon was bone weary. Steven had to be far more exhausted. On top of that, Steven knew the hospital bills were insurmountable, especially for a man who, like most Amish, didn't have regular health insurance. Instead, they had some sort of co-op through the Amish. Landon hoped it would be some help.

He had to admit, though, that Steven didn't seem to be fazed by the reality of paying on this bill for the rest of his life. He somehow managed to tune out that pressure, and after he visited his wife, every day he went home and played with his children as if he felt good and rested.

Landon stood. He'd sat for too long. He needed to find some place out of the way where he could pace. On his off days, when it was his rotation to stay with Phoebe, he paced the room, talking to her, playing the recordings, or reading aloud.

Landon eased into the hallway. Steven was at the end of it, leaning against a wall, talking with several Amish. Landon went the other direction.

"Landon."

At Steven's loud whisper, Landon turned.

Steven motioned for him. "Where are you going?"

"Looking for a place to pace," Landon explained as he reached the group.

"Ah." Steven clutched Landon's shoulder. "I'm just making sure you aren't skipping out on us. I appreciate that you chauffeured most everyone who's here today."

"Not a problem."

"You won't go far, right? The nurses said it would be just a few minutes before we get a report."

"I'll be here for whatever you need."

"The surgeon said that women in Phoebe's condition have an almost-miraculous turnabout once the baby is delivered."

Landon had overheard the doctor say that, but he'd also heard too many conflicting reports to put much stock in what one doctor said. "I hope it works that way for Phoebe too."

"Ya." Steven nodded, scratching his cheek. "I told Samuel to have everyone stay at the orchard. Do you think that was the right decision?"

If Phoebe survived, it was the right decision. She'd remain in a medically induced coma for at least a few more days, and when they did bring her out, she'd be under heavy sedation as they spent a day or more weaning her from the ventilator. "Yeah, it was the right decision."

Landon's phone vibrated, and he dug it out of his pocket. His granny. "I should take this."

"Sure. I need to get back anyway." Steven went down the hallway.

Landon slid his finger across the screen

and held the phone to his ear. "Hey, Granny, what's up?"

"How is everything there?"

"I was going to call you in a bit. Phoebe's in surgery. They're taking the baby today."

"Oh, okay. My stuff will keep. Call me with an update later."

"What stuff?"

"Someone wants to rent my old store, and I don't want to give an answer you might not agree with."

"Rent it for what? It's a run-down eyesore that isn't even wired for electricity."

"It has good bones."

Her retort reminded him once again what she'd said many times — she'd loved running her store back in its day. "Yeah, I guess it does at that. What do they want to do with it?"

"To fix it up, live in it, turn it into a store for the Amish. We're talking long-term, I think, and since my house and property will be yours one day, I just want to be sure it's okay with you."

His? He hadn't ever thought that far ahead. "Let's not talk like that. I want you around, but it sounds like someone's thinking right about that spot. It's in a good location for that kind of store." He knew a group of Amish were keenly interested in moving to Maine, where good farming land was affordable. "You'd make some money off the rent, and I see no reason not to give them a fifty-year lease."

"Landon, it's Leah who's asking. She and a man named Crist came by here."

His heart skipped a beat, and he tried to find his voice. When he couldn't, he focused on breathing. He hadn't even gone on a date. Was Leah already making plans with Crist?

But he wanted her to be happy, and with some tender, loving care, his grandmother's store could be a great place to live and work. Leah had never intended to work the orchard long-term, so maybe this would be her escape — a way to make good money and yet have store hours and not have to toil in the cold. "Yeah, Granny, work out a deal with them, a good one for Leah, and I'll make it up to you, okay?"

"You know this means you'll have to see her regularly, especially if you choose to move back here."

Landon paced, shaking his free hand to release some of his pent-up emotions. "I'm hundreds of miles away, and I see her all the time, whether awake or asleep. Just do it, and don't tell her you asked me. Let this be between you and her . . . I mean, them.

Actually, I would rather not hear anything else about it, okay?"

"Yeah, sure."

Steven's Daed hurried toward Landon, gesturing. "Steven is asking for you. The baby's been rushed to NICU. But while the doctor was delivering the baby, Phoebe's oxygen levels bottomed out."

Landon hung up on Granny and hurried down the hall. Had they gone through all this angst, prayer, and expensive medical treatments for Steven to lose Phoebe?

God . . . please . . . don't let that happen!

THIRTY-FIVE

Jacob pushed the air-gun hammer against the roof and squeezed the trigger, putting another round of nails into place. He stood, removed his hat, and wiped the sweat from his brow. The water in the in-ground pool below lapped against the sides, creating an oasis and releasing the faint smell of chlorine into the muggy air. Being on a roof in July was a world away from being in an orchard in Maine.

Bailey and Althea were inside with the windows and doors shut and the air conditioner running. They'd helped him earlier, but Althea had started feeling bad, and Bailey told her they were taking an afternoon siesta. Esther had gone in for a bit to check Althea's blood pressure and make sure she'd taken her heart meds.

Esther . . .

Jacob put his straw hat back on and looked through the thick foliage of an oak tree, hoping to catch a glimpse of her. But all he saw were the sawhorses they'd set up hours ago, which held an antique door she'd scraped and shellacked to use as a counter-top for the outdoor kitchen.

The metal ladder rattled, and he peered down. Esther was climbing it. *This* is why he'd boarded a train and made the trek here from Maine as often as he could — time with Esther. They'd spent days together on four separate occasions since he'd returned to patch up their relationship. And they'd spent untold hours on the phone. He'd even increased his monthly coverage to unlimited time.

She shook a red Solo cup. "Thirsty?" She climbed to the third or fourth rung from the top and held out the drink. He knew better than to invite her up. After almost falling off a roof as a child, she didn't get on them. So what had happened in her past that made her so leery of romantic relation-ships? There had to be more to it than the jaded views that came from helping preg-nant girls who'd been abandoned by their boyfriends.

"You didn't drink out of it, did you?" He took the cup and tried to keep a serious face.

She raised one eyebrow. "Maybe."

He took a long drink, and sat, ready to

chat for as long as she was willing to stand on the ladder.

After he finished roofing, he and Esther would spend the rest of the day side by side — some work, some play, all of it fun. They shared such camaraderie. He'd never known that with anyone before. Love, yes. But his relationship with Esther was different in ways he knew in his heart yet couldn't define.

How long before she could make herself admit they were more than friends? What held her prisoner from letting a relationship blaze its own path?

She propped her elbows on the top rung. "I got a call while you were up here. Remember the house I told you about, not the one we gutted before they tore it down, but the one that's supposed to be remodeled in a few weeks?"

"I do. Did they accept your offer?"

"It was actually your offer since it was your idea, but ya. They've flagged certain items to be salvaged, and I get to do the work and keep the items. You're a genius to come up with the idea of letting people know that all profits go toward running a home for unwed mothers. I've always tried to hide that part, thinking that it should be kept private and that if people knew, they'd be less likely to help, not more."

He took a long drink, enjoying the cold water. "If you set up the home as a nonprofit and people knew the old crown molding, windows, or flooring they want hauled away could be taken off their taxes as a donation, you'd get even more items and could make a bigger profit."

"I'm not sure how I feel about making the home a nonprofit, and I doubt the church would back going through the government for such a thing. But that aside, would you care to ride to that house later today? It'd be just for fun because we can't do any work on it."

It sounded like another date to him. Plenty of their outings fell into that category, but she didn't see it that way, and he'd keep that viewpoint to himself for now. "Sure."

Working like this — doing his favorite thing, which was carpentry, while Esther did hers, which was adding character through repurposed goods — felt more right than anything in his life ever had.

Their friendship seemed destined somehow.

When he came right after he and the others received good news about Phoebe, he and Esther spent his first two days ripping up pine floors, taking out entire window units, and removing crown molding from a 150-year-old home. As they'd meandered up and down the staircases, their voices had echoed throughout that old place as so many others had before them. Esther's excitement over what she could salvage with his help had made it a weekend to remember. He wouldn't mind finding another project like that to work on with her.

A couple of weeks after that, he had returned again, and they'd worked in the shop, making sellable items from what they'd gleaned. When time allowed, he and Esther worked on this summer kitchen, which he was in no hurry to finish. Jacob knew that Bailey wasn't in a rush either. The man had what he'd wanted, an excuse for Jacob to be around.

He held the cup toward her and shook it. "I saved some for you."

She pursed her lips and narrowed her eyes. Although determined and organized, she was actually pretty laid back about most of life, taking it as it came. But she had a few pet peeves. One was she hated to drink out of a cup someone else had drunk from. He'd figured that out by accidentally drinking from her cup while they were gutting a house. After that, if he could get hold of her cup, he'd get her attention, and then he'd take a drink. She wouldn't drink out of that cup again. They'd shared laughs about that . . . and she'd given dozens of idle threats.

"Do you want to drink the rest or wear it?"

"Maybe both." He continued to offer the cup. "I think that pool is calling my name."

"Then get off the roof and have at it. There are extra swim trunks in the pool house."

He wouldn't. She'd have to leave, and that would undermine his whole point of being here. "You ever swim?"

"Definitely, and I bring the girls here regularly. Bailey doesn't mind, and the church looks the other way as long as we never do it in mixed company."

"Back home in Pennsylvania, some of the girls would clean an Englisch home practically for free if there was a pool they could swim in when the work was done."

"I don't blame them." She took the cup, met his eyes with a daring look, and then drank from it.

He couldn't move. Was she flirting with him? Since he was on a roof, he was glad he'd been sitting down when she pulled that little antic.

Wow. That was really bold for her. What

did it mean?

After a teasing smirk, she started down the ladder. Was she ready to admit that their relationship was deeper, richer than what she wanted it to be?

"You leaving already?"

"I'm sticking my feet in the water. Kumm."

He didn't need to be asked twice. If he really wanted to, he could finish the kitchen today, or he could drag it out for one more visit. He made his way down the ladder and peeled off his shoes and socks. Esther used his arm to keep her balance while removing her laced-up black tennis shoes. She smiled, her light-brown eyes looking golden in the afternoon light. She sat on the edge, with the water covering most of her calves, and tucked her dress a bit above her knees.

He rolled up his pants legs and sat beside her. The water rippled across the pool, catching sunlight that sparkled off the top and swayed shadows through the depths. Sitting there with her, chatting, he felt a sense of peace that burrowed into his soul. It was perfect.

The funny thing about Esther was that, in her own way, she was every bit as private as he'd been before he met her. So he paced his multitude of questions, asking only a couple of important ones each time he came. Some he'd asked a few times but she'd gently refused to answer or had changed the subject. "So, why house pregnant girls?"

"Because they need it."

"Ya, I get that, but it puts you and your life under a microscope. So you've added to the challenges of the Old Ways by making yourself the object of suspicion and prejudice in your own community."

She watched the water, swishing her legs through it, then shrugged. Obviously, she wasn't ready to talk about her reasons.

He cupped a handful of water and dumped it back into the pool. She seemed lost in thought. Even though they engaged in plenty of lively banter and laughter and talked about lots of serious topics, this subject seemed off limits.

She turned to him. "You know . . ."

He chuckled. "I know that tone. You have an idea."

She grinned. "Late this afternoon we could use the outdoor kitchen and cook dinner. Doesn't eating by the pool in the cool of the evening sound perfect?"

"It sounds nice. Perfect would be that meal at the ocean."

Her eyes grew large. "You're right." She

raised her eyebrows. "After the kitchen is done, let's set up a weekend to get Bailey to take us there as a celebration."

Jacob started to get up.

She looked at him. "Where are you going?"

"If that's the deal on finishing the kitchen, I'm getting back to work."

She laughed. "Sit."

"But I need to work."

"Sit." She patted the concrete. "I know Bailey's schedule, and he can't take us to the beach for at least two weeks."

Jacob sat and plunked his feet into the water, splashing her. Without so much as a flinch, she propped her hands on the cement behind her.

Jacob did the same thing, settling his hand near hers. "I've been thinking, Shark Bait."

She closed her eyes and tilted her face toward the sun, soaking in a few rays. "Ya? What about?"

His brushed his fingers over hers. "Maybe we should . . . think about dating."

She sat upright, eyes wide with disbelief. Was she that surprised? Seemed to him she should be shocked if he wasn't leaning in that direction.

He waved his hand away from himself.

"I'm talking a long, long way down the road."

"Jacob . . ." She shook her head. "Don't do this. Don't ask it. Please."

"You've *never* had that thought?"

"Well, I . . . I have, but thoughts don't matter. Actions do, and we talked about this."

"That was months ago — hours of phone conversations ago, many trips and working side by side ago. Just admit what you feel, what *we* feel, and say it's a possibility in a year or so."

"But it's not."

He scoffed, a bitter laugh that he immediately regretted. "You can't be serious. Why is it so hard for you to own up to your feelings?"

She started to stand, and he grabbed her wrist. "Come on, Esther. Don't get all skittish."

She pulled free and grabbed her shoes, knocking the soles of them together, probably to release some of the angst inside her. "I told you men aren't good at being just friends."

Her words slapped across his soul, and anger rushed to the surface. He stood. "And how many men have been where I am now, Esther? How many have navigated over the line of friendship and landed square in the middle of a budding romance, and then you blamed them for crossing the line because you couldn't admit how you felt?"

"You should go." True to form, her words were softly spoken, but he knew she meant them. *Why* had he started this conversation?

She started walking away. "Esther, wait."

She paused and turned to face him. He studied her, seeing a dozen emotions mirrored in her eyes, and even though she stood right here, he knew she was running from him. Jacob closed the gap. "If it helps you, then let's agree to forget everything I said. You can count it as a moment of insanity brought on by daydreaming."

"It's too late. I can't pretend like that."

"But you could pretend to be married. Doesn't that tell you how mixed-up you are when it comes to admitting who you really are and how you really feel?"

The sliding glass door whooshed open, and Dora stepped outside, carrying a cardboard box about half the width of a shoebox. Squinting against the sun, she angled her head and looked at him. "Jacob?"

His heart sank. "Hi, Dora."

Dora glanced from Jacob to Esther, looking dismayed and offended. "What are you doing here?"

"He's building an outdoor kitchen for Bailey and Althea." Esther took a few steps back, motioning at the kitchen.

"Esther," Jacob whispered. Was she really going to continue the cover-up?

Esther turned her back to Dora, faced him, and whispered, "Leave it alone, Jacob."

Dora walked toward the kitchen, looking at the set foundation, timber framing, and almost-finished roof. Her eyes moved to Jacob.

He'd told her that he wasn't dating her anymore. If she'd accepted that, she wouldn't feel betrayed right now. But how could he remind her of that as they stood in front of her sister? The situation was ridiculous.

"Dora." Jacob bent, rolling down his pants legs, using the time to think. He didn't want to apologize for going out with her. That would only be an insult. And he certainly wasn't sorry for the time he'd spent with Esther. He stood upright. "I know Esther isn't married, but I learned it a month after you and I stopped dating."

"So you're dating my sister?"

"No." Esther shook her head.

Dora pointed the package at Esther. "I found this in the attic, and when I realized what it was, my heart fluttered, thinking you'd found a way for me to make contact with Jacob and for us to have a connection. I'm such a fool. I should've known you hadn't changed. You planned the breakup from the day you met him, didn't you? You'd get him to dump me and chase after you, the pretty one."

"Dora, I haven't told you everything, but it's not like that."

"It's *always* like that! Did she tell you, Jacob? The men are either unworthy of me, so she runs them off, or they look past me to her. What is it about a used-up, older woman that attracts the men, Esther?"

"Dora . . ." Esther's calm response was a huge contrast to Dora's flaring emotions.

"Don't you 'Dora' me! When you learned that a new man in town had asked me out, you promised to stay away from him. You gave your word!" Dora's face was scarlet red.

Esther drew a deep breath. "We ran into each other, almost literally."

Dora scoffed. "I bet that *happenstance* took a lot of planning, didn't it?"

Esther's breathing became labored. Did she have asthma? "You know better than that. You're just upset —"

"What I know is this was the last straw." Dora shoved the box toward her, the package shaking.

Jacob understood better why Esther had hoped Dora wouldn't find out about their friendship until she had someone else. Dora resented her sister to the point that she couldn't balance her emotions with facts and couldn't be reasoned with.

Jacob removed his hat. "Maybe we should've told you that we've become friends. But you and I went on only three dates."

"You liked me, and then you bumped into her. Even after you broke up with me, you kissed me. Did you tell her that?"

She was using any weapon she had to hurt her sister and come between Jacob and Esther — as if they needed any help with that. All by himself he was doing a fine job of messing up what they had. "There was only one kiss, and you kissed me."

Dora blinked, looking shocked. Hadn't she expected him to defend himself? Her surprise soon faded, and she slammed the package on a nearby table. "Esther, don't ever speak to me again. From here on I have two sisters, not three." She stormed to the gate of the blind fence and slammed it behind her.

Esther remained glued in place, seemingly resigned to the ugliness Dora had spewed at her. She sighed. "She meant every word. It could be years before she's willing to forgive me, and make no mistake, she'll view the whole thing as my fault."

Where did this leave him and Esther?

Esther went to the table and picked up the box. "I should've told you the truth from the start, and after you found out, I continued the cover-up with Dora. It makes me a horrible person, and I hate who I end up being because of her, but I never know how to handle her."

"Maybe you should stop trying to 'handle her' and just be yourself and live your life. I can't see how you two could've ended up worse off than you are now."

"I can't argue with that reasoning." Esther flipped the narrow box from one side to another, staring at it. "She was upset and saying things she shouldn't have. Her depictions and insinuations about me aren't true."

The fact that Dora had tried to turn the kiss she gave him into something seductive was his proof that she twisted the truth. "I believe you . . . not that anything in your past changes how I feel."

With his past cleaned up so that he didn't need to hide and his talking to Esther about anything and everything, his thoughts and understanding had become clear. He now saw situations for what they really were. And he knew they weren't just friends. There was a spark and something magical between them. And more than that, each of them had a hope of a future together. That wasn't his imagination lying to him.

"But what is true, Esther? Do even you know?" Could she see that how she felt didn't match how she treated him?

She pursed her lips, tears falling. "Ya. What's true is I can't do this. I know it's me, and I . . . I'm sorry." She put the box in his hands. "This is for you. I've been searching for it since before you discovered I wasn't married. At the time I wanted it to be a thank-you gift. A good-bye gift." She paused, staring up at him, confusion and hurt floating in her misty eyes. "And as it turns out, that's what it is. You take good care of yourself, and find a girl you like who didn't decide never to marry." She hurried across the pool deck and into the house.

Jacob stood there. An outdoor kitchen waited for him to finish it, and he'd complete the job before he left.

He looked at the parcel. He would be twenty-five at the end of this month, but part of him felt as foolish as a child who'd broken his mother's favorite item, one that had been passed down for generations, one he wasn't supposed to have picked up in the first place.

But he'd asked Esther about the two of them dating one day, and now he had no choice — he had to give Esther time before he approached her again. That's what she did when she mediated with the pregnant girls' parents — remained available to the parents and protected their children while giving them time to adjust and think about who they really were and what they wanted to do with the facts of the situation.

He opened the box. A doorknob? He picked it up. It was a particularly plain one that appeared to have been painted black a very long time ago. According to what Esther had shared with him, that meant it'd been in a Plain home — either Amish or Mennonite. It had a tag on it: House, circa 1750. Doorknob, circa 1899. Taken from the one-time home of Moses King on Ashen Wood Lane, Lancaster, Pennsylvania, by Esther Beachy, July 2000.

She would've been fourteen and visiting her grandmother's for a few days that summer. It would've been right before her Daed got sick. Jacob wasn't one for looking back, but wasn't the Moses King at that address the original King homesteader in Lancaster?

How many generations back was he? Even with Jacob's math skills, he didn't know.

He clutched it, feeling the power of a connection that went back hundreds of years. The question on his mind was, could he get Esther to stop holding on to the past and step into the future?

And if he could, how many years would it take?

THIRTY-SIX

Rhoda, Samuel, and Leah sat in the waiting room filled with Amish people. The three of them had arrived almost an hour ago, and although they'd visited with plenty of relatives, they hadn't seen Steven yet. He was allowing his parents and Phoebe's to take turns seeing Phoebe, and the next time he returned to the waiting room, he'd see them.

Her pulse thumped inside her ears. After all this time the next few days would tell where Phoebe and her son would land. Phoebe's lungs had hardened, unable to stretch as needed to absorb the oxygen the machines pumped into them, and the antibiotic-resistant infection wouldn't clear up unless they could get her off the ventilator.

But the doctor who'd said Phoebe should start improving once the baby was delivered had been right. Phoebe was still in ICU, and the baby was in the NICU, but Phoebe had improved enough that now, just three days after they'd taken the baby by C-section, they were going to bring her out of the coma. The elasticity to her lungs would slowly return to normal once she was breathing on her own.

Phoebe's yet-unnamed little one was a fighter. The doctors were pleased with the improvements he was making.

Thankfully, Jacob had returned to Maine unexpectedly early, allowing Samuel and Rhoda to come to the hospital. Crist and Iva were there too, although Iva was staying with the bishop and his wife while Samuel and Rhoda were away. But those three would work the orchard and tend to the livestock and dogs. Jojo would cook for them and run any errands necessary for now, but she was thinking of moving in with Bob and Camilla, at least for a few months until she could get on her feet again.

Rhoda had caught a glimpse of the future for Bob, Camilla, Jojo, and Sophia. Jojo and Camilla would slowly and steadily grow closer. Camilla would get to be the mom she'd never been to her own son, and Jojo would have the mother figure she'd always longed for.

Steven strode into the room with Phoebe's parents. "I thought you'd be here." He hugged Rhoda. "It's almost time for them to bring her out of the coma. Her parents don't want to be in there."

Rhoda looked at Phoebe's Mamm. The woman wiped her eyes. "I can't watch anymore. She's struggling to breathe, and the doctor said when they cut the ventilator off and on to wean her from it, she'll struggle harder for a day or two before it gets easier."

Rhoda hugged her as the woman cried. "You've been watching those grandbabies. She'll be so grateful for that, so don't feel guilty over needing to come away while she wakes."

"Denki." The woman straightened.

"I'm going to take Samuel and Rhoda back now. Once Phoebe is awake and understands what happened to her, we'll swap who spends time with her, for those who want to go in. But it may be hours before she feels oriented, okay?"

The others nodded, and Steven ushered Rhoda and Samuel down the hall.

Rhoda's shoes squeaked against the tile floor. "Will they allow three of us in there?" The last time they were here, the staff preferred that only one person at a time be there, but they didn't question two.

"They'll allow four of us right now, at least

for a few hours if not all day."

Rhoda tried to keep up with the men's long strides. "Four?"

"Landon is with her."

Rhoda grabbed her brother's arm, slowing him a bit. "He's in there while Amish friends and family are waiting for time with her?"

"A lot of people go in for their own comfort, but as odd as it may sound, Landon is the one I draw comfort from. We need to —"

Before Steven could finish his sentence, a nurse approached, talking while falling into step with him. "The doctor is by her side, and Phoebe is starting to rouse. Remember what we said: she's heavily sedated and won't be able to talk with the trach still in."

"When will they remove the trach?"

"The tube will be detached soon, but the trach will remain for several weeks. That way if anything goes wrong and she needs oxygen again, it's in place. She'll have day surgery, possibly at a doctor's office, when it's time to remove it." She clicked her pen. "Remember, she'll look different as she wakes."

"I've been told this numerous times. Is there a reason?"

The nurse stepped in front of Steven,

blocking the door. "There is. You've seen her peaceful for months. You need to be braced for what you may see today. If bringing her around the first time goes badly — if she suffers a seizure or uncontrollable panic — we'll have to put her under and then try again in an hour or so. That pattern may be repeated a few times, possibly over a two-day period. Okay?"

Steven's eyes misted. "Thank you for caring."

The nurse smiled, shoving an ink pen into her pocket. "Let's do this."

A doctor stood at the head of the bed, a tiny flashlight in hand as he forced one of Phoebe's eyes open and flashed the light off and on.

Landon stood, and Rhoda went to him. "Hi."

Without a hint of reluctance, Landon embraced her and then shook hands with Samuel. Wasn't he even a little angry with them? Oh, how good it felt to see her friend again.

"Phoebe, can you hear me?" the doctor called. "Phoebe, can you lift a finger for me?" When Phoebe didn't budge, the doctor turned to Steven. "We may have to let more of the sedatives wear off. We gave her a good dose of tranquilizers before bringing her out of the coma. You try."

Steven took Phoebe by the hand. "Phoebe. Sweetheart. Can you hear me?" Steven stroked her head. "It's time to wake. Rhoda's here. And Samuel. And Landon."

Phoebe turned her head toward her husband's voice, her eyes closed and body unmoving. Steven jerked air into his lungs. "That's it, sweetie." Tears choked him. "It's time to wake."

Her hands moved to her stomach, and her brows knitted tightly.

"You had the baby. We have a beautiful son."

Rhoda moved near the doctor. "Can they bring the baby to her?"

He shook his head. "Neonatal babies don't leave NICU. When Phoebe is well enough, she can go to him."

"Did you hear that?" Rhoda picked up Phoebe's other hand. "When you're better in . . ." She looked to the doctor.

He shoved the little flashlight into the lapel pocket of his lab coat. "Probably in three to six days."

"Ah. You'll get to hold your little one in less than a week." Rhoda squeezed her hand. "That's not long at all, and then you'll get a lifetime with him, ya?"

Phoebe seemed pleased, and a tear slid

down her cheek, but she'd yet to open her eyes. She moved her hands a bit and shrugged, apparently asking what she could not voice.

Rhoda caressed her hand. "You got real sick. Remember?" She recounted the incident as Phoebe woke and then slept, woke and then slept. The four of them — Steven, Samuel, Landon, and herself — took turns explaining the same information, and by the time the hour was up, Phoebe opened her eyes.

Her gaze centered on her husband, studying his eyes before she smiled. If a picture was worth a thousand words, that moment was worth a million. She seemed to understand that she was safe, the baby was healthy, and her husband had lived a nightmare but he adored her.

Phoebe fell asleep again, and Rhoda felt free to ask questions. "What's next?"

"It'll take several days," Steven answered, though he never took his eyes from his wife. "Maybe even a week to wean her off the ventilator. When she's free of it, it shouldn't take long for the bacterial infection in her lungs to clear up. Even after she's released, she'll need months of physical therapy to regain muscle coordination and full brain activity."

"Will you stay with Mamm and Daed during that time?"

"Much of that is up to Phoebe. If she wants to stay in Pennsylvania near our parents and hers, that's what we'll do."

From her chair beside the bed, Rhoda reached through the rail and rubbed Phoebe's arm. "I hope she wants to return to Maine when she's better."

"It might be necessary to stay near the grandparents so they can wait on her and help with the children." Steven put his hand over Rhoda's. "Her fight isn't over, but the battle has been won."

His words brought peace, and Rhoda remembered fearing that someone else would be taken from her, as her little sister had been. And even though she didn't want to imagine a future where Phoebe wasn't with her every day — or Landon or Leah — she accepted that life changed. Whether a person did everything right or nothing right, life never stopped changing.

The only constant was God, who loved, forgave, and strengthened and was the same yesterday, today, and forever.

Relief continued to surge through Landon. Phoebe was out of the coma and was likely to leave the hospital in a week. As he sat in her room, chatting with Rhoda, Samuel, and Steven, he kept an eye on the clock. It'd soon be time to take his appointed turn to go to NICU and feed the baby.

He tried to enjoy the conversation, because it would probably be one of the last with all of them together. Phoebe was awake. The baby was thriving. Surely Steven would soon be ready for Landon to extract his English life from the Amish group.

What he'd like to do is tell Steven bye and slip out of the hospital. Of all the things Landon didn't want to happen today, seeing Leah with Crist was at the very top of the list. "Steven, I should go."

Steven glanced at the clock. "You have nearly twenty minutes before time to feed the baby."

"Before what?" Rhoda seemed torn between awe and confusion.

"Ya." Steven arched his back, stretching. "I figure the baby needs the most familiar voices feeding him, and Landon's been here pretty often, so I talked him into it. Of course, if no one is there at feeding time, the nurses will feed him."

Rhoda and Samuel glanced at each other, and Landon could only imagine what they must be thinking. They couldn't afford for him to infiltrate their Amish lives again.

Steven looked more relaxed than he had in months. "I don't know what I'd have done without Landon these last two months." Steven chuckled. "Do you think there's another Amish preacher who has such a close Englisch friend?" He leaned his chair back on two legs. "He doesn't agree with having a literal interpretation of the Word like the Amish do" — Steven patted Landon on the shoulder — "but we agree on everything that's important, including that without God's grace, it doesn't matter how close any of us get to righteousness."

Maybe he should pinch himself. Was he awake? Steven hadn't voiced any of that to him. But they had spent a lot of time talking, mostly about family, farming, and fishing.

Steven put his chair on all fours. "He has good ideas about what needs to be done to help Orchard Bend Farms become what we need."

Rhoda nodded at Samuel.

"Landon," — Samuel scratched his face just above his blond beard — "Rhoda and I have been talking, and if you'd be interested, we'd like for you to come back."

Landon removed his ball cap and settled it back on his head again, but that did nothing to help clear his mind. "I'm confused."

"Seems fair you should feel that way." Rhoda straightened the sleeve of her dress. "Your presence has certainly confused us enough, but the bottom line is we want you back. If we're disciplined or shunned because of it, then so be it."

"I agree." Steven nodded. "And with all he's done and how much the Amish respect him because of it —"

"They do?" Landon blinked.

"Ya. They're not sure how to act around you, so they avoid you, but I think your returning to the farm is a winnable battle now. Since you left the farm and kept your word about not calling Leah, and have been by my side every free minute, and have toted the Amish around as you've done, I just don't think your returning to the farm can cause a rift between Amish districts."

The sense of being welcomed lasted only a few moments before it faded. Were they inviting him back because there was no chance Leah would want to be with him? Had she fallen out of love with him completely in the three months he'd been gone from Maine?

But that aside, he could see they were welcoming him. "Thanks. Really." He stood. "I should probably get to NICU a few minutes early."

Rhoda followed him out of ICU, and when they went through the unit's double-wide doors, she stepped in front of him. "You're disappointed in us."

Landon stopped and leaned against a wall. "This offer would've meant more had it come months ago."

"I know. I wish I'd realized then that my concerns were founded in fear and that I needed to fight against them, not mollycoddle them and use them to try to control the situation. But I didn't, and we needed time to think and to be sure what was right."

"And are you sure?"

"As certain as one can be about anything."

"And Leah?"

Rhoda gestured down the hall, and Landon turned. His heart leaped as much with excitement as with hurt. She was heading their way

"Landon," — Rhoda pulled his attention back to her — "she doesn't know how we feel, in part because we've known for only a few days, and in part because it seemed fair to tell you first." She lowered her eyes. "I can't undo what my wishy-washy behavior has caused, but all of us ask your forgiveness for that."

"Hey." Leah stayed some ten feet away. "Isn't it my turn to see Phoebe yet?"

Rhoda started down the hall. "Sure. You can take my place. I'd like to visit with my Daed." She patted Leah's shoulder as she passed her.

"Hi." Leah fidgeted with her hands. "How are you?"

Landon longed to take them into his. "Good. You?"

"Thrilled that Phoebe's doing as well as she is. But no one's said much about the baby other than he's thriving."

"He's a good eater. But it takes a while to get him to burp, and when his little hands grab something — a finger or shirt — he's got quite a grip."

"Rhoda's Daed said you'd been helping feed him. From what I've heard, it seems you've won over most Amish."

"I had no clue, but that's sort of what Steven just said. Funny, isn't it? Now that it doesn't matter, they see I'm not such a bad guy."

"It's not funny, no."

"Yeah, you're right about that." He wanted to ask what she thought of his returning to the farm, but he needed to make the decision on his own. She would probably tell him yes because she wanted what was best for him. But he wanted what was best for her, and he doubted that his returning to Maine was it.

She motioned toward the automated, double-wide doors, the ones that led to ICU. "I should go."

"Me too. Good to see you." He took a few steps and turned. "Leah."

She paused before stepping back from the automated door. "Ya?"

"Did you and Granny work out a good deal on the store?"

"We did."

"I hope it goes well for you and Crist."

She returned to him, looking offended. And confused. "You what?"

"I hope you're happy. Really, I do."

Her eyes sparked. "Crist is helping me clean out the store, but he's not a part of the plan."

"But I thought —"

"I can see that. It's a little soon, don't you think?"

"I'd hoped."

"Crist is with Iva. They're dating."

"Oh. Okay. It is a little too soon, but you will find the right someone."

"Like you always said, I'm young and shouldn't be in a hurry."

"You mean you listened to me?"

"Only when life proved you were right."

"That I believe." He chuckled. "So what's the plan?"

"To work on the store over the next year or two as time allows. When my family is back on their feet from this crisis and Samuel has hired and trained the needed field workers, I will move into the store and try to make a go of it."

"Opening a store there is a good idea."

"I thought so."

"If you do this as you say, even *your* Daed will be pleased."

"That's not happening."

"It might."

"I won't tell him this before the store is in livable shape, but I'm not joining the faith."

Power jolted through Landon, making him feel as if he might shoot through every floor above him, like a rocket taking off. He fought to respond as if it were simply interesting information from a friend. "How can you be so sure?"

"When the tug of wanting you vanished, I was left with just me. And the real me, without you, still longs to build a healthy, good life outside of being Amish."

He couldn't believe his ears. So where did this leave the two of them? "Do Samuel and Rhoda know?"

"I haven't said it aloud, but I think they know. Like I said, I'm in no hurry. But" — she moved in closer and tugged on his T-shirt — "I'm a mess, Landon. I don't fit in your world, and I get upset and say things I shouldn't. You've experienced that more than once. I used to think I'd mature and grow out of it and I wouldn't be a spring sky — sunny one minute and rainy the next. But if I live to be ninety, I think those things will be a part of who I am, at least when I'm in the middle of an argument."

"I was ready to put up with your . . . more frustrating side, Leah. I've been known to overreact a time or two myself."

She released his shirt and smoothed it. "Then I suppose that makes you free to choose an ex-Amish girl to be yours or to find an Englisch one who suits you better. But as far as you're concerned" — her gaze met his and held it — "I'm a sure bet."

He'd said the same thing to her about choosing to stay Amish or to live English — that no matter how long it took her to decide, he was a sure bet. She turned toward ICU again, her words echoing inside him.

He grabbed her by the hand, looking for a private spot. Down a different hall was an alcove with a pay phone. He knew it well, and it was usually empty.

He tugged her into the tiny space and pulled her into his arms. "The only girl I want is the only one I've ever wanted. You."

She closed her eyes tight, her breathing choppy. Then she drew a deep breath and looked at him. "Then you're a lucky man, because I am yours and no one else's."

Landon placed his lips on hers, drinking in the woman who was his first, his last.

His everything.

THIRTY-SEVEN

Apple-picking equipment was sprawled from the barnyard to the other side of the house, reminding Jacob of a subdivision with multifamily yard sales. He walked the pathways filled with instruments and equipment, taking notes on paper and on his phone as he inspected bins, crates, ladders, and wagons.

Orchard workers, both men and women, buzzed throughout the yards, moving from one assigned task to another, like bees pollinating an orchard in springtime. Unlike past harvests, all the pickers were Amish, but Jacob had yet to learn some of their names. There seemed to be only one name that really stuck, and he heard it all the time — Esther.

In the last six weeks since he and Esther had gone their separate ways, he hadn't quite mastered ignoring the nagging emptiness. But he'd found a distraction that was a little helpful. With a clipboard in hand, he paused in the middle of the barnyard, tuned out everything going on around him, and tapped out a text message to Esther.

It wouldn't get to her. The phone number where he sent the messages was to the landline in Bailey's shop. But Jacob needed to talk to Esther, and, short of calling her, this was the best he could do. Writing to her like this did nothing for their relationship, but he felt better for it — sort of like going to a cemetery and talking to the ground where a person lay. It just helped. Somehow. He shared everything with her via dead-end text messages — his thoughts, dreams, and hopes. He wrote about what was happening with Phoebe, his sister and Landon, the store he'd helped renovate, the farm, and even Rhoda and Samuel. And, of course, he'd thanked her for the thoughtful gift.

But right now Jacob was writing a joke one of the new Amish workers had told him a little earlier.

An Amish dad, mom, and son are in a shopping mall for the first time when they notice something they've never seen before: an elevator. While staring at it, an elderly woman comes up and pushes the button. The door opens, she goes inside, and the door closes. They watch as the buttons for each floor light, first going up and then down. The door opens, and out walks a young, gorgeous woman. Dad turns to his son. "Quick, let's help your mom get in!"

Just as he was about to hit send, his brother's voice boomed through the air. "Jacob!"

Something came flying toward him.

Jacob almost dropped the phone as he caught a notepad. "Hey. I was in the middle of something."

"Ya." Samuel moved in closer. "And half the youth here are watching you do it. Can you check my figures?"

Jacob glanced at his phone. Samuel's flying notepad had caused several words to delete. He slid his phone into his pocket. He'd fix the message and send it later. "Sure."

The workers who filled the yards had been coming from out of state for days — thanks to Jojo and Landon going to bus and train stations to chauffeur them. Many of the Amish had rented homes that were for sale in the area, and they'd filled the leased places with as many workers as possible, setting up cots and sleeping bags. Others stayed with Amish families in the area. Every house had at least one cook to keep the workers fed. After having six weeks of intensive physical therapy in Pennsylvania, Phoebe had finally returned to Maine a week ago. Even so, Iva and Leah were still the main cooks in the farmhouse, and they helped take care of Phoebe as she continued to have physical therapy and to gain strength.

It was the third week in August, and apple-picking season began in two days. How had Samuel and Rhoda managed all this last fall while he was elsewhere? They were a remarkable team, not only in work, but much more so in life and love.

But as much as they needed him this year, they'd already set him free for next year. When the harvest was over, he'd use his portion of the profits to start his own construction company. It'd be a small one, but it'd be the beginning of his dream. He wasn't so sure he wanted to do new construction anymore. He'd shared that too in his text messages. It'd be nice to get Esther's thoughts on his business ideas.

Maybe he should've kept his feelings about their dating to himself, and he had certainly been guilty of withholding parts of his life from others, but for better or worse, he wasn't any good at keeping how he felt from anyone. She had to be able to admit how she felt. Until then, he'd leave her alone.

He glanced over the list of items Samuel had given him, figuring everything they'd need to make repairs and have all the equipment in good working order for the first day of picking. "I think the closest home-improvement and construction store is probably the Home Depot in Waterville." He'd look it up on his phone later. "I'll merge your info with mine, and when I'm done, I'll get Landon to take me to get the stuff."

"He may still be holding those training classes."

Samuel, Rhoda, and Jacob were implementing numerous new ways to harvest the apples. They wanted to make it easier to train people who'd never picked apples so they could harvest apples and deliver them to the assigned spot without damaging the trees or fruit. If their plan worked, and he thought it would, they wouldn't need to hire many migrant workers in the future. They could hire American pickers, mostly Amish ones.

Samuel picked up a crate, inspecting it. "Before you go, would you check with

Rhoda and Phoebe to see if they need anything else added to your list?"

"Sure." Jacob jotted down the amount of pine they'd need to repair a few more crates.

"Thanks." Samuel nodded toward the orchard. "I'm going to take a look at the orchard again."

Jacob started toward the house. Phoebe and Steven had yet to take over their suite again. Phoebe couldn't climb those mismatched, steep stairs dozens of times a day to make beds, gather laundry, and do whatever else she would need to do with her family's bedrooms on the second floor. So the men had created a makeshift bedroom for them on the first floor — mostly a divider made with poles and sheets. Esther could have created something much more charming that would work even better. But when the harvest was over, Jacob would build interior walls and make a fully functional first-floor suite.

Because of the doctor bills Steven and Phoebe faced, they'd used all their savings, and they'd owe medical bills for a long time, even with the help of the Amish community. So they'd probably share a home with Rhoda and Samuel for the foreseeable future, which seemed to suit both couples just fine.

Jacob's phone buzzed, and he glanced at the text message. His grin couldn't be contained. "Samuel, wait up." His brother must not have heard him, and Jacob hurried that way.

The text was the message he'd been waiting for. Peterman Farms wanted to buy organic apples so they could sell whole and sliced apples to a sandwich-shop chain. But they were in a bidding war with a marketer of a fast-food place that sold packages of fresh, sliced apples and wanted to up their game by going organic. Jacob couldn't believe the prices being offered by these companies. The more money Orchard Bend Farms made, the more he could invest in his new business and could increase his help to Sandra.

Samuel studied the trees, oblivious that Jacob was behind him. Was something on Samuel's mind? Jacob slid the phone into his pocket. He'd tell his brother about this in a bit.

"You and Rhoda should be pleased."

"I didn't realize you were there." Samuel plucked a McIntosh. "It's taken all of us, ya?"

Jacob couldn't argue. "So is something on your mind?"

Samuel tossed the apple to Jacob. "Since

we all agree about supporting Leah, including Steven, I'm wondering if we could go ahead and release her from helping the family."

Jacob took a bite, and juice ran down one side of his mouth. *Excellent.* They'd be at peak flavor starting next week. He wiped off his mouth with the back of his hand. "Are you wondering if we're ready emotionally or financially?"

"Financially. Whenever anything changes on this farm, Rhoda's work load increases."

Jacob took another bite of apple. "Rhoda has Landon again, and after this harvest you can hire several girls to relieve Leah while she gets her store up and running." He dug one hand into his pocket and pressed a button, revealing the text. "Top dollar, Samuel."

Samuel took the phone, staring wide eyed. "I . . . I . . ."

"You're speechless!" Jacob laughed.

"Hey." Rhoda was riding bareback on a horse, and she was coming toward them, leading a second horse. They waved, returning her greeting.

Jacob threw the apple core as far as he could. "On to other fun news. Aside from the bidding war we have going with two companies who want organic apples, Gerber has made a pretty good offer. We won't make as much profit selling to them as we will if Rhoda cans the products herself, but if you are concerned about her being overworked, it'd give her less to do. And it's a good offer."

"When do they need to know?"

He wiped his sticky hand on his pants. "We have a couple of days."

"Thanks for taking over that aspect. Numbers are easy for you, but it takes me hours to work through all that."

"When I'm gone, Landon's your next-best help. He's like you with calculating figures — good, but needs to think about it. What's surprising is how savvy he is about what's happening with major corporations and their fruit needs. He's the reason I contacted those two companies."

"Good to know. Denki."

Rhoda brought the horses to a stop near them. "Samuel, kumm ride with me."

Samuel passed his clipboard to Jacob and reached for the second horse.

"Nope." Rhoda backed up her horse, causing the second one to back up as well. "With me. Same horse."

Samuel made a face. "But you brought two."

She leaned in, flirting with him while patting the horse. "The same horse, Samuel King. The other one is for Jacob."

Samuel gazed up at her. "Then you'll have to get down. I can't mount a saddle-less horse with someone already on it."

Rhoda grinned and extended her hand to him. "I'll pull you up like you do for me when we ride together."

"Great idea, except I weigh a lot more than you. We'll both land on the ground."

Jacob passed the clipboards to Rhoda. "Here." He clasped his hands together and held them for Samuel to use as a step. With Jacob's help Samuel mounted the horse, and Rhoda and Samuel chorused a *thank you.*

Jacob patted the horse. "It seems to take the three of us to get you two on a horse riding off into the sunset."

The words brought him no pain. In fact, he smiled. Whether he and Esther worked things out or not, or if he remained single all his life, Jacob knew Rhoda was not the one for him.

As Samuel reached around his wife, she passed the reins to him. Jacob pulled his phone out of his pocket, tapped in the missing words to his joke, and hit send. He would stay out here for a bit and send texts that would never arrive. It was therapeutic.

"Jacob." Rhoda disrupted his focus.

"Ya?"

"Get on your horse and go home."

"I will."

"Now, please." Rhoda tossed a piece of wadded paper at his chest.

"Go away. I'm taking a break."

"Uh, Jacob King."

His sister-in-law's voice was starting to grate on his nerves, but he looked up.

Rhoda smiled. "You're going to make me say it, aren't you?"

"Probably. What's up?"

"A young lady is waiting at the house for you."

"What?" Jacob dropped his phone. "Who's waiting?"

"Well, I didn't meet her. Leah told me as I was heading this way. It's an odd name."

"Oh." Disappointment settled into his heart as he grabbed his phone. Esther's name was common, like Jacob's. He mounted his horse. Whoever was here, maybe another applicant, he needed to go back.

"I think Leah said it was Shark Bait."

Jacob's heart thudded. "You could've said that sooner!" He slapped the reins, and the horse jumped into action.

"She came to see you," Samuel yelled.

"She's not going to run off before you get there!"

His brother's voice barely registered.

One fact was louder right now than all the silence over the last six weeks: Esther had come to Maine!

THIRTY-EIGHT

Astride the horse and watching Jacob ride toward home, Rhoda snuggled back against her husband. "I think he's in love."

"I agree." Samuel kissed her cheek.

Rhoda angled her head, inviting more kisses. "But it seems to be taking a while for them to work out the kinks."

"Should such a remarkable event happen without time and effort?"

That was similar to what Samuel had said to her on their wedding day, and she grinned, recalling another heartwarming thing he'd said. She took a deep breath. "It doesn't matter whether it begins precisely on time. Only that it begins."

"Exactly." Samuel brushed wisps of hair from her face. "Jacob and I were talking, and the price that canning facilities are willing to pay for apples this year is really good. We could send about half our apples there and make a great profit from them, and we'll make a better profit on the rest that you can."

"What would be the purpose behind doing that?"

"So you don't have to work as hard."

"Ah. Is the honeymoon over?"

"I certainly hope not. Why would it be?"

"This new plan would keep me out of the field and kitchen as much. So are you tired of seeing me every moment of every day whether we're having a meal or working?"

"That is never going to happen. But we have this business on its feet, and now it's time you got off yours just a bit more."

She stared at him. Sometimes it was as if he could read her mind. Even though they had been married only a little more than three months, she was a bit surprised she wasn't pregnant yet. Still . . . as she prayed about it, she realized that the stress of the last couple of years and how thin she'd become because of it was the issue.

"Look." Samuel took the reins from her. "When I first approached you about helping Kings' Orchard in Pennsylvania, you were only going to provide part-time help in spring and summer with your expertise on nutrition and then help full-time during the canning of the fall harvest. Neither of us ever intended for you to work as hard as you have the past two years."

This plan had been his goal from the start. "You want my work schedule such that we're all squared away when we start having babies."

With less hard work and gaining a little weight, she would be pregnant by this time next year. She knew that as fully as she knew Samuel was meant to be her husband. And she also knew they would juggle their children's needs during the harvest and love every minute of it.

Samuel kissed her neck. "I'm a planner, and I love my wife. What can I say?"

She shifted so she could see him. "You can tell me that second part again."

"I love you, Rhoda."

"It's a good thing. I'd hate to have to kick you off this horse. Listen, about that family of ours, I have a plan."

He clicked his tongue, and the horse started for home. "Is it one I'll like?"

"Definitely. Now that so many stresses are over, I think I should aim to put on a little weight . . . and then I'll come up pregnant."

"I don't think eating is what causes pregnancy." He headed the horse toward the barn.

"Hush it. I'm telling you my plan. Remember when the frost came our first spring here and you went by a store and brought huge slices of different cakes for us?"

"I'll never forget that."

"You buy more of those at least once a week, and we'll eat cake by candlelight in our suite until I'm at my goal weight."

"Done."

"You're much easier to get along with than you used to be. Are you henpecked or what?"

"I'm not any different. You're just nicer these days. When we first met, *you* were the problem. Not me." He directed the horse into the barn.

"Keep it up, and after *you* go to the store to buy us cake, I won't share it with you."

"I apologize." He came to a halt and dismounted and then helped her down. "But . . ." He towered over her, smiling.

He stared at her lips as if he hadn't been married to her for more than three months. When he kissed her, the warmth of his mouth on hers made her long for the night when they'd go into their suite and share cake and cold milk by candlelight and swap stories while laughing until their sides hurt — and enjoy all the desires God had intended.

Jacob rode into the area between the barn

and house, looking for Esther. What did her coming mean — that she wanted peace and friendship again, or was she ready to think about their dating? If she could admit that their feelings went beyond being friends, he would accept whatever decision she'd come to.

For now.

But she had to own up to what was in her heart for him. Their relationship didn't have to fit any of the ideal situations he'd texted about. Actually, it was a good thing she couldn't read those texts, or he'd have scared her off permanently. He'd written about his dreams of starting his own construction company, of traveling to various states for months out of each year, of buying some old homes near wherever their home was so he could fix those up during the winter months when new construction jobs were scant and slow. What woman would want to marry a man who didn't intend to be home but half of the year?

He spotted her walking the pathways between groups of equipment, and he dismounted. An Amish youth, maybe seventeen years of age, hurried toward Jacob, his hand held out. "May I cool him off and put him up for you?"

"Sure. Thanks."

"Oats?"

"And a rubdown and fresh water."

"Right away."

Jacob smiled. Amish or not, he could get used to having help when on the farm, and he knew that as a King son who received a percentage of the profits, he'd need to return for a few weeks each year. Actually, he looked forward to it.

Esther looked up, and Jacob closed the gap between them. "This is a surprise."

Her hesitant smile was charming. "I can't believe I'm here."

"I'm glad you are."

"My concern is you won't feel that way when you realize what I've done."

"What does that mean?"

She glanced at the people nearby.

Jacob looked at the lane that led to the main road. He'd never walked that while talking. "Kumm." They meandered that way, and soon they were side by side where no one could hear them.

"It took some effort, but Dora is no longer angry with me. She believes my account and forgives me."

"I'm glad, but what I really care about is understanding why you're here."

She stared down at her hands, flicking her thumbnails together. "Which do you want first, a confession of my sin or the reason I find it so ridiculously hard to trust men?"

He was sure that having a constant influx of pregnant girls, each of whom had thought the father of her child loved her, had a lot of negative influence. "I can appreciate some of why you feel the way you do about trusting a man, but I'd like to understand more."

They meandered in silence, and he knew she was struggling to talk.

"Okay." Her rosy cheeks rounded as she blew air from her lips. "My Daed passed when I was eighteen, and I'd been taking care of him night and day for three years."

"Did you get to date or go out with friends during that time?"

"Not once. I spent those early rum-schpringe years living in the Daadi Haus with my Daed, being his nursemaid and shielding my siblings from the worst of it. I protected Mamm too, actually. She couldn't cope, so I did. It had some good aspects to it. Slowly his gruff side faded. As the illness grew stronger, he grew kinder and more grateful." She shrugged. "I'm sure some of it was the amount of morphine he was taking. But when he was gone, I discovered that life had passed me by."

He was also sure that her Daed's rougher

side already had her a bit leery of men. "I'm sure you felt like a colt released from its stall."

"Maybe. But whatever I felt, I soon discovered I was fresh, innocent prey to a handsome young man who was several years older than me."

Jacob had made plenty of mistakes himself, but knowing that did nothing to temper his immediate desire to flatten the guy.

"Over the next several months, I fell madly in love. And when he had my emotions hooked, he started pushing for physical contact. I longed to forget the years of isolation with my Daed, to feel alive and beautiful."

"Of course you did." Jacob held out his hand for hers.

She stopped and looked at his hand and slowly lifted her eyes to his. Tears welled, and she shook her head.

"Esther, I have no stones to throw."

"And I have no companionship to offer, at least not until you know everything." She slid her hand into the hidden pocket of her apron and jiggled the fabric. "Every single thing."

What could possibly be in that pocket — a diary or pictures or a letter of some sort? Whatever it was, he thought she was too hard on herself and too suspicious of potential suitors.

He grabbed his suspenders, and they began walking again. The thing he now understood about relationships was they didn't have to be like new construction, exciting and fresh. They could be as worn and used as the treasures he and Esther had collected from that broken-down house. He could look at each item for the richness it had and appreciate the character of dents and chipped paint.

She brushed back a string to her prayer Kapp, making the string fall behind her shoulder. "A group of single Amish men used to gather at night in the lot behind Bailcy's store. It was easy to get to and had outdoor furniture to sit on, and no one could see them from the street. They could smoke and drink there without fear of burning the place down. But they started leaving their beer bottles and such, so Bailey intended to catch them and talk to them about it. If they were of age to drink, he didn't care if they used the area. But he wasn't going to come in every Monday needing to clean up their mess of fast-food trash, beer bottles, and cigarettes. Catching them proved difficult because they didn't go there until they'd taken their dates home.

So one night he slept in the back room of the shop, and when he woke, he thought he heard Peter bragging about his plans for me."

Jacob's skin pricked, and he didn't know what he'd rather do — listen and comfort Esther or find this Peter and hurt him. The worst thing Peter could have done was boldly paint word pictures about someone as private as Esther.

"Bailey came to see me the next day. When he told me all he'd heard, I was sure he was mistaken. He'd only talked to Peter a few times. Surely Bailey hadn't heard the voice of the man I loved. Besides, Peter and I were only parking the rig out of sight and kissing . . . thus far. I could've confronted Peter, but my gut said if I wanted the truth, I had to find out on my own. So I asked Bailey not to say anything to anyone, and I stayed in the back room of his shop the next weekend, the room where he had been able to hear them so clearly."

Relief eased the tension in his gut. At least she hadn't slept with him, but the scenario certainly helped explain her desire to house pregnant girls.

"Jacob, I hoped against hope that Bailey was wrong, but he wasn't. By myself in the darkness of that shop, I listened as Peter bragged about how many girls he'd been with — Amish and Englisch. But he was with them only once. He'd win their hearts, take their virginity, and move on, and he told his friends he'd have me in less than two months. Then he talked about looking forward to the next girl on his list, which he had already picked out. I was so humiliated and brokenhearted that I couldn't even confront him. I just sat there weeping until morning."

In all of Jacob's travels, he'd not met anyone as cold and calculating as this Peter sounded. "So now you don't trust men."

She shrugged. "People are people. Some are tender-hearted, and some are merciless. Before my Daed got sick, he could be ridiculously difficult, but I saw it. I knew when he was the problem, whether I was free to voice it or not. But how could I possibly have fallen in love with Peter and not seen through him?"

"Maybe for a season love is blind, only seeing what it wants to. I thought Rhoda loved me when she loved Samuel."

"No, Jacob. It's not the same at all. She did love you. It just fell short of being the marrying kind. Both she and Samuel love you. I could tell that based on what you told me even though I was in Virginia. But I couldn't see who Peter was when he stood right in front of me, and yet he wanted to cut out my heart and watch me writhe. I'll never get past the fact that I fell in love with a horrible man."

She took a deep breath. "A few weeks later an Amish girl about my age from a district in Maryland came looking for me. She'd heard I was seeing Peter, and she came to ask me to stop. In complete brokenness and tears, she confessed she was pregnant. We went to see Peter, but despite our best efforts, he denied being the father and called her horrible names. Her parents packed her bags when they discovered she was pregnant, and . . ."

"You housed your first pregnant girl."

She nodded. "Peter left Virginia for a while, which was a relief, but he eventually returned with a wife. And I attend church with him. I'll catch him looking at me at times. His smirk makes me so angry. He thinks my great heartache over him is why I'm still single. I feel sorry for his wife. No one that out of balance with reality could be any fun to live with. We only get one life, and Amish only get one marriage. But the idea of being stuck in the wrong marriage had me convinced I'd rather be single . . . until you came along. The last time we were together, you asked how many men I've been friends with who wanted a romantic relationship. There haven't been any, Jacob. Since Peter, I've never met anyone I wanted to get close to. Until you."

Hope pounded inside him. "That's all I need to know."

"I'm not quite finished with my confessions . . ." Esther pulled something out of her pocket, keeping it hidden between her hand and the folds in her dress. She took Jacob's wrist and turned his hand palm up, then put a black, hardcover phone into it.

"What's this?"

She stared at the phone, looking hesitant to answer. "It's where your text messages have been going."

Jacob's throat closed, and it became hard to breathe. What all had he written?

Esther tapped the phone with her index finger. "Bailey changed the landline in his shop to a cell phone a day or two before our argument at his house. He brought it to me the first time he received a message, and much to his dismay, and as a testimony of his love, he let me confiscate it. Apparently you didn't realize that a cell phone says *delivery failed* if a text doesn't go through."

"I didn't." His skin prickled. "You could've texted me back and let me know the messages were coming through."

"Maybe I should have."

"Maybe?" He didn't like the edge to his tone, but good grief!

"I needed to know what was on your mind and heart."

His anger relented as quickly as it had assaulted him. "Okay, but just so you know, I'm aware that I came on pretty strong, sharing ridiculous dreams, like a man imagining winning the lottery when he hasn't even bought a ticket."

"I needed every word you shared." She folded her arms and stepped closer. "And you needed to hear all I just said. But . . ."

His heart lurched into his throat. Was she going to bare her soul simply to say they needed to be *only* friends? "Go on."

Her eyes met his. "The full truth of it is . . . since the day you came to the shop to help me," — tears welled and one ran down her beautiful face — "I've been awed by you. I kept convincing myself you couldn't be as amazing as you seemed. The idea of falling for anyone is terrifying, but for someone younger than me? I felt like a fool. But it was the texts that dissolved the last of my reservations."

"Then it was worth every sentence I wrote."

She searched his eyes. "Like my Daed or Peter, men can hide how difficult or manipulative they are until they're married, and then women are powerless in a society that believes God's will puts people together and the man has complete authority in a home."

Jacob brushed a tear from her cheek, and his heart leaped when she didn't pull away. "There are far more good men than bad."

"That's like saying the odds of being struck by lightning are almost nil when I'm standing there having been hit twice already."

"Most of us know our days are numbered, and we only long to love and be loved by those who know us best — by our wives and children." But he knew it would take a lot of years before she could accept what he was saying was true. It was enough for now that she believed it of him. He moved his hands to each side of her neck, stroking her cheeks with his thumbs. "So where does all this leave us?"

She lowered her eyes, and he gently tilted her head back ever so slightly. She drew a ragged breath. "I've been saving my love a long time, Jacob. I just didn't know it until you entered my life."

His heart pounded with relief as unfettered love began to sprout. "Is it too bold to say I'd like to be with you and no one else for the rest of my life?"

She shook her head, seemingly unable to speak.

"No?" He lifted her chin.

"It's not too bold to say it."

The love and respect he saw in her eyes worked its way into his soul.

She tugged on his shirt. "I agree with almost every text you wrote about doing construction work and traveling to various states for a few months each year."

"Really? That's encouraging. What didn't you agree with?"

"That I could stay rooted while you travel for work. I want to go with you as much as possible."

His heart jumped. Could he be that blessed? "Really?"

"It'd be fun, and our excuse for my going with you is I need to do the cooking and cleaning. When you're off, we'll sightsee and explore. Attend auctions, yard sales, and gut a few old houses here and there. And we could begin the first year we're married."

The first year we're married . . . That she spoke those words without hesitation made his heart sing. "And your home for unwed mothers?"

"I've been working on that. They'll be well taken care of, sometimes by me, sometimes by the bishop's wife and other volunteers."

Wow! Clearly his texts had her thinking and planning. He liked that, and it said a lot about how well they could communicate when he was away. "I imagine I'll need to return here during springtime each year." Would she mind?

"I could come with you. I haven't spent time anywhere yet that wasn't completely fascinating in its own way."

He laughed. "A woman after my own heart."

She smiled and tilted her head in a way that welcomed a kiss. "And you are a man after mine, and that includes the kind of man who intends to always be in Sandra's and Casey's lives."

He could hardly take it all in. Esther understood who he was and wanted to help him embrace a good life as much as he wanted to do the same for her. He wrapped his arms around her and lowered his lips to hers, grateful to have found the one. As she melted against him, he knew . . .

What they had now was worth every bit of the long, painful journey they'd traveled to find each other.

EPILOGUE

Nerves skittered through Leah, making her feel flushed as she folded a pair of jeans and tucked them into her suitcase. Music played softly on the digital clock radio beside her bed. A ceiling fan whirred overhead, rustling the knee-length, beige silky dress that hung on the closet door.

Her wedding dress. She'd bought it six weeks ago, and it'd been hanging right there ever since, waiting for today.

The store below her was silent, closed all day for this wonderful occasion. With help from family — some of hers and all of Landon's — she had a thriving business.

Finally, two years after she and Landon had made up at the hospital, they would marry. They'd spent the last two years trying to walk carefully among the Amish as she severed ties as honorably as she knew how.

Her phone rang, and she dug it out of her

jeans pocket, glancing at the screen. *Landon.* She put in her earbud headphones, brushed her finger across the screen, and slid the phone back into her pocket. "Apparently this avoid-the-groom-before-the-wedding thing doesn't include phone calls."

Landon chuckled. "The tradition is that the couple isn't to *see* each other before the wedding."

"Oh." She put the last few items into her suitcase and zipped it. "If you marry me enough times, I'm bound to get it all straight in my head."

He laughed. "It's taken us years to get it done once, but your confusion over traditional English weddings is understandable. It would've helped if you'd been able to attend one before our big day. How're you doing?"

His question hung in the air, and she pondered it.

Even though she was going to be center stage during a rather unfamiliar ceremony, she was beyond excited to begin a new chapter of her life. But it hurt that no one on her side of the family would be allowed to attend her wedding.

"Great . . . and yet a little sad."

"I know. Me too."

She ran her fingers over her dress, enjoying the cool, soft fabric. Landon's mom and grandmother had shopped with her. The trio had spent two days going from store to store before Leah found the perfect dress — not too fancy or too plain. Landon's mom said it was a vintage sundress style with a short waist jacket. Whatever its style, Leah thought it was perfect for a midsummer, Saturday afternoon wedding in a small church. "It's finally our day, Landon."

"It is. I'd begun to think it'd never arrive."

She chuckled. When she was eighteen and they were falling in love, he'd had to encourage her regularly to slow down her desire to get married. This past year *he* had been the one who needed encouragement to continue waiting. But she'd had goals she wanted to accomplish before she wed — like establishing the store, finally getting her driver's license, earning her GED, and being accepted into a community college, where she'd taken a few business classes at night.

More than those things, at twenty-one years old, she had a deep, abiding satisfaction, and even on her worst days, peace guided her.

"Leah, I called to say that I'm leaving in a few minutes. It's your last chance to take me up on the offer to drive you to the church."

"I'm not arriving with the groom. Go."

"Mom and Granny are at the church already, making sure the girly stuff is in the right places, but they wouldn't mind coming back to get you."

"Flowers, tulle, and lighting." She looked forward to seeing the church decorated for her wedding.

"Yeah, like I said — the girly stuff."

As a gift to her and Landon, his mom had been the wedding planner. With Leah staying busy at the store and knowing too little about Englisch weddings, she was glad to turn it over to her. They'd become good friends since meeting almost two years ago. For that, Leah was grateful. Other than giving opinions about the wedding plans, Leah hadn't needed to do any work to prepare for the event. She had even slept late this morning. There wouldn't be a meal after the wedding, just a nice reception that Landon's parents had insisted on paying for. The ladies from Unity Hill were doing the setup, serving, and cleanup.

Her life was so different now, and this was just the beginning. Eighteen months ago, when she'd told her Daed she was moving off the farm and wasn't going to join the faith, he'd railed at her and hung up, and he had refused to speak to her since. He didn't let her younger sisters talk to her either, but her Mamm had written a couple of times — just enough to assure Leah she loved her even though she disagreed with her decisions. Leah didn't know if her Mamm had Daed's permission to write or if she had to sneak around to write and send the letter.

"Leah," — Landon's voice pulled her from her thoughts — "not seeing the groom is a silly tradition most people have set aside these days. How about if we meet on the porch and talk?"

The long pause she'd taken after his earlier question apparently had him worried about how she was doing. "We'll have plenty of time to talk after you're legally bound to live with and listen to me."

"Legally bound to listen?" His chuckle warmed her heart. "I don't think there's a law that covers such a thing."

"I may have to work on that." She grabbed her shiny, heeled sandals off the bed. "Look, I know everyone at the farm would come if they could, and they'll make it up to us when the dust has settled. So trust me when I say I'm coping just fine, okay?" She was strong enough to carry the hurt and still fully enjoy her day.

"Okay."

But she knew Landon wanted to give her what he couldn't — a wedding day without any lingering sadness.

When she'd made it known to the Amish community that she wasn't joining the faith, Samuel, Rhoda, Steven, and Phoebe had supported her without fail. But for giving her their support, they'd been held accountable by the church for several violations of the Ordnung: not taking the proper stand against the person leaving, creating an atmosphere that encouraged Leah's independence from the Amish, and helping her establish a business with the intent of leaving her Amish roots. The final charge was opposition to the will of God.

Since Leah had been born into an Amish home, the church believed it was God's will she remain there. So Samuel, Rhoda, Steven, and Phoebe were shunned for six weeks and had to retake instruction classes concerning the Amish belief on how to deal with wayward loved ones. Steven had lost his right to preach during that time too, which had to be embarrassing. But despite what was equal to six weeks of public flogging, the four hadn't wavered in their backing of her.

Jacob and Esther supported her too, but since they didn't live here, they hadn't been held accountable for helping pave the way for her to leave the Amish.

She moved to the window. Landon was below, looking up. Fresh gratefulness stirred excitement about her future. The store was under her, Landon was beside her, and God was in and around her. This was the life she wanted.

A few months ago, before they announced to the community that they were getting married, Landon had quit his job at the farm, hoping to diminish the church's outcry at Samuel, Rhoda, Phoebe, and Steven. Landon would return to work on the farm when those who were so angry with Leah for leaving the Amish and marrying an outsider were no longer looking for someone to blame.

If people were over the worst of their anger before apple picking began at the end of next month, Samuel would hire Amish workers again. If people were still too upset to work for Orchard Bend Farms, Samuel would hire migrant workers. By Leah pacing her severing of ties, she had tried to leave her family in a good place emotionally and businesswise.

Still, even with their love and encouragement, she and Landon had dealt with anger, disapproval, and harsh words of judgment from some in the district. The disapproval of the Amish community directly affected the success of her store, but she couldn't live her life based on that. Her next goal, which would take a few years to achieve, was to establish a strong connection to the non-Amish in the area.

She grabbed her keys and took one last look at Landon as he stood on the gravel parking lot staring up at her window. She was so very, very grateful that he'd been willing to walk this journey with her. "I love you, Landon Olson."

Inside a pole barn, Jacob stood behind a row of mismatched, unlevel tables filled with junk and treasures. All of it represented the life span of a stranger who'd passed.

Only a few minutes earlier, he and Esther had been passengers in a car, and this wasn't their original destination. But he had spotted the Estate Sale sign, and it had been his idea to stop. Of course Esther had been excited at the prospect, and once out of the car, she sent him on a mission to hurriedly search for goods, because they had to leave soon.

His intentions were good. If a worthy item was here, he wanted to help find it. But right now, rather than searching, he couldn't stop eyeing his wife. She was on the next aisle from him, quickly moving down the tables of items.

Yard sales and auctions were a favorite pastime of theirs, something they had done just for fun on Saturday mornings the last two summers. They'd had only two summers together thus far, but the idea of a lifetime of seasons with her made his heart pound with anticipation and enthusiasm. She called Saturdays their minivacations, and no one was quite as good at productively wasting a day as he and Esther. Last spring when Jacob and Esther were in Maine to visit and help with the orchard, Landon had pointed out that "productively wasting a day" was an oxymoron — a contradiction of terms. But that didn't stop Jacob and Esther from spending their Saturdays in that fashion.

Since the beginning of their courtship, they had gotten up early on Saturdays, gone out for breakfast, talked over coffee and delicious food, and then spent half the day finding a few hidden treasures. Most often they walked through the yard sales and auctions like they walked along the beaches Bailey drove them to — hand in hand.

She glanced up. Her beautiful, radiant smile warmed his day even more than the

July sun. Privately he called her Sunshine. Truly, she brought warmth and light into every moment of his life.

They'd courted for a year before marrying, and as courtships were intended, they'd gotten to know each other better and had fallen so deeply in love he couldn't imagine life without her. Looking at her now, he found it hard to believe how difficult it'd been to get to know the real Esther. But after she came to Maine to see him almost two years ago, letting him know she'd chosen to dismantle her armor for him, he'd never known a more honest and open person.

They'd been married nine months, and they'd learned yesterday that she was expecting. Their firstborn was due early next spring. Jacob had never imagined being this excited about anything. Before the wedding they'd bought a small, older home less than a mile from the Daadi Haus where she used to help unwed mothers-to-be full-time, but now she did it only part-time. At Esther's warm and sincere invitation, Sandra had moved to Virginia and now lived in a good school district only a few miles from them.

Esther looked up again. This time she mouthed the words *you ready to go?*

He grinned and shrugged, finally scanning

the stuff on the table in front of him. He quickly scrounged through various boxes.

She joined him. "Having trouble concentrating?"

"I am," — he opened the lid to a dilapidated box about the size of a toaster — "and I blame you for being entirely too intriguing. Did you find anything?"

"No. I searched every table except this one and had no luck, but we need to go."

Jacob jiggled the box, making it rattle.

She peered inside it and laughed. "That's not fair."

He'd stumbled upon a box of antique doorknobs, plates, and keys. "Apparently you didn't need to go in search of treasures. You only needed to wait for me."

She put her arm around his waist and kissed him on the cheek. "*That* is the story of my life."

Rhoda came out of the bathroom, freshly showered and wearing a new dress. Her almost air-dried hair cascaded down her back as she gathered the items for pinning it in place. Was that humming she heard? She followed the sound and found herself tiptoeing to the nursery and peering through the barely opened door.

Samuel stood beside the empty crib, his

daughter snuggled in his arms as he swayed her back and forth. He turned, radiating the peaceful contentment of a man in love with life.

When they werc shunned for supporting Leah's leaving, it'd been unexpectedly hard on Samuel, and they'd discovered that Rhoda was as much help to him in that situation as he was to her when tragedy made her sense of intuition run amuck. She'd grown up being isolated and ostracized due to her intuition, and he'd grown up as a King, knowing only respect from everyone. But the birth of their daughter had freed him from people's opinions, because he'd realized all that truly mattered was what was in his heart toward his family and others.

She moved in closer and cradled her daughter's head, enjoying the downy softness of her scant blond hair. Three months old today. Rhoda had been completely clueless how much she and Samuel would fall in love with their child — and with each other all over again. Was this normal? "She's so beautiful."

They'd named her Emma, after Rhoda's deceased sister.

"She is." Samuel met Rhoda's eyes. He ran his hand through her hair and to the base of her neck. With Emma asleep in the crook of one arm, he pulled Rhoda closer.

She rested her forehead on his. He gazed into her soul before he slowly kissed her full on the lips.

"Hello?" Phoebe called, sounding as if she was at the foot of the steps.

Samuel slowly stopped kissing Rhoda. He drew a deep breath and winked. "In the nursery."

Numerous footfalls could be heard on the steps, and Rhoda knew Phoebe had at least two of her three children with her.

Phoebe was quite healthy, had been for the last eighteen months, but since she liked having her living quarters on the main floor, Samuel and Rhoda's space was permanently upstairs. With Leah living above the store and Iva married to Crist and living in an apartment above his parents' carriage house, these days the home housed only two couples and their children.

A few moments later Steven eased open the door. Isaac and Arie hurried into the room, and Steven's two-year-old son, Karl, was in his arms, grinning. Steven and Phoebe had fought so hard to keep Karl alive, and they would probably never get all the hospital bills paid, but he was such a blessing to the household and a bundle of boundless joy, energy, and smiles.

Arie slid her hand into Rhoda's. "Is Emma asleep again?" she whispered.

Rhoda bent and kissed Arie's forehead. "Ya." Arie wanted Emma to play, and thus far her little cousin had proved to be a disappointment.

Phoebe held up a black apron. "Freshly pressed."

"Oh, gut." Rhoda put it around her waist, and Phoebe helped pin it in place.

Steven gestured toward the front of the house. "Jojo's here."

Rhoda jolted. "Already? I'd better get moving. I need to get my hair pinned up and find my shoes." Since Emma had been born, Rhoda seemed to have lost her sense of timing.

"We're here to help." Phoebe glanced under the gliding rocking chair and then pulled out Rhoda's missing shoes.

Samuel grabbed Emma's diaper bag. "I'll take Emma down. By the time we have the children strapped in their car seats or seat belts, you'll be ready."

"I'll hurry." Rhoda scurried out of the room to find a hairbrush.

Jojo worked for them full-time now. She and Sophia had rented a tiny house between here and Camilla's. Sophia loved her grandmamma, and the little girl thrived, learning music under Camilla.

Rhoda rushed through the last bits of getting ready, and within five minutes she was walking out the front door. The van doors were open, the children were strapped inside, and Samuel stood in the yard nearby talking to . . .

Rhoda grinned. "Jacob King! What are you doing here?"

He turned, smiling. "Well, look at you, Rhodes. You're a little thinner since the last time I saw you."

"I hope so." She'd been eight months pregnant when she'd seen him last. "Where is your wife?" The two were just about inseparable. But maybe he'd chosen to come alone in order to protect her.

Jacob gestured toward the van, and Esther came around the side of it. "I was admiring your daughter." Esther hugged her, and Rhoda had a surge of joy go through her. Maybe it'd been the brief glance she'd witnessed between Jacob and Esther, but Rhoda was sure Esther was expecting. Jacob hugged Rhoda, and when they parted, Rhoda grasped Esther's hands. "I didn't know Jacob was coming, but when I saw him, I thought maybe you'd stayed home this time." She squeezed her hands and then released them.

Esther looped her arm through Jacob's. "If he's in trouble, I'm in it with him. But we didn't know you guys had decided to go until Jojo picked us up. Does Leah know any of us are coming to her wedding?"

"Not yet." Samuel rested his hands on Rhoda's shoulders. "No one around here knows we're going, including Crist and Iva."

It'd been one thing to help Leah establish a store *before* she moved out of the farmhouse and *before* she'd told her father and the community that she didn't intend to join the faith. But to condone a union between an ex-Amish woman and an Englisch man by celebrating their wedding day with them could be far, far more punishable.

Rhoda slid her arm around Samuel's back. "Keeping our plans private was our only way to avoid the Amish boycotting her store before or after her wedding. When we're questioned by the church, we'll make it clear that Leah and Landon are innocent in what we're about to do."

"We should go." Samuel caught Rhoda's eye and held her gaze. "Whatever the cost of attending, I don't want to miss a minute of the wedding."

Rhoda paused, letting the others get into the van ahead of her and Samuel. As she looked across the farm, taking in the view, she sensed that through the years, love and faith would do far more than just see them through the good times and bad. It would rise to meet every challenge with joy and hope.

Samuel held out his hand to her. "You ready?"

She put her hand into his, feeling more than just ready for whatever was ahead. She was happy to embrace it.

APPLE SCONES

1 2/3 cups all-purpose flour, plus some for patting out the dough

1 1/3 cups old-fashioned rolled oats, plus some for topping

1/2 cup brown sugar

1 teaspoon ground cinnamon

1/4 teaspoon ground nutmeg

2 teaspoons baking powder

3/4 teaspoon baking soda

1/2 teaspoon salt

1 1/2 sticks cold unsalted butter, cut into pieces

1 1/2 cups peeled and diced Granny Smith apples (about two apples)

2/3 cup cold buttermilk

raw turbinado sugar for sprinkling over scones (Turbinado sugar is simply raw sugar.)

Preheat oven to 400°. Combine all dry ingredients (flour, oats, brown sugar, cinnamon, nutmeg, baking powder, baking soda, salt) in a large mixing bowl with a whisk. Cut in cold butter with a pastry blender, or with your fingers, until the mixture resembles coarse crumbs. Add the apples and buttermilk, stirring until the dough just comes together. Divide the dough in half, and place both halves on a lightly floured surface. Pat dough into two circles, about two inches in thickness. Cut each circle into 6 wedges to make 12 scones. Using a spatula, gently lift scones onto nonstick baking sheets, leaving about two inches between them. Sprinkle the tops with oats and raw sugar. Bake 20-30 minutes or until golden brown. After removing from the oven, let the scones cool on the sheets for about 10 minutes. Serve warm or at room temperature.

MAIN CHARACTERS IN
SEASONS OF TOMORROW

Rhoda Byler — A young Amish woman who is skilled in horticulture and struggles to suppress the God-given insights she receives. Rhoda and Jacob King were courting when Samuel King fell in love with her.

Samuel King — The eldest of three sons. Loyal and determined, he's been responsible for the success of Kings' Orchard since he was a young teen.

Jacob King — The irrepressible and accepting middle brother. He worked among the Englisch and had a tangled past before he courted Rhoda.

Dora Beachy — A twenty-year-old Amish woman who lives in Virginia and goes out with Jacob.

Esther Beachy — A twenty-seven-year-old Amish woman who lives in Virginia and befriends Jacob. She is Dora's older sister.

Bailey Hudson — A fifty-two-year-old non-

Amish man who owns Hudson's Decorative Ironwork. He is a longtime friend of Esther Beachy's.

Althea Hudson — Bailey's wife.

Leah King — The eldest King daughter and the only one who moved to Maine with her older brothers Samuel and Jacob to help establish a new orchard.

Landon Olson — A single, non-Amish man who has worked as Rhoda's assistant and driver for several years. He's a loyal friend of Rhoda's who has reluctantly and with many reservations fallen in love with Leah.

Erlene — Landon's grandmother, whom he calls Granny.

Steven Byler — Rhoda's older brother who moved to Maine to help found the new Amish community.

Phoebe Byler — Steven's wife.

Isaac Byler — Steven and Phoebe's son.

Arie Byler — Steven and Phoebe's daughter.

Emma Byler — Rhoda's younger sister, who was murdered several years ago.

Iva Lambright — A twenty-one-year-old Amish girl from Indiana who moved to Maine to work the orchard.

Eli King — The youngest of the King brothers. He remained as the caregiver of the storm-torn orchard in Pennsylvania when his brothers moved to Maine.

Benjamin King — The father of Samuel, Jacob, Eli, Leah, and their two younger sisters, Katie and Betsy. He runs the family's dairy farm.

Mervin King — Benjamin's brother. He's an Old Order Amish preacher in Lancaster and owns a construction company that Jacob sometimes works for.

Karl Byler — Rhoda and Steven's father.

Crist Schrock — One of the single Schrock men who moved to Maine with his family after the Kings and Bylers founded the Amish settlement about nine months earlier.

Catherine Troyer — Samuel's former girlfriend. She's also the sister of Arlan, a friend of Leah's.

Rueben Glick — A young Amish man. He destroyed Rhoda's fruit garden in book one, *A Season for Tending.*

GLOSSARY

ach — oh, alas

alleweil — now

begreiflich — easy

Bischt du allrecht? — Are you all right?

Daadi Haus — grandfather house

Daed — dad or father (pronounced "dat")

denki — thank you

Duh net geh neh die Haus. — Do not go near the house.

Du hungerich? — Are you hungry?

Du muscht net kumm im. — You must not come in.

Eens. Zwee. Drei. — One. Two. Three.

Englisch — a non-Amish person

Es iss Zeit esse. — It's time to eat.

geh — go

Geh zu die Scheier. — Go to the barn.

Gern gschehne. — You're welcome.

gross dank — many thanks

guck — look

gut — good

hallo — hello

Hausfraa — housewife

Heemet — home

Ich bin do. — I am here.

Ich bin ganz gut. — I am quite good.

Ich bin hungerich. — I am hungry.

Ich lieb du. — I love you.

iss — is

Kann Ich helfe? — Can I help?

Kapp — a prayer covering or cap

kumm — come

Mach's gut — literally, "make it good" but used as "take care," "so long," "good-bye"

Mamm — mom or mother

nee — no

Ordnung — means "order," and it was once the written and unwritten rules the Amish live by. The Ordnung is now often considered the unwritten rules.

Pennsylvania Dutch — Pennsylvania German. Dutch in this phrase has nothing to do with the Netherlands. The original word was Deutsch, which means "German." The Amish speak some High German (used in church services) and Pennsylvania German (Pennsylvania Dutch), and after a certain age, they are taught English.

rumschpringe — running around. The true purpose of the rumschpringe is threefold:

to give freedom for an Amish young person to find an Amish mate; to give extra freedoms during the young adult years so each person can decide whether to join the faith; to provide a bridge between childhood and adulthood.

Willkumm. Es iss gut du kumm. — Welcome. It's good you came.

Wunderbaar — wonderful

ya — yes

ABOUT THE AUTHOR

Cindy Woodsmall is a *New York Times* and CBA best-selling author of thirteen works of fiction and one work of nonfiction whose connection with the Amish community has been featured widely in national media and throughout Christian news outlets. She lives outside Atlanta with her family.

If you'd like to learn more about the Amish, snag some delicious Amish recipes, or participate in giveaways, be sure to visit Cindy's website: www.cindywoodsmall.com.